Praise for *Zeppelins West*:

"Irrepressible, irreverent and unpredictable, this hilarious fantasy with nostalgic touches of yesterday's SF shows off the narrative skills of an inventive author altogether comfortable in his metier....This novel is one big joyride from start to finish."
—*Publishers Weekly*

Praise for *Flaming London*:

"Lansdale's homage to Twain, Verne and Wells is sci-fi fun at its boisterous, silly best."
—*Publishers Weekly*, starred review

"One of the wildest -alternate-worlds, rip-in-space-time, sf-pastiche romps this side of fifties B movies."
—*Booklist*

Praise for Joe R. Lansdale:

"A folklorist's eye for telling detail and a front-porch raconteur's sense of pace."
—*New York Times Book Review*

"A zest for storytelling and a gimlet eye for detail."
—*Entertainment Weekly*

"Like 10-alarm chili, Lansdale is pretty strong stuff...a cult figure."
—*People Magazine*

"Lansdale is a storyteller in the Texas tradition of outrageousness... but amped up to about 100,000 watts."
—*Houston Chronicle*

"Lansdale is an American original with a storytelling style distinctively his own."
—*Publishers Weekly*

"He may be violent, gruesome and shocking, but [Joe] Lansdale is also one of the greatest yarn spinners of his generation: fearless, earthy, original, manic and dreadfully funny."
—*Dallas Morning News*

"Lansdale's style is breezy, fun and full of black humor. To achieve this effect, he borrows from, praises, buries, and reinvents an impressive array of genres. The books are filled with noirish double-crosses and hidden agendas, droll observations, melancholy, and amateur sleuthing—all told in the author's distinctive, shit-kicking Texas twang."
—*Edge*

"Be thankful [Lansdale] crafts such wild tall tales...cunning, humor so salty it burns, and a fevered, cleansing imagination..."
—*Chicago Sun-Times*

"Lansdale writes about the poor, emotionally traumatized, violent and stoically heroic better than almost anyone. His characters can be off-the-charts weird, yet lovable in a strange S&M way."
—*Marin Independent Journal*

"Reading him [Lansdale] is like riding the best tilt-a-whirl you've ever been on while still keeping your lunch down."
—*Washington Post*

"Black humor and bad taste abound in Lansdale's Edgar-winning body of work..."
—*Details*

"The ever-prolific Joe R. Lansdale...certainly knows from fucked-in-the-head."
—*Austin Chronicle*

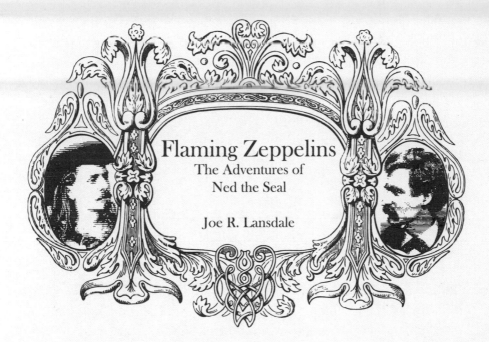

Flaming Zeppelins
The Adventures of
Ned the Seal

Joe R. Lansdale

Flaming Zeppelins

The Adventures of Ned the Seal

Containing the Novels

ZEPPELINS WEST & FLAMING LONDON

by

JOE R. LANSDALE

Cover design by John Coulthart
Interior design by Elizabeth Story

Tachyon Publications
1459 18th Street #139
San Francisco CA 94107
415.285.5615

www.tachyonpublications.com

Series Editor: Jacob Weisman
Project Editor: Jill Roberts

Printed in the United States of America by Worzalla

First Tachyon Edition: 2010
0 9 8 7 6 5 4 3 2 1

ZEPPELINS WEST

Table of Contents

ZEPPELINS WEST

IF VIEWED FROM BELOW, the twelve of them appeared to be brightly colored cigars. It seemed God had clumsily dropped them from his humidor. But fall they didn't. They hung in the sky, floated on, and from time to time, as if smoked by invisible lips, they puffed steam.

If you listened carefully, and they weren't too high, you could hear their motors hum, and if it were high noon and the weather was good, you could hear the John Philip Sousa band out on the promenade, blowing and beating to knock down the heavens or raise up the devil.

Inside the main cabin of the lead zeppelin, called *Old Paint* due to its spotted canvas, Buffalo Bill Cody, or what was left of him, resided in his liquid-filled jar, long gray hair drifting about his head. He waited for Buntline to turn the crank and juice him up. He certainly needed it. His head felt as if it were stuffed with cotton.

Problem was, Buntline was drunk, passed out beside the table where Cody's head resided in the thick jar with the product name MASON bulged out in glass at the back of him. He was grateful that Morse had put the logo at the back of him. The idea that he might look out at the world through the word MASON for the remaining life of his head was depressing.

Cody supposed he should be grateful that Doctor Morse and Professor Maxxon had put him here, but there were times when he felt as if he had given himself over to purgatory, or perhaps worse, a living hell.

The liquid in the jar, what Professor Maxxon called activated urine — it actually did contain a quarter pig urine, the rest was one-hundred-proof whiskey, and an amber chemical called Number 415 — kept his head alive, but it couldn't keep his brain from feeling dull, sleepy even. To think right, to have the juice he needed...well, he needed Buntline to turn that goddamn crank.

Through the cabin's louvered windows, Cody could see it was high morning and the sunlight was warming up his jar. He had the horrible feeling it would heat up so much the liquid would boil and cook him. He wondered how the rest of him was doing in Morse's laboratory in Colorado. They could preserve the body all right, and they could make the heart beat, and of course they were keeping his brain alive here, but did it matter? Would head and body ever reattach?

It was too much to think about.

The lip of the brass mouth horn was fastened just inside his jaw, and when he bit down on it and talked, his voice, due to the liquid, gurgled, but he could be heard, thanks to Morse's device fastened tight in the center of his throat. He called, "Buntline, you dick cheese, get up."

Buntline did not get up.

"I'll have you tossed off this goddamn craft."

Still no Buntline.

Cody gave it up. When Buntline was truly under a drunk, which these days was most of the time, you couldn't wake him with a toot from Gabriel's horn or a kick from Satan's hoof.

Cody closed his eyes and tried to think of nothing.

But as was often the case, he thought of whiskey, women, and horseback riding. A trio in which he could no longer participate.

Wild Bill Hickok awoke from Annie Oakley's beautiful ornate bed with a hard-on like a shooting iron, but Annie was gone. The bed was still warm from her and smelled of her sweetness and the sheets were wet in the center where they had made love.

Hickok suffered a tinge of guilt because he was glad Frank Butler, her former husband, was dead. Frank had been a good man, but death had certainly opened up opportunities that Hickok now dutifully enjoyed. The drawback was Annie still pined for Frank, and sometimes, after their lovemaking she would arise early to sit out on the enclosed zeppelin deck so she could feel guilty and no longer a child of God.

Hickok thought God was a fairy story, so, unlike Annie, that didn't worry him. He felt worse about Frank's memory. He thought Frank a hell of a guy, not as famous as himself, or Cody, or many of the others on board, including Annie. But like Annie, he had been a human being superior to them all.

What had made Frank good was Annie. Hickok was looking for that in himself. When he was with Annie, he felt as Frank must have, that he was worthy. That there was more to him than his speed with guns, his skill with cards, his way with whores.

Jesus, he thought. What am I thinking? I need to get the hell out of this Wild West Show and back to the real West. Away from Annie and her goodness, back to gunfights, card games and stinky whores like Calamity Jane — mean as a snake, dumb as a stone, crooked as a politician, with a face like the puckered south end of a northbound mule.

It was safer that way. You didn't get high-minded. You didn't have to stand by any morals. Calamity didn't smell good and when she left a wet spot it was something to attract insects and stick them to it, like flypaper. A woman like that you didn't attach to.

But a moment later, dressed in a long-sleeved, red wool shirt, buckskin pants and beaded boots, his long blonde hair and mustache combed, his face washed, Hickok went looking for Annie.

Annie Oakley, Little Miss Sure Shot, twirled her dark hair with one hand, thought of Wild Bill Hickok and their lovemaking, and hated to admit he was far better in bed than Frank had ever been.

But a lady wasn't supposed to think about such matters. She turned her attention away from that and back to Frank, and though she missed him, knew she still loved him, his image failed to come into total focus.

It faded completely when she saw Hickok coming along the deck toward her. His tall figure, shoulder-length hair, the manly nose, the cut of his hips and shoulders, made her a little queasy.

Out here on the zeppelin deck, covered by glass and wood and curtains, she thought perhaps she could think clearly. That away from his charms she could work up the courage to tell him it was over. That she would now do what she was supposed to do. Wear black till her grave and never love another man.

What courage she had summoned to do such a thing, dissolved as he sat in the deck chair beside her.

"I woke and you were gone."

"Can't go far on this craft. I'm easy to find."

He laid his hand on top of hers. "I suppose that's true."

She gently moved it away. "Not in public, Bill. I'm going back to my cabin now. To be alone. Perhaps we'll talk later."

"Certainly," Hickok said. Those clear sharp brown eyes of hers were like the wet eyes of a doe. They had the power to knock holes in his heart. He stood, watched her go away, her long black dress sweeping the hardwood decks.

Strolling outside on the promenade deck, Hickok saw Sitting Bull standing by the railing, a colorful blanket around his shoulders, his braided hair shiny with oil, decorated with a single eagle feather that fluttered in the breeze.

Hickok practically floated up to Bull, using all his woodsman's skills, but when he was within six feet of the old Sioux, Bull said, "Howdy, Wild Bill."

"Howdy, Bull," Hickok said, stepping up beside him. Down below, the earth went by in black and green patches, the Pacific Ocean swelled into view, dark blue and forever.

"Been across big water many times," Bull said. "Still, fucks me over."

"Me, too," Hickok said.

"Deep. Big fish with teeth. Makes Bull's tent peg small."

"I hear that. But this beats the way we used to go. By ship. I don't know how we used to stand it. Slow. Storms. I mean, you get them up here, but you can rise above a lot of it. Course, get too high you can't breathe. Always a drawback."

Bull grunted agreement, studied Hickok. "How life, Wild Bill?"

"Good…good."

"Gettin' plenty drink?"

"Yeah."

"Good. Got tobaccy?"

"Yeah. Sure."

Hickok took out a long twist and gave it to Bull. Bull clamped down with his hard white teeth, gnawed a chunk off, began to chew. He gave Hickok back the twist.

"Gettin' pussy?"

"Oh, yeah."

14

"Good. Little Miss Sure Shot?"

"Gentlemen don't discuss such matters."

"That why Bull ask you."

Hickok laughed.

"And if you gettin', don't tell. Little Miss Sure Shot like daughter to me. Could take your hair."

Captain Jack Crawford, the poet scout, appeared on deck. He was dressed in his beaded buckskins and wore a tan hat, the brim of which snapped in the wind. He was seldom seen without his hat. What most didn't know was that his hair, though long on the sides, was bald on top. Scalped by Cheyenne summer of '76 was the story he told, but in actuality he had been held down after a poetry reading by some miners, and with the help of Oscar Wilde, who was touring the West at the time, they had scalped him as punishment for his poetry. Literary criticism at its most brutal.

Captain Jack stood next to Hickok, looked down at the Pacific. "Ah, the waters," he said. "Those big blue deep waters wherein, down below, the fishes hide. Where great monsters unknown lurk, and cavort..."

"Would you shut up?" Hickok said.

"Make stomach turn," Bull said. "Make tobaccy taste bad."

"Sorry," Jack said.

"Save it for those want to hear it." Hickok said. "If that's poetry, I don't want any more. All right?"

"Well, I doubt I'll be doing any recitations in Japan," Jack said. "They don't speak English."

"How bad of Japanese not speak English," Bull said. "Like dirty Indians who speak Indian words, not English."

"Custer killer," Captain Jack said.

"White eye motherfucker in wrong place at wrong time," Bull said. "Know Custer your friend, Hickok, but Custer still motherfucker."

"Probably right about that. Audie would poke water in a bar ditch he thought there was a fish in it, and him with that fine lookin' Libby."

"Our Savior would not want us expressing ourselves in such a manner," Captain Jack said.

"Thought white father spoke Hebrew," Bull said. "Bull speakin' English. Or almost English."

"He speaks all languages," Captain Jack said.

"Good for him," Bull said. "Him one smart God fella."

There was a moment of quiet, then Captain Jack worked the conversation back to what he wanted. "The samurai who fought with Custer. Did they make account of themselves, or did they run?"

"No arrows in yellow men's backs, not unless we sneak up from behind. They brave. Soldiers brave enough. Custer, he shit pants and shoot self."

"That is not true!" Jack said.

"True," Bull said. "Was there. You writing poetry, Bull watching white men and yellow men gettin' shot, cut, scalped. Have many swords from yellow men. Much hair from yellow and white."

"Custer had his hair," Jack said. "When they found his body he had it all. And he wasn't mutilated. So I know you're lyin.'"

"Did not want hair. Ashamed of him. Custer cut it short. No hair to take. Bull hear that story how Custer not cut up. Story lie for lady Custer. He Dog cut Custer's willie off and stick in Custer's mouth. It look like it belong there. Real asshole, Custer."

"I won't hear of this," Captain Jack said, and went away.

"Good work," Hickok said.

"Bull think so."

"Custer *was* a friend of mine."

"Sorry."

"That's okay."

"No. Sorry Custer friend. Show Wild Bill got bad taste."

"If Yamashita had arrived on time with his planes, Terry with his zeppelins, the outcome would have been different."

"Ugh. If Bull's ass wider, deeper, could store nuts and berries for winter."

Hickok laughed. "I see your point."

"Got bottle?"

"No, but there's one in my room."

"Sound good. But must tell you. On shield, back home. Got skin off Custer's ass stretched on it. Asshole right in middle. Cleaned after bad moment on the Greasy Grass. You know. Custer shit self. Wild Bill friend of Custer, so thought you should know."

"You cut his ass off?"

"No. He Dog. He give to me. Said, 'Here asshole.' Have thought on that long and hard. He Dog like Bull only little better than Custer."

Hickok nodded. "Well, Custer was a friend, but you're a friend now. And frankly, I always thought that Libby Custer might have somethin' for me, and that Audie could have treated her better."

Like Bull said, Custer friend, now Bull friend. Wild Bill's taste no better."

Hickok grinned. "Let's me and you have that drink, Bull."

Japanese biplanes buzzed them in.

The little aircraft were like hornets, flicking this way and that. They weaved in and out between zeppelins, the long white scarves of the pilots trailing like the tails of kites.

They flew near the huge cargo zeppelins where the faces and bodies of buffaloes and horses could be seen through portholes. They glided through the zeppelins' bursts of steam, were pushed back by it. They flew close enough to hear the machinery in the gear house of the zeppelins clicking and clashing like a frightened man's teeth.

On the promenade deck of *Old Paint*, Sousa and his band struck up a lively tune, tuba blasting, Sousa horn wailing, bass drum pounding.

Cody's head, in its jar, sat on the shoulders of a steam man, its silver body glistening in the sun. From behind, his hair, floating in the preserving and charging liquid, looked like seaweed clinging to a rock.

Hickok, Annie Oakley, Captain Jack, Bull, and Buntline, a few assorted cowboys and Indians, Cossacks, and Africans, all dressed in their finest, surrounded Cody.

The Japanese pilots flew so close to the front of *Old Paint*, Cody and his companions could see the slant of their eyes through their big round wind glasses. Everyone waved except the steam man. That was more trouble than it was worth.

Inside the steam man's chest, a midget named Goober worked the levers that worked the steam man. The interior of the steam man was hot and the fan that blew down from the steam man's neck only gave so much air. The grating Goober looked out of had limited vision; therefore, as the mind and reactions of the steam man, Goober had limited response.

Buntline was drunk again, but at least he was standing, his black suit looked only slightly wrinkled, his bowler hat was cocked to one side. His boots were on the wrong feet. He was trying to remember his real name before he took the name of Ned Buntline as his pen name. He smiled as he finally remembered. Ed Judson. Yeah. That was it.

He had one hand on the crank that attached to the battery in Cody's jar, and from time to time, with much effort he would crank it, giving Cody the juice. When he did, the liquid glowed, Cody's head vibrated and his hair poked at the amber fluid like jellyfish spines.

Frank Reade, the inventor of the steam man and the airships (he had improved on the German design), had donated the steam-driven man to Cody to promote his line of products. Reade had come to prominence pursuing Jesse James and his gang across the U.S. with his steam-driven team of metal horses, and now his products ruled the United States and were spreading rapidly across the world. Even if he had failed to capture James.

The steam man Cody used had been modified. The head with its conical hat through which steam had been channeled, had been removed, and the steam now puffed out a tube in the back, a tube that carried the steam above the jar and spat it high at the sky like periodic orgasmic eruptions.

Where the steam man's hat had been, Cody's jar now fastened, and on top of the jar was a great big white hat with a beaded hatband.

On the steam man's feet were specially made boots of buffalo leather, dyed red and blue, decorated with white and yellow beads. On the toes of the boots there were designs of buffaloes cavorting.

In his room, Cody had a pair that were similar, only on the toes of the boots the buffaloes were mating. He wore those when he went out with the boys.

As the zeppelins dropped, escorted by the Japanese biplanes, Japan swelled up to meet them, showed them fishing villages of stick and thatch and little running figures. Farther inland the sticks gave way to thousands of colorful soldier tents tipped with wind-snapped flags as far as the eye could see. Samurai, in bright leather, carrying long spears with banners attached and swords at their sides, lifted their helmet-covered heads to watch the zeppelins drop. From above, the Japanese in their armor appeared to be hard-shell beetles waiting for a meal to land politely into their mandibles.

As the zeppelins glided toward the long runway, bordered by soldiers, the band went silent, and Cody yelled to Goober through the talk tube.

"Turn me and raise a hand."

Goober worked the controls. The steam man hissed and turned, raised a hand. Buntline, from experience, adjusted the talk tube so that it faced the crowd on the deck.

Cody boomed and gurgled. "My friends. This is an important mission. Relations with Japan over the Custer fight are strained. We are here to entertain, but we are also here as ambassadors. As role models for the others, I must ask special things of you. I need advise Mrs. Oakley not at all, but men. Stay off the liquor. They have a particularly nasty drink here called sake. Don't touch it. Keep your Johnsons in your shorts. Pass this word along... No offense, Annie."

Annie blushed.

"And men, try not to get into fights. I have dealt with the Japanese. For a time I was an ambassador to Japan. They are extremely good hand-to-hand fighters. They have a thing they call Daito Ryu Jujitsu. Boxing and brawling stand up to it poorly. They can tie you in more knots than a drunk mule skinner. Trust me on this. And in case you have not noticed, you are outnumbered. They have few guns, on the planes mostly, but they are absolutely magical with the weapons they carry. Stay in camp. You will be treated well. Abide by all the rules I have laid out, or I'm gonna be madder than the proverbial wet hen.

"So now. What do we say?"

Up went the cry: "WILD WEST SHOW FOREVER."

"Hickok," Cody said sharply.

"Oh, all right," Hickok said, his face red. "Wild West Show Forever. Okay, now I've said it... I didn't hear Bull say it."

"Bull?" Cody said.

"Hey, me say thing," Bull lied.

Once moored and disembarked, The Wild West Show — seven hundred strong, escorted by a clutch of Samurai and a robed translator who was also the Shogun's Master Physician — was amazed and delighted and a little frightened by the variety of armor and weapons, the ferocious appearance of the Japanese warriors.

Fragrances of food and body oils unfamiliar to them wafted through the air and stuffed their heads like mummy skulls packed with incense and myrrh, a musty beetle or two, a slice of raw fish.

They gravitated toward a great black tent, the peak of which was tipped with a pole and black pennant wriggling in the wind like a small ray with its tail pinned by a rock.

There was much formality. The Americans tried to bow at the right time and look pleasant. Cody, in his jar, could only grin. In his steam man arms, Cody carried a red and blue Indian blanket wrapped around gifts from President Grant. So heavy were they, he could not have carried it with his own natural arms. The gifts were for the Shogun, Sokaku Takeda.

When the rituals were complete, Cody spoke through his tube. "From President Ulysses S. Grant to you."

Since the steam man could not bend completely over, Hickok and Bull came forward, took hold of the blanket on either side and lifted it from the steam man's arms. Sweat popped on their heads as they lowered the blanket and its burden onto a bright runner at the front of Takeda's tent.

Takeda, a small man dressed in colorful robes, his hair bound up and pinned at the back, sat, and magically, a retainer produced a camp chair. It was beneath Takeda's rear even as it appeared he would fall backwards.

Takeda spoke a few sharp words and two more retainers appeared, unrolled the blanket. Inside were eight bars of gold and eight of silver, a bright Henry rifle, two black oak-handled revolvers, their silver barrels shiny as cheap fillings in a miner's mouth. With them were two black buffalo-leather holsters pinned with silver conchos. There was also a bandoleer of ammunition.

Takeda grunted. In response to this noise, a retainer brought forth a wrapped parcel, unrolled it at the steam man's feet. Cody could not bend his neck, so the contents of the blanket were lifted and unwrapped by Hickok and Bull for his inspection.

Inside the blanket was a long sword and a short one, encased in what looked like black bone scabbards, but were in fact, highly lacquered leather.

Words were exchanged. It was determined a demonstration would be given of Grant's presents by Annie Oakley.

They retired to a large patch of land next to the tent. Annie strapped on the holsters and the black-handled revolvers. She was wearing a black hat, black dress, black stockings and lace-up black shoes. She turned to Hickok and smiled.

She was so beautiful, Hickok felt his knees weaken. Then he remembered it was his job to reach into the bucket provided and toss glass balls at the sky. He snatched one, threw it high. The guns jumped from Annie's holsters. BLAM, a blast tore from one of the revolvers and the ball burst. Hickok reached in with both hands, tossed high with his right, then high with his left, snatched up other balls and flung them rapidly, one after the other.

Annie fired first one revolver, then the other. She seemed casual, as if she were thinking about something else. But each time the balls exploded. Soon Captain Jack was helping Hickok toss. The guns snapped and the balls exploded. Annie reloaded three times, never missed.

A deck of cards was produced. Captain Jack took one from the deck, held it with the edge facing Annie. She loaded and holstered the pistols. Took a breath. The revolvers leapt from their hutches, coughed. The edge of the card was cut in two places, torn from Captain Jack's hand.

Now Bull came forward, a fat cigar in his mouth. He was puffing savagely, trying to get as much from the smoke as he could. He stood sideways, the ash on the cigar standing out a quarter inch.

Annie slowly lifted the right hand pistol, shot off the ash. She lifted the left hand pistol and shot the cigar in half. Bull pocketed the butt and stepped off the field, saying, "Machin Chilla Watanya Cicilia."

In Sioux this meant "My daughter, Little Miss Sure Shot."

Now Annie picked up the Henry, cocked it. "Let 'er rip," she said.

Hickok, Captain Jack, Bull, and an African Zulu king named Cetshwayo grabbed from two buckets of glass balls and charged them at the sky. The rifle went up, moved left and right, up and down, barking at every change in direction. The balls exploded all over the sky.

Finished, Annie placed the butt of the Henry on her lace-up shoe and bowed ever so deeply. Takeda grunted. A retainer stepped forward, yelled words, the Samurai let out a roar of approval.

It was then decided Takeda would demonstrate.

He rose from his chair, which had been placed in the field, and yelled. Two armored men came charging out of the ranks, their hands lifted to strike. They struck at Takeda with extreme ferocity, but, with minimal movement, Takeda sent them flying.

They rose, came again. An arm cracked, a man screamed. Takeda struck quickly at the other. Down he went. Silent. A puff of dust from the field hung over him for a moment, thinned, disappeared.

The Wild West Show applauded politely.

The translator and Master Physician came forward then. Said to Cody, "We would like two of your men to try Master Takeda. It would be an insult not to. And it would be an insult not to try and hurt him. They must come at him hard."

Cody asked for volunteers. Hickok decided, why not, and stepped forward. With him came the tall African, Cetshwayo. Takeda nodded at them. Hickok and Cetshwayo charged. Hickok's plan was to throw a hard and powerful right, clock the little dude.

His right whistled through the air, and he knew he had Takeda, his fist was almost to the little man's temple.

Then the little man wasn't there. Hickok felt pressure on his hip, then he was falling. Cetshwayo attacked by reaching for Takeda's throat with both hands. Next thing he knew, he was sailing through the air.

Jumping up, Hickok grabbed Takeda's right hand with both of his. Cetshwayo rose, struck hammer-fist style at Takeda's face.

Next thing they knew, their arms were entwined and they were both on the ground, held there by Takeda's left foot.

Takeda raised his hands, his army cheered. Politely, so did The Wild West Show.

Humiliated, Hickok and Cetshwayo skulked back to their group, trying to figure on how Takeda had done it.

Takeda was handed a scabbard and sword. He poked the scabbard through his thick cloth belt. Two naked men were brought forward, they were given swords and shoved toward Takeda.

"What's happening?" Cody asked the translator through his voice horn.

"Chinese prisoners," said the translator. "They have been told that if they kill Master Takeda, they are free to go."

The Chinese, charging together, attacked the little Japanese, swords lifted high.

Takeda swayed left, then right, his sword a flash of light as it left its scabbard. One Chinaman dropped his sword, took a step, then the top half of his body fell off the bottom half. A split second later, the bottom half collapsed. While this was in progress, Takeda made a slice at the remaining swordsman.

The last Chinaman survived with only a cut across his chest. He attacked again. His sword hand went away, his wrist pumped blood. Takeda moved and let out a yell, his sword went through the man's solar plexus, out his back. With a whipping motion, the sword was freed and the man fell, as if absorbed by the earth.

"That is how the sword is used," said the translator.

"I see," Cody said.

Takeda spoke in his harsh voice. The translator bowed, spoke to Cody. "He asks if you, or in this case, one of your retainers, would like to use the sword. We have spare Chinese."

Knowing that a trap had been laid, that Takeda was testing him, Cody said, "I would not dare make an inaccurate stroke with these metal arms. I am incapacitated. Nor would I insult Master Takeda by using a retainer. I would not want anyone else to touch such a magnificent gift as the swords given me by him, and if another sword were offered for my use, it would be an insult to his generosity."

This was duly translated. After a moment of consideration, Takeda nodded. His army cheered.

Annie had not meant to let it happen again, but by nightfall she had invited Hickok into her bed. They made love for a long time, then lay together looking at the ceiling, bathed in soft lantern light.

"Takeda murdered those men," Annie said.

"Yes he did," Hickok said.

"Savages."

"Not too unlike what we did to Bull's people."

"Not like that. Surely, it wasn't like that."

"I guess you never heard of Sand Creek?"

"I don't want to."

"Neither do most white people. Especially since innocent Cheyenne were slaughtered there for the amusement of white Colorado Volunteers. Women and children were scalped. Tobacco bags were made from parts of their skins, their private parts. And the Little Big Horn. My friend Audie was killed there, and made into a hero, but he was a fool. The Sioux and the Cheyenne were merely protecting themselves, and we call it a massacre."

Annie rose up, put her back against the oak headboard. Though normally modest, now mad, she allowed the sheet to slip away, revealing her breasts. In the lantern light the nipples stuck out like the tips of .44 caliber slugs, the rings around her nipples were dark as burnt powder.

In spite of her anger, or perhaps because of it, Hickok felt aroused again.

"Are you saying I don't care about what was done to Indians? You know better. Bull is an Indian and I love him dearly."

"I'm saying, you're human. Like me. We don't see what's in our own country as bad, any more than these folks do. Or by the time we do, it's too late."

Annie relaxed. "You've changed, Bill. I never knew you to feel this way."

"The Wild West Show, which I don't care for, I might add, changed me. I don't like all these plays and speechifying, but when you spend enough time with people with different skin you start thinking of them differently."

"You're a real pain, Bill. Frank never disagreed with me."

"I'm not Frank."

"You certainly aren't."

"Is that good or bad?"

"I'm beginning to think it's good." Annie took hold of one of her breasts, arched her back, and in a voice Hickok had never heard before, said, "Baby, you want to nurse?"

"Oh. You betcha."

Inside the black and yellow tent of the Master Physician, Sokaku Takeda, thirty-third grandmaster of Daito Ryu Aikijujutsu, sponsor of the diplomatic invitation to The Wild West Show, Shogun, soon to be ruler of Japan, watched as two soldiers held the monster's lashed down left leg firm.

When the soldiers had it held tight, the Master Physician sawed off the remaining piece of the monster's left foot, not bothering to cauterize the wound. There was no point. There was no blood in the creature. It was, however, decided it would be best to screw a block of wood to the ankle so they could walk the thing back to its cell and not have to lift it from the carving table and carry it.

Though the monster had no blood, no beating heart, it lived. Its oily black eyes rolled in its greenish face, it shook its head, causing its long, greasy, black hair to thrash back and forth like a veil in a crosswind.

Alive or not, as the soldiers put the block to its nubbed ankle and pushed in the screw with a driver, it bellowed like a bull, began to curse Takeda and all his descendants in guttural English.

The chunk taken from the monster's foot was placed on a small wood-block table. The Master Physician cut, sliced and diced the piece of dead flesh into a dozen pieces, placed the particles in a little bronze bowl, poured scented oil on it and set it on fire.

The flame leapt green, yellow, subsided. The physician ground the remains into a fine black powder with a pestle. He used a thick piece of cotton to pick up the bowl and pour the smoking ashes into a bowl of water. This in turn was run through a white cloth, leaving black residue on the surface. The residue was placed in a rice paper envelope, folded, sealed with wax, given to Takeda, the Master Physician bowing low in the process.

"How long will he last?" Takeda asked.

"He feels pain, but his body is not really harmed like that of a living man. Master Takeda, he will last a long time. I believe he will be alive when only the head is left. Doctor Frankenstein developed a process that causes his brain to live and make the body function. There is blood, but it has nothing to do with life. It congeals more than it runs."

"Does he eat?"

"He must eat."

"Does he defecate?"

"Like a water buffalo, sire. He has all the urges of man, but he is a false man. He does not bleed true blood, just the congealed goo. He does not sweat."

Takeda turned to where the naked monster lay lashed to the table. The creature was tall, and in a way, attractive. But his legs didn't match. You could see scars where the legs had been fastened with thread and bolts to his hips, same for the knees. His shoulders, elbows, wrists and ankles showed the same sorts of scars. His genitals were massive; testicles like grapefruits, a penis like a dagger scabbard.

The face was the thing, however. It was greenish, the eyes gray and watery. There seemed to be too much bone for the available skin; it didn't fit right. The lips were black as charcoal, the teeth horse-like and of poor quality.

"You are strange," said Takeda in Japanese.

The monster, having been a captive now for six months, a piece of him whittled away daily, could understand enough Japanese to know what was said. He replied in English.

"You eat of my flesh to make yourself hard, and you say I am strange. Yours is a life of oddness and ritual, the bizarreness of the living. Like my former creator, Victor Frankenstein, long lost now among the ice floes of the Arctic in a skating accident, I have only simple dark words for you. Eat shit, little man."

Of course Takeda did not speak English, nor did the soldiers. The Master Physician did, but he lied to Takeda, told him the monster was asking to be freed.

"Only when the last of you is gone," Takeda said. "Think of it this way. What residue of you my body does not absorb is passed through my bowels. That is how you will escape. As turds."

Takeda exited the tent with his little envelope of burned, ground flesh.

Sokaku Takeda headed back to his tent where naked women waited. He had learned from the Master of Apothecary that there was something in the flesh of the creature that, when prepared properly, served as an aphrodisiac. It gave him the energy to spread his seed among his concubines. For if there was one thing he wanted, it was a male heir. He already had several daughters. So many he had sold some of them to Chinese merchants and one American who wanted a pet. What he needed was a son. Someone to teach Daito Ryu to. Someone to hand down his kingdom to, for it was just a matter of time before the old ruler collapsed under the weight of his army and ambition. And, in the meantime, this son business, well, it was fun trying to make the little guy.

When Takeda had departed and the soldiers had taken the monster away, the Master Physician seated himself in a corner and opened a drawer hidden in his desk. From it he took a little machine with lettered keys and extensor antenna.

When he had the antenna pulled to its full length, he began to tap out a message on the keys.

Inside Cody's cabin, on the dresser, next to the jar that held his head, a duplicate machine began to snap. Cody opened his eyes, yelled through the voice tube for Buntline.

Buntline, pinning a chair to the floor with his butt, rose, staggered to the machine, grabbed up a pad and pencil, wrote out the message.

He read it to Cody.

Cody spoke to Buntline. A moment later, Buntline was tapping the keys.

Next morning was full of pomp and circumstance. The Wild West Show in all its colorful glory, paraded between the Japanese tents and soldiers, Sousa and his band playing "Garry Owen."

There were livestock, stagecoaches, covered wagons, buckboards, all manner of riders and rigs, and, of course, the beautiful Annie Oakley waving from the back of a big white horse. Last, but certainly not least, came the head of Buffalo Bill Cody. Cody rode in a buckboard, on the lap of Buntline, who was not overly drunk this day. From time to time, Buntline would raise the jar containing Cody's head, lift it to the left, then to the right.

There were cheers, but they were more polite than inspired.

"Tough bunch," Buntline said.

"They only cheer when they're supposed to," Cody said. "Takeda runs this show."

"Not The Wild West Show, he doesn't," Buntline said, hoping Cody would remember this later and offer him a bottle from his good stock of special whiskey.

"Not yet," Cody said. "But he makes me nervous. This is the first show where cutting up a man was part of our arrival celebration. Cast and crew, Annie I know, were more than a little upset. Could affect their performance, and if it's one place we want to look good, it's here."

"Would you like a little crank?" Buntline asked.

"Not just yet," Cody said.

They rode the rest of the way in silence.

Parade over, The Wild West Show was quickly constructed. The show was a traveling community with carpenters, painters, blacksmiths, tailors, doctors, barbers, stock handlers, gunsmiths, boot and shoemakers, washers and ironers, cooks and prostitutes. Everyone had a job and did it with speed and precision.

Tents leapt from the ground, poked summit poles at the sky. Corrals snapped together and the stock was thunderously yee-hawed inside. Water tanks were filled, food tents were packed with supplies and tables.

Inside Cody's tent, the tip of which was peaked with the American flag, the steam man was in the process of being painted so he would appear to be wearing a buckskin jacket, cream trousers, and a crimson shirt dotted with blue and white prairie flowers. Over this, colored beads and soft leather tassels would be glued in the appropriate places. The jar containing Cody's head would be attached, different boots would be placed on the steam man's feet; they would be dark-chocolate-colored knee-highs with bright red suns on the toes as a goodwill gesture to the Japanese empire. Last but not least, a wide-brimmed, white hat with a beaded hat band would be pushed down over the top of the jar.

Goober, the midget, would be inside the steam man, out of sight, wearing nothing more than a g-string, fighting the heat, fighting the gears, the little steam-powered fan in the neck of the machine blowing hot air down his back.

When the show was over, Goober would be hosed down, laid out and fanned by four assistants. Cooled, Goober would be hosed again, dried, fed, then allowed to sleep.

The steam man would be cleaned with turpentine and soap, dried, ready to be repainted. Cody had discovered long ago that, with the exception of the boots and hat, dressing the steam man made him look too bulky. This method kept him streamlined. From a distance, even relatively close, no one could tell it was paint and showmanship instead of clothes.

That night, electric lights powered by the show's steam generators, as well as strings of bright Japanese lanterns strung on high poles, illuminated the scene. Around the field The Wild West Show had thrown up rows of bleachers as well as concession stands where taffy, popped corn, parched peanuts, cotton candy and American beer could be bought.

Once the show started, the crowd, though not particularly loud or rowdy to begin with, went stone silent. Soon Annie was at work doing her trick shooting. Her husband and helper, Frank, was gone, but now she had Hickok to assist her, keeping her guns loaded, her props in place. She started by having Hickok release four clay pigeons simultaneously.

The moment they were sprung, she ran toward the bench where her guns lay, leapt over it, grabbed up a Winchester, and burst all the launched targets before they could touch the ground.

A roar went up from the crowd. They were not only amazed at her marksmanship, but at the rifle itself, as Japanese exposure to fine firearms was limited.

More clay pigeons were released and burst. A playing card was cut. Strings dangling from a hat were picked off one by one at a great distance. One impossible shot after another was made.

Finished, Annie raised her arms, slowly bowed. The normally sedate Japanese warriors broke into a cheer. Takeda, sitting on a stool at the front of his tent, stood and bowed to Annie.

A rider burst out of nowhere on a black horse, galloping toward Annie at full speed. He extended a hand. Annie grabbed, swung onto the back of the saddle, and away the horse thundered. Again the crowd cheered.

Shortly thereafter came a horde of cowboys, doing tricks on horseback, roping and shooting at targets. Cattle were released. The cowboys roped, threw, and tied them.

Stagecoaches thundered around the makeshift arena, pursued by Indians who leapt onto them from their horses. Mock fist and knife fights took place, cartridge blanks snapped and exploded.

Scouts of the Prairie, a play, was performed in the center of the arena with Hickok, Captain Jack and Cody. It was translated by the interpreter who called out the words in Japanese over a megaphone. His words were in turn passed throughout the crowd by other Japanese armed with megaphones.

It was not an entirely successful moment. The play was bad to begin with. There was the language barrier. And every time Cody moved there was hesitation as Goober responded to orders tossed down the pipe. The interpreter sometimes mistook these words as part of the play, presented Cody's commands, curse words and oaths to the perplexity of the crowd.

The next act bought the crowd's enthusiasm back. A small log cabin was fastened together quickly in the center of the arena. Thatch was tossed over the top to serve as a roof. A clothesline was hastily erected, a wash pot and scrub board were placed nearby. A woman and her children, a boy and a girl, appeared. The woman pretended to do her wash in the wash pot. She hung a couple of items on the line.

Suddenly, out of nowhere came a horde of Indians. The mother and her children retreated inside the cabin. A window was opened. The mother poked a rifle out, shot at the Indians as they circled the cabin on their horses, hooting and hollering and firing off blanks.

Then a torch was thrown on the cabin's roof. The prepared straw and kerosene sprang to life. It looked as if the woman and her children would be burned alive. An Indian leapt off his horse, grabbed at the cabin door.

The lock snapped free, the Indian rushed in. The woman and her children were pulled into the yard. The roof of the cabin blazed. An Indian in heavy war paint pulled a tomahawk from his belt, and just as he was about to cut down on the woman, there was a bugle blast.

Twenty men in cavalry uniforms, Cody at their head, his steam man torso mounted on one of Frank Reade's shiny steam horses, rode into view. The steam horse hissed clots of vapor, its metal hooves stamped the ground. The Indians released their captives, bounded onto their mounts and fled, the cavalry and Buffalo Bill Cody in hot pursuit.

Saved, the women and children ran out of the arena. A steam-powered fire engine chugged up. The cabin's roof was doused with water from a large hose. Men dismantled the cabin, and away it went, providing room for the next feature.

Off-stage Cody was lifted from his horse with a crane. When the steam man was on the ground and the cowboys had unfastened the harness, Buntline appeared with a screwdriver, and removed Cody's head from the torso.

While he was doing this, Goober opened the door in the steam man's ass and slid out backwards like a plump white turd. He got up with dirt sticking to his sweaty body, and without a word, wandered off to be hosed.

Annie and Hickok were nearby, cleaning the weapons Annie had used in her act. A cowboy rode up. He said to Cody's head, "You heard them yellow men got them a fella they're cuttin' up?"

"What?" Cody asked.

"A fella. They're cuttin' on him. And he ain't no Chinese or Jap neither. I think he's a white feller."

"Say he is," Cody said. "Where did you hear that?"

"That boy, Tom Mix."

"The elephant handler," Cody said. "Well, it's most likely a damn lie. But I'll look into it." Then to Buntline: "Get my head inside the tent. These electric lights are making me hot. I feel hungry, too."

The cowboy rode away.

"You don't eat," Buntline said.

"I know that, you idiot. How in the world did you ever write my adventures?"

"Hell, I just do what you do. I make them up."

Buntline picked up Cody and started for their tent.

Annie said to Hickok, "They're cutting up a man? You mean like those poor Chinese?"

"I don't know," Hickok said. "It wouldn't surprise me to discover they're cutting on someone most of the time. But I won't lie to you. My curiosity is getting the better of me."

Hickok laid the Winchester he was cleaning on the bench, wiped the gun oil from his hands, headed for Cody's tent, Annie walking alongside.

Hickok threw back the flap on Cody's tent, peeked inside. Cody's jar had been placed on a crate. The lid of the jar had been removed, and Buntline, with a long straw, was poking through the liquid into a hole in the top of Cody's head.

"Oh, yeah. That feels good. I feel like I'm eating something."

"What's it taste like?" Buntline asked.

"Anything and everything," Cody said, "but I'm going to think it's a big buffalo steak with a burnt potato. And beer. Plenty of beer."

"I don't mean to interrupt you at mealtime," Hickok said. "But we overheard that cowboy out there, and since it's none of our business, we thought we'd ask what that was all about…a man being cut up and all."

"Come in," Cody said. "That Annie with you? Why sure, come in, darlin'. Good show. You've never been better. *Scouts of the Prairie* certainly went over like a lead balloon, didn't it, Wild Bill?"

31

"Far as I'm concerned, it always does."

"What exactly is it you and Ned are doing?" Annie asked Cody. "Or should I ask?"

"I'm eating. Sort of."

"Doctor Chuck Darwin came up with it after the accident," Buntline said. "Him and Morse. Darwin discovered that if you stimulated certain parts of the brain in rats, they thought they had eaten. You could do this until the little buggers died of starvation. But they'd think they were full. Having worked on rats, Darwin thought it would work on Buffalo Bill, his ownself. And it does."

"Won't you starve to death too?" Annie asked.

"Not in this fluid," Cody said. "And Morse is taking care of the body. Someday, we'll reconnect them. And I'll be slimmer to boot. Morse told me last time we talked that he'd allowed the body to shed a few pounds."

"About this man being cut," Hickok said. "Know about it?"

Cody was silent for a moment. He said, "Ned. Put the lid on the jar, then I want you and Annie to listen, Bill. I know who it is being cut up. It's why we're here."

"I thought we were here for a Wild West Show," Annie said.

"I thought we were here on a kind of diplomatic mission," Hickok said.

"Yes and yes...and no," Cody said. "President Grant thought after the disaster at the Little Big Horn, all those Japanese warriors being slain under Custer's fool command...well, we needed some diplomatic work. But there's more."

"I don't keep up with politics," Annie said. "Enlighten me."

"Ever since the Japanese discovered America's West Coast, and the Europeans discovered the East Coast, there's been tension. In the last few years our expansion has outdone that of the Japanese, and both nations have crushed the Indian in the middle. We've even worked together at doing it. Now, well, frankly, after the Civil War and the founding of Texas as a Negro state, it seems the U.S. is interested in removing the Japanese from our continent. The recent annexing of Canada as the twentieth state, and with all the western territory we now own, Grant would like to see us own all the land to the western coast.

"But the Japanese won't sell. Takeda, he's the most powerful ruler in

Japan. With our help, or without it, he will eventually rule all of Japan. But with our help it would be easier. That's why I presented him with firearms. To give him some idea of their usefulness. Japanese firearms are so primitive."

"He's going to use a rifle and a couple of handguns to rule Japan?" Annie said.

"If he likes what he sees," Cody said, "President Grant will supply more. And the guns will, obviously, make his conquest easier.

"In fact, on this trip, I have secretly had a case of Winchesters presented to him, along with a case of ammunition. For our assistance, he is supposed to sign a pact with our country offering us the West Coast. Only, there have been some recent flies in the ointment."

"Such as?" Hickok asked.

"Such as Mexico. They're still mad about San Jacinto. For the last thirty years or so they've been looking to stick it to us. They're offering the Japanese the same guns, but they're not asking them to give up land. They merely want them as allies."

"Didn't our country just give Mexico guns they didn't have a couple years back?" Hickok asked. "Some kind of diplomatic gift?"

"We did," Cody said. "Now they make their own. And good quality, too."

"So why are we here wasting our time?" Hickok said. "If they can get the guns from Mexico without having to give up land, then we're kind of done in, aren't we?"

"We didn't know that when we set out. I received the information by telewire this morning. The Verne satellite beamed it in."

"We seem to have lost our fella that was gettin' cut up," Hickok said.

"We'll come back to that," Cody said. "I came here as a diplomat for our president, but I had an ulterior motive."

Cody paused as a cheer resounded in the arena.

That would be the stagecoach trick, thought Cody. It made him feel good to hear that cheer. It always did.

Hickok offered Annie a camp stool, folded out one for himself, sat down. Cody suggested they break open a bottle, and Buntline was quick to grab it from Cody's private stash. Whiskey was poured for Hickok and Buntline. Annie declined. Cody, of course, was forced to pass. He said, "Drink a bit for me."

"You betcha," Buntline said.

"Give me a crank, Ned. Give me two."

Buntline complied. Cody's hair stood on end and the jar glowed. When the moment passed, Cody's hair collapsed in the fluid to float. And Cody began to talk.

"Once up a time I had a body with this head. Pretty damn good body, I might add. I've told many tales about how I ended up this way, but, as you might suspect, they are all lies, some of them concocted by my friend Buntline here.

"My head was not cut off with a tomahawk, as has been reported, nor did I have an accident learning to fly an airplane or drive one of those horseless carriages. Nor was I in an incident with a herd of swine. That's one I didn't make up, I'm quick to admit. That was one of Buntline's. Turn the crank, will you, Ned."

Ned took hold of the crank and went to work.

"That's better. It all happened back at my place, The Welcome Wigwam on the North Platte. Christmas of two years ago. It was a great night at home. It was cold as a castrated pig's nuts in a tin basin, and it was snowing. Louisa and I had guests. Sam Morse and his wife. Their friends Professor Maxxon, his lab assistant, B. Harper, and his lovely wife Ginny. Also present was the beautiful young stage performer, Lily Langtry. They were spending the night with us. The Morses and Maxxons in the guest house, all others in the main house. There had been much playing of the piano and singing aloud around the Christmas tree. The usual holiday frivolities.

"Truth was, Morse, Maxxon and Harper were there to do scientific work in my outbuildings. They were trying to bring a cadaver back to life. A horrible thing, I assure you, but fascinating nonetheless, and I was anxious to have them there because they were such good company, and because Miss Langtry was a dear friend of Sam Morse's. A lovely woman, clothed or unclothed. Wonderful as a spring morning, only a lot more fun.

"The good news was my wife, Louisa, went to bed early. And I went to bed not much later. With Miss Langtry. The bad news is my wife, normally a sound sleeper, slept less soundly this night, and Miss Langtry, a vocal nightingale under any circumstance, hit a high note during our visitation. It awoke Louisa. She discovered us together, took the fire axe from the dining hall and struck me from behind.

"It wasn't a killing blow, but it nearly severed my head from my shoulders. Once Louisa realized what she had done, she let out a scream that awoke Morse and the others. Miss Langtry began to scream as well.

"Morse immediately set about stopping the flow of blood, and with the aid of Harper and Maxxon, got me out to the lab they had made in one of my outbuildings. They immediately placed me in the bathtub there and packed it with snow. I don't remember feeling cold, or feeling much of anything. I vaguely remember the tub was where they cut up dead bodies for use in their research, and now I was in it. But I didn't give that much thought. I was sailing away, folks, that's what I was doing. The Happy Hunting Grounds had done thrown me up a teepee.

"Well sir, Maxxon and Morse struck upon a bold plan. They had had no success in reviving a corpse, but perhaps their knowledge could save me. Morse contrived the battery jar, the fluid was a creation of Maxxon's. He had been using the fluid for some time as a preservative for body parts.

"They had been working on the theory that if you charged Morse's electrical energy into Maxxon's chemicals, it would not only act as a method of preserving, but would actually cause the nerves in severed limbs, and perhaps even brain cells, to continue to function.

"Since I didn't have a lot of options, they decided to operate. My head was completely removed, placed in this jar you now see, and an electric current was applied.

"Obviously, it worked. Later, the battery, the cranker, and the voice horn were added. Then of course Frank Reade provided the steam man's body and Doctor Charles Darwin has made a few suggestions. But the bottom line is yet to come. And that is Victor Frankenstein."

"Frankenstein?" Annie said. "I thought that was just a story. This all sounds like a story. One of your stories."

"This one's true, Annie. And Frankenstein, he's real. And so is his monster. Morse and Maxxon were much aware of Frankenstein's work, but had been unable to duplicate it.

"Maxxon had tried to produce a man out of chemicals, what he called the very stew of life, but had failed. As you might suspect, he was not vocal about his results, for obvious reasons. He had failed, and the fact that he had tried was enough for some authorities and citizens to rise up in arms and maybe lynch him. The very idea of it was aberrant to many."

"It's aberrant to me," Annie said.

"I just recently learned that word," Cody said. "And I've been wanting to work it into conversation. How did I do?"

"Good enough," Hickok said.

"So, it's aberrant to you, Annie," Cody said. "But think about it. Without it, I wouldn't be here."

"But you weren't created," Annie said. "You were saved. That's not the same as bringing back the dead, or creating a human being out of electricity and chemicals."

"True," Cody said. "That kind of business upsets the Christians, and I don't think it does the Moslems any good either. But it can be done. Frankenstein managed to cobble dead bodies into a man, and with a charge of lightning, brought it to life.

"Morse and Maxxon teamed up, decided to try and approach Doctor Frankenstein, and Doctor Momo, another scientist working on the problem, to see if collectively they could find an answer. Something more successful than a living dead man. They felt with Maxxon's knowledge of chemicals, Morse's of electricity, Frankenstein's knowledge of anatomy, and Momo's understanding of surgery, they would be able to fill in the blanks for one another.

"How would this help you?" Bill said.

"In the process of learning how to create a human being, they felt assured they could, with Frankenstein's help, refasten my body to its head. Use me as a kind of lab rat. An experiment in preparation for the greater experiment.

"However, Momo was eliminated immediately. He had left England some time before and had not been heard from since. It was rumored he had lost his marbles.

"Then it was learned that Frankenstein had gone to the Arctic in search of his creation. It was his intent to kill it. Story isn't clear, but it's said the doctor was lost in the frozen waste, perhaps killed by his creation. Certainly the monster killed Frankenstein's wife, so the creature was capable of it."

"How horrible," Annie said. "That's the kind of result you can expect, tampering with nature."

"Perhaps," Cody said. "But the creature turned up in Russia, was captured, sold to Takeda. This we knew. Takeda bought him with the express purpose of making aphrodisiacs by cutting off pieces of him and turning them into a powder. This was on the advice of his Master Physician, who has ulterior motives. Like finding out what makes this creature live."

"How do you know that?" Bill asked.

"Because the Master Physician is an agent for the United States. He has scientific interests that are smothered by Takeda's war interests. He's been turning information over to our country with the understanding that he may come to the U.S. to live, and there have the opportunity to expand his knowledge and interest in medicine.

"The Master Physician offered the creature to our country along with the information he was providing. Our country was not all that interested in the thing, but I was. And so were the good doctors who saved me.

"So, when there was an opportunity to take The Wild West Show here on a diplomatic mission, I jumped at the chance. I thought I might kill two birds with one large rock. I'd make a good deal for our country with Takeda, then maybe make a personal deal for the monster, take him home for Morse and Maxxon to look over and study. The first part of the plan is shot. I know that now. And I doubt that helps the second part of the plan. So, what we're going to do is something different."

"How different?" Hickok asked.

"We're gonna steal the old boy and hustle him home to Welcome Wigwam where the boys, wives and assistants, and of course the smug Louisa, wait to do their work. They on the monster, Louisa on me. Her tongue is as sharp as any scalpel."

"How did it work out with Miss Langtry and your wife?" Annie asked.

"Louisa apologized, but I got to tell you, an apology for something like that, it just doesn't have the impact you'd hope for. I forgave her, but I didn't forget. I'm thinking of divorce.

"As for Miss Langtry, she was disappointed in the whole state of affairs, especially since we failed to finish our mission of that night, but pledged silence. She went home on the next train. I suspect she's doing now what she's always done. Performing in stage shows."

"With donkeys and her tied to a barrel," Annie said.

"What was that?" Cody said. "Speak up."

"I said, you can't really blame your wife. You're not exactly the most faithful husband in the world."

"Well, dear, not everyone can be like your Frank, God bless his soul. I was at fault, no doubt, for I love a skirt, or rather, and pardon my boldness, what is under it. But chopping off my goddamn head. Now that's severe."

"Not in my book," Annie said.

"I'm not trying to force anyone to get involved with my plight," Cody said. "But if I can convince just a few, for it is a mission better accomplished by a few, to help me, then I have a chance to live a normal life. The creature will be spared a slow death, brought home for honest scientific study."

"Won't he be cut up there?" Annie said.

"Possibly," Cody said.

"Then what's better about his situation?" Annie asked.

"Oh, hell," Cody said. "I admit I'm more worried about my situation. Look at it this way. He's dead already, so what's to lose?"

"Nothing says he'll certainly be dissected." Hickok said. "Am I right?"

"Right," Cody said.

"Then at least he's better off for a while, and maybe forever," Hickok said.

"I don't feel right about it," Annie said.

"Count me in," Hickok said.

"Ned?" Cody asked.

"I get whiskey out of this deal?"

"You do."

"I'm in."

"Annie, darling. What about you?"

"I don't like it," Annie said. "But since the Japanese are double-crossing our government, and it gives the monster some chance at freedom, why not?"

"Good," Cody said. "It's wonderful to have you. There are a few others I'm going to ask for assistance. But only a few. A small group is best. And we'll only need a skeleton crew to operate my personal zeppelin. We'll send everyone else home, then...well, let's just hope the Japanese don't read Homer and the Master Physician is as trustworthy a spy as he seems. He did, after all, study at Harvard, Ned. The time."

Ned removed his pocket watch from his pants pocket, opened it, told Cody the time.

"Two hours from now, the Master Physician will be ready to receive a message. Ned, this is what I want you to tell him..."

When the show came to an end that night, and ceremonies were observed, Cody set a crew of men to work. By morning the mules were pulling a large wheeled platform into the arena, near the edge, next to the great tent of the Master Physician.

The platform was thirty feet long, twenty feet wide and five feet deep. On it sat a Conestoga wagon fashioned from the lumber of prefab animal pens and leather. It had been worked on carefully by Cody's craftsmen: carpenters, tailors, etc. It was a beautiful thing. The leather covering of the Conestoga — mocking what should actually have been canvas — was brightly painted with trees, buffalo and a rising sun. Inside the Conestoga were a number of gifts. Indian blankets, beaver hats, jerked meat, jarred jellies, and a fairly lifelike female sex doll fashioned from leather, paint and human hair. The doll had been pumped full of air, and had the proper anatomical adjustments.

Almost instantly after the delivery of the Conestoga, The Wild West show folded and loaded. The zeppelins rose, their steam-driven motors kicked in, and they sailed west, leaving their gift behind.

The delivery of the wagon had not gone unnoticed by the Japanese. The departure of the American fleet had been rude and unceremonious, but at least they had left a box of treasures. Takeda surveyed them, had the wagon searched for trap doors and the like, found none. He gave a few of the gifts to select soldiers, placed the wagon under guard, then retired to his tent with the leather blow-up doll and the intention of testing its function.

Deep in the night, the wind came down out of the north and brought dampness with it, spread it over the great camp of Takeda, and over the unlucky guards protecting the gift from The Wild West Show. The air turned chilly, and so did the soldiers.

The Master Physician, feigning insomnia, came from his tent smiling, carrying a gourd full of sake. He offered some to each of the guards in little wooden cups he carried in a knotted rope bag coated in wax. Shortly after swallowing the liquor, all of the guards collapsed into a deep sleep. Later, early morning, they would be awakened by their skin being removed slowly from their bodies with a sharp piece of bamboo. Their reward for failure.

When the guards collapsed, the Master Physician gave the side of the wagon's platform a hard kick. Hesitated. Kicked again. Then kicked twice. He immediately disappeared inside his tent.

The sides of the platform on which the wagon rested opened, and a very hot and uncomfortable group of men, and Annie, all dressed in black, their faces smeared with ash, (except Cetshwayo, whose skin was already black as the night sky) slid out into the darkness and rain, and slipped into the nearby tent of the Master Physician.

Inside there was only one lantern burning. But Hickok, Cetshwayo, Annie, Bull and Captain Jack had enough light to see the Master Physician and a man seated on the ground, dressed in a blue and white kimono. He had a leather mask over the lower half of his face, his feet — one foot actually and a block of wood — were bound in front of him, his hands behind his back. For insurance, he had been wrapped in strong silk cord.

"We must hurry," said the Master Physician, "otherwise, we are up what you Americans call shit creek."

"This is the creature?" Annie asked.

"It is," said the Master Physician.

"Why, he looks like any other man. Except for that block of wood on his foot."

"And the green skin," Hickok said.

"Him look sick," said Bull.

"What happened to his foot?" Annie asked.

"It would take too long to explain," said the Master Physician. "And remember, looks can be deceiving. He is not like any other man. Stand closer, away from the direct glow of the lantern. His skin is strange. Touch him. It's like touching a corpse. He is a corpse."

"Important thing is to grab the rascal, and haul ass before Takeda figures out what's going on," Hickok said. "Send the message, Physician."

The Master Physician opened the secret panel in his desk, brought out the machine, raised the antenna, began to tap out a message.

Hickok cut the silk rope around the creature's legs and body. He and Bull raised the creature to his feet. Hickok was amazed at the size of the man. He must have been over seven feet tall, with shoulders considerably broader than his own. Hickok said, "You can understand English, can't you?"

The creature nodded.

"Good. Now I know you can't talk with that gag on, but you can listen good. I got a .44 here, and if you mess with me I'm gonna blow what brains you got — whoever they originally belonged to — all over this place. Savvy? Nod your head if you do."

The creature nodded.

"You would have to splatter his brains for him to really be affected," the Master Physician said. "Remember. He is not a man."

Hickok ignored the physician, spoke firmly to the creature.

"Remember, I'm here to save your patchwork ass."

The creature nodded.

"I'm gonna have my friend Bull here cut your legs loose when the zeppelin shows up, and you're gonna go with us. Can you stump on that block of wood all right?"

The creature nodded.

The Master Physician stood at the front of the tent, near the flap, looking out at the night and the rain, which had begun to hammer the camp. "A light," he said.

He was referring to a light from the zeppelin. As planned, all other lights on the craft had been turned off, but the foredeck beam blinked once through the night and the rain, went black.

A moment later, three rope ladders coated with a glowing chemical were dropped from the zeppelin. The Master Physician was the first one out of the tent, the others followed. Hickok, Bull and the creature brought up the rear. The creature with his wood block foot was no runner. He stumped and sloshed mud.

As they grabbed the ladders, began to climb, a cry went up in the camp. They had been spotted. From the ground, at first glance, it appeared they were ascending glowing magic ladders hung in the air; it was only with a bit of eye strain that one could see the shape of the zeppelin through the night and the rain.

The zeppelin's foredeck and open promenade lay under the great interconnecting cells of helium; the ladders were fastened to the railing of the promenade. Annie was the first on board, then the Master Physician, followed closely by Cetshwayo, and Captain Jack.

On the last ladder was Bull, the creature, and Hickok bringing up the rear. The creature, heavy and slow, was climbing with difficulty. An arrow whistled by Hickok's head. He turned and looked.

Down below fire burned in pots, hissed in the rain, coughed white smoke. The flames, fueled by some remarkable propellant, leapt orange and yellow through the smoke. From high above, they were like redheads and blondes hopping on the balls of their feet, bouncing their heads above a morning mist.

Hickok hung to the rope with one hand, jerked his revolver loose with the other, fired at the pots, bursting four of them, smashing the fires in all directions.

More pots were lit, and more arrows were launched. One went through Hickok's trousers, hung there, just below the knee. Hickok slipped his revolver back in the sash at his waist and tried to climb faster, but all he could see was the monster's legs, the block of wood, and under the kimono. Hickok was disgusted to find that he could see the monster's big nude butt. He banged on the creature's leg. "Move it, buddy."

The zeppelin's motor was fired. Steam kicked out of the boiler room, whistled whiteness into the wet night. The zeppelin jumped toward the sky, nearly jerking Hickok loose of the ladder.

Faster and higher the zeppelin went, the ladder, with Bull, Hickok and the creature, flapping like clothes on a wash line. Arrows buzzed all around them.

Then the zeppelin was too high for arrows. The camp lights receded. Turning, Hickok could see the airfield, the planes there outlined by lanterns and fire pots. Half a dozen of the little Japanese hornets rose up in the airfield light, dissolved into the darkness. Hickok could hear them buzzing.

Hickok prodded the creature again, and he began to climb. Bull had long ago reached the top, was looking over the railing, calling to the creature. "Green face. Get move on."

The creature had to work carefully to free its woodblock foot from the ropes with each step, but finally it reached the railing, and Bull, with the help of Cetshwayo, pulled him on board.

Hickok was swinging back and forth as the storm increased in savagery and the zeppelin rose faster and higher.

Cetshwayo and Bull began pulling the ladder up. Eventually, Hickok rolled over the railing and collapsed on the promenade deck. He sat up, and removed the arrow from his pants leg.

Buntline appeared on deck, a clutch of Winchesters under his arm. He passed them to Hickok, Annie, Bull and Cetshwayo.

"You, physician fella. Get that damn green man inside."

The Master Physician grabbed the monster at the elbow, led him off the promenade, onto the enclosed deck. Through the great glass windows he could see the vague shapes of the biplanes in the darkness.

Annie was the first to fire. Her shot, as always, was a good one. She hit a pilot in his cockpit. The plane jerked, dove. Moments later there was an explosion and a flash of light as the biplane slammed into the shore near the Pacific Ocean.

The biplanes were trailing the dark cigar shape, firing their simple guns. *Blat*. A beat. *Blat*. A beat. *Blat*. The guns were designed to fire with the beat of the propeller, slicing through at the precise moment of the blades' spacing. It was clever. It was tricky. And it didn't always work.

Hickok was glad they were not the new German planes which fired dual Gatling guns as fast as they could work till the ammunition ran out.

On the downside for them, the zeppelin had no real maneuverability. They were like a dying albatross besieged by falcons.

Wood splintered on the promenade deck, bullets pocked, cracked, or exploded glass on the main deck. One bullet went through the glass, drove splinters into the creature's face. A bullet tore through his upper left arm.

He didn't bleed.

Another bullet took Buntline's bowler hat, caused him to prostrate himself on the deck. The monster stood his ground, glass dangling from his chest. His kimono was torn and burned where the bullet had ripped through it and through his arm.

The planes were attacking the zeppelin itself. Bullets slammed into the great rubber casing, and though it was designed to take terrific impact from hail, flying birds, and small arms fire, the heavy bullets were succeeding in pounding through.

Hickok heard a hissing sound as the zeppelin let loose some of its helium. The good news was the big bag was actually a series of smaller gas cells. It could lose considerable helium and still stay airborne. The bad news was there was a limit to anything.

A biplane passed in front of the promenade deck. Bull shot it the finger, then they all raised their Winchesters and fired at its rear end.

Their shots smacked into the biplane's tail assembly. A stream of fire raced along the fuselage, rolled around the plane as if it were a hoop the craft was jumping through. Then the flames grabbed at the seat and the pilot, burst him into a human torch. The plane spun. The blazing pilot freed himself from his seat, and even as the plane turned over and over, he dropped free, a burst of meteoric flame driven hard into the ocean.

The plane exploded on the water. Flames spread on the surface, waves leapt wet and fiery until the fuel burned itself out.

The zeppelin sailed along rapidly, propelled not only by its motors, but by a strong tail wind. The Japanese pilots no longer exposed themselves to the zeppelin's defenders; they knew how unerringly accurate they were. Instead, they flew high above it, firing at the defenseless structure of the craft, causing it to collect damage.

On the zeppelin's bridge, pilot William Rickenbacher needed more steam. He was not used to working without a copilot, but Cody had insisted on a skeleton crew. William felt sick. Why had he agreed? Cody had given him a choice. He could have gone back with the others. His copilot, Manfred Von Richthofen, had been eager enough. But no. He wouldn't let him. He didn't want a dumb kid in command of his ship. Wanted to spare him the danger. What an idiot he had been. He had a wife and children. This was idiotic. He wasn't a spy, and he wasn't a fighter pilot. He was the captain of a luxury airship.

Jesus. What had he been thinking?

Had he been thinking?

Not only were the biplanes tearing his craft apart, the storm was slamming it about. He was no longer sure of the difference between sea and sky. The only thing to do was to try and let the ship rise, propel it forward with full throttle.

"Gib eet more steam," he called through the command tube, trying to shape his words carefully, so his heavy German accent would not be misunderstood. "Gib eet more steam. Power ees dying. Ve are losing altitude."

In the steam room the workers struggled valiantly with coal scoops and chunks of wood, tossed them into the great oven. The heat was unbearable. Steam hissed. Motors hummed. Men groaned. The ship moved slightly faster, rose gradually.

A biplane buzzed the bridge. William saw it as it passed. A moment later it turned in the darkness, came back. It fired a shot that blew out a fragment of the glass. Cold air embraced William, the blast nearly knocked him down. He turned, could see the plane's shape, flying fast toward him.

In that moment he knew there was no time to do anything, knew what was about to occur. His last thought was not of God, but of his wife Elizabeth, and his children, especially his favorite child, his little boy Eddie.

Then a bullet spat from the biplane, zipped through the already destroyed window, caught Rickenbacher in the throat, opening a wound that looked like two rose petals falling apart. He fell face forward against the control console, blood rushing over the gears and dials.

Before William's corpse fell against the panel, the biplane's pilot realized he was in trouble. In getting close to the zeppelin's bridge, he had not allowed himself enough time to turn. He didn't even pretend to work the control stick. The pilot threw his hands over his eyes as the plane struck the command deck, knocked off the propeller, and was driven into the side of the zeppelin like a dart. The front of the plane rubbed William's body into a red smear. Fuel dripped from the damaged plane, trailed into the night air. Some of it dripped along the floor of the command deck, ran toward the door, slipped under the crack, fled along the corridor, was absorbed by the carpet.

When the plane struck the zeppelin, there was such a jerk, on the promenade, Captain Jack was tossed forward. He caught the rail, and just when it looked as if he would regain his balance, the zeppelin lurched once more, and Captain Jack went over the side and was silently swallowed by darkness.

Hickok tried to grab him as he went, but it was too late. The zeppelin tilted dramatically. All the defenders were tossed about. They struggled valiantly to hang on, grabbing at the rail, scratching at the promenade deck with their nails.

Buntline felt himself flying forward, toward the broken window on the main deck. He knew he was a goner. Through the gap in the glass he went, out into blackness. But just when he was trying to remember the Lord's prayer and decide if there was time to say it before he was splattered all over the Pacific, his jacket collar was snagged, and he was jerked inside, tossed on the floor.

Buntline looked up to see the creature looking down on him with a solemn expression.

"Thanks, old boy," Buntline said. "You're peachy by me."

Frankenstein's creation did not reply.

In Cody's cabin, the collision of the plane hurled his head off its perch on the dresser. Had it not hit Goober in the side of the head, knocking him down, it might have smashed against the wall.

The jar lay on its side, the liquid in it sloshing. Cody yelled through the tube. "Get me up. Get me out in the open where I can die like a man."

Goober, a knot forming on his head, put one hand to his wound, got his feet under him. He picked up Cody's head, tucked it under his arm, darted out into the slanting hallway.

"Check the bridge," Cody said.

Goober rushed forward, his head feeling as if it were giving birth to a child. When he reached the hallway that led to the bridge, he could smell the fuel from the Japanese plane. He hustled along, feeling colder as he went.

When he reached the bridge, he saw a lumpy red smear that might have been Rickenbacher. It was smeared all over the console. The Japanese plane's nose poked through the side of the zeppelin, and the pilot lay slumped in his seat. A freezing spray was blasting in from the outside.

"Goddamn," Cody said, when Goober turned his head upright, moved the jar around so he could see.

"We're done," Goober said.

"Hush your mouth, shorty. You are not dead till you're dead. And you do not quit till you quit. I thought I was dead when I fought my duel with Yellow Hand. He was a tough customer. I was about ready to give up and die. But something in me said, 'Don't do that, Buffalo Bill. You stick in there.' So, I stayed with it. Yellow Hand slipped on his own knife, stabbing his ownself to death. You got to stay with things. You never know how they will work out."

"I got a pretty good idea," Goober said.

"Quick," Cody said. "Back to my cabin."

"I thought..."

"Just do it!"

Out on the promenade deck, the zeppelin began to roll back level. The Japanese planes were now closing for the kill. Bullets slammed the deck from all directions. Cetshwayo took a shot in the side, let out a yell.

Annie and Hickok grabbed him under the arms, hauled him onto the main deck, laid him down. As they did, a plane came by so close its dual wings edged only six feet from the promenade railing.

Bull, the only one left on the railing, slammed several shots from his Winchester into it as it retreated. At first he thought he had failed. Then the plane's motor cut and there was a whistling sound as it went into a dive. This was followed by an explosion and a flash of light.

Glancing over the railing to see if planes might be coming up from below, Bull was greeted with the sight of the glowing, dangling ladders.

"Damn," he spoke to himself. "That how them follow so easy in dark. See ladders."

Bull tossed the Winchester to his left hand, pulled his knife from under his jacket, moved around the railing hacking the ladders free.

The steam man had a fire in its belly. Cody had ordered it kept going until they were out of this business. He wasn't sure what he might need the steam man for, but he wanted to be prepared.

His jar fastened to the steam man, Goober inside to work the controls, Cody returned to the bridge. Calling commands to the midget, the powerful steam man's body shoved at the plane. The pilot, who they thought was dead, lifted his head just as the steam man managed to shove the plane through the wound it had made in the zeppelin's side.

"Sayonara," Cody said.

The pilot just looked sad as the plane fell backwards, said in Japanese, "Typical."

Cody, Goober and the steam machine were hurled backwards as the zeppelin, relieved of the plane's weight, leapt skyward.

Out on the promenade, Bull was slammed face down on the deck so hard his nose bled. Inside the main deck, the zeppelin's defenders experienced the same moment of surprise.

The advantage, although not immediately known, was that the zeppelin was now lost to the biplanes. They could no longer see it in the dark and the rain. They were also running out of fuel, so there was nothing left for them to do but turn back.

The downside was the zeppelin had suffered many wounds in its rubber skin. Helium had been lost. The bridge was damaged. The zeppelin had no pilot. The steam man had been damaged by the sudden rise of the ship; it had caused the steam man's legs to crimp, and it had fallen. Somehow, Goober had gotten the front of his trousers hung up. As the machine lay on its side near the gap in the wall, Goober said, "I'm coming out of this thing, Cody. I'm jammed up in here. It's pinching my pee-pee."

Goober worked the trap door open, tore the front of his trousers loose and slipped out on the floor. He hastened to unfasten the clamps that held Cody's head in place. Finished, he clutched the jar under his arm as they stood looking at the wheezing steam man lying on its side.

Cody, peering through the glass, said, "I'm gonna miss that dude."

"Not me," said Goober. "It pinched my pee-pee. And it's hot. And it's hard work, too."

"Give me a crank, will you?"

Below in the boiler room all was panic. The great furnace had been in the process of being loaded when the plane came loose and the zeppelin jumped. Flaming hunks of wood and coal had been tossed from the furnace; the three men in the boiler room were frantically attempting to put out the flames with small tanks of water.

It was pointless.

The zeppelin dropped as if the bottom had come out of the world, and the ocean, like rolling concrete, came up to meet it on the way down.

When the zeppelin hit the stormy sea the hot furnace exploded. Flames danced on the water, then hissed out, leaving boiling white smoke, charred lumber and stinking rubber in its wake. Waves crunched the decks and cabins, wadded up what was left of the helium-filled tubing as if it were onion skin paper. The rain cried on the remains. Lightning slashed yellow sabre cuts across the sky.

The corpses of the boiler room workers, par-boiled, popped to the top, bobbed on the waves like corks. Floating with them was the jar containing Cody's head. He was cursing violently, calling for Goober.

The waves shoved Cody up, dropped him in a trough of foaming water; he saw the corpse of Goober float by face down. Then the whitecaps turned his jar and tossed him; water ran down the speaking tube, joined the mixture inside his container. Cody licked at the water. Salty, of course. But it did kind of neutralize the pig urine.

For once, Cody was glad he didn't have a stomach; all he could feel was a kind of dizziness.

Nearby, clinging to planks, were Hickok, Annie and Bull. Cetshwayo and Frankenstein's monster were nowhere to be seen.

There were oil-fueled flames burning on the water. In the light they provided, Hickok, clasping his plank, saw the others. The dead boiler room workers, Goober popping about, Annie and Bull clinging to a plank together, and finally, the head of Cody, surfing the waves in his sturdy Mason jar.

Hickok paddled over to Bull and Annie, pulled his bowie knife from its scabbard, stuck it in his plank, said, "Bull, we got to get hold of Cody, then find a way to lash some of this junk together."

Bull nodded.

Hickok swam to Cody's jar, grabbed it, swam it over to Annie. Then he and Bull set about building a raft. It was tedious, but by dog paddling about, grabbing planks and cutting strips of floating rubber, they were able to fasten a half-dozen pieces of wood together.

By the time they finished jerry-rigging a raft, got Annie and Cody loaded on it, they were exhausted; the sun was burning through the haze, the rain was dying out, and the ocean was beginning to settle. Then the sharks came.

Hickok said, "No rest for the wicked, and the good don't need any."

Unconsciously, Hickok reached for his guns. But his sash was empty. They had been lost. He had even lost the bowie knife.

There were about a dozen of the beady-eyed bastards circling the makeshift craft. One of them came near, rolled on its side, showed its dark dead eyes. It opened its mouth to reveal a hunk of dark flesh dangling from its teeth. Part of an arm actually. They recognized it. It belonged to Cetshwayo.

"That not good," Bull said.

Cody, in his jar, was singing drinking songs.

"He's starting to lose it," Hickok said.

"It's the salt-water in the jar, mixed with his chemicals," Annie said. "And he could use a crank."

Hickok cranked him.

Cody went silent for a moment. Hickok held the jar in his lap, tilting it so he could look down into Cody's face.

"It's all right, pard. Or as good as it could be under the circumstances." Hickok turned the jar so Cody could see the contents of the raft. "We're the only survivors."

"All I want is a body so I can fight," Cody said. "If I can go down fighting, I'm all right."

Hickok placed Cody in the center of the raft, leaned back, waited for it to get hot and unbearable. He thought of food briefly, thought of water longer, then the flames on the water died and the sun rose high and hot and their flesh began to burn. The water in Cody's jar began to bubble.

Annie thought of Frank. For a long moment she remembered how he held her. Hickok held her, too. He was a passionate lover. But there was an urgency about him, a desire to get on with the act. Frank wasn't like that. He was slow about his business. God she missed him.

She opened her eyes, looked at Hickok. He had his eyes closed. His long hair was wet and matted. His clothes clung to him, drying slowly in the sun. She thought he was gorgeous.

She closed her eyes, tried to grab back her memories of Frank. But this time, they wouldn't come. She thought of Hickok again, back on the zeppelin, in her cabin, in her bed.

Bull looked out at the great expanse of water and thought of the Greasy Grass. Greasy Grass was what his people called the Little Big Horn, where Custer and his soldiers died. The Greasy Grass had looked like a sea of grass, and this ocean, right now, looked much the same way.

The Greasy Grass. What a fight.

Bull thought: Bad day for white guys. Big day for red guys.

He wished he had participated, but it was over by the time he tried to join the fight. He had always felt slighted by that.

Bull closed his eyes, saw Crazy Horse standing before him, wearing only a loin cloth, lean and strong with braided hair. He wore war paint. Spots on his body. He had the corpse of a hawk fastened to the side of his head.

He thought of how Crazy Horse had died. Held by his own people, bayonetted by soldiers.

"Sorry, friend," he said softly in Sioux. "I will soon join you."

Buffalo Bill dreamed of women. All the women he had known and loved. He dreamed last of Lily Langtry. Her long white limbs, her thick dark hair, the darker patch between her legs.

God, at least Louisa could have let him finish. She already had him dead to rights. What would another half a minute have mattered?

Oooooh, that was one evil woman.

Yeah. He had made up his mind. He got out of this pickle, he was divorcing that bitch.

By midday the sharks had become so bold it was necessary to use one of the two planks they had kept for paddles to fight them off.

All Hickok could think of was one of them coming up from below, hitting the center of their leaky, poorly lashed raft, sending them all into the ocean to be sorted out by hungry sharks.

The evil fish came more often. Hickok and Bull fought them back constantly, banging at their snouts, poking at their eyes. Bull wounded one of them bad enough it bled. The others turned on it, biting, ripping, pulling at strands of gut.

"Maybe reservation not such bad idea after all," Bull said. "Wish Bull fat ass there. Not here."

"I'd rather fight a whole parcel of Sioux than deal with this," Hickok said. "No offense."

"Fuck you, Hickok."

The day burned on. They ached from thirst. Then, as night was about to fall, they saw the fin of an enormous shark.

No. A whale.

But whales didn't have fins like that.

Huge. Slicing the water like some kind of prehistoric fish, speeding directly toward them.

Rising from the water, spilling bubbles over its side, it revealed a long snout and bulbous black eyes. The brute crackled with illumination.

"What are you waiting for," Hickok yelled at it. "Eat us or go away."

The strange beast made a creaking noise. A flap opened in its top and, like Jonah freed, a man scrambled out of it. He was lanky, bearded, wore sailor-style clothes and a fur cap. He had a large revolver strapped to his hip. His arms hung impossibly long by his sides.

"Ahoy," he said in an exotic voice. "You people seem in a bad way."

The insides of the great fish hummed. Behind them lay the eyes of the fish, which were actually a great, tinted, double-bubbled water shield. Before them was a long hall.

The sailor who had spoken to them and helped them onto the craft, sealed the round lid above them with a twist of a wheel. Two more sailors appeared. They looked just like the first sailor. Lanky, hairy, and long-armed. Close up, it was revealed they did not wear beards at all. Nor were those things on their heads hats. It was part of their heads. They had sharp teeth. They seemed to be large monkeys with good backbones.

They were carrying white fluffy robes. The first drew his revolver and pointed it at them.

"Put them on," he said.

"The guns aren't needed," Hickok said.

The one with the gun ignored him, said, "Take off your clothes. Put the robes on."

"I beg your pardon," Annie said.

"We will avert our eyes," the sailor said.

"Like hell you will," Hickok said.

The sailor pointing the pistol cocked it. "Please," he said.

Bull and Hickok, Cody's head under his arm, turned their backs for Annie while she undressed and slipped on the robe. Next, passing Cody's head to Annie, Hickok and the others slipped on their robes.

Later, Annie admitted that the sailors had been most polite, actually averting their eyes while she changed. Hickok thought they were certainly unlike any sailors he had ever heard of.

Once in the robes, the sailors escorted them down a long hallway tricked out in thick red carpet. They entered a large room that housed a magnificent library; the smell of books was rich, laced with the stench of cigars, a bit of spilled whiskey, a hint of perspiration and the stout stink of fish. There was a soft-looking red velvet couch and cushioned chair, a mahogany desk and a wooden chair. And the source of the fish smell.

A seal was perched in the stuffed chair, tail curled, holding a book with its flippers. It wore glasses on its nose, and a large, square, metal hat. It was obviously engrossed, flicking not a whisker or turning its head to observe them. Beside it, in a bowl, were the remains of several sardines — heads and fins.

As they watched, one of the seal's flippers moved, turned a page.

Bull, Annie and Hickok looked at one another, looked back at the seal. Hickok, who had ended up with Cody's head, lifted the jar so Cody could see what they saw.

"You don't see that often," Cody said.

"I think he's actually reading that book," Annie said. "And it looks as if he has thumbs on his flippers."

"Oh, I assure you," said a voice, "he is reading the book, and those are thumbs of a sort."

They turned, saw a tall gentleman dressed in a soft white shirt, blue velvet trousers, woven sandals. He was nice looking with wide-spaced eyes, a large forehead, dark skin, and silvery hair.

All of the sailors, save one, disappeared. The remaining sailor edged backwards out of the way, but at service. He was the sailor with the gun. He dropped it by his side, but made no move to holster it.

"Ned, that's the seal, becomes deeply involved," the man said, "but

53

the mere smell of a fresh fish will jerk him out of his concentration."

"What do seals read?" Hickok asked.

"Actually, his personal reading habits aren't up to snuff. He likes dime novels. *The Adventures of Buffalo Bill.*"

Bill cleared his throat. It sounded more like someone spitting water.

"Good Lord, is that a living head?" the man asked.

"I certainly am," Cody said. "I am Buffalo Bill Cody."

"No shit?"

"No shit."

The man took the jar from Hickok and examined it carefully. "You do look like him."

"It's him," Annie said.

The man gave the jar back to Hickok, studied Annie. "My, but you are lovely. And who are you?"

"I'm Annie Oakley, this is Sitting Bull, and Wild Bill Hickok."

"Well I will be twisted and peed on. I am honored. I know of all of you. My name is Bemo. Captain Bemo to my friends. This ship is my creation, the *Naughty Lass.*

"I named her that because she was a bitch to build," Bemo said. "My original name for her was *Sea Shark*, but no one in my original crew liked that one. Lots of grumbling about the name. I changed it to *Nasty Sea Shark*, but that didn't excite anyone either. I even considered *The Real Nasty Sea Shark*, but by that time I'd lost everyone. I should have just called it what I wanted. I didn't have to answer to anyone. Not then. But, I wanted to please. Finally, I decided on the *Naughty Lass.*"

"By the way, we've heard of you, too." Hickok said. "And the *Naughty Lass.*"

Neither Hickok nor the others mentioned Bemo had been considered a pirate, noted for destroying vessels on the high seas. It had been his way to combat war, destroying the ships that made war or carried goods for war. Every navy in the world put a price on Bemo and his ship, but the bounty came to naught. Since the attacks on ships ceased, it had been thought for the last few years that he had lost himself at sea.

"But you're supposed to be dead," Annie said.

"Don't believe everything you read," Bemo said. "And while I'm on the subject, there were some photos that got out. Me...unclothed, and well...I just want to say, if you saw those photos... Well, it was cold."

54

"Photos?" Annie asked.

"Taken by a disgruntled crew member. A female crew member, I hasten to add. I posed for them, caught up in the moment, you might say. Quite a mistake. They appeared in some French periodicals. So, again, don't believe everything you read, or see. In fact, I'm certain those photos were doctored. They can do that sort of thing, you know."

"Don't believe everything you read is right," Hickok said. "Including the stuff in Buffalo Bill dime novels."

"Some of it's real," Cody said. "And I thought it was *Naughty Ass*. Not *Naughty Lass*. I'm a little disappointed."

"Come," Bemo said. "Sit. I'll have food brought. All of it from the sea. Afterwards, seaweed cigars."

"I hate I'll miss that," Cody said.

"You're being snide," Bemo said. "But you really will miss out. This seaweed is high in nicotine. Quite tasty. Better than Cuban, actually. The only thing missing is it isn't rolled on the thighs of Cuban women. That's how it's done, you know."

"If that's true, I miss it already," Cody said. "The Cuban cigars, that is."

"These were actually rolled on the thighs of my crew," Bemo said. "That's not something I like to consider while I'm smoking."

"By the way," Hickok said. "Who is your crew? They are unusual."

"Ugly," Bull said.

"Yes, they are," Bemo said. "They're monkeys. Or they were. They have been altered through surgery, genetics and chemicals. Their intelligence has been raised, and for the last twenty years or so, they, and...others, have been receiving training in all the basics. Reading, Writing, Arithmetic. The last part gives them trouble, but they try. I think their English is quite good, don't you? Come. Please. Take a seat."

The seal didn't give up his seat. He gave them a quick, uninterested glance, went back to reading.

There was plenty of room on the couch, and soon they were seated, telling their story, each filling in a little bit here and there.

"The Frankenstein creation," said Captain Bemo. "Ah, yes. I've heard of him. Lost to the waves, you say. Not exactly a prosaic life, his, now was it? Or maybe it was overly prosaic. Depends on how you look at it, I suppose. Met the monster's creator once. Convention of inventors and scientists in Vienna. This was before he made news with his creation. Quite the bore, actually. Couldn't stop talking about anatomy, brains and venereal disease. Had one, if I remember correctly. A venereal disease, of course. I'm sure you know he had anatomy and a brain, but the part about the disease, that is most likely news to you. Ghastly subject matter, venereal disease, isn't it?"

Annie said, "Thanks for rescuing us."

"When the storm finished I thought it would be more energy-saving to travel on top of the sea, rather than under it. We found you entirely by accident. Think about that. We surface, and there you are. The proverbial needle in a haystack. Of course, since we weren't looking for you, you weren't even that. A happy accident. But this isn't exactly a rescue."

The zeppelinauts considered that statement, let it hang.

"About the seal?" Hickok asked. "I'm curious, is he just doing a trick? You were kidding about him reading, right?"

"Him like that hat?" Bull asked.

Bemo grinned. "That's not a hat. It's a brain enhancer. A bit of surgery was required, and now the brain, having grown to three times its size, needs more room. Thus, the hat, as you call it. Hat and brain have long since fused. The glasses are for bad eyesight, of course. And yes, he can read, and from the notes he takes, it's apparent he understands what he reads quite well. When left to his own devices, his reading habits are quite atrocious, but he can read heavier material if put to it. He's a good researcher. Takes insightful notes."

"Notes?" Annie said. "He can write?"

"It's a bit messy," Bemo said. "But legible. He's working on it. Wears a pad and pencil around his neck."

"Can he talk?" Hickok asked.

"Don't be ridiculous," Bemo said. "Isn't it enough he can read and write and use the toilet? He can stand a bit more upright than the average seal, however. He's had some adjustments. He does have a tendency to lose his glasses, and that's why we've added a chain to the ear pieces, so that he can hang it, along with his pen and pad, around his neck."

"You did that?" Cody asked. "Expanded his brain. Taught him to read."

"Oh, no. I'm talented. But my abilities tend to be more of the mechanical, ecological nature. This is the work of Doctor Momo."

"Momo?" Cody said. "I thought he might be dead."

Bemo grimaced. "No. He's quite alive, I assure you. Ned is sort of on loan to me. I have him read certain texts, evaluate them, write up his notes. He also takes dictation from me."

"What's he researching?" Annie asked.

"Material for Doctor Momo," Bemo said. "There are a number of items Momo needs for his experiments that only come from the sea. I acquire these for him, and do some research. With Ned's help, of course."

"I've wanted to meet Doctor Momo for some time," Cody said. "I have friends who would love to meet him as well. Sam Morse. Professor Maxxon. Chuck Darwin. Many others."

"My goodness," Bemo said. "Famous people, all. This is wonderful. Your friends may not get their wish, but you will, Mr. Cody. And the friends with you. You will meet him. We are, in fact, on our way to Momo's island."

"You're jerkin' me," Cody said.

"As how there's little to jerk," Bemo said, "I doubt that. And by the by, how did that happen, good man? The head business and the jar, I mean?"

"Cut myself shaving," Cody said.

"Very well, your business," Bemo said. "No need to discuss it."

"And you're not jerking me about Doctor Momo?"

"I said as much. And beyond the physical, neither am I jerking you in a figurative sense. We are indeed on our way to see Doctor Momo."

"I suppose you two are great friends," Annie said.

"No, actually, I hate the sonofabitch, but..." Bemo stood from his place on the couch, turned to reveal the back of his head.

It was missing. A large chunk of hair and skull had been removed. There was a shiny bulb screwed into his brain, the gray matter around it pulsed.

When Bemo turned to face them, he said, "You see, I'm in a bit of a pickle. Wrecked the *Naughty Lass* on his island once. I was grievously injured in the wreck. My crew was killed. Doctor Momo saved me. But, knowing who I was and what I could do for him, he cut out a bit of my brain, fastened in an apparatus that makes me submissive to him and in need of frequent bowel movements. I talk a little fruity, as well. I'm a kind of zombie."

"Good Lord," said Cody.

"Yes," Bemo said. "And in short time you will meet my master. And you won't like it that much, I assure you. An absolute asshole, Momo. Absolute."

The rescued zeppelinauts spent the night in comfort in separate cabins, Cody's head in the library on a shelf. In spite of Bemo's disconcerting revelations about the zombie business and the comment about them not going to like Momo, for the first time in three days, mostly due to exhaustion, they slept well and awoke rested.

During the night their clothes had been cleaned and dried, left folded at their bedsides before morning. Annie had been supplied with a large box of brushes, combs and hair pins. She used them minimally, looking lovely with little effort.

Early morning, for their benefit, just before arrival at the island, Bemo had taken the *Naughty Lass* down. They stood at the great water shield and watched. Hickok held Cody's jar. The sea foamed about the nose of the sub, then overwhelmed it. They dropped deep, burned a bright exploratory light that revealed all manner of fish and water creatures. They saw reefs. They saw shipwrecks.

"I really would like to have shown you Atlantis," Bemo said, "but, alas, we are nowhere near it, and I'm afraid I don't choose for myself much anymore. You know how it is, the bulb and all."

An hour before they reached the island, a breakfast was provided. There was stewed kelp, salmon, fish eggs and kippers. There was a kind of coffee made from dried seaweed. There was bread ground from an underwater plant. It was all delicious. Cody, unable to eat, was the table centerpiece.

A mile out from the island, they surfaced. The *Naughty Lass* entered the island of Doctor Momo via an inlet bordered on both sides by a monkey- and parrot-filled jungle.

Bemo allowed them on the sea-slick deck of the *Naughty Lass* as they sailed in. Hickok carried Cody's head. Bull watched the monkeys leaping and chattering with the same deadpan expression as always. Blue and red parrots exploded from the jungle, water birds burst toward the sky in blues, whites and grays. Huge water snakes were spotted.

Bull blinked once, having thought he saw a female head poke from the water, but when he looked again, there was only a huge fish tail flipping up and dropping away.

Annie had Ned the seal at her side. She had tried to pet and coo to him the night before, but the seal wasn't having any until she explained the head in the jar was that of Buffalo Bill, the hero of the dime novels Ned loved. After that, the seal was her companion.

Annie attempted to introduce Ned to the head of his hero, but Ned was too nervous. Hero worship prevented it. But he had taken to carrying a copy of one of Buntline's dime novels under his flipper. It was titled *Buffalo Bill's Journey to the Centre of the Earth*. Also included, *Richard, Lord of the Jungle, or, the Swinging Dick*.

Upon arriving at the dock, they were greeted by a strange sight. A hunchback and a metal man.

"We have a welcoming party," Hickok said.

"Yes," Bemo said. "I used the Marconi Wave to send news ahead."

The hunchback was excessively hairy. His face was dark with it. Hair pushed out of the back of his shirt and through the front where it buttoned. He scuttled hurriedly onto the deck as if he might be receiving candy. He had a wandering eye, a left foot larger than his right, a buck-toothed smile, and a less than conventional dress pattern. He wore a white shirt, a bow tie and a jet-black bowler hat and thatched sandals. He seemed nervous, as if ants had taken to his rectum.

The metal man was even more amazing. Sleek, well-formed, his face appeared to have been modeled after the Greek god Apollo. He flashed in the sun like a rifle barrel. Like the hunchback, his manner of dress was unusual. He wore a pair of knee-length red shorts, a black vest that was wide open, revealing his rippled blue-metal stomach and swollen chest. He had pink painted toenails.

A chain was fastened to the left side of the vest; it stretched across the gap, where it disappeared into the right vest pocket; the pocket bulged with the shape of an enormous turnip watch; it could be heard ticking, like the beating of a small tin drum.

"Oh," said the hunchback. "What we got here? Oh, my goodness, she's so lovely. You're a lovely, lovely lady."

When he spoke there was a chattering to his voice, as if he had learned English from monkeys.

Annie smiled. "Thank you, sir. And your name?"

"Jack. At your service." He scooped the bowler off his head, bowing low. "May I escort you to shore?"

"That would be most gracious," Annie said.

Ned took her hand in his mouth, began to lead her toward the dock.

"Ned!" Jack said. "I just offered my services."

Ned paid no attention. With Annie laughing, he guided her off the boat, onto the dock. Jack followed, paying close attention to the swing of Annie's ass.

Hickok shifted Cody to the crook of his left arm, and out of habit, reached to touch the butts of his guns.

Of course, there was nothing there.

Warily, he proceeded ashore.

As Bull stepped off the submarine with Bemo, he said, "Any place to do business?"

"Business?" Bemo asked.

"Number two?"

"Number what?"

"Shit? Need shit."

"Oh, why yes. I'll show you one of the outdoor facilities."

They were led to a great house made of native logs and thatch. It was stately, two stories, surrounded by a compound with palisades and a massive gate.

There were inhabitants in the fort. They were monkey men. No monkey women were visible.

The Wild Westers were given rooms. Annie and Hickok insisted on a room together, and their wish was granted. Cody also had a room. He was placed on a dresser with the back of his head to the mirror; seeing his head floating in a jar was just too much for the vain Cody and he insisted he be placed that way.

Heated water was brought in and poured for baths by the monkey people. White cotton trousers and a white jacket were supplied for Bull, Hickok and Annie. There were also little cotton shoes with thatch soles.

Cody's jar was cleaned and the big tin lid was polished.

Their doors were locked from the outside.

FLAMING ZEPPELINS

Late in the day, their doors were unlocked by the metal man, who told them in his metallic voice that his name was Tin. He carried Cody, led the others along a corridor and into a fine dining room that connected to a sunlit veranda, a long table and tall-back chairs.

Ned, the seal, waddled into the room, and when he saw Buffalo Bill being carried by the Tin Man, he brightened. Bemo followed shortly behind, looking pleasant enough for a man with a pulsing bulb in the back of his brain.

At the table, Tin introduced them to the middle-aged, gray-haired Momo who was already seated, dressed in white cotton shirt and trousers, drinking a very dark wine, spots of which dotted the front of his shirt. He smiled at them with gray, slightly bucked teeth in a tan face. His eyes looked like the ass end of silver bullets.

Tin guided each of the guests to their seat. Hickok was on the left of Momo, Annie the right. Cody's head was placed in the middle of the table, and Bull was placed at the far end, facing Momo. Bemo sat next to Bull. Tin and Ned did not take a seat. They stood near the edge of the veranda, watching and waiting.

A moment later, Jack scuttled into the room, scraping and shuffling, his bowler hat in his hand. With him came a faint aroma that might have been dung and sweat sweetened with urine.

"Sorry I'm late, Doctor," Jack said. "So sorry."

"Very well," Momo said. "Tell Catherine she may serve now."

"Yes, Doctor," Jack said, put on his bowler and scuttled from the room. When he returned a moment later, he removed his hat, squatted next to Momo's chair.

The meal was served by an attractive woman with thick black hair. She was short and well built and had a curious way of moving. Her eyes were bright green and her mouth was broad and thick lipped. She wore a short yellow dress. It was just to her knees and the boots she wore were black and laced and very tiny.

Catherine moved quickly and carefully until everyone was served. When she bent to serve him, Hickok noted that she had a pleasant musky aroma about her.

Finished, she disappeared from the room, silent as a cat.

The food, though tasty in design, was hard to consume because of Momo's dining habits.

The hunchback sat in a chair next to Momo and fed him his dinner bite by bite with a long wooden fork. Sometimes, if the meat being served was not tender enough, the hunchback pre-chewed it for Momo, placed it on the fork when it was properly soft and soggy, and fed it to the good doctor.

Even Bull — who had eaten grubs and maggots, boiled dogs and raw buffalo livers, picked corn kernels out of horse shit, and was accustomed to poking food into his mouth with his fingers — was appalled.

"I am most glad to have you here as guests," Momo said with a jaw full of food, then stopped suddenly, reached a probing finger into his mouth, pulled out a wad of graying meat. "This still has gristle," he said to Jack.

"Sorry, Doctor," Jack said, took the food from Momo's finger, poked it into his own mouth, began chewing vigorously.

While Jack was at work on the meat, Momo said, "This island is my island, and I welcome you. Of course, you won't be leaving."

"And what's to stop us?" Cody asked.

"Tin," Momo said sharply. "Come in here, please."

The metal man stepped forward. Momo said, "Demonstrate."

Tin picked up one of the empty chairs, wadded it into curled splinters with a slight movement of his hands.

"He can also run fast, see extreme distances, and for reasons I won't go into here, he's very dedicated to me. There are also other obstacles you would face escaping from this island. My servants and guards. The ocean itself. It's best just to be comfortable."

At that moment, Catherine, the servant, reappeared with a tray containing dessert and coffee. She set both in the center of the table, poured each of them a cup of java, served them heavy devil's food cake and left the room. As she passed, Doctor Momo patted her on the behind.

"Good girl," he said.

Hickok said, "We would prefer to leave, Doctor."

"I'm afraid I must insist," Momo said. "Nothing bad will come of you if you stay. I mean, in one shape or fashion you will carry on. It's not so horrible here. We have a large house, plenty of rooms, built by the island's labor. And I believe you will find me an amusing host."

"I'm already amused," Annie said.

"Good," Momo said.

"Who are these islanders?" Cody asked.

"Actually, when I arrived, this island was populated only by animals."

"You're saying they are your creations?" Cody said.

"Very astute," Momo said, lifting a hip, cutting a fart sharp enough to use as a bread knife. "I've been most busy. Our servant, Catherine, or as I sometimes call her, Cat, was produced from a small species of wildcat on the island. Not a large cat, I might add. But look at her now."

"Ridiculous," Annie said.

"And Jack here. He was once a chimpanzee." Momo reached out and tapped Jack on the head. Jack smiled, and for the first time they could see that his teeth had been filed off to appear more human.

"All right," Annie said. "In his case, I believe it."

"I am aware of your work," Cody said. "But I've never heard that you actually created human beings."

"You're aware of my old work, Mr. Cody. It is nothing compared to what I'm doing now. Captain Bemo told me of your friends. Samuel Morse. Professor Maxxon. Who else? Darwin? I understand you also had in your possession Frankenstein's creation."

"That's correct," Cody said.

"A shame you lost the creature. I'm sure it would have made quite a toy for the island. And these friends of yours, Morse, Maxxon. Good minds compared to yourself and the average moron, but compared to mine, their brains are doo-doo."

"Doo-doo?" Hickok said.

"Yes, doo-doo," Momo said. "And this monster Frankenstein created…child's play. Nothing of real importance. Cobbling a body out of corpses. That's not creation. That's re-creation. My work…that's creation. Tell them, Jack."

"It's very creative," Jack said.

"Damn, he's cute," Momo said. "I love this guy. I can remember a time when he only ate bananas and played with his balls. But look at him now. He looks near human. Ugly, but human. Still, look at him. He doesn't just eat bananas now. Eats meat as well. Still plays with his balls, but you can't accomplish everything in one fell swoop."

"What we would like," Annie said, "is for you to allow Captain Bemo to deliver us home. That is all we ask. Once we arrive, we would be glad to pay you for your inconvenience."

"Ah, my beautiful Little Miss Sure Shot. Your reputation precedes you, and I would be very amused to see you shoot sometime, and I would very much like to see you with your naked butt turned over a log, but, I cannot let you go."

Hickok jumped to his feet. "Don't you dare speak to her that way. I challenge you to back up your mouth, Mister. Guns. Knives. Bare hands."

"I'll use Tin," Momo said.

Tin slapped Hickok on the shoulder, knocking him to the ground.

"Sorry about that," Momo said. "Tin, help him up."

"I can manage," Hickok said.

Tin pulled Hickok to his feet anyway, sat him in his chair. Annie leaned over, put a hand on Hickok's knee, whispered, "Take it easy. He's about a quart shy a gallon."

"The problem is," Momo said, "you will not forget you have been here. I know human nature better than that. Mr. Cody, wouldn't you like a body to go with that head? Wouldn't you want to see my research go on until I'm ready to reveal it to the world? Not have some do-gooder who thinks I am evil rush out here to the island to put a ruin to my work? Think of it. Goddamn Christians tromping around on this paradise. Destroying what I have accomplished. Putting up churches. Trying to teach my people about God. A fool's mission. I am not even sure they have souls."

"Fuck Christians," Bull said suddenly.

Everyone looked to the end of the table. Bull raised his drinking glass. "Death to Christians," he said. "Dirty shit-heads." Bull took a long pull at the wine in his glass.

"Well now, a kindred spirit," Momo said.

"No," Bull said, pouring himself more wine. "Bull not like Christians. Pretty much think you asshole."

"Honesty is the best policy," Momo said. Then to Cody: "But that body to go with your head. You would like it, would you not?"

"I would," Cody said. "In fact, I have a body. My old one. Back home. On ice. Powered by electricity and batteries. All that modern science allows keeps it alive, waiting until a method can be discovered for reconnecting my head to my shoulders."

"Why wait?" Momo said. "I can do it for you now."

"You can?"

"You bet your ass I can," Momo said, "Then again, you don't have an ass, do you?"

"You all ass," Bull said.

"Mr. Indian Man," Momo said, "do not push me."

Bull grinned.

"I do not want just any body attached to my head," Cody said.

"Posh. I do not work that way. I will grow you a body. From your own cells. It would be like the body you had before. Only younger. Stronger. It is no trouble. Not really. I have never done it before, of course. Not having any humans to work on, but I have done it with animals, and I'm ready to give it the old college try, and all that. I am certain I can do it. Whoa. Hold on."

Momo let a fart fly. Jack went to fanning immediately.

Annie said, "I hope you can grow some manners while you're at it."

"Understand, on this island I set the standards for behavior," Momo said. "And I delight in violating the old rules. Makes me feel in control, you know. Kind of a flaw actually, but there you have it. And you know what, young lady? I may just see you naked and bent over that log yet. In fact, I may brand you on the hip. A big fat M for Momo."

Angry, Hickok eyed Tin. Tin, as if reading his mind, was eyeing him. Hickok thought about it a moment, decided it was best to bide his time. He forced himself to turn his attention to dessert and coffee.

After his first forkful, he glanced at Bull. Bull had already eaten his dessert and was pouring himself more coffee. He seemed to have lost all interest in the conversation.

Bull was like that. Paid attention until it didn't seem necessary to pay attention anymore. Kept his feelings to himself most of the time, but now and then, as with his comments about Momo, he'd let an opinion loose.

Bull said, "Got cigar?"

Momo eyed Bull for a moment, then... "A proper suggestion," Momo said. "Bemo prepares these from seaweed."

"So we know," Hickok said, waving a hand at Bemo. "Why have you done...*this* to Bemo?"

"I found him and his sub in one of my coves. His crew was dead. Bemo was badly injured himself. The only survivor. The *Naughty Lass* had been injured badly as well. I, of course, knew about him, his activities on the high seas, his strong stance against war and all the machines of war. I didn't really give a shit about that, but I thought I could use him, so, I made some adjustments in his brain, as well as gave him medical attention. He got better, and I created a crew for him...literally. They were originally howler monkeys, every one of them. The island is covered in my monkey creations. All male. Bemo, like the monkey men, though less willingly, does my bidding. Correct, Bemo?"

"I'd rather not," Bemo said. "But yes."

"But yes," Momo repeated. "If he doesn't, I don't replace the special bulb in his gray matter on a regular basis, and he dies. I can control him quite easily if he becomes annoying, or decides, as now, to adopt a sort of smart attitude in his voice." Momo produced from his pocket a chain, and what looked like a watch.

"No," Bemo said.

Momo pressed the device. Bemo screamed, fell out of his chair, onto the floor.

"I will be good. I will be good." Bemo repeated over and over.

Momo ceased pressing the watch. "Careful, Bemo, you'll burst your bulb on the floor there, and that wouldn't be good. And you are damn right you will be good. Jack, see to some cigars. Get a big fat one for Bemo. I have a feeling he'll need it. Miss Oakley? A cigar for you? Any kind at all. You know what I mean. You know of Freud, do you not? A real cigar? A symbolic one that I personally can provide?"

"No thank you," Annie said.

Ned, who had stood silent near Annie, eased forward, touched her elbow with his cold nose. When she looked down at him, she could see he was trembling and there were tears in his big black eyes.

The Wild Westers were given limited run of the island. They could visit one another in their rooms during the day, could venture about the house and veranda, but were not to go upstairs to Momo's private quarters, nor were they to go to what Momo called the Barracks. This was a chain of small buildings at the edge of the compound where his "people" lived and where his laboratory was located. The laboratory he referred to as the House of Discomfort.

They also had access to the closest beach, but were asked not to wander off in the woods, or to the beach on the opposite end of the island.

A few days went by, and one night in their room, Hickok and Annie, having finished lovemaking, lay close and talked. "What kinds of wild animals would be on an island like this one?" Hickok asked.

"Pigs?" Annie said. "Rabbits. Squirrels, maybe."

"I suppose."

"Crocodiles possibly. Isn't there some kind of saltwater crocodile?"

"I don't know," Hickok said. "I believe there is."

"Monkeys, of course. And parrots. Other kinds of birds. Snakes maybe. Rats. Ships could have brought in creatures like that. I would guess different kinds of lizards. Cats. He said Catherine was made of a wildcat, if you believe that."

"Why not? I believe he made those guards from monkeys. And Jack from a chimpanzee."

"I suppose you're right, but she looks to have been a more successful experiment. Wouldn't you say?"

"She's all right," Hickok said, giving the classic male answer when a female asks a man's opinion of the appearance of another female. He quickly changed the subject. "No big predatory cats would be here," Hickok said. "Regular ship cats were most likely marooned, mated, produced a wild species, but hardly anything life threatening to humans. Certainly not bears. Not on an island this small."

"So what are you saying?"

"I'm saying, Annie, that Momo admits to creating humans from animals, if you can call a creation like that human, but at worst, his source for these creations is house cats, monkeys, possibly wild hogs, or dogs. Nothing truly dangerous. But why would he not want us in the woods, or the far side of the beach? What could harm us?"

"The creations themselves?"

"We've seen them. Think about Bemo's sailors. Long arms. Very hairy. Didn't have sense enough to look at you when you were naked. They carry guns, but, unless given direct orders, they seem harmless enough. Not dangerous by nature."

"He said the one he calls Jack was developed from a chimpanzee.

Could chimpanzees be deadly?"

"Probably brought the chimpanzee to the island himself. And I don't believe chimpanzees are by nature particularly dangerous. Unless provoked, that is? Again, I'm no animal expert, but I say what's to harm us? What's his fear? And does he truly care about our welfare? He doesn't strike me as all that worked up about anyone other than himself."

"Why does it matter?"

"Why wouldn't he want us to wander about other than for our own protection? Could it be he fears we might find a way off the island? A boat perhaps. Is that what he's keeping us from?"

"So, of course, you want to investigate."

"Of course. But right now there's something else I'd like to investigate...a flat brown mole on the inside of your right thigh."

"That's not a mole."

"No?"

"Believe it or not, it's a powder burn."

"Say what?"

"I've only told Frank this, but when I was young, learning to shoot, I became enraptured with guns. I handled them like a gambler handles cards. Handled them nude even. I once had an old Colt revolver without a trigger guard, just had the trigger hanging out. I thought, what if I turned it upside down, between my legs, barrel pointing out like a man's...you know..."

"Johnson."

"Yes...well, I wanted to see if I could pull the trigger with the muscles in my...you know."

"Vagina."

"I believe I would have said the lips of my Venus Mound, but yes. And, I did."

"I'll be damned."

"But the barrel was short, the load was heavy, took a powder flash, burned a spot into my thigh and it's been there ever since."

"Did you hit the target?"

"I hate to report it was a miss...but the second time I tried it, I hit it. And I didn't burn myself."

"Can you still do it?"

"I don't know, I haven't tried it since. But you know what?"

"What?"

"There are other things I can do."

Hickok rolled on top of her, said, "I know that."

"Yeah, well, there are some things I know you don't know about. Yet."

"I doubt that."

"Years of marriage teaches possibilities."

"Show me."

She did. And she was right.

That afternoon, out on the beach, Bull walked with Annie and Hickok. The seal followed from a distance, thinking itself hid. Ducking behind rises of sand from time to time, clumps of bush.

Hickok said to Bull, "We were thinking about violating Momo's orders."

"Bull good at no follow orders," Bull said. "Momo crazy white eyes. Like to cut him. Think it fun to scalp little man. Like his hat."

"Jack, you mean?" Annie asked.

"Ugh."

"It would look good on you, Bull," Annie said. "The hat. Not the scalp."

"Where Cody?"

"With Momo." Hickok said.

"Him need help?"

"His own choice," Annie said. "Maybe he thinks he can find out something that will help us if he buddies up to Momo. And I think he'd like a new body to go with that head."

"Can't blame him for that," Hickok said. "But I've known him a long time. He always comes around when the chips are down."

"Let's walk," Annie said.

"What about our tagalong?" Hickok said, jerking his head toward Ned.

"I think Ned likes us. Especially Cody. He reads the dime novels. All of us are in them. He idolizes us."

In an outbuilding stuffed with beakers, test tubes, wires, lights and colored liquids, Momo worked a booger free from his nose with a dirty finger, wiped it on his pants, said, "I doubt your friends understand what I'm trying to accomplish here, but you, Mr. Cody, being perhaps the most worldly of the bunch...I believe you must."

As Momo talked, Buffalo Bill's head was placed dead center of a long wooden table by Jack. The liquid in Cody's jar had changed colors, gone pale. Cody felt stranger than usual. The turning of the crank by Jack did little to stir the cobwebs in his brain. Cody was beginning to feel — and he had to laugh when he thought it — disconnected; as if his soul were being stretched like taffy.

He supposed there were a variety of reasons for this. The fouled liquid in his jar. The aging and watering of the mechanical devices attached to his neck; the wires that were traced to his brain; the unoiled mechanism of the crank.

At the table's end, directly in front of him, was a square glass receptacle placed on a six-inch-thick metal platform. The glass contained a howler monkey's head. The head was alive, juiced by a power pack situated on top of the container. From the power pack, cables ran into the side of the glass, plugged directly into the monkey's brain. There was no liquid in the container. The monkey looked alert. Its neck swiveled on a rotator.

"He can turn and look in different directions merely by stretching muscles in his neck and cheeks," Momo said. "It took a bit of effort to teach him, but a man could learn it rather quickly. An afternoon or two, would be my guess."

"And if you smile too hard," Cody said, his voice coming weakly through the speech tube, "do you spin about like a top?"

"It takes a special kind of effort. Not hard, but more effort than you would have smiling, or frowning. Or eating."

"Of course, the monkey doesn't eat," Cody said.

"Oh, he does," Momo said.

"But how? It would run into his neck, fill up...he can't."

"He can, and does. Jack!"

Jack scuttled about in the back, clanking this, clanking that, finally showed up with a flexible tube, fastened it to the sides of the metal platform; the opposite end of the tube was dropped into a metal container, a large can to be exact.

The front of the glass case was snapped free. Jack produced a wild plum, held it up to the monkey's mouth. The teeth snapped as Jack jerked the plum back. The monkey worked its mouth, frantic for the fruit.

"That is quite enough of that business, Jackie-Boy," Momo said. "Tease him when I'm not demonstrating. He has such fun with that silly monkey head."

Jack laughed, placed the plum so the monkey could eat it.

It gobbled hungrily as Jack moved his fingers out of the way of the monkey's teeth.

"This way," Momo said, "though the monkey has no stomach, it can taste the plum. The refuse runs through a gap in its neck, into the box on which the contraption rests. From there it's sucked out by the tubes and into the metal stomach, as I like to call it. Is that not some clever shit?"

The plum gone, Jack turned a key on the side of the box. It began to pump, pulling the plum refuse from the box and into the metal stomach. Cody could hear it plopping into the bottom with a thud.

"For the monkey, it doesn't matter," Momo said. "He doesn't need food. I give the head an injection daily. This injection provides all the nutrients the brain, the skin, the eyes need. The cables are there for extra help, but I've improved my work so much, he really doesn't need them. An electrical charge is no longer necessary...do you miss taste, Mr. Cody?"

"I do."

"I thought you might. Put the monkey away, Jack. In fact, get rid of it. I've had it long enough. Perhaps we'll have a new use for our apparatus. A more important one. Huh, Mr. Cody?"

Jack produced a screwdriver, unfastened the head from the platform, pulled it free of wires and tubes with a plopping sound. Holding the creature's head by its fur, Jack shoved the back door open, tossed the head up slightly, gave it a sharp kick, causing it to disappear into the distance.

"Plenty monkeys where that one came from," Momo said.

They walked along the beach, and as they walked the jungle to the left of them grew thicker and darker and the sounds from it intensified. The ocean crashed over the algae-covered rocks to their right, foamed around them, crashed against the beach.

They were soon past the point Momo permitted, and they kept walking.

The natural sandy beach changed, became more barren, narrow and rock-laden. The jungle turned ever darker and thrived closer and closer to the sea. The sounds of birds and animals intensified.

Once, Hickok stopped suddenly, looked at what he thought was a face poking out of the foliage, but when he blinked, it was gone.

"Did you see that?" Hickok asked.

"What is it?" Annie asked.

"It looked like a wild hog, with large tusks, but..."

"But what?"

"Its face was nearly six feet off the ground. It had to be standing upright. But that can't be."

Bull grunted. "Was hog. Hog man. Saw it."

Hickok and Annie looked at Bull. Hickok said, "You saw it too?"

"Bull see."

"Maybe Momo did have a positive reason to keep us away from the jungle and the other side of the beach," Annie said. "Maybe he has other creations. Not so successful ones. He said something to that effect. I didn't realize he meant they were...out here."

"Could be," Hickok said, "but I'd still like to see the other side. I don't cotton to being stuck on this island forever. Not if I can find a boat. Or someone who can get us off."

"Perhaps we could take the *Naughty Lass*," Annie said.

"I wouldn't know how to control it," Hickok said. "We'd sink."

"Bemo might help us."

"Not with that thing in his head. He might want to, but there wouldn't be any way."

"Talk less," Bull said. "Walk more."

They continued along the beach, keeping a wary eye directed toward the jungle. In time they came to a wad of seaweed and driftwood on the beach. As they neared it, they saw something was entangled in it. It was a large man wearing the shreds of a Japanese kimono.

It was the Frankenstein monster, minus an arm. Like Cetshwayo, the sharks had torn it off. Unlike Cetshwayo, the monster had survived. The block of wood had been wrenched from its foot, and now there was only a nub of bone visible.

"My God," Annie said. "Is he...alive?"

"Fact is," Hickok said, "he was dead before he was what he is now.

Whatever that is."

"Please see," Annie said.

Hickok went to check. He raked back some seaweed, touched the creature's neck. "No pulse," he said. "But I don't know that means anything."

It didn't. The monster slowly raised its remaining arm, opened its hand and clasped it over Hickok's.

"For lack of more accurate words," Hickok said, "it's alive."

Bull stayed with the monster while Annie and Hickok returned to the compound. Momo was on the veranda sitting in a wicker chair, drinking a tall mint julep served by Catherine, the woman who had been a cat.

When Hickok told Momo what they had found, Momo's countenance clouded.

"You went beyond the point I asked of you," Momo said.

"It was an accident," Hickok lied. "We just got carried away. It was so beautiful. The weather was so nice. And then we saw the monster. I hope you'll forgive our trespassing."

"Very well," Momo said. But he didn't sound very forgiving.

Momo sent a rescue party in a motorized vehicle. Behind the hooded motor was an enclosed, two-seat, black cab. Inside the cab rode Tin and Jack. Tin operated the craft with a stick he wobbled left and right; a pedal he pushed with his foot. At his left was a crank he used for a brake. The cab pulled a flatbed cargo carrier made of wood panels. Annie and Hickok rode on that. The vehicle moved an exciting five miles an hour on flat-rimmed metal wheels. The motor made a sound like something dying and whining in pain.

Eventually they came to the spot where Bull sat on a hunk of driftwood, and nearby the monster lay tangled in seaweed.

When the vehicle was stopped, Jack bounded over to the monster, sniffing the air. "He stinks. He stinks good."

When Tin saw the monster lying there, he startled so much his body made a noise like teapots slamming together. "He is so big."

"Yeah," Hickok said. "He's a big one."

"And he is made from the parts of other men?" Tin asked.

"That's the story," Hickok said. "And I believe it. In a way, he's not living at all. He moves. He thinks. But he's not really living."

"Neither am I," said Tin.

Hickok rapidly changed the subject. "Let's load him up."

They laid the monster on the flatbed, turned the vehicle around, started back. Bull joined Hickok and Annie on the bed with the monster.

They hadn't gone far when the creatures appeared.

They came out of the woods and stood in front of the vehicle, which Tin slowed to a stop just in time to keep from running over them. They didn't seem to realize that the vehicle could crush them. There were at least twenty of them, and shortly thereafter, twenty more. Their numbers kept increasing as they slipped from the woods to surround and crowd the vehicle.

They stood like men, wore rags of clothes, but were more animal in appearance than human. Theirs were the faces of hogs, dogs, goats, bears, cows, a lion, a wolf and even one reptilian face. Some of them seemed to be two or three animals blended.

Yet, their bodies were different from their animal sources. There was a greater intelligence about them, a deeper curiosity. They ran their hands over the vehicle, sniffed at it. Their hands sometimes had five fingers and a thumb, sometimes not.

Several of them climbed up on the wooden bed, sniffed at the prone body of the monster.

"We thought you were bringing us another man," said the one who looked like a wolf. His yellow eyes were intense, and his lips dripped foam. "We have not had a new man among us in some time."

Tin and Jack had gotten out of the truck. Jack was carrying a coiled whip in his hands. When the creatures saw it, they cowered instinctively.

"There is no man here," Jack said. "Not like you, anyway."

"Yes, this is another man," Tin said. "He has been hurt. We are taking him to the doctor."

"To the House of Discomfort?" asked the wolf.

"No, Sayer of the Law," said Tin. "He is to be treated for wounds. He has done nothing wrong."

"And who are these men?" asked Sayer of the Law. "Are they the creations of the Lord Father?"

"Yes," Tin said quickly. "We are all the creations of the Lord Father Momo."

The wolf creature, Sayer of the Law, moved closer to Tin, said, "If this is so, and if this man," he gestured toward the unconscious monster, "is not of the Father, then who is he of? And if he is of other than the Father, then is the Father not the father of all?"

"He is," Tin said. "But there are some things too complicated to explain. He is the father of this man, as he is your father. That is all you need to know."

"Then if he is of the Father," said the Sayer of the Law, "and he is being returned to the Father, then he has violated the law, and he should be punished in the House of Discomfort. Is that not the law?"

"Of course," said Tin. "But first the Father will make him well, then he will punish him."

The creatures were silent. They gathered in a semicircle, moved close to Tin and Jack.

"Say the law!" Jack bellowed, and cracked his whip. The creatures jumped back, snarling. Jack cracked it again. "Sayer of the Law," he said. "Recite the law."

With head bent, the Sayer began to recite:

"Not to go on all fours; that is the law. Are we not Men?

"Not to suck up drink; that is the law. Are we not Men?

"Not to eat meat or fish or anything French; that is the law. Are we not Men?

"Not to hump each others' legs, but to have better aim; that is the law. Are we not Men?

"Not to smell each others' butts; that is the law. Are we not Men?

"Not to lick our private parts; that is the law. Are we not Men?

"Not to chase, bite, beat, or molest other men; that is the law. Are we not Men?

"Not to dig in the Father's flower beds at night; that is the law. Are we not Men?

"Not to leave our piles to be stepped in; that is the law. Are we not Men?

"Not to claw the bark of trees or the faces of others; that is the law. Are *we not Men?"*

The Sayer ceased quoting, said, "There might have been another verse in there, but if so I've forgotten it."

"Close enough," Tin said. "Now let's talk about who's who. Come on, now. Do it. You know what I'm after."

There was a moment of shuffling. Finally the Sayer led off with the chant and the others followed:

> *"His is the House of Big Bad Pain.*
> *"His is the hand that makes stuff.*
> *"His is the hand that wounds stuff.*
> *"His is the hand that heals stuff.*
> *"His is the Great Swinging Hammer of Delight."*

"The what?" Annie asked.

"You don't want to know," Tin said.

"Now, go about your business of men," Tin said. "And leave the business of other men, the Father's main men, to them. It is not yours to wonder why, it is yours to do as the Father says. And if you do not...the House of Discomfort."

Tension hung in the air thick as brick. Slowly, the animal-men moved away from the vehicle. Hickok thought he heard one of the creatures mumble something about, "I got your house of discomfort," but he couldn't be sure.

Tin climbed inside the cab with Jack, and away they went. From the wooden bed, Hickok looked back at the throng of creatures. They had gathered in a knot on the rocky beach, staring after the vehicle's departure.

Suddenly, one of them lifted its head and howled.

Bull swung around on his knees, pulled down his pants, and gave the creatures a look at his bare ass.

"Same to you," cried the Sayer of the Law, but by that time, the vehicle had turned out of sight around a projection of sand dune and jungle.

"Did you see the way they were looking at me?" Annie said.

"Yes," Hickok said. "With no women creatures among them, I can see how they are disgruntled."

Momo, with Tin and Jack in his laboratory, stood over the body of the monster. They had strapped it to a long table. Jack and Tin had used tweezers to pick maggots from the wounds, had scoured them out with water, then alcohol. When this was finished, Momo took a scalpel from the little sliding metal table at his side. He held it up, examined it, watched it wink in the light.

"Is he awake?" asked Momo.

Jack slapped the monster's face. The monster moaned slightly. Jack produced a pail of water, poured it over the creature's face. It shook its head, throwing beads of water like tossed pearls from its hair.

"Who are you?" it asked.

"We are some nice people who are going to give you back an arm and a foot," Momo said. "But boy is it going to hurt."

"Must he be awake?" Tin asked.

Momo looked at Tin, surprised. "Since when does it matter?"

"They need not always be awake," Tin said. "You can make them sleep. You can make him sleep. He need not have to feel the pain."

"That's true," Momo said. "But what fun would there be in that?"

Momo turned, looked down at the monster and smiled. "I'm going to attach some little cells, some elements of monkey embryo, mix in some special chemicals. It will fasten itself to your arm and foot with a vengeance, dear monster. It will take twenty-four hours, and you will have a new arm and foot. To attach this little packet of goodness to you, I will need to cut you, and sew into you this magical gift. And it will hurt... Dear monster. Dear...*thing*... Welcome to the House of Discomfort."

"Yeah," Jack said. "Glad to have you."

Outside, next to the House of Discomfort was a large garden. Hickok and Annie sat there with Bull, wondering about Cody, whom they had not seen since the day before, wondering what was going on in the building next to them.

The walls of the House of Discomfort were well designed. Inside the structure the monster's cries of pain were loud enough to shake the rafters. Outside, in the garden, the trio could not hear them at all.

That night, while dinner was served to the others, Tin sat in the House of Discomfort by the table where the monster slowly sprouted a new arm, grew a new foot. The monster lay naked, clean, and sweeter smelling now. Tin had anointed him with oil, had pushed his black hair back from his face and bound it there with a band of leather.

The monster opened its eyes.

"Who...who are you?"

"I am Tin."

"You are beautiful. More beautiful than Hans Brinker."

"Say what?" said Tin.

But the monster, exhausted from pain, had slipped back into sleep.

In the dining room, they took their previous positions at the table, Cody dead center. Jack stood by Momo, of course, and tonight, since Tin had been asked to take care of the monster, he was guardian to the creature and not present.

Since Hickok, Annie and Bull had gone on their little adventure, they had been watched much more closely. A monkey man with a pistol followed them around, stood near the table by Doctor Momo and Jack. Just the idea of a monkey man with a pistol made Hickok nervous. He felt he might be able to overpower the critter, but it was a long way from where he sat to where Momo and Jack and the monkey man were. He was one, they were three. Certainly Bull and Annie would join in to help him, but still, it was iffy. Hickok decided it was best to lay low until the right moment.

Cody looked very happy. He was in a new container of glass. There was no liquid. All of the wires had been removed, and at the base of the glass was a metal platform, and when Cody so chose, with the slightest use of the muscles in his face and neck, he could turn his head in any direction.

"How do you feel?" Annie asked Cody.

"It's not perfect," Cody said. "A body would be perfect. But this sure beats the old setup. And see what Momo has done to my throat? No tube. I can speak in a voice that is almost my own. A little squeaky, but not bad."

"Perhaps I can adjust that," Momo said. "A tweak of the pliers. I might even be able to grow you new and better vocal cords."

"Grow them?" Annie asked.

"Yes, in a dish. Of course, some monkey will lose an embryo, won't she, Jack?"

"Oh, he will, Doctor Momo, he will."

"She will. Of course, we'll have to shop for a female monkey."

"Yes sir, whatever you say."

"You said before, all your creations were male. How come there are no females in your animals?" Hickok asked.

"There have been. Cat, of course."

She appeared so human, Hickok had forgotten her.

"I find that when both sexes are available they become a bit too independent. I've tried it. Had to kill off the females. They sort of civilized things; gave the male creatures too many thoughts about themselves and their future. Wanting to raise children and the like. Civilization is much harder to rule than anarchy is to control. If you're the one in charge, that is. The great thing about anarchy is the most powerful is always in charge. I'm the most powerful. So, I rule. Of course, there are some wild female monkeys. I keep them about to re-create my crop, so to speak. And for experimental embryos."

"You have the monkey men here," Annie said, "but the others, why are they in the jungle?"

"Obvious," Momo said. "They were not so successful. Very ugly, aren't they? I don't like looking at them. I raised them all from pups or kittens, or cubs, or whatever. I taught them to read and speak, and to think a little. Not too much, but a little. The creatures other than the monkeys and my chimp here," he patted Jack, "were a little too independent. Even the dog creatures. Who would have figured that, huh? I think it was the women did that to them. I had to get rid of them. In the House of Discomfort. You know. Chop, chop.

"After that, well, the other animals weren't worth a flying shit in a snowstorm. Most of the monkey men I made later, after knowing better how to do it, and knowing not to use women. Women screw up everything."

"Then why Cat?" Annie said.

"Well, women do have their benefits. Is that not right, Mr. Hickok?"

Annie sat silent, fuming. So did Hickok.

They eventually ate. From time to time a tube was attached to the platform that supported Cody's head, and the contents of his meal was drained into a bucket. This, in turn, well-chewed, was deposited on

Momo's plate for his consumption.

"It's the teeth," Momo said when he saw the astonishment on his guests' faces. "I'm good at repairing most anything, but I have the hardest time with myself. It's like they say about the blacksmith. His own horses go wanting shoes. The shoemaker's family goes wanting shoes. The doctor always has a canker. Or in my case, bad teeth. I really must take the time to do some work on them. Sensitive beyond reason, really. I'm attempting to discover how to grow myself an entirely new set."

"What of the monster?" Hickok asked.

"Ah, yes," Momo said. "Growing a new arm and a foot, right now as we speak. Tin's watching after him."

"You can actually do that?" Annie said. "Grow an arm or foot...from nothing?"

"I wouldn't call it something from nothing. Let me give you an example."

Momo stood up, unzipped his pants, produced his member, which he plopped on the table across his plate of pre-chewed food. The member was absolutely enormous and very dark in color, like an overripe banana.

"Used to be horses on the island," Momo said. "I brought them with me. Two of them. A stallion and a mare. Worked them for a while, then experimented with them. This is all that remains of Dobbin. It's quite functional, you know. The mare, Mattie, didn't care for it much, and I had to stand on a bucket to use it. It was entirely functional, you see, but I just was not tall enough to do the job properly. Got kicked once. Sometimes, in a moment of excitement, the mare would pull me off the bucket. It resulted in some injuries. Both to me and the mare. Eventually, we ate the mare. Though I did have her sexual equipment grafted onto Catherine. Would you like to see that?"

"Heavens no," Annie said, her face red as fire. "Please...put it up."

"Very well," Momo said.

Momo, almost sadly, dunked his dong back into his drawers, food particles and all.

Bull downed a glass of wine. "Big deal." He stood up, pulled down his pants, tossed his hammer on the table, smashing his mashed potatoes flat. "They not call me Bull for nothing." Bull shook his penis. "Only little smaller than doctor's. Not ugly. Not come off horse. Come with Bull. Get damn big when happy."

"Most impressive," Momo said, gritting his teeth.

"Catherine," Bull said. "She your squaw? Or she free range?"

"Oh, free range for sure. But she's quite in love with me, I must admit. No use trying there."

"Put it up, Bull," said Hickok. "You're offending the lady."

"Oh my, yes," Annie said, but she took a good long look anyway.

"I knew a fella with one bigger than either one of you," Cody said. "He got ready for the deed, so much blood went to it he passed out."

"You're making that up," Hickok said.

"No," Cody said. "No I'm not. It's true. Every word of it. At least the words in between that I'm not lying with."

Cody laughed and so did Momo and Jack. Bull even thought it was a hoot. Then again, after two glasses of wine, Bull thought everything was funny and was willing to do almost anything, though this was the first time Hickok had seen him take his dick out. It was quite a show stopper. Too bad it couldn't be used in The Wild West Show.

When the monster awoke, he saw Tin sitting in a chair near him. He thought the Tin Man was gorgeous. His metal skin was smooth and flowing, like silver flesh; his face was like that of a god. The monster tried to sit up, but the straps restrained him. He was amazed to discover his arm had regrown itself completely in a matter of a few hours. It was not sewn on at the shoulder like the other, it was an arm grown from the shoulder out.

His foot had regrown as well, except for the toes. Momo had explained that since it had been amputated longer, was not as fresh, it would take a bit more time.

"Here," said the Tin Man, "let me release those."

"Are you not afraid I will seize you?"

"I am not. You see, I am strong. Very strong."

Tin released the straps. The monster swung to the side of the table, but suddenly felt dizzy. He lay back down.

"It will take some time," Tin said. "When you get ready, there are some clothes for you on the chair. And some sandals."

"Thanks. You asked him to give me anesthetic. And though he did not, I appreciate the gesture."

"Momo enjoys the pain of others. Mine included."

"You feel pain?"

"I feel pain. Of a different sort. The metal feels nothing, but in here," Tin tapped his chest, "in my body of gears and clockworks, wires and springs, I feel much. But I am not human. I have no heart. Except this watch that beats like one."

Tin pulled the huge turnip watch from his vest pocket. "It was given me by a man who I thought was a wizard, but I realize now, after all this time, was a fool. No heart, and because I am not human...no soul either."

"There is a heart in this chest, but in one sense neither chest nor heart is mine," said the monster. "It was borrowed by my creator from a dying man while it still beat. In me, the heart beats slow. The blood flows slow, like honey in winter. And like you, having been made, I have no soul, for in the greater sense of things I am not alive. I move. I think. I consider. But I am dead."

"I am called Tin," said the metal man. "What do they call you?"

"Monster is common. Sometimes Creature. 'There He Is' is used a lot. I used to think my name was 'Get Him,' or 'Kill Him.'"

"You are making a joke?"

"A little one. Now and then I'm called Frankenstein after my creator, poor dumb fuck that he was. You have heard the stories, have you not?"

"Stories?"

"About the murder of his wife...the murder of Frankenstein himself. Both said to be committed by me."

"Were they?"

"In a manner of speaking."

"Look, I have a past too. Perhaps we could share our stories. I like you. I do not fear you. Do not fear me."

"I do not."

"Good...so, shall I call you Monster?"

"Though I have no given name, I actually have taken one for myself. One I overheard, liked, and prefer to call myself."

"Then I shall call you that. What is the name?"

"Bert."

"Bert it is. Would you like to come to my cabin where we can talk?"

"Will that cause trouble with your boss?"

"He said to watch after you. He did not say how. Besides, I care less and less about my boss. I think, like the man who claimed to be a wizard and told me this watch was a heart, what Momo has promised me he can not and will not give."

"And what was that?"

"The thing we both crave most. A soul."

It just happened. A kind of magnetism. One moment Tin and Bert were in Tin's cabin, Tin showing him his collection of clocks, and the next moment their bodies were pressed together, Tin's smooth metal lips against the dead rubbery ones of the monster.

It worked, those lips together.

Bert carefully removed Tin's vest with its shiny watch chain and turnip watch, and slowly, Tin removed Bert's new clothes, dropped them to the floor. The next moment they fell in bed together. The room ticked and thundered clocks.

There was a problem. Tin didn't have any place for Bert to put the old see-saw.

"Look," said Tin, rubbing Bert's chest. "I know it's unconventional, but I can take care of you, and there is a way you can take care of me... Between my legs there's this loose bolt, and if you touch it with your finger...for I have touched it many times with my own, and you shake it a little, well, it does something to me. The gears and clocks inside of me run faster, seize up, stop, let go furiously, and I feel warm all over. It is a heavenly experience, and in that moment, when I feel that charge...just that one little moment...I feel as if I not only have a soul, but that it can soar."

"In other words, you want me to kind of finger that little bolt there until you get off?"

"Yeah, oh yeah, oh heaven's yes, that works. Yes. That works. Faster, my love."

When it was over, Tin lay on his back. His body was alive with whirling gears and clacking clocks. He felt as if he had levitated and that lava flowed over his gears. It was far better than when he had serviced himself. Bert had the touch.

"I was built of tin," Tin said. "I was built to help clear wood to make lumber. I remember nothing other than one moment I stood up and an axe was put in my hand. I was given orders, and I did them. Then one day I did them no more. I was rusted in the forest.

"I was saved by a trio of travelers and a dog. There was a girl named Dot. The dog was called BoBo. There was a lion that walked on its hind legs and was called Bushy, because of his mane, and there was a man made of straw. He was called Straw.

"They seemed nice enough. Especially the young girl. The dog was cute. But Bushy and Straw, though nice, there was just something about them. The way they followed Dot. The way Straw's arm would linger on her shoulders, brush her bottom. It didn't seem quite right, you know?

"They all wanted something. The girl Dot wanted to go home. She claimed a storm had carried her to our world inside a house. A little bit of a tall tale, perhaps. Bushy wanted strength and courage. Straw wanted a brain. And he needed it. He wasn't that smart. The dog was just along, you know. What the hell does a dog want."

"This sounds like a very strange place," Bert said.

"To me it was normal. It was where I was born, where I lived. It was called XYZ."

"Ex-ee-zee?"

"Close enough," Tin said. "It is a world that lies somewhere sideways to this one. That is the best I can explain. I asked Doctor Momo about it once. He said my world most likely lies in another dimension. I can't say. I only know that I am from XYZ, and now I am here."

"And how did you get here?"

"They were all on their way to see a mighty wizard, to get the things they wanted. You see, Dot, she was from a parallel world too. But not XYZ. She wanted to go home."

"Are there many of these worlds?"

"I cannot say, but I suppose. The world Dot spoke of might well be this world. Actually, I thought she was lying. A little dotage in the Dot, you see. Now I know she was telling the truth."

"Did you find the wizard, did he help?"

"We went to see him. It was said he could give me a heart. He gave me a watch and told me it was as good as a heart. He gave Straw a funny hat and told him it was a brain. Well, stupid as he was, he believed it. He gave the lion a gun, told him he didn't need to be strong and courageous, he could just shoot anyone that bothered him.

"Well, those were simpler times and it was a simpler place, and we bought that crap. A little later we realized our wizard was a fraud who had drifted into our country out of a mist from a place called Kansas. He claimed it was the same place Dot lived."

"What about Dot? Did she go home?"

"He planned to sail away in his balloon back to his world. He kept saying there was a dark air draft on up high, and that if he entered it at a certain time, it would suck him home. He said he would know when the mist showed up. Dot was to go with him, but during the night, he crept away and went by himself. You see, the mist showed. It looked like silver dust spinning. Maybe he did not have time to wake her. I cannot say. But it is my guess he never meant to bother. I hope he was struck by lightning.

"Anyway, he left me with a watch and no heart. I am full of watch work, so maybe he saw that as a joke. Momo promised me a real heart. A heart taken from one of the animals he experiments on. He said he could fasten it inside of me and it would pump. But he lied. I am sophisticated now. You can not make heart and clockwork click in unison. Not and have it mean anything. A clock does not pump blood through its veins. And a soul...I realize now I was never meant to have that. Never."

"Then we are alike," Bert said. "I am told God cannot love that which has no soul. So I am doomed to be nothing."

"If we are both nothing, perhaps we can be nothing together."

"Perhaps that is, in fact, something."

Tin smiled, the metal rippling slowly across his face, revealing his shiny tin teeth.

"Did Dot have to stay in XYZ?" Bert asked.

Tin narrowed his eyes, a drop of oil squeezed out, ran along his face. "For a time," he said. "Tell me your story, Bert. Tell me how you came to be."

"I will," Bert said wiping the oil drop away with his fingers. "But finish your story. How did you get here from this world of yours? Sometimes it is best to discuss the things that hurt us."

"Very well. Here is the hard part. Dot, the little girl. She was supposed to leave by wearing the silver shoes given her by a witch. It is a long story, but when the wizard didn't work out, a witch gave her some shoes. All Dot had to do was put them on, click the heels together and say something about how it would be nice to go home. Something about computer chips inside them. Anyway, that's what the witch called them. I have no idea what that is. The witch said they sent surges through the shoes, activated a grid on which Dot could ride through space and time to her world. Had Dot listened, I suppose she would be home now.

"But Straw, that filthy scarecrow, talked her into staying another day, to visit with us — me, the lion, and himself. She did just that.

"Poor Dot. She didn't understand that Straw's obsession had grown renegade. And the lion followed along. He was up for whatever Straw wanted. Together they added up to bad.

"I slept late the next morning, awoke to a sound. Down the halls of the palace I heard a muffled scream. I got up, went out. I heard scuffling in Dot's room, and when I got there, well, Straw had her on her back and she was fighting him. I grabbed him and tore his head off. Then I ripped straw out of his chest, and jerked his legs and arms off. But it was too late for Dot. She had died from the assault. Her little dog, BoBo, lay in the fireplace, burning, its head twisted at an odd angle.

"The lion shot at me. The bullets bounced off. He tossed the gun aside. So much for his courage. He bolted. I found him in his room cowering in a closet. I was so angry at the lion, I tore him apart, limb from limb. I was an absolute savage, no better than they.

"Then it occurred to me that the palace guards would think I murdered the two to have Dot to myself; and that I then raped and murdered her."

"No offense. What would you have raped her with? You don't have a... Well... You know."

"It wouldn't have mattered. They might have thought I did it with my hand. A substitute penis like a fireplace poker. Who is to say? I was frightened, bad as the lion. Know what I did?"

"No, Tin. I do not."

"I took Dot's silver slippers from her feet, put them on, and clicked my heels three times, just as the witch had told her, and I said, 'get me home, you betcha.' It worked. Everything went foggy. I seemed to be falling through space. I realized as I was swept away, I did not have a real home. Maybe I would go to Dot's home. Or my original place of creation. Wherever that was. It did not matter. All that mattered was that

I be away from the palace at XYZ."

"And you ended up here?"

"Not quite. I awoke in a great heap of scrap metal. This was, in fact, my home. A place where metal was collected. Was I not a metal thing run by clockwork and gears? It so happened that Momo worked his way through scrap yards, gathering odds and ends for his laboratory, which at that time was in a place called London. That is how I came to be with him."

"That must mean you were first built in London but somehow were transported to XYZ. Then, back to London."

"There are no real answers. Just this stamp of a name on my foot."

Tin held up his foot. On the bottom was stamped: RETURN TO H. G. WELLS THIS METAL CHRONONAUT. Then there was an address.

"Did you try the address?"

"I did not. Momo had me. I was grateful at the time, and felt he was my savior. Besides. He was offering me a real heart. Not a watch. But let me tell you, he is a horrible man, Bert. He is soulless, even though he has a heart.

"Do you know what he did in London? He disguised me in a hat, long coat and pants, horrible shoes, and we took to the streets of Whitechapel. He had a thing for women, Bert. Not unlike Straw. Except, he cut them up. He did horrible things to them, took pieces out of their bodies and took them home for his experiments. The police searched everywhere for him, but, obviously, never caught him. He wrote them taunting letters, calling himself Jack the Ripper. He dropped clues. He wrote in American vernacular. He played games with them. And then one day, he heard of an island in the Pacific, and he went there, taking me with him. And here I am now."

"What became of the silver slippers?"

"I still have them. When I ended up in the metal yard, I removed them, hid them inside a secret place in my leg. Let me show you."

Tin touched what appeared to be a smooth place in his leg. It popped open. Inside were the silver slippers.

"Yes," Tin said. "I can see by your eyes that you have noticed the obvious. They are not very attractive and the toes are ripped out, the sides broken down. My feet were bigger than Dot's. I have never tried them again. For one thing, I thought Momo was a noble man about noble experiments and he would give me my heart. I was naïve. I knew what he did to those women was bad, and still, I helped him. He was no better than Straw and Bushy, and I killed them. I was such a coward, Bert. I wanted that heart."

"With the shoes you could leave at anytime."

"I have been thinking of trying them on again, letting fate carry me where it chooses. Then you came along. Now I do not want to go anywhere without you. I thought...you might try them. That you might escape this madhouse."

"Why would I go anywhere without you?" Bert said.

Tin squeezed closer to Bert. "That is the sweetest thing ever said to me...goodness, I have done all the talking. Tell me your story."

"Not much to tell. Not here one day, here the next. Victor Frankenstein constructed me of dead bodies. Was disappointed with my appearance, and with what he had done. Laid a lot of guilt on me. You would have thought he was Catholic. Then he cast me out. I will not lie to you, I was pissed."

"About Frankenstein's wife?"

"We are both murderers, Tin. And both of our murders came from good intentions. You see, I was in love with Victor's wife, and she with me. From the first time she saw me lying on a slab, it was there. She was a necrophiliac, you see. That is why she was attracted to my creator in the first place. He played with dead bodies...and, well, I was just...if you will pardon the pun, just what the doctor ordered."

"So you go either way?"

"Until now...but as for Elizabeth, well, when it all went sour we were about the deed that we had done many a time behind Victor's back — and I assure you, I am not proud of that. But this time we were doing it, she decides she wants to be dead like me. Or near dead. She is not planning on a permanent thing. So she says, 'choke me,' and I will not lie to you, I found it kind of appealing, so I choked her. And choked her. Only I choked too long and too hard. She died. I had to flee then, and Victor brought the hounds of Hell down on me.

"Some months later, after fleeing all through Europe and elsewhere, I ended up at the Arctic Ice Skating Championships. A new sport recently designed by Hans Brinker, who was a noted winner of the old Silver Skates championships, and quite a looker, I might add. You remind me of him, only far more attractive."

"You flatterer."

"I was quite the skater actually. Victor taught me. Back when we were friends, I decided to enter the championships. You see, I thought I was home free. Had escaped Victor completely.

"Turned out, he was right on my tail. In the midst of the championships, me in third place — and mind you, it was cold and we were all bundled heavily, so we looked like bears on ice — Victor and his thugs came out from behind an ice floe on skates and went for me. I fought back. Just natural. I tossed the two thugs about until they were unconscious, then there was only Victor. As we struggled, other skaters went by. I said to Victor as I held him by the throat, 'You are going to make me lose this championship over some woman I did not even mean to kill and who was unfaithful to you, and in addition, you will be dead. Is this not silly?'

"He agreed, of course, and then an amazing thing happened. I not only let him go, we began to skate together. Him encouraging me to skate well, to cross the finish line, and me skating for all I was worth. Soon I had left him behind, but I could hear his voice calling to me, encouraging, like a father. Then the voice went silent.

"I turned, looked over my shoulder. Victor had fallen through a gap in the ice. I turned back, could see the finish line. It was cross the line or save Victor, who moments before had tried to kill me, only to turn and give me the encouragement I had always wanted from my creator. I had to make a decision.

"Well, you know I turned and went back for him. How could I not. But fate, as it always does, turned against me. After skating perfectly for the entire contest, as I went back for him, allowing the other contestants to pass me, I slipped. That is the best I can explain it. One moment I am skating like a veritable arctic god, and the next, I have slipped. I hit on my butt, feet forward, and one of my skates struck Frankenstein in the face, hard. He let go of the edge of the ice, and was gone with a sound not too unlike *Blurp*. That was it. He was drowned.

"Well, of course the way the crowd saw it, I deliberately skated back to him, jumped, slid on my butt so I could boot him in the face with a skate.

"I was arrested. Shortly thereafter the Brinker committee decided the best thing to do with me was to sell me to a Japanese delegation that had attended the contest, and the next thing I knew, I was in Japan, being sawed on. That's what happened to my foot. They were cutting off pieces of me to be made into an aphrodisiac."

"My goodness."

"My goodness indeed. I was rescued by Hickok and the others, and when we were shot down at sea by the Japanese, I was separated from them, partially eaten by a shark, and would have died had I not been carried along by dolphins for a goodly distance, and finally, with their assistance, reached this island's shore, only to be rescued by Hickok and his friends once again."

"Why would dolphins help you?"

"I cannot say for sure. I think they helped me for one reason, and one reason only. They don't like sharks. And, they are in fact, often mistaken for them."

"An amazing story."

"As is yours."

"Bert?"

"Yes."

"Do you think we could snuggle?"

"Of course," said Bert.

Ned was nervous. Assigned to assist Cody in his cabin, he found that he was all flippers. The attached thumbs seemed worthless. He couldn't hold anything without dropping it. The whiskey Cody wanted to taste, the hose that pumped out the waste box, everything Ned touched he fumbled.

"Take it easy, Ned," Cody said. "I won't eat you. Though, under certain circumstances a seal steak might be acceptable."

Ned blinked his big black eyes.

"Just a little joke," Cody said.

Ned relaxed.

"So, you're quite the fan of my little adventures, huh?"

Ned nodded.

"Well now," Cody said, feeling well tucked into his element as a teller of tall tales, or as many had called him, a goddamn liar. Cody said, "Did I ever tell you about the time I fought off half the Sioux nation? Why of course, I haven't. We've just actually met, haven't we? Well, climb up in that chair there and let me give you the story. First, let me say I have a motto. 'Do right.' And I have a little motto goes with that. 'Do right 'cause it's right.' How's that, huh? Good, is it not?

"Well, now, once out on the plains, all by my lonesome, 'cept for my horse, Ole Jake, I was beset upon by the entire Cheyenne — what's that?"

Ned had raised a flipper, halting the story. He adjusted his glasses on his nose, quickly lifted up the notebook and pencil that hung about his neck on a chain. He had written: SIOUX NATION. HALF OF THEM.

"Ah, yes," said Cody. "Wrong adventure. That was another time, actually. Not nearly as hair-raising as this one, even though there were more of them. Why I bet there were three times the number of Sioux as Cheyenne. But this time I meant to tell you about, it was Cheyenne, and I was on my horse, Will."

Ned's note pad went up again. JAKE.

"Yes, of course. Jake. Not Will. Totally different horse. So there I was..."

It was near dark when Cody ceased telling stories, drinking whiskey that Ned held to his lips, and having it pumped from the waste box by the enraptured seal.

Finally Cody became too tired to continue. He nodded off. Ned placed a blanket over the container that held the great frontiersman, then, turning down the lamps, curled in a chair and slept, thinking happily of Buffalo Bill.

As Ned and Cody slept, and the zeppelinauts remained in their rooms, locked in by Momo's assistant Jack, a great storm struck a ship out on the ocean, some twenty miles west of the doctor's island.

The storm was a real piss and vinegar of a churning belly-whirler. It bullied the ocean, shoved it, slapped it, threw it high and made it foam. It pushed the sea so hard great valleys of water were built. Then the storm collapsed the walls, tumbled them down, sprayed wide and wet.

The ship popped and bobbed, tossed and rolled. The sea lathered against its sides like custard. Inside the ship, inside a coffin, the dark man had just laid himself down to sleep. It was not the sleep of the living, but a different kind of sleep. A sort of hibernation. There was no breath. There was no heartbeat. There was only sleep.

But in the moments before the strange condition claimed him, he thought of his country of blackly wooded mountains and shadowy forests, and of what had been.

Many years past he had been a powerful ruler. A man feared and respected. Now, through a series of circumstances involving murdered priests, tripping over a holy relic, the cursing of God, he had been cursed in return. But not with words. With the curse of the undead.

He had made the best of it, had learned to love it, then hate it, then love it again. Now he felt nothing but the need to exist in his undead condition. And to do that, he must have blood, for the blood is the life.

But on his way to the Far East to taste Asian food, a storm had lost them on the deep blue for way too long, and when it ended they were drastically off course. During this time he lay down in the ship's hold in his coffin — thought by the captain to contain the body of an eccentric American who wanted to be buried on Asian soil for some reason or another — and waited.

Waiting, the dark man became hungry. He could hear the heartbeats of the crew, could in fact hear the blood rushing through their veins, like water through viaducts. Above it all he could hear the new storm. One more powerful and ferocious and determined to consume them than the one that had driven them off course. Compared to this, that storm had been a high wind.

He was disappointed. He had plans. He had tasted what Britain had to offer, had not cared for it. Except for young women with powdered necks and perfumed ears, the place was a disappointment.

He had gone to savage America, had not cared for it much either. Too many men in smelly buckskins and shit-stained longjohns. Worse, too many women in smelly buckskins and shit-stained longjohns. The West was glamorous not at all.

So now he was set to try Asia.

Along the way, however, he could not contain himself. He had been forced to feed on the sailors. He had been so famished he had ripped out their throats and sucked them dry, instead of milking them slowly night by night.

It was a part of his nature he hated. As much time as he had on his hands he would have thought by now he would have learned to be patient.

He had instead sucked the life out of most everyone on board, save a handful of crew and the captain. Last time he had seen the old man he was lashed to the wheel, fighting the storm. He still lived, but barely. The dark man could hear his heartbeat and the slow slush of blood in his arteries. The beat of his heart was erratic. He was frightened both of sea and what lay below in the hold. He didn't understand it, but he knew it was horrible.

The dark man knew all this and reveled in it. Cursed himself at the same time. He had, by feeding so violently, left himself in dire straits. Without sufficient crew, he could be lost at sea.

The ship tipped and righted itself a half-dozen times, but the last time the wave was too big and the tip was too far, and over it went. The sails were snatched away, the mast cracked against the sea, turned to splinters. Water rushed into the ship, filled it from top to bottom. It began to sink.

The captain and remaining crew abandoned ship, but were instantly swallowed by the waters and taken down deep and away.

Under the ship went, sawing back and forth beneath the ocean. Then, out of an open storage hatch, up popped the coffin. It shot to the surface like a cork, bobbed in the sea.

It bounced and heaved for hours. Then, suddenly as it had begun, the storm died down and the ocean went smooth. The coffin washed toward the island of Doctor Momo.

The tide moved it onto shore. The lid popped, slid sideways. A hand grasped it, pushed it off. Slowly, a hand grasped either side of the coffin, and a mustached, white-faced man with angular features, wearing a dark outfit with a black cloak lined with red, rose effortlessly from the box, stood, turned his red eyes toward the jungle.

Out there, in the jungle, Momo's creations saw the coffin and the man. They were bunched up behind a clutch of trees. The Lion Man said, "Is that a man?"

"It walks on two legs, does it not?" said the Sayer of the Law.

They watched as the tall man stepped out of the coffin and waded after the coffin lid. He was making a terrible noise in a language the beast men did not recognize.

Finally, after much thrashing and falling into the seawater, the dark man was able to rescue the lid, drag it and the coffin onto the beach. He paused a moment to kick a crab loose from his ankle.

"I know you're out there," he said to the jungle. "I can smell your blood, hear your heartbeat. I can smell your breath and your unwiped asses."

The man smiled at the darkness. His teeth were white and shiny. Like the beast men, he had long canines.

The Sayer of the Law edged out of the woods. "Are we not men?" he said. "Not to run on all fours, that is the law. Not to roll in dead things, that is the law." (The Quoter was overcome with joy; that was the part he had left out the other day when quoting to the newcomers.)

"Not to..."

"Silence," said the tall man. "You bore me."

The others came out of the jungle now. The pig-faced creature snuffled about the dark man, trying to intimidate him.

"Do not speak to the Sayer of the Law that way," said the pig in his choked voice. "It is not the way of men."

In answer, the dark man grabbed the Pig Man by the neck, and with one violent rip, tore the creature's throat out.

"Oh, shit," said the Lion Man. "That had to hurt."

The Pig Man toppled to the ground spouting blood. The dark man hissed as the others circled him. "By God," said the Goat Man, "he's ripped out Jerry's throat."

The Sayer of the Law bent over the Pig Man, said, "He's dead." Edging closer to the dark man, the Sayer of the Law said, "Not to kill, that is the law. Are we not men?"

"No," said the dark man in his accented voice, "you are not men. You are beasts walking around on your hind legs like men. You are playing like you are men. But you are not men."

"See there," said the Lion Man, "I told you, Sayer. We are *not* men. Just like I been saying all along."

"He did say that," one of the beast men said.

"But I thought..." started the Goat Man, but he trailed off. "Goddamn it. We've been bumfuzzled."

"And to think I gave up meat," said the Lion Man. "You know how much I like meat."

"That wasn't a big problem for me," said the Goat Man. "But now I know why my back hurts."

"Who's to say this man knows anything!" said the Sayer. "He has merely violated the law. He is not the law. Who is he to say who we are? Are we not men?"

"I don't know," the Lion Man said. "I think maybe, considering what he did to Jerry, we ought to just go with it. You know."

"You are such pathetic things," said the dark man. He bent over, grabbed Jerry's carcass, began to suck at the wound in the creature's neck.

"Oh my," said the Lion Man. "Oh God, that looks good."

The dark man tossed the corpse aside, as easily as if it were made of straw. "Have a taste, my friend. You were born to it."

The Lion Man slowly dropped to all fours, edged toward the corpse.

"Don't listen to him," said the Sayer. "Not to go on all fours, that is the law. Not to eat meat or fish, that is the law."

"Don't get in my way," said the Lion Man, "that is *my* law."

"Silence," said the tall, dark man. "I am the law. I am the power. Try me, if you think I am not."

The crowd watched Bill tear at the meat that had been Jerry the Pig Man. The creatures who had been birthed from meat eaters filled their nostrils with the smell of Jerry's blood, eased toward the kill. The others slowly bent until their hands rested in the dirt. From them went up a sigh of relief.

As the carnivorous among them tore at the meat on the ground, and the others watched, the dark man turned to the Sayer, said, "I am Vlad Tepes. The Undead, former ruler of Transylvania and once upon a time a little chunk of Turkey. Or so I think. The memory fades a little with age. From here on out, I am your master."

The Sayer dropped to his knees.

"Yes, Master, you are the law."

"From now on, I will call you Wolf."

"Yes, Master."

"What of Doctor Momo, our Father?" asked one of the creatures, perhaps a mixture of cat and squirrel.

"Whoever he is," said Vlad, "he is nothing compared to me. I am the power and all the power you need or know. Forget this one you call the father. I am more powerful. And where I come from, the strong rule."

Vlad's voice made the air tremble, worked inside of them like a parasite, seized their skulls and shook their gray matter.

"The nose in the crotch," Vlad said to the Sayer, whom he now called Wolf. "You can stop that. And do not sniff my posterior either. It annoys me."

Behind them the sky had started to lighten.

"I will return to my coffin now," said the Transylvanian. "You and your friends carry me to some place soft, not out in the open, bury me before daylight. The light greatly disturbs my eyes. By the way... Is this Asia?"

The beast looked puzzled.

"I thought not. Now do as I say."

With that, the dark man climbed back into his coffin. Wolf fastened on the lid. The beasts picked up the box and carried it into the jungle.

As daybreak broke, Hickok and Annie found themselves exhausted. They had tried to trip their door's latch from the inside, but failing that, they had spent the night making love, which was not a bad consolation prize.

Now, as daylight trickled in through the barred windows and exhaustion set in, Hickok wished he had spent at least a portion of the night sleeping.

Annie rose naked from the sheets, walked to the bathroom in that beautiful way only a well-built woman can walk, ran a bath. She loved the way the water got hot out of the tap. She had always had to have her water heated on a stove. There were good things about Doctor Momo and his island. But not many.

While she waited for the water to reach the right temperature, she returned to the bedroom, said, "And what are our plans now?"

"I would say, at least until nightfall, intercourse is not in the near future. I think I've pulled something."

Annie smiled. "Actually, I think I could interest you rather quickly."

"Yes," Hickok said. "But please don't. I hope to have this little item for future years to come, and not lose it in one exciting and lovely day. You are most energetic, my dear."

"You know what I can't help but think about, in spite of myself?" Annie said, losing her smile.

"What?"

"Poor Bull. Locked alone in his room with nothing to do."

"Goddamn. That hurt, Cat," Bull said.

"Sorry," she said.

"No. It hurt good. Keep on doin' what Cat doin'."

She did. When she finished, she said, "Bull, do you love me?"

"Love? Love too soon. Only first date."

"Date?"

"Never mind. Stupid thing white men do."

"Doctor Momo tells me that he loves me. He always says it before he mounts me."

"Bull love," he said, taking her from behind.

Doctor Momo, reluctant to rise from his bed, screamed for Jack. Jack bolted into the room. "Yes, Doctor."

"Where is Cat?"

"I don't know, Doctor. Haven't seen her."

"It is time for her to have her reading lesson."

"I thought you usually put the old horse dick to her about now."

"True. But reading is close behind. And she must take her shot. Find her, will you."

Jack bounded out of the room, yelling, "Cat! Cat! Get your ass in here."

Inside Bull's room, Cat heard Jack screaming for her as he ran down the hall.

"Oh no. The doctor is looking for me. It's time for what he calls dorking."

"Dorking?"

"What we have been doing."

"Oh."

"Then I have my reading lesson and my shot."

"Shot?"

"He gives me, and himself, an injection with a hypodermic. If he does not, he will lose his horse member. And I...I will convert back to neither what I am now nor what I was. I will be like the others on the island. The beast men.

"I will not be a success, but a failure. That is what the doctor calls the others on the island. Failures. Jack and I are his successes. I must go. If he finds me here, he will have me whipped. He might not give me my shot. And we are in the middle of an excellent Dickens novel as well. I want to know what happens to little Nell. You understand, do you not?"

Bull nodded. "Go, Cat. Go."

As Cat pulled on her clothes, she said, "I will have to trip the latch from the outside again, so he will not be suspicious."

"Give Bull key."

"It fits all the rooms. Hide it."

Cat gave Bull the key, and when she left, he locked himself in from the inside.

After Doctor Momo saw Cat and did his thing and did her thing and gave her a shot and one for himself, he went to Cody's room. When he opened the door, Ned opened his eyes.

"Ah," said the doctor. "You are keeping our guest company?"

Ned nodded.

"Good. Good. Take that blanket off his head."

Ned removed it.

The doctor removed the lid from the case, tapped Cody sharply on the head with his knuckles.

"Hey, goddamn it," Cody said. Then: "Why, Doctor Momo. My apologies. I was asleep."

"Quite all right, my good man. Interested in that body today? Hhmmmmm? Hhhhmmmmmmmmmm?"

"Yes. Yes I am. Might it be too much to ask that Ned here accompany us? I have grown quite fond of him."

Ned rose in such a way as to seem at attention. Or as close to attention as a seal can get. Doctor Momo studied him. "Why yes. That will be quite all right. Come, Ned. Jack. Get in here."

Jack, who had been waiting outside in the hallway, bounded into the room. "Get Colonel Cody's head, will you?"

Jack put the lid on the container, picked up the whole affair, including the waste box, and away they went.

Hickok and Annie bathed together, then dressed. Both were in need of breakfast and coffee. They were discussing that when the door was unlocked, pushed aside, and there stood Bull with Cat.

"Horse dick in shack with Cody's head," Bull said.

"It's a laboratory," Cat explained. "It is the House of Discomfort." She shook. "I was created there. It is a terrible place. Once when I was sassy he took me there. He will be there for hours. I can show you to the other side of the island."

"You have been to the other side of the island?" Annie asked. "We made it about halfway, I think. You've been beyond that point?"

Cat nodded. "Before...before I was Catherine. When I was just...a cat. I remember some of it."

"The other side of the island isn't hard to find," Hickok said. "You just walk around the beach. The problem is the monkey men. We are now under house arrest. They won't let us leave the compound."

"Not to worry," Bull said. "Cat have plan."

Good, thought Hickok, a former house cat with a horse vagina has a plan.

Cat unlocked Doctor Momo's room, and they entered.

"Where is that little weasel Jack?" Hickok asked.

"With the doctor. He is nearly always with the doctor."

There was a crystal container on the nightstand, a hypodermic needle.

"What is this?" said Annie. "Is the doctor some kind of addict?"

"It is the serum that keeps me from turning back to what I was."

Annie took the glass knob out of the top of the container and sniffed. "Bull, you have a good nose. Tell me what you think?"

Bull sniffed. "Water."

"No. That is the serum," Cat said.

"No. Bull said, that water."

"But it is the serum."

"Then serum water," Bull said. "Bull can smell good."

"Provided you have bothered to bathe," said Hickok.

"No," Bull said. "Can smell with nose good."

"He injects me and himself with water?...But why?"

"Control," Hickok said. "You see him do himself, it makes it more believable. You don't need this."

"But, Cat, why did you bring us here?" Annie asked. "To show us that? The serum?"

"No." Cat rushed them into the next room. There was a large hand-woven carpet in the center of the room. Cat flipped it back. There was a trap door underneath. Cat opened it. There were stairs. They dropped down into darkness.

"It leads to a spot in the jungle," Cat said. "Doctor Momo has told me all about it."

"You've never actually been through it?" Annie asked.

"No. But, sometimes, when he drinks too much, he talks of it. He had it built when he first claimed the island. He has showed me how to open it many times."

"Probably built by the monkey men," Hickok said. "They seem the smartest and most energetic of his creations. With the exception of yourself, of course, Cat. You have certainly learned a lot in a short time. Way you speak. What you know."

"I am Doctor Momo's greatest success."

"Ugh," Bull agreed.

"We'll take a look," Hickok said. "We find something, we've got to come back for Cody."

"He is no longer your friend," Cat said.

"You don't know that," Annie said.

Cat shrugged.

"Cody will come through all right," Hickok said. "I've known him for years."

"What about the Frankenstein monster?" Annie said.

"We find a way off, we'll take him too," Hickok said.

"Why?" Cat said. "He's just a monster. Made from dead bodies."

Hickok and Annie exchanged looks. Cat had become all too human.

"Do you know how long Doctor Momo will be busy?"

"All day. Until four o'clock sharp. I serve tea then. I have to prepare it at three."

"Then let's have a quick looksee," Hickok said.

There was a switch on the wall. Cat flipped it. Electric lights flared in the tunnel. Once inside, Cat pulled the trap down, then used a string that went through the trap and attached to the rug. When she tugged it, it pulled the carpet back in place.

They proceeded along the tunnel rapidly, soon came to a short flight of stairs. At the top of the stairs was a bolted door.

Bull pushed aside the bolt, lifted the trap, climbed out.

The others followed, found themselves standing in a small clearing surrounded by thick trees.

Cat pointed. "Over there is where they live. The beast men."

"We have met them already," Hickok said.

"Ugh," Bull said. "No like."

"We have to be very quiet, and go out and along the beach," Cat said. "They will hear us making noise if we stay in the jungle. Sometimes they are bad tempered."

"Then we should walk carefully, by all means," Annie said.

"Now," said Doctor Momo to Cody. "We can go about this different ways. Each has its strengths and drawbacks. Before we start, I would like to outline them for you."

They were in Momo's laboratory. Cody's head was on a work table. Jack was in the corner, eager to respond to Momo's orders. Ned was nearby, positioned so he could see Buffalo Bill.

"We could graft," Momo said. "This means we take appendages and sew them to you. Not the best way. You would be not too unlike the Frankenstein monster, except you would never have been dead. Least not completely. Also, you might not be able to match all the body parts. And, right now, it would be monkey body parts, since that's what's available. So, we will agree, not a good way?"

"Not a good way," Cody said.

"Two. We use a large fragment of human flesh, mix it with chemicals, graft it to your body, and it will grow, reproducing whatever it should reproduce. It's a complex method. You have to code the cells to work in coordination with little tidbits in your brain that already know how to reproduce."

"Then why don't they?"

"That's my discovery, Colonel Cody. Reading Darwin put me onto it. It caused me to dismiss my other methods, the methods I used on the animals. Catherine is made up of both methods. Grafting through surgery. The mare's reproductive organs, for example. And cell regeneration. Here's an example. Take a lizard. It can lose its tail, and can grow another. Inside our brains is a kind of signal that tells the body to repair itself. It does that in small ways. Healing wounds for example. Fighting disease. But it is only successful to a certain point. You lose an arm. Or, as in your case, a body, the brain can not replace that. It knows how, actually, but it can't do it, because for some reason that ability in man lies dormant. Go figure. You would think that would be something we would need and nature would keep, but let me tell you, nature is not organized. That bullshit about how everything fits together in nature and it's organized is three million pounds of wet bullshit. It is chaotic my friend. Evolution is chaotic. There is no grand design. That ability lies dormant in us all. What I have done is I have found a way to activate it."

"Then why do you need to add flesh at all?" Cody asked. "Can't you just spur that ability, have it grow what it needs?"

"Alas, that is my goal. But I am not there yet. So far I can duplicate what all my colleagues have done. I can bring things back from the dead. Never works out. They want a soul. They do not like themselves. They want to be loved like children. Just a disaster. I can duplicate the work of Professor Maxxon. I can grow flesh in chemicals. But, it turns out a little messy. An eyeball here. An eyeball there. That kind of thing. Surgery. Well, that's okay, but not good enough. Surgery with a bit of chemical growth, that was my best way until lately. The beasts that call themselves men, they were successes until I found my most recent method. Then they no longer seemed successful, so I put them on the other side of the island. I don't like looking at my failures. This is some clever shit, that's what I am trying to tell you. And I will become cleverer yet when I activate the brain to the extent that chemicals and flesh are not needed. At that point, I will be ready to return to the mainland and claim my prizes of recognition. I love prizes...I'm sure you could introduce me to some important people once we were ready to do that...return to the mainland. You could, couldn't you? People with money?"

"I suppose...so we can begin today?"

"We can. And we will. But it will only be a partial success today."

"Partial?"

"It is best, Colonel Cody, if I do what we need to do for today, and we discuss what we can do in the future later. Are you ready?"

"I am...will it hurt?"

"Oh, you bet. Especially the way I do it.

"Jack, take the good colonel out of the jar will you, and leave the battery and important items intact. We would not want any little accidents, would we, Colonel Cody?"

"I presume not."

"Oh, Colonel, let me tell you, there is no presuming. It would not be positive. Your head would be good for nothing more than something to kick about."

Jack looked up. The idea seemed to appeal to him.

"Yes, then, be damn careful of my battery," Cody said.

"Jackie," Momo said. "No little accidents for your own pleasure. You do that, Doctor Momo will graft something funny onto you. Understand?"

Jack drooped. "I understand, Doctor."

"Then do your job. And when it's done, will you please get a piece of my old penis from the refrigerator."

"Penis?" Cody said. "What the hell is that for?"

"It is sort of like sourdough starter, Colonel. I add it to my chemicals, it melts, produces a kind of plaster. I apply it to your body, activate the regeneration area of your brain, at least as much as I am able to reactivate it, and it begins to grow."

"An entire body? I'm not going to be just a big dick, am I?"

"That is part of the drawback. No. Only kidding. Some might think you're already a big dick."

"Watch your mouth, buster."

"Oh, are you going to spring off your neck and bite me, Colonel?"

Cody fumed.

Jack laughed.

"Relax now. Let's not worry our pretty head over words. Right now, you have to deal with the pain."

Cody's head, battery intact, was placed directly in front of the doctor on a tray. Jack went to the refrigerator. Doctor Momo picked up a scalpel. He held it up to the electric light. "Good. It is sharp. On the monster I had a dull one. He found it most uncomfortable. Even for a dead man."

"Is your penis in a pink bowl, or one of the metal ones?" Jack called.

"It's just a small piece of flesh, Jack. In one of the metal bowls. Please do not mix it up with one of the other chunks. Those are all different animals and such. We would not want the colonel's new body parts to be covered in hair. Or if you get that diseased piece, oh dear, that could be a real mess."

"Is it just the tip of your dick?"

"That is the one. Oh, now, Colonel. Do not look so concerned."

Ned tugged at Doctor Mormo's sleeve. The doctor looked down. Ned had written a note. He held it up. It read: WILL BUFFALO BILL BE OKAY?

"Well now, Ned. We certainly hope so."

Jack put the bowl with the tip of Doctor Momo's penis on the table. Doctor Momo laid his scalpel on the tray, added a vial of pink liquid to the bowl. He reached for a semi-clear liquid with chunks of pulp in it, started to pour. Jack caught his hand.

"Isn't that our lemonade?" Jack asked.

"You know, it is. I left it out. Probably no good now. Looks just like the elixir. Take this and pour it down the sink. Oh, here it is...Jack...this is it, is it not?"

"That's it, Doctor."

"Good. I am so glad. If it wasn't, I just wouldn't have any idea where it could be, and I am not up to mixing a new batch. I don't have the dick to spare... Well, I have it to spare, but you know what I mean."

"Will you get on with it?" Cody said.

Doctor Momo poured a splash of the concoction into the bowl with the penis tip and the pink liquid. When he did, it began to steam. The penis tip melted, spread like a plop of pancake mix slopped on a griddle.

"I have found the ding dong to be about the best thing there is for this stuff. Testicle's second, facial parts third. Internal organs fourth. Fingers and toes fifth. After that, kind of a toss up."

"Just get on with it," Cody said. "And be careful."

"Careful is my middle name... Oh, goddamn it."

Doctor Momo had put his hand down on the scalpel. "Mother of God. Holy asshole of Satan. I've punctured my palm."

Doctor Momo lifted his bleeding hand. The scalpel fell out, landed on the tray. "Shit," he continued, "that little shiny sonofabitch is sharp."

Jack brought a piece of cloth to Momo, who wrapped his hand.

"I'm okay, now," he said. "Goddamn that hurt...now, Colonel—" Momo picked up the scalpel, flicked the blood from it, sending a streak of it across the white page of Ned's note pad hanging about his neck. "Shall we get on with it?"

"Doctor," Cody said, "you never really completed outlining the drawback of this method."

"Ah, screw it. It will be all right. I will tell you the rest of it later. Now grit your teeth, this is going to hurt like the proverbial sonofabitch."

When they reached the far side of the island they found a rocky beach. The surf crashed against it savagely, throwing a fizz of white ocean high into the sky, dropping it to burst on the rocks in a stinging mist.

There was no boat. There was nothing really. Just rocks and the surf.

"Now we've seen it," Annie said.

"Yes, and it doesn't look good," Hickok said.

"Could build raft," Bull said.

"We could," Hickok said. "Provided we could steal tools, slip out here every day for a week or so. Course, if we did manage that, soon as we dropped it in the water, the waves would smash it, and us, against the rocks."

"Not good plan," Bull said.

"There is another alternative," Annie said. "We could take Bemo's submarine."

"It's probably covered in those monkey men," Hickok said. "And say we do take it, how do we drive it?"

"Ned," Annie said.

"Ned?" Hickok said. "Why would he do that?"

"Because," Cat said, "he adores your friend, Cody."

"It's something to consider," Hickok said.

"Sun show two o'clock," Bull said. "That something to consider."

"Right you are," Hickok said. "Let's head back."

The left side of Cody's neck was cut. The mixture was applied to the incision. Wires were fastened to the wound and the other ends of the wires were plugged into a machine festooned with whirligigs and blinking lights. A switch was thrown. Dynamos groaned. Machinery clattered, screeched, coughed black puffs of choking smoke. Electrical power bolted through the wires, lit Cody up like a flaming meteor. His face wriggled. His hair stood up like porcupine quills. His eyes poked almost out of his head. His lips peeled back to show all his teeth. He made a sound like "Ahhhhhhhhrrrrrrruuuuuuugah."

The dynamos whined and wooed for a time, then went silent. Cody's hair dropped. His very pink skin stopped moving. For a moment, he smoked pleasantly on the metal tray like a hog's head just pulled from a vat of steaming water.

On his neck, where the scalpel had opened his flesh, the wound had closed and there appeared a kind of wrinkled knot. It quivered, as if a worm were inside it.

The knot grew bigger. It quivered more than before.

Bigger yet.

The quiver turned into a shake.

"As you Americans say," said Doctor Momo, "now we are cooking."

When they reached the mouth of the tunnel, Bull glanced at the sky. "Three o'clock white man time."

"Then we have to hurry," Annie said.

"I have been thinking," Cat said. "To do what you want to do, you must ask Tin and the monster."

"I thought the monster was just a monster," Annie said.

"True, but you need them."

"Even if we do," Hickok said. "Tin wouldn't be of any use. He's Doctor Momo's man."

"He loves the monster," Cat said.

"Say what?" Hickok said.

"Men," said Annie, "they are so dumb. I realized that the day Tin saw the monster lying on the beach. I thought he was going to melt."

"But...they are both...men," Hickok said.

"For one who thinks of himself as worldly," Annie said, "you know very little about love. Some men love men. And in a physical way."

"Well, I mean...yes, I've heard of it. I know it exists. But where do they put...it."

"Think about it," Annie said.

"But that is just wrong," Hickok said.

"Once you thought it was okay to kill Indians merely because they were Indians," Annie said. "Now you think that is wrong."

"That right," Bull said. "What about that, Wild Bill?" Then to Annie: "But me wonder too. Where thing go?"

Cat and Annie looked at one another, exasperated. "We'll explain it to you later," Annie said.

They went into the tunnel, flipped the switch for light, latched the door back in place, rushed along the corridor.

At this same moment, Doctor Momo, the quick-scooting Ned, and Jack — who was carrying Cody's babbling, smoking head on a platter as if it were that of John the Baptist about to be presented to the wife of Herod — were proceeding back to the living quarters of the compound.

The explorers had no sooner pulled the rug in place, eased out of Doctor Momo's door and locked it, than they heard Cody running on about this and that, reciting some tall windy he had told them all twenty times before, but in a manner that indicated he was out of his head. Which, considering the circumstances, wasn't something he could spare.

Hickok and his crew hustled quickly down the hall, just out of sight as Doctor Momo, Jack and Cody turned the corner.

They all ducked into Bull's room, quietly locked the door.

Cat said, "I can only stay a moment. It is time for me to bring the doctor his tea. He gets upset if I do not bring it on time. But, I want to leave this key with you. Bull has one. You must be very careful."

"Thanks," Annie said.

They eased the door open. Cat glanced down the hall. "I must go," she said. She kissed Bull quickly and made her exit, leaving in the room the faint smell of musk.

Bull made a horse whinny under his breath.

Doctor Momo stopped off in his room for a drink. He placed Cody's head on the table while he sipped whiskey. This time he did not offer Cody a drink. He stared down at the Westerner, shook the colored liquid in his glass.

Cody's hair was dripping sweat. His skin was less pink now, but it had a kind of glow to it. Cody felt great. He could feel himself changing.

The twisting knot on his neck had expanded, producing a large segment of shoulder. Underneath the shoulder, tendons were visible, and there was a spot of bone; blood dripped onto the metal tray, filled it.

Cody was about to ask for a taste of whiskey, when Doctor Momo spoke. "Drain that tray, will you, Jack?"

Jack bent over, began lapping blood from the tray.

"Good boy," Doctor Momo said. Then: "Colonel Cody, we have come to what I must call the moment of truth. Before this day ends you will have a shoulder, and perhaps a complete arm. A little luck, a hand and fingers. No more. There is hardly enough flesh and elixir left to provide more for you. I can brew up a bit of the beasts around here, make you part of them. But the ideal situation is a volunteer."

"Volunteer?" Cody asked.

"One of your mates. You need human flesh. I have offered up some of my own. And, might I add, without any selfishness. But, to do this right, to give you a complete body, and for it to be entirely human, we need a subject."

"You mean a flesh donor?" Cody asked.

"Of course. There's one little problem. I would really like to have someone not only donate a bit of flesh, but, in fact, donate their entire self."

"You mean kill one of them?"

"I dislike that word. Kill. It brings all sorts of nasty things to mind. Sacrifice is not a good word either. I suppose we could ask their permission, but, I am afraid, no matter how well they hold you in high esteem, donating their body to you might not be what they had in mind."

"I can understand a hold up on that," Cody said.

"But we are in a position, if we choose, to pick someone. We invite them to a special meeting, promise them something. Then we clip that sonofabitch in the head, and into the mixture they go."

"My God, Momo. I couldn't do that. They're my friends."

108

"Hey, your choice," Doctor Momo said. "You can be a head, a shoulder, an arm, and maybe a hand. But I wouldn't bet on much else. Or, we can choose one of the monkeys. You will most likely turn out a little hairy and have a craving for bananas and a desire to throw shit. I tell you what. I am going to have you taken to your room. Ned here will be left to serve you, and you may consider our discussion. But tomorrow, I would like an answer. I would like to pop someone before breakfast. Because, you see, Colonel Cody, I have other plans. I would like to do more with this flesh than reanimate you. I can build all manner of things from humans and animals. I can make you your very own Catherine. Would you like that? I can give you a body. A woman. If you go along with me, not only will you have your body back, but you and I can return to civilization, touting my work, and the both of us will become not only wealthy, but famous. I see myself as taking to cowboy hats, actually."

"I am already famous. And I am sometimes wealthy. When I don't waste it."

"Of course," Doctor Momo said. "I understand. And I am asking you to do a dreadful thing, no doubt. But, you either want your body back, or you do not. It really is that simple."

"My God," Cody said. "Think what you are asking. Civilization will not be glad to know we murdered humans for their flesh. And I won't be glad of it either."

"We do not have to tell the exact truth. Accidents happen. People die. There are ways around it. But, do not give me your answer immediately. To your room to rest. And to wait and see what my little experiment does. You may find yourself quite happy with the results. Jack. That is quite enough. Quit licking. The tray is shiny."

There was a light knock on the door.

"Ah," Doctor Momo said. "That will be Cat with my tea. Jack, will you see Colonel Cody to his room. And Ned, watch after him. And Colonel, give some real thought to picking out one of your little friends. If you do not pick one, I will pick one. And later, I will pick another. And when they are all gone — though I may keep Miss Oakley around for other reasons — Captain Bemo will bring me more. It will happen one way or another. The difference is, if I pick, you do not profit. In fact, I am sure you have considered this, but your head is flesh. And I don't believe in waste. A few slices, and you would fit nicely into the mixing bowl. Give it some thought, will you?"

As the day settled, well before dinner, Annie and Hickok decided to take a flyer. They crept out of Bull's room with the key Cat had provided, moved along the corridor and tapped slightly on the door Cat said was Tin's room.

Tin opened the door, shocked to see them.

"We are friends of the monster," Hickok said.

"Bert," Tin said.

"Bert?" Hickok said.

Tin stuck his head out, looked in both directions, hustled them inside.

Bert lay on the bed nude. He was not the least bit embarrassed. Annie took him in with one quick look, then glanced away.

Then she glanced back.

Then away.

Then back.

And away.

"For heaven's sake, cover yourself," Hickok said.

"Heaven," Bert said, "has not been all that kind to me. I see no need to do anything for heaven's sake. Has your lady not seen a naked man before?"

"Do not tempt fate," Hickok said.

"I thought you were friends?" Tin said.

"I suppose we are," Bert said. "He and his friends saved me from being ground to powder. They carried me away and later found me here on the beach. They saved me again. I suppose I at least owe the lady some respect."

Bert rose from the bed, snatched the sheet off and wrapped himself in it. "You may look now, lady, and forgive my manners. I have become quite the card as of late."

"Tin," said Hickok. "Will you help us?"

Tin said, "Help you? I should turn you in."

"But will you help us?" Annie asked.

Tin looked a question at Bert.

Bert said, "We could listen."

Hickok explained simply that they wanted to leave the island, that the best method might be by Bemo's submarine.

Tin said, "I will help you. I love Bert. I want to be with him."

"And I with you, Tin," Bert said.

"That is so sweet," Annie said.

"The problem we have," Hickok said, "is we have no weapons. We don't know how to navigate the *Naughty Lass*, and Bemo, who of course does know how, can't help us. He's controlled by Momo. What do we do?"

"Ned," Tin said. "He can operate the *Naughty Lass*."

"That's what we heard," Hickok said.

"I don't see why we don't just grab Momo and make him do what we want," Annie said.

"Because the monkey men protect him," Tin said. "They would tear you to shreds."

"We could threaten to kill Momo if they bother us," Annie said.

"They would still tear you to shreds," Tin said. "You might kill Momo, but they would kill you...oh, goodness gracious. How can I talk like this? Doctor Momo has been good to me."

"He has also lied to you," Bert said. "That heart business, remember."

"I remember. I am just so confused."

"We get out of this," Bert said, "we can go somewhere where we will not be bothered. Somewhere where we can live a life together."

"And where would that be?" Tin said.

"Maybe Annie and I can come up with something," Hickok heard himself say, and was amazed at the sound of his own voice. Just what was he thinking? He and Annie, a Tin Man and a monster who were sissy on each other.

"Another thing about the monkey men," Tin said. "You will not even get close to Doctor Momo. They seem to be out of sight a lot of the time, but they are near. They wait until he commands, or for that matter, looks in distress. When we eat dinner, behind the wall, to the right of Momo's seat. That wall is transparent from the opposite side. A kind of mirror. Monkey men wait there."

"Can we get guns?" Hickok asked.

"There are guns," Tin said. "I had not thought of that. We can get guns, but it will not be easy. There is a storehouse for such things. It is for the monkey men. Mostly it houses weapons they do not know how to use. Weapons the men who worked for Momo left. He sent them all away when he created the monkey men. He wanted complete obedience. The monkeys are less scheming than men."

"What about this storehouse?" Hickok asked.

"Guarded by the monkey men. But I can get in."

"Do you think Ned will operate the *Naughty Lass*?" Annie asked.

"He loves your Buffalo Bill Cody," Tin said. "I think he might. But then again, only if Cody wants to leave."

"And why would he not?" Hickok said.

"The body," Annie said. "You know that."

"And I know when the chips are down, Cody does the right thing."

While Ned sat in a chair in the corner, curled up with a dime novel Buntline had written, titled, *Buffalo Bill Battles the Steam Dogs of the Prairie*, Cody lifted his new shoulder, flexed his arm, closed his hand and wiggled the two fingers and thumb he now had. It felt good, looked like his old arm, only stronger; in fact, he felt so vibrant he thought he might somehow be intoxicated from the chemicals used in the operation.

He was trying to consider who to offer Doctor Momo. Annie was out. She was just too sweet.

And Hickok. They had been friends a long time. He did not really want to have him boiled up and made into goo.

Bull. Bull was also a friend. But he was an Indian. Cody considered that he had certainly killed a lot of Indians in his time. Maybe one more wouldn't matter. Maybe that was the way to go. Just add to the record. On some level, Bull would understand that. He was a practical man.

Then again, would Indian flesh work with his flesh? Did that matter?

Cody let that run through his head for a while.

Bull became his favorite candidate.

In his coffin in the jungle, under three feet of dirt and leaf mold, Vlad Tepes, Dracul, could not sleep.

He hated that kind of thing. You needed to sleep. Wanted to sleep, and just could not.

It was terrible.

He had only recently started to have trouble.

112

Used to be, he lay down, his head hit the cushion in the coffin, and he was out like a dead man.

Oh, that was good. Dead man. He wished he had someone to share stuff like that with.

But...that was out.

Instead he was here with these creatures. They were not even proper men. They were made from this and made from that, and if the boar man he had tasted was any indication, they were a lot like the British Bland. He had always preferred ethnics while in Britain. An Indian. A Chinese. They had some taste.

Their taste caused him to consider Asia in the first place.

Oh, the Americans had been all right, in spite of the smell. But they gave him indigestion.

Sometimes, no matter what you did, you just could not win.

Dracul closed his eyes and counted backwards from a thousand.

...eight hundred and seventy-one... Oh, this is not working. Not in any kind of way is it working. Eight hundred and seventy. Eight hundred and sixty-nine...

When he got to seven hundred and seventy-nine he lost count because he fell asleep.

The sun slowly sank toward the ocean. It was so red it appeared to be heated. The beast men gathered at the edge of the woods to watch it go down.

It made them nervous.

They knew they had to dig up their master when it was low down and the dark was high.

They knew they had to do that, and they would, but they feared doing it, and it was not just because Vlad Tepes, Dracul was ill tempered. It was something else. Something they sensed and could not explain.

The Lion Man said, "I know. Why don't we just dig him up now and eat him."

This was considered, and agreed to be a good idea.

Vlad heard the ground being scraped away.

He sent out a telepathic message. *NOT YET, YOU FOOLS.*

The digging stopped.

Then it resumed.

I SAID STOP.

A pause.

The digging started up again. Now Vlad could hear them scratching on the lid of the coffin.

Oh, boy, was he going to whip some ass if they pulled off that lid.

The lid creaked, groaned, was lifted.

Beast faces looked down on him. Directly above his own face was the face of Wolf, formerly the Sayer of the Law.

The red rays of the dying sun fell inside the box and burned Vlad. He quivered, smoked, but could not make himself rise. The sun owned him.

I CANNOT STAND THE SUN. I MUST NOT HAVE SUN. REPLACE THE LID. NOW.

Wolf heard the voice in his head, and he wanted to do as he was told because he was afraid, but he wanted not to do what he was told because he was a beast and he was no longer a man and he did not have to listen to men, even one as powerful as this one.

"You ate Boar," Wolf said. "Bad man."

"Bad man," the beasts said together.

Vlad was cooking now, screaming, folding up inside his clothes.

But before he dissolved entirely, the beasts, in a frenzy, feasted on him, eating the smoking flesh quickly and finding it good.

If a bit bony.

Two hours later, dark, the beasts sat on the beach and watched the waves explode in the moonlight, crawl over the rocks like some kind of frothy parasite.

"The bad man tasted good," Lion Man said.

Wolf stood up. He was wearing Vlad's cloak. He ran around the beach on his hind legs so that the cloak was caught up by the wind and flapped behind him like wings. The red underside of it looked orange in the moonlight.

Lion Man, who was wearing Vlad's vest, and nothing else, stood up and scratched himself.

"Momo, and all those men, they can kiss my ass. I am through with them. I am a beast. I can run on all fours."

He sprang about on all fours, shouting:

"I am free. ARE WE NOT FREE?"

The other beasts joined in. "We are free! We are free!"

"We bend to no man!" screamed the Lion Man. "We can eat anything we want. We can eat anybody we want. We can eat Doctor Momo if we want."

Wolf bounded into their midst.

"Oooooh. I don't know about that. Is he not our father?"

"Is he not meat?" said the Lion Man. "Do we not eat meat?"

The Goat Man said, "I'm sticking with vegetables."

They howled at the great big moon. They danced on the beach. They made love to each other. They drank spoiled fruit juice. They had a big time.

Of course, the next morning they were mighty sick, two of the creatures had bleeding asses, and the Lion Man, high on fruit juice, had eaten one of the goats.

Cody was ecstatic about having a shoulder, arm and a partial hand. But the ecstasy soon passed. He wanted more. He decided he hadn't really liked Bull all that much anyway.

Bull it was.

He worked the muscles in his jaw, turned on his rotor and looked at Ned, curled in a chair, using his flippers and thumbs to read the Buntline book.

Old Buntline, Cody thought. Always there for me. Except when he was drunk. Or asleep. Or chasing whores. Well, there for me the rest of the time. Turned my crank when I lost my body. Listened to my bullshit stories. Made up bullshit stories about me that made me rich.

They had done all manner of things together. Back when he had a body.

God, he thought. A body.

Cody missed Buntline, but he missed his body more.

Damn, he thought. Ned Buntline. Ned the seal. What a coincidence.

Ned finished the dime novel, closed it, lifted his head, saw Cody looking at him. He smiled his little seal teeth. His whiskers wiggled.

With furious movement he laid aside the novel, pushed his glasses on his nose, grabbed up his pad and pencil, began to write.

Scooting down from the chair, Ned eased over to where Cody was, lifted the pad to show what he had written: I ADMIRE YOU.

"Why thanks, lad. That is most kind of you. I think you are quite the little cutter, yourself."

Ned began writing again. He held up the results: IT IS YOUR CODE OF HONOR I MOST ADMIRE. I HAVE NEVER KNOWN ANYONE LIKE YOU. I READ WHAT YOU SAID ABOUT LOYALTY TO FRIENDS. I WANT TO BE LIKE THAT.

Cody developed a lump in his throat.

"Why yes, little friend. That is important."

Ned jerked the page off, wrote on another, held it up: I WILL LIVE BY YOUR CODE. DO RIGHT 'CAUSE IT IS RIGHT... YOU HAVE CHANGED MY LIFE.

"Good...how good. Well now, I think I should close my eyes and rest, Ned."

Ned writing again. He held up what he had written: OF COURSE, SLEEP WELL. YOU ARE MY HERO. AND I KNOW YOU HAVE ALREADY DECIDED TO PASS ON THE DOCTOR'S OFFER. I AM SO PROUD OF YOU.

"Very nice," Cody said. "Very nice."

Cody closed his eyes to feign sleep. Maybe he could talk to Momo about banging the little seal in the head. Something quick and from behind, so he never knew what hit him. Have Jack do it. Better yet, Tin. Tin could hit hard and he seemed methodical. Jack would enjoy it too much. Jack would probably eat Ned when he finished. Must make sure that doesn't happen, thought Cody. No eating Ned. Just a quick bang and it's over.

During dinner Jack chewed a lot more of Doctor Momo's food than usual.

Bert joined them for dinner this time. He sat by Tin, but they did not show any obvious affection toward one another. Beneath the table, however, their feet touched, and a couple of times, for what seemed like no reason at all to the other diners, the bolt between Tin's legs rattled.

Hickok sat and thought about all the monkey men Cat told him were behind the see-through wall. Hickok looked and saw only solid wall. Amazing. Was it true? Could there really be monkey men on the far side of the wall watching them?

Considering all the things he had seen here on Doctor Momo's island, there seemed little reason to doubt it.

Captain Bemo said not a word during dinner. He drank heavily and his face was gloomy.

Doctor Momo noted this with enjoyment, said, "Bemo, look at it this way. There is no use worrying over your plight. You are alive. You would have been dead. As for the rest of your life, well, it is mine."

After dinner, Bert was assigned his own room. Doctor Momo thanked Tin for watching after him. Tin escorted Bert to his room, presumably as a prisoner, but he left Bert's door unlocked. Jack led Annie and Hickok to their room, locked the door.

Doctor Momo himself carried Cody back to his room, Ned following.

Four armed monkey men helped the intoxicated Bull to his room. Bull had his arms around a couple of them, and was telling them a story in the Sioux language. They put him in his room and locked the door. One of the monkey men bent over and looked through the keyhole.

Bull staggered to his bed, sat down, stooped his shoulders, then fell backwards on the bed and lay still.

When the monkey man's eye went away from the keyhole, Bull sat up on the edge of the bed, straightened and smiled, sober as a minister at a baptism.

Inside Tin's room, Tin packed a small bag. It included: Machine oil. Polishing rags. A toothbrush. Mint water for a mouth wash. He opened the compartment in his body and took out Dot's silver slippers. He put the slippers in the bag, then pushed the bag into the opening in his leg.

Packed.

In their room, Hickok and Annie kissed. After kissing, they exercised their fingers. Stretched them, bent them this way and that. They always exercised their fingers before they did any kind of marksmanship.

Of course, they were usually sure of having guns.

Bert sat in a chair and thought about the skating championships. Shit, he had lied to Tin. He had purposely kicked that goddamn Frankenstein in the mouth. He had gone back for just that purpose. He would have to tell Tin the truth.

Then again, why?

They loved each other. Wasn't that all that counted?

Captain Bemo looked at himself in the bathroom mirror. He looked the same, but knew he wasn't. He hadn't been the same in a long time, and he didn't like it. He would never be the same, and he didn't like that. Even the load he had just dropped felt different. He had no desire to fornicate anymore. Food was a chore. When science, eating, fucking and shitting were no longer fun, what was there?

He got a smaller mirror, turned so he could look in it; he could see the back of his head in the main mirror.

The bulb pulsed a dull yellow.

He remembered long ago, building the *Naughty Lass* with his original crew. He remembered how the crew jumped to his every command. Now he was lucky if someone would pass the salt.

Not worth it anymore, he thought. Being Momo's zombie is not what I had in mind for my life.

Bemo laid the mirror down, selected from his shaving kit his straight razor, and without opening it, using the mirror again, he pinpointed the bulb in the back of his head. Reaching over his shoulder, he used the closed razor to tap the bulb.

It was sturdy. It took the hit.

He did it again, but this time like he meant it.

The bulb popped.

Before Bemo fell to the floor, truly dead, he had the sensation of being on board the *Naughty Lass*, diving down quick into deep dark waters.

In Doctor Momo's room Cat grabbed a few things and put them in a satchel. A razor for shaving her legs. She still had a lot of fur to contend with, even if it did make her look as if she had a wonderful head of hair. She even had a faint mustache, but she stayed on top of it. No reason for anyone to ever know. She packed a toothbrush and a container of baking soda. Baking soda was really good for the teeth. Gave fresh breath, too. She packed two Dickens novels and a small bottle of flea killer. She also packed two dresses and no underwear.

As he adjusted Cody's head on a dresser top, Doctor Momo said, "Did you give it some thought? About who goes to the meat machine, I mean?"

"I did," Cody said.

"And?"

"You can take your flesh-growing business, all your test tubes, and stuff them up your ass, if there's any room in there after Jack climbs in."

"I beg your pardon?" Doctor Momo said.

"Hell, boy," Cody said. "You heard me. I don't stutter."

Ned snickered.

Doctor Momo's mouth collapsed and sucked wind. "You ungrateful American peasant. I will have you ground up and mixed with monkey meat. I promise you. Ned, take this talking head to my laboratory. Now."

Ned, glasses on his nose, jerked up his pad and pencil, began to write.

"What are you doing?" Momo said to Ned. "I didn't ask you a question. I gave you an order."

Ned turned the tablet around so Momo could read it: KISS MY LITTLE BLACK SEAL ASS.

"Why you ungrateful, glorified fish."

Ned wrote quickly, held it up: MAMMAL. YOU SHOULD KNOW THAT.

Doctor Momo reached in his pocket, pulled a flick blade knife, snapped it open.

"I will have you gutted, sliced, cooked and put on crackers, you piece of sea lard."

Doctor Momo slashed at Ned.

Ned moved just in time. For a seal on land, he was pretty fast.

"Leave him alone, you coward!" Cody yelled.

Doctor Momo turned, swung his hand at Cody's head, knocking it and the container that held him flying.

Cody rolled across the floor, slammed up against the door. Cody's new thumb popped back into his face and poked him in the eye.

"Owwwwwwww."

Doctor Momo turned his attention back to Ned, said, "Now where were we?"

Ned wrote quickly: YOU WERE TRYING TO CUT ME, YOU ASSWIPE.

Tin walked out to the weapons shack. There were two monkey men guarding it. They gave him a quizzical look. When he walked between them and took hold of the door, they began to chatter. One clutched his arm. Tin grabbed the monkey man's head and twisted it violently. It came off in his hands, messy and wet. He turned and threw it, striking the other guard full in the face. When the guard tried to get up, Tin stepped on his head. Tin was heavy. The monkey man was small. There was a sound like someone stepping on a pile of brittle sticks, followed very soon by a sound like someone stepping through a large pile of cow pies.

Tin shook the monkey man off his foot, grabbed the door to the shack once again, ripped it free. Inside was a virtual cornucopia of arms. Tin chose holstered revolvers, bandoleers of coordinating ammunition. He draped them over himself. He picked up a Gatling gun as if it were a pencil, as well as belts of ammunition. He tucked the Gatling under his arm. With his free arm, he scooped up a pile of rifles and shotguns, headed back to the compound.

On the way two monkey men approached Tin.

"What are you doing with that stuff?" one asked.

Tin tried to think of a quick answer. Nothing came to mind.

"Doc Momo said stuff was not to be touched unless he said so," the monkey man continued. "You are not doing some kind of bad thing, are you?"

"Well," Tin said. "Yes, I guess I am."

Tin kicked the inquiring monkey man in the testicles so hard the critter went out. The other one screeched, drew his revolver. But before he could fire, Tin dropped the Gatling, took hold of the monkey man's gun barrel, twisted it.

Next he twisted the monkey man.

When I'm oiled, he thought, I am one quick sonofabitch. He picked up the Gatling, kept going.

Ned ducked Doctor Momo's swipe, rushed between the doctor's legs, knocking him down. In the process, Ned took a cut to his back.

Ned grabbed up Cody's jar, tucked it under a flipper, jerked the door open with his other, rushed out into the hall.

"Treason," yelled Doctor Momo. "Attempted murder. My seal has lost his mind. He's got Cody. Catch them!"

Monkey men appeared almost magically in the hall, sliding out of trap doors, slipping out of sliding walls. Ned saw them, but he didn't slow down, he went through them with his nose forward, his eyes half closed. He wasn't moving very fast, but he had some momentum. He knocked several of them over before a pile landed on top of him and hammered him to the ground.

When Bert heard the noise in the hallway, he cracked open the door, saw the seal and Cody's head taking a beating. Monkey men were hammering the little seal, clanking on his tin head-guard, kicking Cody's jar about. The jar slammed up against a wall and cracked, fell apart.

Cody stuck out a hand he had not had when Bert saw him last, grabbed the ankle of a monkey man and tripped him.

Bert rushed out into the hallway, grabbed a monkey man by the throat, squeezed until the throat went small. Then he grabbed up the dead monkey man by the ankle and went through the hall swinging the beast, knocking monkey men from wall to wall.

The monkey men went for their revolvers. The gunfire was loud in the hallway. Shots struck Bert. They hurt him, but they did not stop him. The monkey man he was swinging no longer had a head, just a red, wet stump. Bullets dove into Bert.

Annie and Hickok opened their door, saw the action.

Hickok burst out of the room, grabbed a revolver from one of the dead monkey men, started firing.

Every shot was a winner. Four monkey men fell dead. Then Hickok snapped the revolver on an empty chamber. The other cylinders were empty; the owner of the gun had already fired two shots at or into Bert.

Hickok grabbed up more revolvers, and now Annie was in the hallway, and she did the same. But by the time they did, a large number of the monkey men were dead by Bert's hand, and the others were fleeing so fast they were falling over one another.

Doctor Momo, who had been watching the action from down the

hall through his partially opened door, closed it slightly and locked it.

Rushing to the wall behind his bed, he threw open a secret panel, hit the alarm button. He hit it twice. That was the signal for all the monkey men to congregate at his room.

On the other side of the compound, the alarm went off: a blaring horn, flashing lights placed strategically here and there.

The monkey men came together in a heap, chattering.

One of the monkey men, a survivor of the hallway fight, arrived with three of his comrades. He said, "That's the alarm. We all know what to do, but I think we might not want to. Big guy in there is wiping the floor with us. Ugly business. Monkey guts and brains from wall to wall. Bullets just piss him off."

"Doctor Momo calls," said one of the fresh recruits, "we're supposed to go."

"We been," said the first. "Didn't like it much."

"Doctor Momo needs help."

"You know," said the monkey man, unfastening his gun belt, letting it drop, taking off his shirt, scooting out of his pants, socks and shoes, standing hairy in his underwear, "I've been thinking about eating fruit up in a tree. A lot."

"Me too," said another of the monkey men.

Others chimed in with the same sentiment.

Bending over, touching knuckles to the ground, they ran off into the jungle.

One diehard, still dressed as a human, said, "But what about Doctor Momo?"

"Fuck Doctor Momo," one of the monkey men called back.

The diehard stood for a moment, looked around the compound. He glanced hard in the direction of Doctor Momo. He glanced back at the open gate.

Beyond, the jungle, lush, full of fruit and grubs, beckoned him.

He slipped off his clothes, dropped to all fours, began to hoot and run for the jungle.

Doctor Momo pressed the button again.

"All right now. Where are you simian sonofabitches? Things are not looking good here. Get your asses over here."

Jack pounded on the door. Doctor Momo looked through the peephole. He opened it, let Jack in.

"Where are those monkeys?"

"They stripped off and tore out for the jungle," Jack said. "They almost ran me down."

"Damn," Doctor Momo said. "What about Cat? Why is she not showing up?"

"I haven't seen her. But I did see Tin."

"Good."

"No, not good. He took a shot at me. He was carrying a bunch of guns under his arms, including a Gatling. He saw me and put them all down, took a rifle out of the batch and shot at me. I was lucky he was such a crummy shot."

"Why would he do that?"

"I think he's in with them, Doctor."

"Them? You mean Ned and Cody?"

"All of them. Hickok, the split tail, the whole lot."

"Bemo. We can escape in the submarine."

"No, that's not going to work."

"And why not?"

"Thought of that. Went by his room to get him, bring him here. He didn't answer the door, had to unlock it. He was on the bathroom floor. He popped his bulb. Was already starting to smell."

"All right. All right. If that's how they want it. They can have it. We'll use the tunnel. Out on the beach, under a series of false boulders, I have a very fine boat. With a motor."

"A motor?"

"That's right, a motor. I built it with Bemo before I made you. You were a chimpanzee then. The boat is large, has a roof, plenty of room so we wouldn't have to share a bed, very fine equipment. It is well stocked. Dried foods. Water. Playing cards with nude women on them in compromising positions with farm animals."

"We could turn this into a holiday," Jack said.

"Just what I have always taught you, Jack. When life gives you lemons, make lemonade. Get the work books, my notes, and you and I will haul out of here. I will set the device to blow up the compound. It will blast their asses all the way to the moon."

"What about Cat?"

"Been nice knowing her," Doctor Momo said.

As they entered the tunnel the explosive device started to tick. It was designed to blast the island into a large series of swirling dust motes. It was programmed to go off in forty minutes.

It took twenty minutes to get to the other side of the island.

It would take two to three minutes to activate the boat.

Then they would be gone.

Plenty of time.

The minutes ticked off on the bomb's counter.

One...

Hearing a commotion at the compound, gunshots and such, the beast men out on the beach gathered in a huddle.

"Doctor Momo's got some action going," Lion Man said, pushing his vest open, clutching it on either side like a happy politician.

Wolf agreed. He was still wearing Vlad's cape, and he had come to think of it as a sign of authority. Once it was the law, now it was the cape. Either way, he was the big cheese among the beast men and he intended to keep it that way.

Two...

"I say we go over there and eat Doctor Momo," Lion Man said.

"I don't know," said a creature so mixed of animals it was hard to know what he was. He was called Patch by the others. "He is still Doctor Momo."

There was another Goat Man in the crowd, and he thought of something he might want to say, then hesitated. After last night, after his friend had been eaten, he thought it best if he sort of went along to get along. He faded back into the crowd, tried not to bleat. He thought happy thoughts.

"I say we eat everybody," Lion Man said.

Three...

Patch, gathering his courage, said, "I didn't want to bring this up, but, I think I should. There's a time when it has to be said. I think if we are going to live together, and if we are going to eat meat, that is all right. But I think a certain someone amongst us needs to learn to draw the line. And we can't eat everybody all in one day. Do that, all the food for you meat eaters will be gone."

"I don't know," Lion Man, said, "there are always lots of monkeys."

"Food must be handled carefully," Patch said. "There is no such thing as an endless supply."

"That's a point," Wolf said to the Lion Man. "And, eating Billy, come on. He thought you and he were friends."

Lion's head drooped. "I couldn't help myself."

"And," said the other Goat Man, finally finding courage, "not all of us eat meat. I just don't have the teeth for it."

"All right, all right," said Lion Man. "I agree. Not to eat friends, that is the law."

"That's good," Wolf said. "I will put that on our new list. Not to eat friends."

"But," Lion Man said, "I still think we should eat Doctor Momo, monkey men, and that little Jack guy. Some of the others."

"That sounds good," Wolf said. "Let's march over there right now and get to eating."

"We can dig holes and put what we don't eat in the holes," said a Dog Man. "It tastes better after it's been in the ground awhile."

"That'll work," Wolf said. They started for the compound.

Four...

Five...

Six...

The monkey men were surprised to meet the assorted beast men at the edge of the jungle. It was not a happy surprise. A real wholesale slaughter went on.

Seven...

Monkeys were torn and ripped, thrown this way and that. A few fled into the trees, but they were heavier than when they were monkeys. They weren't as agile. Tree limbs broke. Feet slipped. It was not a good day for the monkey men.

Eight...

When wet monkey parts were spread from one end of the jungle to the next, the beast men continued their march to the compound.

Meat could be buried later.

Nine...

Bert, Tin, Hickok, Annie, Catherine, Bull and Ned, carrying Cody's head, all came together near the dock where Bemo's sub bobbed in the dark blue water.

They arrived just as the beast men were coming out of the forest.

Ten...

"We see you!" the Lion Man yelled.

In response, Hickok and the others looked up to see the creatures charging toward them. There must have been a hundred of them, foaming at the mouth, cussing, one wearing a cape, another a vest, some in remnants of clothes. They were growling, running on all fours.

Eleven...

Tin, who was still carrying the weapons, dropped everything, called out, "Grab something."

Tin himself grabbed the Gatling gun, pulled out the props, adjusted a belt of ammunition, told Bert, "Guide the belt. Feed me, baby."

Hickok and Annie snatched up rifles, poked revolvers in their pants. They shoved ammunition in their pockets. Hickok said, "Ned, can you get the submarine started?"

Ned nodded.

Twelve...

"Take Cody on board, start it up."

Ned hustled Cody's head onboard the submarine. Free of the jar, Cody was idly waving his arm about. Ned plopped Cody on the sub's deck while he worked the hatch with his two thumbs and flippers. It was a pretty tough job, but finally he jerked the lid open.

He grabbed up Cody, ducked inside, left the lid open for the others. The Gatling gun began to bark.

Thirteen...

Creatures dropped. Wolf got a hole shot in his cloak. The goat took one in the stomach. Patch got a leg blown off.

A few of the charging beasts got past the Gatling barrage. Hickok, Annie and Bull blasted away, killing the creatures. Cat managed to shoot the ground twice, knock fruit out of a tree, and nearly deafen Bull, she fired so close to his ear.

"Be better off, shoot self with that," Bull said.

"That's mean," Cat said.

Fourteen...

The beasts were on the run now. They grabbed up their wounded and fled into the jungle.

A cheer went up from the defenders.

Fifteen...

Patch and the goat were dead before they had been carried twenty feet into the jungle. The creatures stopped, laid their comrades down and looked at them.

Sixteen...

"They were brave," Wolf said.

"They were," Lion Man said. "Let's eat them."

"No eating friends, that is the law," one yelled out.

"Hey," Lion Man said. "Did we say anything about dead friends?"

"Well, now," Wolf said, "that's a point. It's not in the law. So, I suggest we eat them later."

Seventeen...

This seemed agreeable. Their bodies were once again picked up, and the beasts, fed up with the Gatling gun, fled for the other side of the island.

Eighteen...

The zeppelinauts and their comrades climbed into the submarine with their bags and guns. Hickok closed the hatch and Ned took her out.

Nineteen...

Doctor Momo and Jack reached the end of the tunnel and attempted to lift the trap.

It moved only slightly.

"My God," Doctor Momo said. "It's hung. Give it a push, Jack."

Twenty...

Jack gave it a push. It would not budge at first, then it gave.

It gave because the Lion Man, who had stopped to rest, was no longer standing on it. He had felt the movement beneath his feet and had stepped off.

When the trap opened, and out came Jack and Doctor Momo, the Lion Man and all the other beasts he had created were waiting.

Twenty-one...

Wolf, the leader, said, "Well, Doctor Momo. What a pleasant surprise. For us, anyway."

"Welcome to dinner," said the Lion Man.

Twenty-two...

"Just who do you think you're speaking to?" Doctor Momo said.

"Why, to you," said the Lion Man, reaching out to place a hand on Doctor Momo's shoulder.

Doctor Momo slapped the hand off. "I am your father. I am your creator. You will show respect. Sayer of the Law. What is the law?"

Twenty-three...

"I don't do that anymore," said Wolf, the Sayer.

"The hell you do not," said Doctor Momo. "Say the goddamn law."

Wolf was surprised to hear himself say: "Not to run on all fours..."

The others began to quote it with him.

Jack grinned from ear to ear.

Twenty-four...

The Lion Man let out a bellow. "Stop! This is not our law. This is his law for us. We aren't his servants. Let's eat him."

The beasts stopped quoting the law. They exchanged glances.

Twenty-five...

"Wait," said Doctor Momo. "I am your father. Without me you would not exist."

"Not exist as we are," said the Lion Man. "We were something before you made us this. We are that again. Animals. I eat meat, Doctor Father. I like meat. You are meat."

"NO! I am not to be eaten. But you must be satiated. I see that now. I was wrong to deny you."

Doctor Momo wheeled, extended his arm, jabbed a finger at Jack, said, "Take Jack."

Jack looked sharply at Doctor Momo.

Twenty-six...

"Doctor," Jack said.

But it was too late. Momo still had a certain power of command, and he had offered the Lion Man what he wanted.

Meat.

Twenty-seven...

The Lion Man sprang on Jack. The meat eaters leapt, ripping. Jack screamed. Briefly.

The nonmeat eaters cowered at the back of the crowd.

While the frenzy went on, Doctor Momo slipped away from the huddle, slid through a clutch of trees, broke for the beach.

Twenty-eight...

The *Naughty Lass* was still on the surface, cruising for deep water.

Twenty-nine…

Thirty...

The beasts ate in a fury. They tore off Jack's head. It bounced above the crowd, every hand and paw reaching up to poke it.

Soon they were kicking Jack's head about the clearing.

Thirty-one...

Thirty-two...

Doctor Momo reached a pile of black rocks on the beach. They were built up high. Odd. Unnatural looking.

Because they were.

He bent over, pulled at one of the rocks.

It snapped open. Under it was a lever.

Thirty-three...

Doctor Momo pulled the lever.

The ground slid open. There was a short flight of stairs.

Doctor Momo went down. Inside, in a hangar, was a large, streamlined boat. It was designed and painted to look like a black shark. It bobbed up and down in a channel of water.

Thirty-four...

Doctor Momo opened a hatch, climbed inside, pulled the hatch cover closed. He sat behind a V-shaped steering device. In front of him was a large, slanted window. All there was to see was darkness.

Thirty-five...

Doctor Momo worked a switch on the control board.

In front of the boat the rocks split open and there was light and the ocean.

Thirty-six...

"Sorry, Jack," Doctor Momo said aloud. "I can make another man, but there is only one Doctor Momo."

Thirty-seven...

Doctor Momo pushed a lever forward and the boat jumped like a porpoise. It leapt into the light, tore out across the water in a burst of foam.

Thirty-eight...

The beast men quit kicking Jack's head about. The Lion Man took it and started to gnaw on it. He said, "Hey, where's Doctor Momo?"

"Gone," said Wolf. "He outsmarted us again."

Thirty-nine...

"Let's get him," said the Lion Man.

But, of course, it was too late.

Forty.

The island rumbled, seemed to grow in the middle. The ground rose up and split. Trees fell. The compound trembled.

Then the whole island blew.

It blew with one terrific rumble and a blast. It knocked dirt, trees, manmade structures, beast men and every living thing on the island into a mix of churning dirt and whirling explosives.

The explosion made the sea ripple. It made the sky dark. It spat a cloud up high and white as fresh sperm. The cloud spread. It took the shape of a mushroom.

The sea shook as if it were gelatin. Momo's craft wobbled violently, but stayed afloat. It was making hot time, burning miles and splitting water.

It was doing great.

Momo laughed out loud.

Then the boat hit the side of the still surfaced *Naughty Lass* and blew into a thousand pieces.

It didn't do Doctor Momo any good either.

He went all over.

A chunk of him slapped up against the side of the sub's conning tower, hung there, then slipped off slowly and glided down gently into the water.

The impact knocked a hole in the side of the submarine big enough to drive a boat through.

The *Naughty Lass* took on water and began to sink.

Inside, Ned scurried with Cody's head toward one of the exit portals. He stood on the ladder and held Cody by the hair with his teeth. His little flippers and thumbs worked at turning the wheel that opened the hatch to the surface.

It sprang open, and up and out Ned and Cody went.

Bull and Cat came running down the corridor, saw the open hatch, water sloshing in through it.

Bull pushed Cat toward the ladder, up she went, and up he followed.

They leapt over the side.

Tin and Bert were trapped in the library. The water had flooded in and was already up to their chests. There were only moments left.

"We've got to swim for the main hatch," Bert said.

"Never make it," Tin said. "We'd swim, then the thing would sink and take us with it. There may be another way."

"What way?"

Tin reached down, opened the compartment in his leg, took out his goods, pulled out the silver slippers.

"Yes," Bert said. "You can escape."

"Don't be silly. We both can or neither of us can. And this just might work."

Tin pushed the shoes onto his feet. His toes poked through the tips, his feet pushed out the sides.

The water was almost to their chins.

"Hold me tight, Bert," Tin said.

Bert clutched him. "I love you," he said.

"And I you. If it works, there's no telling where we will end up. It could be worse."

Bert looked at the rushing water, felt the sub start to tilt.

"And it could be paradise," he said.

Tin clicked his heels.

Nothing.

"It's not working," Tin said.

"It's the water," Bert said. "You probably have to click them harder. Give it all you got."

Clinging to one another, Tin moved his feet close together as the

Naughty Lass tilted. He snapped his heels together with every ounce of metal and clockwork power he possessed.

The sub went under spinning.

But Tin and Bert were gone.

Hickok and Annie, once on the submarine, feeling they were home free, found Bemo's cabin and fell in bed together. They just couldn't contain themselves. Blood and violence made them horny. They were making love when the bomb went off on the island. They thought it was in their heads.

They were laughing at the joy of the moment when Doctor Momo's boat hit the *Naughty Lass.*

The boat collided exactly where their cabin was, ripped through. They never knew what hit them.

They were cut in half in their bed by a slice of metal fragment from the boat.

Far out at sea Ned swam gracefully.

He had flung Cody's head on his back, tying it around his neck with Cody's long hair.

He had not bothered to check on Cody. He didn't know the water had shorted out the battery and breathing device in Cody's neck. Unaware of this, Ned swam on and on with the shriveling head of his deceased hero nestled on his back.

Two hours later the sharks took him.

Exhausted as Ned was, there wasn't even a serious fight.

When Bull and Cat leapt from the sub, they were fortunate enough to clutch to a piece of Momo's wrecked boat. A long seat cushion made of wood and leather.

It supported them for a full day before falling apart.

That night, they took turns with one swimming, holding the other up. Daylight, they continued the same program.

The next night while Bull was swimming, holding the fitfully sleeping Cat, he looked up at the stars. They seemed to be the eyes of lost friends, looking down.

He thought of Cody, Hickok and Annie. He was unaware of their fate, but assumed they were all dead. He thought little of Ned, Tin and Bert. He hardly knew them.

Cat slept so deeply, Bull swam long after he felt he could swim.

Next morning, as it was turning hot and the skin on his lips was peeling in strips, just when he considered it might be best to go under, Bull spotted something.

Men on horses.

They were coming across the water.

They rode slowly.

They clopped their horses right across the top of the water and the waves curled at their feet like greasy grass.

As they neared he saw they were the faces of warriors he knew.

Crazy Horse. He Dog. Spotted Calf and several others he did not know.

Crazy Horse was dressed for war. He wore a dead hawk fastened to the side of his head. His face was painted with black dots and lightning bolts. His great white horse was decorated with painted hand prints, red and black.

He Dog wore nothing.

"My brothers," said Bull in Sioux. "Why is it that you come here?"

"We come for you, my brother," said Crazy Horse.

"For me?"

"For you and your squaw."

"I would ask you what horse pussy feels like," He Dog said, patting his mare's side. "But I already know."

All the warriors laughed.

"Here," Crazy Horse said, and extended a hand.

Bull took it.

He was pulled onto the back of Crazy Horse's mount.

When Bull looked down, Catherine lay asleep in a field of blue waving grass. He Dog climbed down, picked her up, and lifted her onto his horse. Spotted Calf reached over and held her sleeping body upright while He Dog climbed up behind her and held her with one hand and held his bridle with the other.

"Do not ride too close," Sitting Bull said.

He Dog laughed.

The riders tugged at their reins. The horses lifted their heads and rose to the sky, their legs working the air.

When Bull looked back, there was only the sea.

"You're awake."

Bull sat up. He was nude with a sheet over him. A man wearing a heavy blue coat and watch cap, smoking a pipe, was looking at him.

"Where am I?"

"On board a ship. We found you and the woman at sea. We sent out a smaller boat, pulled you inside, brought you here."

"So, did not die?"

"No," said the man.

"Woman?"

"She's all right. We have her in another cabin."

"No horses on water," Bull said.

"Excuse me?"

"Nothing. Bull thank you."

"That's all right... Are you the famous Sitting Bull?"

Bull nodded.

"I saw you in The Wild West Show once. You and Buffalo Bill. Just relax. You're on your way home now."

The man rose and went away. Bull lay back and pulled the sheet up under his chin. He closed his eyes. He dreamed briefly of the riders. Then he dreamed of Cat, and what they would do when they regained their strength.

The thought of it made him feel stronger already.

Somewhere, in a time out of joint, there's an island and a beach. It's a better island than the island of Doctor Momo. It is full of trees and animals and the beaches are wide and made of pristine white sand.

Surrounding this beach is water more beautiful and a brighter turquoise than that of the Caribbean. The waters are full of fish. At night two moons race across the sky and the black between the stars is always filled with burning red comets.

The silver slippers hang from the limb of a tree bursting with fruit.

Tin and Bert live there.

Bert has fish and fruit to eat.

Tin uses oil made from plants and fish to keep himself functional.

All day they talk and walk and at night they lie together.

The sun comes up. The sun goes down.

The moons come up. The moons go down.

The Tin Man's chest feels warm, as if a heart beats there.

Bert, the monster Frankenstein built of dead bodies, feels very much alive.

And the two of them together, feel rich and full of soul.

FLAMING LONDON

Before my career as a best-selling novelist, I lived an active life. I knew Captain Bemo, Doctor Momo, Buffalo Bill — still my hero — Annie Oakley — a peach of a woman — Wild Bill Hickok — a man's man... well, a seal's man as well — Sitting Bull — who invented the word *stoic* — I knew many others as well. I cruised beneath the seas in the *Naughty Lass*. I lived on the island with Doctor Momo when he made his beast men, and I am, in fact, a product of his handiwork. I even knew Tin, who came from a world far away, and I knew the Frankenstein Monster, who was one hell of a fine fella.

And I was there when the Martians came, and all the horrors that accompanied them. I was a companion of Samuel Clemens, otherwise known as the great novelist Mark Twain. I knew his friend, Jules Verne. I knew H. G. Wells. I knew the Lost Island. And I knew London when it was in flames. In my life, I have eaten many fish.

—From *The Autobiography of Ned the Seal,*
Adventurer Extraordinaire

Part One:
Invaders

One: A Dark Moment
for Humankind

ONE HUNDRED AND FORTY MILLION miles across the vast expanse of blackness and prickly white stars, on the planet we call Mars, the red sand shifted, and out of it rose a magnificent, blue-black, oily machine with twenty-six enormous barrels. The barrels were cocked and loaded.

The barrels fanned wide, greased gears rotated and lifted them into their trajectories. Then there was a sound in the thin Martian air like twenty-six volcanoes erupting simultaneously. The great guns spat shiny silver cylinders dragging blue-red flame toward our Earth at a blinding speed.

From Earth the eruption was noted by astronomers, but there were no definite conclusions as to the cause. Nothing like it had ever been seen.

Twenty-six objects sped toward Earth. They were observed in our day and night skies as twenty-six flaming streaks.

They all smacked the Earth or its waters. Several in America, several in Europe, one just outside of London, one in a lake in Darkest Africa, another in India, several in the Siberian wastes, four in the Atlantic, four in the Pacific. One in the Sandwich Islands.

There were all kinds of guesses as to the source of these objects, but no one knew at the time that it was the beginning of an invasion from Mars, or that more flashes of light would follow.

And no one knew about another problem.

The very fabric of time and space was in jeopardy.

Two: Huck Bites It
and Mark Twain Moves Out

In the Casbah of Tangier, Samuel Langhorne Clemens, better known as Mark Twain, sweaty as nitroglycerine, drunk as a skunk and just as smelly, resided in his stained white suit on a loose mattress that bled goose down and dust, and by lamplight he pondered the loss of his shoes and the bloated body of his pet monkey, Huck Finn.

Huck lay on the only bookshelf in the little sweat hole, and he was swollen and beaded with big blue flies. A turd about the size and shape of a fig was hanging out of his ass, and his tongue protruded from his mouth as if it were hoping to crawl away to safety. He still wore the little red hat with chin strap and the green vest Twain had put on him, but the red shorts with the ass cut out for business were missing.

Twain was uncertain what had done the old boy in, but he was dead and pantsless for whatever reason, and had managed in a final gastronomic burst to stick that one fig-sized turd to one of the two books on the shelf, *Moby-Dick,* and his distended tongue lay not far from the other book, *20,000 Leagues Under the Sea,* written by Twain's good friend Jules Verne.

Huck, bookended by sea stories, lay in dry dock.

Twain rose slowly, bent over his pet and sighed. The room stank of monkey and monkey poo. With reluctance, Twain clutched Huck by the feet, and as he lifted him, the tenacious turd took hold of the heavy tome of *Moby-Dick* and lifted it as well. Twain shook Huck, and *Moby-Dick,* along with the turd, came loose. Twain then peeked carefully out the only window at the darkness of the Casbah below, and tossed Huck through the opening.

It was a good toss and Huck sailed.

Twain heard a kind of whapping sound, realized he had tossed Huck with such enthusiasm, he had smacked the wall on the other side of the narrow alley.

It was a cold way to end a good friendship, but Twain hardly felt up to burying the little bastard, and was actually pissed that the beast had died on him. Huck had wandered off for a day, come back sickly, vomited a few times, then set about as if to doze on the bookshelf.

Sometime during the night, Twain heard a sound that he thought was the release of his own gas, but upon lighting the lamp, found it in fact to be Huck who had launched that sticky, fig-shaped turd. He saw the little monkey kick a few times and go still.

Twain, too drunk to do anything, too drunk to care, put out the lamp and went back to sleep.

A few hours later, hung over, but sober enough to wonder if it had all been a dream, lit his lamp to find that Huck was indeed dead as the Victorian novel, but without the shelf life. Flies were enjoying themselves by surveying every inch of Huck, and due to the intense African heat, Huck had acquired an aroma that would have swooned a vulture.

No question about it. He had to go.

With Huck dead and tossed, Twain decided to pour himself a drink, but discovered he had none. The goatskin of wine was empty. Twain dropped it on the stone floor, stood on it, hoping to coax a few drops to the nozzle, but, alas, nothing. Dry as a Moroccan ditch in mid-summer.

Twain removed his coat, shook it out, draped it over the back of the chair, seated himself. He sat there and thought about what to do next. He had sold all of his book collection, except *20,000 Leagues*, which was signed, and the be-turded *Moby-Dick*. He didn't even have copies of his own books.

It was depressing.

When he was strong enough, he rose and made coffee in his little glass pot. It was weak coffee because there were only yesterday's grounds left, and the biscuit tin contained only a couple of stale biscuits which he managed to eat by dipping them in the coffee.

By the time he had finished breakfast, light was oozing through the window and he could hear the sounds of the Casbah below. Blowing out his lamp, he recovered *Moby-Dick* from the floor, wiped it clean with a cloth and the remains of the coffee. It left a slight stain, coffee, not shit, but he hoped it wouldn't damage what value the book might have.

Tangier was full of readers of most anything in English (except his books, it seemed) *20,000 Leagues*.

It would be just enough money for a real meal of fruit and olives, and a bit of wine, as well as the rent. Which seemed pointless.

What after that? There was no place for him to work, and his new novel was going about as well as his life had. Everyone he knew and loved was dead. Well, almost. There were a few friends, Verne among them.

Twain searched about and found his missing shoes, then he grabbed a big white canvas bag and stuffed it with a few belongings, his manuscript in progress, gathered up the two books and headed out into the Casbah. As he climbed down the narrow stairs and rushed into the street, he came upon Huck's body being feasted upon by dogs.

The biggest of the dogs, a mongrel with one eye and scum around it, wrestled Huck away from the others, and darted down the street with his prize, the monkey's tail dragging on the flagstones.

Twain sighed.

Perhaps when he died, that was what was to become of him. Tossed in the street, eaten by dogs.

It was better than being savaged to death by book critics. The sonsabitches.

The street stank of yesterday's fish and today's fresh fish. Blood dripped from the tables and gathered in little rust-colored pools and slipped in between the grooves in the stones. The reek of ripe olives bit the air and chewed at Twain's nostrils. He wandered the crooked streets, which just six months ago he would have found harder to navigate than the Minotaur's maze, and came upon Abdul laying out his sales goods on a worn but still beautiful Moroccan rug of blue, green and violet. Among the items on the rug were a few books. Twain recognized titles he had written, books from his very own collection. Each one of them reminded him of the few coins he had contributed to drink and women, mostly drink.

Abdul eyed Twain with his bag and two books under his arm.

"My friend. More books. You can see I do not need them."

"These are my last books, Abdul. I sell these, I'm taking the ferry to Spain."

"And what there? You should stay here among friends."

"You old pirate. You've given me little for what I've sold you. These are fine books."

"They are not worth much."

"I sold you copies of my own novels, signed."

"Alas, they are not worth much either. Perhaps had they not been signed."

"Very funny, Abdul. If I didn't feel like an elephant had sat on my head, I would give you a good old-fashioned American ass whipping."

Abdul pulled back his robe and revealed in his belt a curved, holstered blade with an ornate handle of jewels and silver.

"Well, maybe I wouldn't," Twain said. "Will you buy the books, Abdul?"

"Promise you have no more?"

"I promise."

Twain squatted, laid them on the blanket Abdul had stretched out on the ground.

"What's this stain on *Moby-Dick*?"

"A fig got squashed on it. My monkey did it."

"Where is Huck?"

"He leaped out of the window this morning and committed suicide. Landed right on his head."

Abdul looked at him.

"Even monkeys fall out of trees," Twain said.

"Very well, I will give you..."

"In dollars, Abdul."

"Very well, I will give you four dollars."

"Jesus Christ, the *20,000 Leagues* is signed to me by Jules Verne. The both of us certainly have some coinage for collectors."

"Okay. How about I give you ten dollars?"

"How about you give me fifteen?"

"Deal."

Three: A Ferry Ride,
an Injured Seal

It was more money than Twain expected to receive for the books, so he bought some figs, a skin of water, and boarded the ferry to Spain. It took most of the day, and the sea was choppy. Twain lost his figs and water early on, throwing them up in a brown stream over the side.

As he leaned over the railing, watched the water churn below, he considered losing himself as well, but gradually came to his senses. He realized that he was feeling better as the wine wore off, realized too this was the first time in six months he had been truly sober.

It wasn't a great feeling, but it really wasn't that bad either.

Upon arriving on the coast of Spain, he and the passengers, as well as a dozen goats and a cage of chickens, disembarked. It felt good to be on solid ground, and after buying some coffee in a little outdoor cafe, fending off a half-dozen souvenir peddlers and a fat Spanish whore who wanted to sell him a quickie, or for half the price, squeeze him off between her legs, he decided to splurge another coin and catch a cart ride to where Verne was staying, working on yet another successful novel.

Twain envied Verne. He seemed able to write at any time and under any circumstance. As of late, all Twain could think about was the death of his wife, Olivia, and the death of his daughters. Susy by disease, Jean, drowned in a tub while having a fit, and Clara, married and gone from him, living somewhere in Europe, a place unbeknownst to him since beginning his wanderings. He hoped her life was good. He hoped he would find her again someday. He hoped even more that some of his old self would return to him, like a lost dog, worn out and tired, looking for a familiar bed, a currycomb, a pat on the head and a good meal.

As the cart clattered along, Twain noted the beautiful coast. Perhaps this was the key to Verne's success. A beautiful view. The Casbah was interesting and exciting in its own way, but it wasn't beautiful, and too much excitement and noise did not a good writer make. Here you had the ocean and the shoreline with natural white sand, and there were the rocks upon which the ocean foamed, and way out beyond that fine blue water, a thin brown strip that was Africa, the coast of Morocco from which he had come.

As they neared Verne's residence, Twain stopped the driver, paid him, and in spite of his old aching bones, decided to walk along the coast and wind his way to where Verne lived in a beautiful villa on a rise of white rocks overlooking the sea.

As he walked along the beach, his bag slung over his shoulder, Twain discovered a strange thing. A large black shape with something shiny attached to it lay near the ocean on the sand. At first he couldn't place what it was. It appeared to be an oilskin bag with something metal hanging out of one end, but upon closer examination he was amazed to discover it was a seal. A seal with a metal object, a box, fastened to its head. There were a number of deep red cuts in the seal's body, and a chunk had been taken out of one flipper by what were obviously some very nasty teeth.

Shark teeth, Twain figured.

Twain bent over the seal, nudged it with his foot. The seal opened one eye.

Very slowly the seal rolled over. Twain saw there was a cord around his neck, and fastened to that was a writing tablet without paper, and a stubby pencil. There was also a chain around the seal's neck, and from that hung a pair of sand-sprinkled spectacles.

He discovered there was another thing even more amazing than a seal with a metal cap, pad and pencil, and reading glasses about its neck.

There were little thumbs growing from its flippers.

Four: The Great Jules Verne, Ned's Story, a Shape beneath the Canvas

When Twain arrived at Verne's villa pulling the seal on his formerly white coat, Verne was on the second-floor landing, sitting with pen and paper, working on a dark novel about Paris, thinking about how old he felt, the loss of his wife and children, who had gone off to live somewhere in France with the explorer Phileas Fogg.

The dirty bastard.

Verne tried to concentrate on his work.

He had submitted pages of his novel to his editor, but the editor had been appalled. Much too noir for them, lacked the glitter of his other novels, and they felt his readers would be disappointed.

It certainly was a dark book, and not optimistic in the least, but the thing was, Verne wasn't feeling too optimistic right then, and the novel reflected that. He felt he had fallen into a trap of writing only what many were now calling children's adventure stories. He longed to reach deeper and write darker. He wished he had his children back, and his wife had a hot croissant up her ass, and Fogg had one too. Neither croissant buttered, and both day old and stiff.

He did have his experiments, his plans for devices that he worked on from time to time, and they had of course made some impact on the world, but so far their use and knowledge of them were restricted primarily to himself and his servant, Passepartout, and to a handful of rich associates; the devices were far too expensive to give away, and patents had to be protected.

He was thinking about these things as he pondered his maligned manuscript with distracted concentration, so when he saw his old friend Samuel, Mark Twain to the world, he was surprised and heartened to have a break from his work and editorial troubles, as well as curious to discover what his bedraggled friend was pulling on top of his coat.

Downstairs, Verne met Twain in the front yard and saw what he had. When Verne spoke English, his French accent was noticeable, but not too heavy. He had been practicing his English for some time, and had learned much about American colloquialism from the works of Twain, though he still had the occasional French phrasing. When he spoke to his friend, he called him by his real name, Samuel.

When Twain saw Verne, he smiled. "Jules."

"My friend, Samuel. You have a seal on your coat."

"Yes, I do."

"He is dead, monsieur?"

"No, he's not. He's been bitten by sharks, but he's alive. See that metal hat. It's bolted to his head. Fixed that way. Look at that stuff around his neck. What do you make of it?"

"I make nothing of it. Shall we put him in the barn?"

In the barn, Verne used a hand pump and water hose to wash down the seal, then examined his wounds. "We'll need someone who can sew good stitches. I'll make a call."

When Verne left, Twain made the seal as comfortable as possible, saw a large canvas draped over a large form. At the bottom of the canvas, he could see something shiny. He wondered what was beneath the canvas, and under ordinary circumstance, might have taken a look, but he didn't wish to leave the injured seal, and besides, his age had caught up with him a bit. Now that he had gotten comfortable, sitting on the ground, he didn't want to get up unless it was absolutely necessary.

Verne went to the house, cranked the phone and spoke in Spanish. When he came back to the barn, Twain was holding the seal's head up, giving him a drink from a water dipper.

"That is strange," said Vern. "He takes that like a man."

The seal raised its flipper, and working its thumb against the skin of the appendage, made a snapping sound.

"Well, I will be, how is it you Americans say? I be damn."

"Close enough."

The seal tapped the pad on its chest, took hold of the pen.

"My God," Twain said. "He wants writing paper."

"That is not possible."

The seal snapped both thumbs against his flippers and made a kind of whistling sound with his mouth, then slapped both flippers against the pad and took hold of the pencil with one thumb and flipper and made a writing motion.

"Now I've seen it all," Verne said.

"Not if he actually writes something, you haven't."

Verne ran to the house, procured paper and a better pencil. When he returned with the writing materials, the seal sat up on its hind end, folding its flipper-tipped tail beneath it, cocked its back against the water pump, placed the glasses on its nose, took the writing supplies and wrote in big block letters.

MY NAME IS NED. I WAS THE BOON COMPANION OF BUFFALO BILL CODY, WHO WAS EATEN BY SHARKS. I WAS INJURED BY SHARKS. I LIKE SLOW SWIMS AND BIG LIVE FISH AND SOMETIMES A BEACH BALL TO BALANCE ON MY NOSE, THOUGH I KNOW IT'S IMMATURE.

I DO NOT LIKE SHARKS.

I DO LIKE FISH. DID I MENTION THAT?

"Holy shit," Twain said. "A goddamn note-writing seal."

The seal continued to write, passing along pages as he filled them in his large block printing.

HERE IS MY STORY. I WAS MADE BY A MAN NAMED DOCTOR MOMO. HE LIVED ON AN ISLAND. I SPENT MUCH OF MY TIME WITH CAPTAIN BEMO ON THE NAUGHTY LASS. ONCE I WAS A REGULAR SEAL. NOW I AM SPECIAL.

"Holy Mother of God, give Jesus the apple," Verne said. "I wrote a novel based on this very interesting man, Captain Bemo. Not all true, a novel mind you, with name changes, but with much biographical detail. This is amazing. This seal claims to have known the real Captain Bemo, on which my Nemo is based. I have also heard of this Momo. A scientist. About half-crazy was the rumor. H. G. Wells has written a story about him. He calls him Moreau."

"Let him write, Jules," Twain said.

I HELPED BEMO AND MOMO DO RESEARCH. I WAS ABLE TO DO THIS BECAUSE DOCTOR MOMO ENHANCED MY ALREADY CONSIDERABLE INTELLIGENCE WITH THIS DEVICE YOU SEE

ON MY HEAD. HE DID THINGS TO MY BRAIN. AMPLIFIED IT. THE DEVICE COVERS MY BRAIN, PROTECTS IT. MOMO BECAME STRANGE. HE GRAFTED A HORSE PENIS ONTO HIMSELF. HE MADE PEOPLE OUT OF ANIMALS AND PIECES OF FLESH. BUFFALO BILL, WILD BILL HICKOK, ANNIE OAKLEY AND SITTING BULL ALL CAME TO MOMO'S ISLAND, HAVING CRASHED IN THE SEA. BUFFALO BILL WAS ONLY A HEAD. IT WAS IN A JAR POWERED BY BATTERIES AND SOME KIND OF LIQUID. THEY HAD THE FRANKENSTEIN MONSTER WITH THEM. THERE WAS A TIN MAN WHO WORKED FOR DOCTOR MOMO. HE AND THE MONSTER FELL IN LOVE. I THINK THEY MAY HAVE DROWNED ON THE *NAUGHTY LASS*, AS DID WILD BILL HICKOK AND ANNIE OAKLEY, AND I SUPPOSE SITTING BULL AND A WOMAN MOMO MADE NAMED CAT. BUFFALO BILL'S HEAD WAS EATEN BY SHARKS. I WAS BITTEN BY SHARKS. I SURE COULD USE SOME FISH.

"What happened to Momo and Bemo?" Verne asked.

Ned shook his head, wrote: I DO NOT KNOW. I THINK THEY ARE DEAD. MOMO'S BOAT RAMMED THE *NAUGHTY LASS* AND SUNK IT, I THINK. HE WAS PROBABLY ON BOARD. THE ONLY WAY HE COULD HAVE LIVED IS IF HE COULD LIVE IN PIECES, LIKE A PUZZLE. DO YOU LIKE THE DIME NOVELS ABOUT BUFFALO BILL CODY? DO YOU HAVE ANY FISH?

"I don't have any fish," Twain said, "but I do like the novels about Buffalo Bill. Can't say they are well written, but they are entertaining. Ned, I am Samuel Clemens, though I go by the name Mark Twain as well, which is the name I write under. This is Jules Verne."

Ned stiffened. His whiskers wiggled. He slapped his flippers together. He snatched up the pencil, wrote:

AFTER THE ADVENTURES OF BUFFALO BILL AND THE DIME NOVELS, I LIKE YOU TWO BEST. ABOUT THE SAME, ACTUALLY. I HAVE READ *HUCK FINN* AND *TOM SAWYER*, AND I HAVE READ *JOURNEY TO THE CENTER OF THE EARTH*, *FROM THE EARTH TO THE MOON*, AND IF YOU WILL FORGIVE ME, I TRIED TO READ YOUR STORY ABOUT BEMO. HE WAS NOTHING LIKE THAT. HE WAS QUITE SHY, ACTUALLY. HE DID DO MUCH THAT YOU WROTE ABOUT, BUT NOT ALL OF IT. MIND YOU, I WASN'T THERE DURING ALL THOSE EVENTS, BUT I DID HAVE THE LUXURY OF

KNOWING THE MAN.

HE HAD GAS PROBLEMS. THAT'S ANOTHER FACT NOT WELL KNOWN. YOU MIGHT WANT TO WRITE THAT DOWN IN CASE YOU DO A REVISED VERSION OF YOUR BOOK. SEALS DON'T REALLY MIND THAT, HOWEVER. REMEMBER. WE EAT RAW FISH. AND, OF COURSE, FISH EAT US. SHARKS TRIED TO EAT ME. I TRIED TO SAVE THE HEAD OF BUFFALO BILL... DID I SAY I DO NOT LIKE SHARKS AND THAT I WOULD LIKE SOME FISH?

"Yes," Verne said, "you did. And I read something about Buffalo Bill being a living head powered by batteries. Some kind of accident. Saved by a scientist, some such thing...And I remember reading in the papers about part of The Wild West Show being lost over the Pacific Ocean. I think this little seal is telling the truth, Samuel."

Ned slapped a flipper on the ground. Hard.

He wrote: OF COURSE I AM. DO I LOOK LIKE A LIAR TO YOU?

The man Verne had called arrived and stitched up Ned to the sound of grunts and squeals while Verne and Twain held the poor seal. Once, Ned was able to snatch up the pencil and paper Verne had provided. He wrote: WHERE'S THE ANESTHESIA? WANT IT. GOT TO HAVE IT. WANT IT BAD. TELL THIS HORRIBLE MAN TO GET OFF OF ME AND TAKE HIS NEEDLES WITH HIM. OH, YOU ASSHOLES.

Twain wrestled the pencil and paper away from Ned, said, "Sorry, Ned. For your own good."

"My God," the veterinarian said in French. "He writes."

"Yes he does," Twain said, being able to understand French well enough. "And neatly."

"How is that possible?" asked the vet.

"It's a trick." Twain said.

"With mirrors and such?" the veterinarian asked.

Twain looked at Vern. They both looked at the vet.

Verne said, "Of course. Mirrors."

Five: A Meal, Pleasant Conversation,
a Duck Toy

That evening they dined in Verne's fine dining room, waited on by a servant dressed in crisp black pants, white jacket and black bow tie. Verne was now dressed in smoking jacket and loose pants and Moroccan slippers. He had provided a similar outfit for Twain.

Earlier, while removing these items from his closet, Verne had stumbled over a red fez with a golden tassel that had been given him by a friend. He had never worn it. Ned saw this while waiting for Verne to supply fresh clothes for Twain. It was obvious to Verne that Ned was taken with it, so he gave it to the little seal, fastened it over the metal box on Ned's head. Ned looked rather suave in the fez, like a seal of great importance and wealth with a harem.

With his stitches in place, Ned forgave them for holding him down. The pain had passed. And besides, he had a neat as hell red hat.

Ned was placed in a portable Victorian-style tub with fresh water. Next to it was a long low table on which sat bowls of fresh sardines, fish oil and wine. And, of course, a napkin. Floating on the water was a rubber duck toy. At first, Ned resented it, but discovered it squeaked when he squeezed it, and he eventually found it comforting. He balanced it on his nose and made seal sounds.

The servant, Passepartout, who had been with Verne for years, appeared to be totally unperturbed by an injured seal near the dining table in a tub with a rubber duck. He looked as if he had seen it all, and then some. He poured the seal's wine with the same panache he poured all wine.

Upon completion of pouring, Ned took his pencil and pad from the little table and wrote: THANK YOU, KIND SIR.

In French, Passepartout told Ned he was quite welcome. Then, said the same in English.

Verne thanked Passepartout, and the servant went away, saying, "Very good, monsieur."

"When we finish," Verne said, "we will retire to the study for cigars."

Ned took up his pad, wrote, and held up what he had written:

NO THANK YOU. SMOKING IS BAD FOR YOU.

"Very well," Verne said. "Then, for you, smoked herring. Will that be sufficient?"

Ned wrote again, held up his pad on which he had written:

SMOKED HERRING IS NOT BAD FOR YOU. HOW MUCH SMOKED HERRING?

"A lot," Verne said. "And tomorrow, I have another present for you. Something I designed some time ago."

Ned, in anticipation of the herring, ate his sardines and drank his wine, dozed in his tub, dreamed of female seals with long eyelashes. From time to time the sound of the duck being squeaked could be heard.

Six: Cylinders from Space, a Hole in the Ground, a Strange Ray

While the three companions were enjoying dinner on the beautiful coast of Spain, on the outskirts of foggy London the first of the bullets, or cylinders as some described them, screwed open with a hiss of steam and a red and yellow wink of light.

The screwing motion caused the lid to fall off, smack in the dust. A crowd, which had gathered at the rim of the crater caused by the impact of the cylinder, watched carefully. They had been watching for nearly a half-hour.

"It's opening," said a short stocky man in the back of the crowd.

This was, of course, obvious. The short stocky man had been giving them a play-by-play since the crowd first arrived. As there was little to see other than the cylinder, he took it upon himself to describe the steam coming from the interior of the device, and was quick to describe it in excruciating detail, as if everyone present was blind.

"See the steam coming out. More steam than before. A lot of steam's coming out," he said.

This was true.

"Now the lid has fallen off. See that?"

Everyone saw that.

"Now there's some light. Do you see the light?"

The light was pretty obvious. Red and yellow.

"There's something moving in there. Did you see the shadow?"

Suddenly, without warning, a little man in the crowd screamed something impossible to understand, leaped on the explainer and began beating him. "We see it. We see it, you dumb bastard."

Police arrived and promptly jerked the small man off of the explainer, hauled him away, stuck him in the back of a police wagon. The police returned to the scene.

"Thank you, officers," said the explainer. "He had gone mad, he had.

157

Oh, look, look, the shadow is growing larger."

Indeed, it had grown, and something was starting to come out of the cylinder.

"It's a bloomin' octopus," said the explainer.

In fact, a tentacle, reminiscent of an octopus, was waving out of the opening, as if hoping to snag something floating in the air.

"They've got a bloomin' octopus in that tube," said the explainer. "Can you see that? A bloomin' octopus. Now he's comin' out. More of him. You see that?"

The police officers looked at one another.

"Ah, two tentacles."

The higher-ranking officer turned to the other. "Go let the little man out of the cage, will you?"

"Certainly."

"It's crawling out," said the explainer.

"Excuse me, sir," said the officer. "That is quite clear to all of us. Would you please shut your bleeding mouth."

"Why, I can't believe that. Did you hear that, friends? The officer told me to shut my bleedin' —"

It was just one quick shot of the billy club, between the eyes, and down went the explainer. The little man who had been caged came back with the lower-ranked officer, stood with them, glanced down at the unconscious explainer.

"Should he awake," said the officer, "one word from him, you have our permission to finish what you started."

A shriek went up from the crowd.

A bulbous head with two red eyes peeked out of the mouth of the cylinder. Its two arms, which continued to wave, were joined by two others. It did very much look like an octopus.

It glanced up at the crowd with its odd red eyes, quivered its beaklike lips, omitted a sound like someone trying to breathe after running a fast mile, then retreated into the cylinder.

"It's frightened," said the little man who had jumped the explainer.

"You're not going to start now, are you?" said one of the officers.

Inside the cylinder, there was a sound like something being snapped together. Then there was a guttural sound like someone displeased. This was followed by more snapping and more guttural noises, as if some sort of trouble was being had with the fastening of a device.

Martian Translation of Gutteral Noise:
"It goes in the other hole, Gooldaboo."
"Which hole?"
"That hole."
"I don't get it. This hole?"
"No. One of your assholes. For heaven's sakes, give me that. Damn. That got me in the eye. You are always dooddiddledooin something. That could have put my eye out. There...I'll take care of this. You just sit there. And don't touch anything, Gooldaboo."
"Yes sir/ma'am."

As the people watched, metal tubing poked out of the cylinder, followed by what looked like an octopus with rectal pain. It scooted along the rough ground making a number of faces with its flexible skin and long broad mouth, which was quite unlike an octopus. It set the little framework of tubing on the edge of the cylinder, rotated it.

The other creature appeared, carrying a long thin tube of light. This was placed in one end of the cylinder. The octopus reached a tentacle around the end of the tubing and pulled. It extended. He rotated the cylinder again, pointing the tip of it at the crowd.

"What do you think he's doin'?" asked someone.

"Could that be a gun?" someone else said.

"Shit," said one of the policemen.

And then there came a guttural sound from one of the creatures —

— good-bye funny things —

— and the tube spat out a rod of light. The light hit the crowd. The crowd glowed. The crowd disappeared. Left in its place were piles of black dust.

The creatures flapped their tentacles wildly, made sounds that even humans would have recognized as laughing. One of the Martians climbed up on the edge of the crater, turned both assholes to where the crowd had been and cut an excruciating fart that flapped the edges of both his anuses, turned and said:

Take that, you inferior fuckers.

Seven: A Meteor, a
Tidal Wave, the Martian Machines

Meanwhile, back at the villa...

Vern, Twain and Ned had gathered in the study. Ned was enjoying pickled herring while his rescuers smoked large cigars amongst thousands of volumes of books. One side of the room, the only side without books, was made up of numerous glass windows, and there was a fine view of the moonlit ocean. The waves came in white and silver whirls and burst against the white rocks on the shore and sent up spray that, in the moonlight, looked like an explosion of pearls.

"Look," said Twain.

The night sky, as if clawed, was bleeding a horde of red marks.

"Meteors, I presume," said Verne.

"Yes," said Twain. "Most beautiful."

"Look at that," said Verne, "they do not seem to be burning up in the atmosphere. Why, look there."

One of the red scars stripped across the sky and grew in size until it was a ball of red.

"My god," Verne said. "It's going to make landfall."

"More like wet fall," Twain said.

The great ball of fire struck the ocean with a hard blast of white steam. The ocean waters rolled up high and dropped down and came upon the shore with a rush that caused the waves to rise as high as Verne's house on the hill, all the way up to the glass windows of the study. It struck them with such force the glass collapsed, the water washed in, overturning furniture, knocking books from the cases, lifting Twain and Verne and Ned up and down, and then the water washed out again, fast as it had come in, took the three with it, but crashed them against a wall, left them lying on the floor amongst wetness, seaweed, fish and the wet pulpy pages of books.

Ned darted for the fish, finding one large creature to his taste. He tore into it instantly.

"Damn," said Verne. "Now that was unusual."

"What I'm wondering," said Twain, "is what happened to all the others."

"Others?"

"The meteors," Twain said.

"What I'm wondering is how much of my home has been ruined."

Next morning, Verne called in workers to clean up his library, replace the glass. During the day, he, Ned and Twain took the dampened books — only a handful had been ruined — out into the sunlight, opening them to dry on the rocks beneath the warm Spanish sun.

Twain had been given a new set of clothes by Verne, a nice white suit and shirt with white socks and black shoes.

Verne had provided this because he did not like to wear white as much as Twain. He was dressed as usual in a black suit and white dress shirt. He had even bothered to tie a loose, thick, black tie about his neck in a bow.

Ned had received the present Verne had promised. A device Verne called the Air Cruiser. A floating device, powered by air and by a core of uranium. The device had a fold-down step, and this led through a flap-open gate, a wraparound body. It was large enough for Ned and two others, if the three were willing to be pressed together tight.

Inside the open-air machine, standing slightly higher than the encircling railing, was a control box on a post. There were but a few switches. It was essentially a disk with a railing and a gear box on a support.

"It runs about six inches to twelve inches over the ground. A friend of mine in London invented the fuel core. He thinks that it will allow him to travel through time, this fuel. I think he is an idiot in that respect, but in all others he is a genius. The device is designed to create a current of air beneath, and this current will carry you over either land or water. One thing that is most unique, is that by pulling the red lever the sides will collapse and the surface on which you stand will also collapse, forming a kind of disk. The disk is very light, and can be reinstated by gripping the sides with your hands, or thumbs in your case, Ned, and pulling. You must watch though, for it will spring to life and knock you on your ass. Place it on the ground, so that when it springs, it will spring up, and you will be standing to the side. But it is ready now. Climb in."

With Verne at his side, Ned learned to work the device, and with the tassel on his fez popping in the wind, Ned rode about over the shoreline and even over the water, cruising at a fairly good clip.

Ned was so excited he squealed. Verne had also provided him with a new pad. It was not made of paper, but was more like a white board. The pencil, which hung by a strong cord from the pad, was one with which you could write on the board, and erase with a wipe of your hand. Strangely, it left no stains on flesh or seal skin.

"This way," Verne said, "you need not worry about paper, or for that matter, the whole thing becoming damp. You can swim with it around your neck. There's a light vest that goes with it, and you can push the pad against the vest, and it will stick. I call this, well, I call this sticky. Water will not loosen it, but with a quick flip of flipper and thumb you can remove it and write on it. There is also a cord attached around your neck for added insurance."

After an hour or so of experimenting with the near silent craft, Verne was confident Ned had it. They coasted back to shore where Twain waited.

"What a device, Jules," Twain said. "You are truly a genius. Like me."

Jules grinned.

"Passepartout is as much genius as I. Or as you. He actually put it together. I provided the blueprint, the idea. And my friend in London —"

"Would that be Wells?"

"It would, provided, as I have said, the fuel. Shall we continue our work?"

It was midday, and the books were drying well. Because of this, and his time spent with the delighted seal, Twain noted that Jules' depression, due to the destruction of part of his house and books, was passing. He was glad. Jules was a good man. A little more successful than himself... Well, a lot. But a good man. He just wished he were the one who was successful and Jules had a corn cob up his ass.

Or sometimes he wished that.

He felt bad about wishing that, but, alas, there it was.

He had liked being rich and famous, and now he was only famous, and he realized now that rich was probably better. And, frankly, he wasn't sure how famous he was anymore.

He missed America. He missed his home. He missed his dead wife and daughters. Wondered where in Europe his other daughter resided. They had, due to him and his adventures with John Barleycorn, lost contact.

While Twain was reflecting on this, as well as examining a copy of *Don Quixote,* he heard a noise, lifted his head, spotted something rising from the sea. It was a machine. It had long, flexible, metallic legs and a body like a grand daddy long-legged spider. It stood high up on its shiny silver legs and it moved quickly, as if its feet were on a hot griddle. The torso, if it could be called that, was fronted by a window of glass[1], and behind the glass were two strange creatures flailing with octopus arms at numerous controls. They almost seemed to be struggling with the gears and levers.

A little rod rotated under the torso of the machine, and out of it burst a ray of light that hit the rocks between where Verne and Twain stood, disintegrating them. The explosion knocked Verne and Twain winding. Ned was able to avoid the brunt of the blast, but he too was knocked by the shock waves.

"Jumping horn toads," Twain said, as he pushed himself to his feet. "Shit, Jules. It's still coming."

And it was. It was on land now, and the two creatures behind the glass were definitely struggling at the controls. The way their tentacles whipped about, they looked like confetti in a windstorm.

Interior of the Martian War Machine, and we've got:
mine! ultu gets to kill.
no. mine. ultu can suck my asses.
fatty.
smelly.

---

1   It appeared to be glass to Twain, Verne and Ned, but actually it was a kind of Martian plastic, very hard, and waterproof.

Twain and Verne could not have known that the aliens, though wise and developed in the ways of machinery and invention, were, as far as emotions, as immature as six-year-olds. Even as Ned, Twain and Verne climbed into the device Verne called an Air Cruiser and made their exit, inside the war machine a fight broke out.

mine!
    no. mine!
    remove your tentacles, you assholes.
    you. you assholes.
    i got your assholes, you bilbo sucking —
    Gears were touched that shouldn't have been touched. The legs of the stalking device twisted and wadded up, and down went the device, striking the glass, shattering it, rolling over and over, and finally, with the glass now pointing toward the sky, one of the creatures pushed at the shattered pieces and finally worked them free and scuttled out of the machine, bleeding green ichor.
    mine, said the creature.
    To the ears of humans, these words would have sounded like coughs and sneezes.
    all mine.
    The creature crawled over the rocks, and one of its tentacles, which had been cut badly in the crash, came loose and stayed behind.
    orifice excrement, it said. that is not some good at all.
    Inside the machine, the other creature did not move. One of its eyes had come loose of its tendons, cut on a fragment of smashed metal, and it rolled out on the rocks and lay there like a giant medicine ball with an iris painted on it.
    The crawling creature soon ceased to crawl and lay on the beach. Quite still, and quite dead, looking for solace, poked one of its own tentacles up its ass.

Looking back, observing this, our formerly escaping trio shot the cruiser back to where the creature lay sprawled on the sand like a beached squid.
    "What in hell?" Twain said, climbing down from the machine, poking at the beast with the toe of his shoe.

Verne followed. The fez-festooned seal kept his place at the controls, nervously checking out the sea and the surrounding landscape for more attackers. He also wondered if the creatures were edible. They looked like things he had eaten. Only what he had eaten had been smaller. But they looked very similar.

"The meteors," Verne said. "They contained these life forms. It's the only possibility. My guess is, due to recent articles I've read about canals on Mars, and the relative closeness of Mars to Earth, these, my good friend, are, in fact, invaders from that world."

"No shit?"

"No shit. I wonder what happened here? How they crashed?"

"A malfunction of some kind. Whatever, it was good for us."

Ned made a whistling noise, slapped his flippers together, pointed toward the sea with one of them.

Out there, rising out of the water, were more of the machines.

"Damn be it all and such," Verne said, trying to sound American but failing miserably. "We must warn Passepartout. Would you do that, Samuel? I will prepare our escape. I know just the thing. Meet me in the barn."

Twain raced off for the house, while Verne and Ned headed toward the barn in the cruiser.

Eight: Passepartout's Blueprint, Pursuit at Sea, Mooned by Aliens

In the barn, Verne leaped from the cruiser, proceeded to the tarp and using a pocket knife cut the ropes and removed it.

Beneath lay a shiny craft. It was long with a point on one end and glass slanted into a windshield. It had one great fin that started on the roof and ran to the tail.

Twain and Passepartout came racing through the open barn door. Twain said, "If you've got a plan, might I suggest you put it to use. Those things are everywhere now, out of the sea, making kindling out of your house."

"I have this machine, my friend."

"Please tell me it does more than open cans."

Verne produced a key from his pocket, stuck it in the side of the machine. There was a hissing sound, like the air coming out of a bicycle tire, and a trap door came open slowly, guided by hydraulics and a puff of steam.

"Climb in," Verne said.

Ned rode the cruiser inside and managed by himself to collapse it. He nosed it up and rolled it behind a curved couch at the rear of the craft.

Once they were all inside, Verne closed the door, set about spinning a wheel that battened down the door firmly.

"Watertight," Verne said. "Powered by Mr. Wells' invention. As well as steam."

Verne hustled to the front of the craft. The same key that opened the door fit into a slot on the instrument panel. Verne turned it, the machine hissed, the panel lit up like the U.S. on the Fourth of July.

"That's pretty fine," Twain said. "But does it do anything besides look pretty?"

Passepartout said, "Might I suggest we strap ourselves in the seats. Tight."

Passepartout hastened to do just that, but not before he strapped Ned into his seat. Ned's seat was behind Verne's, Passepartout was behind the seat that Twain took, which was to the right of Verne.

"How do you say it," Verne said, "grab you ankles and kiss your asshole, because here we go? Or, I hope. This is its maiden voyage."

"What?" Twain said.

"First time, monsieur."

"But where do we go, Jules? The barn door is over there, to the right."

There was a big lever on Verne's left. He popped it free, jerked a small gear forward, put his foot on something, and the sleek machine rose up on a set of rubber-wrapped wheels (one front, one rear), pooted a burst of fire and steam out of its ass and leaped.

It seemed as if suddenly the barn wall jumped at them.

Twain threw his hands over his eyes.

The craft hit the wall with a sound like grapeshot, then they were through it amidst a crack and a rain of splinters.

The craft hit the shoreline in an instant, dove into the sea, raced across it like a shark, water spraying the windshield like bulldog drool.

"My God, a submersible," Twain said. "Like in your book. *20,000 Leagues.*"

"No, it does not go under," Verne said. "Not completely. It is a very fast boat. In fact, I call it a speedy boat. And it can serve as a land vehicle. And, like a flying fish, it can fly, or rather leap, short distances."

"Damn, that was some takeoff," Twain said. "I think I'm sitting a foot higher in my seat, if you know what I mean."

"If you feel the need," Verne said, "There is a toilet in the back. The feces are absorbed by chemicals, flushed out the rear of the boat. I believe once the chemicals do their work it is harmless."

"I take my hat off to your skills at invention. Or would, if I had a hat."

"I contributed. I borrowed ideas from Wells. But Passepartout is the builder," Verne said.

Twain turned in his seat, looked at Passepartout, and nodded.

"Thank you."

"Thank Mister Verne, he hired me for both my butler skills and my machine-designing skills. But many people must be given credit for their discoveries from which we borrowed, and the machine itself was constructed with Mr. Verne's money, and a team of experts. I provided the blueprint and turned a few bolts myself, monsieur."

Ned was writing furiously. He held up the pad so Twain and Passepartout could see it.

PLEASE TO PAT EACH OTHER ON THE BACK LATER. MACHINES WITH UGLY OCTOPUSSIES STILL OUT THERE. WE ARE OUT THERE. WE ARE JUST ONE MORE INGREDIENT IN THE SOUP. DO WE HAVE SOUP ON BOARD?

Twain read this aloud so Verne could hear it.

"The seal is quite right; let us see if we can lose our enemies. See the device to your right, Samuel. I have one on my left."

"The mirror?"

"Ah, but it is arranged so that by looking into it you can see behind you. There are a series of mirrors alongside the craft, each feeding images into the other."

Twain looked. The Martian machines were running through the water toward them. And they were running fast. Twain could see at least five machines. White foam splashed up around the legs of the machines. One of them stumbled, fell, disappeared beneath the water, rose up again and continued its pursuit.

"This way, we can keep watch on what's behind us," Verne said. "The good thing is, they are behind us."

"They're catching up," Twain said.

"Yes," Verne said. "They are fast. But, can they manage the deep water?"

As if in answer, out of the heads of the machines came the hot rays. The beams hit all around Verne's racing craft, and where they hit, the water steamed and hissed.

"They may not need to catch us," Twain said, looking into the relay mirror. "They can boil us in here like sardines in a can."

"I hardly think we would boil, sir," Passepartout said. "I think we would explode."

OKAY. THERE'S NO SOUP. BUT SARDINES WERE MENTIONED.

DO WE POSSIBLY HAVE ANY OF THOSE? ANY KIND OF FISH? I'M
WRITING HERE.

Twain patted Ned on the head. "Later, Ned. Later."

They went far out fast and furious, and the water grew deep, and the
silver machine rode up high on the waves and dipped and reared, and
finally the walking machines began to fall deep. Pretty soon the water
was up to the bulk of the machines, up to the windows that showed
the tentacled aliens working at the controls as desperately as one-armed
paperhangers.

Then one machine went under and did not come up. Then another
went down. Metal legs thrashed. One tried to rise. A wave took it and
washed it back and under. It rose up again. All that could be seen was the
top of the machine. The window. Green-gray heads behind it, flashing
tentacles.

One of the beasts pressed its double anus against the glass. It and
its companion Martian, its copilot, screamed and cursed. But the sleek
silver craft darted over the waves, out of sight and sound of their grunts
and sneezes, coughs and wheezes, and pretty soon the speedy boat, as
Verne called it, was just a silver line, a shiny needle shooting through
water, sewing up the ocean like a Neptunian tailor.

All of the Martian crafts floated to the surface. None was lost. They
had crashed in the sea and had come out of the sea. They were prepared
for that business. But they weren't ready to race across water. They could
slide out of their "meteors" inside their little watertight, air-filled suits,
click the machines together as fast as a kid could line up jacks. They
could enter into their machines through their watertight, air-controlled
hatches. And they could make the machines crawl across the bottom
until they could stand tall and step on shore.

But that crossing the water bit, on the surface and fast, they had left
that out of their plans. Someone had snoozed.

They stalked back to shore. The machines stood there on the sand.
Tall, wet and shiny. Inside the machines, the Martians, their critter faces
pressed to their windows, looked out at the ocean and the world they
intended to conquer, and they were seriously pissed off.

Nine: A Warm, Sweet Day off the Coast of Spain, Followed by Disaster and Further Surprise

Twain thought: Could he actually be back in Morocco, dozing, wine-sodden, out of his head, Huck on a shelf, shitted all over, fly-swarmed and dead?

He pinched himself.

Ouch.

Didn't seem that way.

The craft went bumping over the waves. It made Twain sick at first, but in time, his stomach settled. There was the smell of the ocean being channeled through the top of the machine by a whirligig that pulled the air throughout, and in the beginning made the interior too cool and too strong with the smell of salt. But in time it became refreshing.

The stalking machines were long left behind, and now there was only the water and the jumping craft, bouncing up the waves and down them, in the ocean that was home to Gibraltar and the Pillars of Hercules. Just the thought of that made the historical-minded Twain happy. He could envision himself and his companions as ancient Greek heroes who had sailed this stretch of sea.

He tried to recall which heroes he had read about, which ones had sailed the sea on which they bounced.

Who was it?

Jason?

Odysseus?

Theseus?

All of the above?

He couldn't remember, but it was fun trying. And it was better than thinking about the machines. Twain was certain there were many more of them, and that they were spotted about the world. Had to be. If the meteors were in fact not meteors, but machines, craft from space, then there were many more. And had it not been for this fact, he would have enjoyed his trip.

That was nice to consider.

His life had been so miserable for so long, so lost without his wife and daughters, he had not considered the possibility of fun. Solace maybe, out of the contents of a bottle.

But fun?

Who would have thought? He actually felt good to be alive.

Of course, it was a partial kind of fun. The boat ride was nice. But what had gone on before, and might go on after, was bound to be less than fun.

Another snag was that Verne and Passepartout kept exchanging looks; Verne looking over his shoulder at the butler, his face scrunched up like fruit too long on the vine.

"What's wrong?" Twain said. "Something's wrong? Am I right? There's a snag. Right?"

"There is a snag that is small," Verne said. "Or, to say it another way. We are about to be snagged."

"How's that?"

"This craft, it is a prototype."

"So."

"So, it isn't designed to be...permanent."

"How's that?"

"The sides, the bolts, they are screwed in, okay, but not great."

"Why? Why would you do that?"

"Well," Verne said, looking at Passepartout, "we thought there were other things needed. So, the sides were designed to come loose easily, until certain changes were made inside. Designs, decorating."

"Decorating?"

Ned made a seal sound and twisted his mouth so that one side seemed to be wadded up. He slapped his pad, wrote, held it up. It said: I NEVER EVEN GOT TO TRY THE SHITTER.

Passepartout said, "It may hold long enough for us to reach land. Farther along, closer to Italy, that's our goal. But it's quite a ways, and though I think we'll arrive safely —"

The left side of the craft came off and water gushed up over the side. Passepartout said, "And maybe we shall not."

Ned wrote:

SHIT!

"To the rear," Verne said, "I shall hold its course. Hurry!"

Harnesses were unsnapped. Verne leaned the boat on its right side. More water crashed in from the left, rushed about their ankles. The top blew off and Twain and Passepartout and Ned were thrown to the rear.

Passepartout gestured to the circular couch, said, "Grab one end."

Twain struggled to his feet, did as he was told.

"Now push your end toward mine."

Twain did as he was told. The couch stretched as a partition came out of it, and it continued around until it clicked into the other end, forming a circle. Twain noted that there were thick rings placed strategically all around the top of the couch.

"The craft is losing its right side," Verne yelled.

Ned wrote on his pad: SNAPPY, SNAPPY, SNAPPY.

But no one was paying attention.

Passepartout climbed into the ring of the couch, sat on the cushioned seat, bid Twain and Ned to do the same. Twain helped Ned climb over, then they hoisted the cruiser into place. Passepartout took hold of the bottom edge of the couch and pulled. Thick wooden sections sprang out, snapped together, filled the gap.

"What good is a couch pulled into a circle?" Twain said.

Ned whistled and wrote. NOW IT HAS A BOTTOM. IT'S A BOAT.

Passepartout made no comment to either.

The right side of the boat shredded, just crunched up like an invisible hand had squeezed it. Verne righted it just in time to keep from being swamped. They were essentially jetting across the water now on a leaky, silver V.

The couch slid precariously to the left.

Passepartout lifted up one of the couch cushions. There was a box under it. He took out the box and set it in the center of the couch bottom he had made, opened it quickly. It was full of cables and the cables had snaps.

Passepartout snapped them into the rings around the top of the couch. The cables went from the couch, into the box, and in the box was something folded up. It was bright orange and of an odd texture.

"Stand back," Passepartout said, reaching into the box. He yanked something, a lever perhaps, and up jumped a balloon, hissing and filling and swelling up large. The cables struggled as they might yank the balloon back into the box.

"Jumping Horny Toads," Twain said. "All that was in that little box?"

"Sir," Passepartout yelled. "Master Verne. Please. It is time. It is past time."

The balloon was throwing off the boat's balance even worse, slowing it down, causing it to wobble. The back end dipped, the front end rose.

Verne unfastened his harness, careened and wobbled from his seat, lunged over the side of the couch onto its cushions.

"Grab your nuts, monsieurs," Passepartout said. "Master Verne, if you will assist me."

What happened next happened very quickly.

Verne leaned over one side of the couch, as did Passepartout, and grabbed at something.

Twain peeked, saw on Verne's side that the couch was fastened to the floor by a cable and bolts, and there was a lift lever attached to the cable.

"One," said Passepartout, clutching a similar lever on the other side.

"Two," said Passepartout.

"Three," they said together.

Verne and Passepartout pulled the levers and the cables let go of the bolt.

They sprang to the heavens.

The motion was so hard Twain's neck was popped and he and Ned were nearly tossed out of the craft.

An instant later, beneath them, the boat wadded up and went to pieces in a million silver directions.

Out in the distance Twain saw an enormous swordfish jump, as if it were triumphant about the whole dang deal.

Ten: The Nature of the Device, Sailing Along, High Up, Full of Bread and Honey

"I can't believe it held as long as it did," Twain said. "With the balloon tugging, the wind, the speed."

"It may be a strange thing to say," Verne said, "considering it has come apart beneath us, but it was of an extremely sound design. Just wish we had not left the bolts loose."

"Yes, Passepartout. I do believe that furniture and decoration could have waited. But, alas. Millions of francs down the old shit hole."

"How does the balloon work?" Twain said. "It's not hot air."

"When the box was opened," Verne said, "the lever was pulled, and it was rushed full of the helium."

"Helium?"

"A gas. It works very good to make things float. Passepartout designed it so that a small compressor filled the balloon instantly."

"All of that helium out of that little box."

"A new design," Verne said. "A new way to condense helium. You will note the compressor in the bottom of the box."

"Amazing," Twain said.

"Yes," Verne said. "It is. The gas is very hard to come by, and it is very seriously compressed. Passepartout's design is years and years ahead of anything anyone else is doing."

"Thank you, sir," Passepartout said.

"You are quite welcome, my friend."

"It's certainly obvious that it is advanced," Twain said. "Like the boat."

Verne nodded, "Like the boat."

That got Twain to thinking.

"Is this a prototype too?" he asked.

"In a way, my friend, it is. Yes," Verne said. "We have never used it before, but, it is better constructed... But..."

"But what?"

"There is a problem."

"Figures. And that is?"

"It is not designed for the too long flight, you know. It will lose its buoyancy after a time."

"A short time?" Twain asked.

"Maybe not so short," Verne said.

"Maybe?"

"Who knows?"

"Great," Twain said. "We might as well shit on ourselves and call it lilac water."

The balloon kept rising and the sun was high and yellow and dripping over their balloon like a runny egg yolk. They sat in the shadow made by the balloon, and the wind carried them along, very fast, along the coast of Spain. Down below they could see the stalking machines.

Many of them.

Rays flashed. Farmhouses burned. They could see people running.

"Sweet Virgin," said Verne.

"I hope they don't look up," Twain said. "Those rays have quite a range."

They didn't look up.

Our heroes sailed along for some time, and then from under one of the cushions, Passepartout brought out a container of water, some food, bread and honey, utensils, and they ate and drank.

"How do we know we're going in the right direction?" Twain asked.

"That is one of the drawbacks," Passepartout said. "We do not. We have no navigational equipment on board."

"Oh, good," Twain said. "And, for that matter, what is the right direction? Where are we going? If we had a compass, at least, we could chart a course."

"If we could control the balloon's direction," Verne said. "We can not."

"No," Passepartout said. "We can not."

"Priceless," Mr. Twain said. "You don't have a plan?"

"My plan was to save our asses," Verne said. "Our asses are saved. At least for the moment."

"We won't go any higher, will we?" Twain said.

"No," Verne said. "Or, we shouldn't. And, in time, when land is near, we will leak the helium, bring us down. The important thing is we are away from those machines and our dissolving boat."

"I suppose," Twain said, finishing off a slice of bread with honey, "that is for the better."

In time they all lay about on the cushions and slept, Ned snuggled up close with Twain, his nose under Twain's chin.

The balloon, a giant tangerine in the sky, sailed on.

The storm hit them like a fist.

It came down out of the sky like the howling vengeance of Zeus, wrapped itself around the balloon and tossed it this way and that, nearly throwing them all into the foaming ocean below. They managed from one of the containers under the couch cushions a large tarp that fitted almost snugly over the top of the basket. They fastened it there with the ties sewn to it, cowered under it, fearing any moment the balloon would be snapped from its cables. Or the basket would rip. Or the tarp would be torn off and they would be tossed like dice into the ocean.

The storm raged on and the balloon sailed on, making Ned so sick he stuck his nose out between tarp and basket and let loose with a stream of fish-smelling vomit.

The smell of long-ago eaten fish came back to him on the wind, and strangely, made him a bit peckish.

When Ned was finished with this, he poked his head completely free of the tarp and looked out and tried to determine most anything there might be to determine. This proved no small feat.

He could not tell if they were directly over the water or high in the sky. The storm had become so furious it had balled up the world.

All Ned knew was that the ball he was in was a mixture of black and gray and bursts of lightning. And that in some manner, shape or form, they were between sea and sky, but if they were high or low, he could not determine.

He thought that if it were not for gravity, they could be flying upside down and he would never know it. He listened for the crash of his friend, the sea, but nothing.

There was just the howl and cry of the wind, the pounding rain and the strips of lightning that tossed about them as if they were spears being thrown from heaven.

How long before one hits, thought Ned? How long?

After a particularly ugly chain-reaction of hot lightning, so close the smell of ozone stuffed his nostrils like a rag, the wet-nosed seal pulled his head in under the tarp and lay down and tried to sleep to the toss and whirl of the basket. The sleep of the exhausted and the fearful overcame him as it did the others, and he spiraled down deep. In his dreams he was tossed into the sea, his home. The sea, though turbulent and frothed with storm, was smooth and silent beneath the waves. Full of fish. Great fish. And he took the fish, and he ate the fish, and finally he dreamed not at all.

The basket became a kind of bassinet, rocked by Mother Wind, rolled to the slam-pat-whammy of the cold, driving rain, the unmelodious lullaby given voice by the loud mouth of Captain Thunder and the snap crackle pop percussion of Old Man Lightning.

Sometime while they slept, the storm ran its course. The sun poked out and it grew warm, finally hot. Twain rose up in a sweat and removed the tarp, folded it, put it away. The air was dry and heavy as chains.

None of the others moved. Ned lay on his back, his tail flipper in the air, his arm flippers folded over his chest. Twain thought the look on his face was one of satisfaction, as if he had just gobbled a tuna. Verne and Passepartout lay back to back like an old married couple.

Twain peeked over the side. A calm blue sea. He looked out, up and around. A calm, clear, blue sky and a huge yellow sun. But there was one peculiarity.

The sky seemed to have a rip in it. Like a painting of the sky that had been torn and pushed back together. Between the edges of the rip, Twain thought he could see movement, but he couldn't identify it. The rip went from way on high, down to the sea, dropped into the horizon.

Peculiar, to say the least, Twain thought.

Cloud formation?

He couldn't decide. Gave it up.

They lived. That was the important thing. They lived.

Twain lay back down, surprised himself by falling asleep again. And he slept well.

There were flashes of light and waves of darkness in the crack in the sky. Shiny things. Dull things. Moving things. And then the crack narrowed.

Eventually it would be nothing more than a fine blue line.

Then that too would fade away.

But, before it did, something sailed out of the crack, onto the dark blue ocean below.

Black sails.

The Jolly Roger.

A large ship.

Pirates.

Part Two:
Extracted from the Diary and
Journals of Ned the Seal

Eleven: The Mist, Ripped, the Terrifying Descent

Once upon a time I was a normal seal. This was before I was captured by Captain Bemo and given a great brain in this tin hat beneath this fine fez by none other than the infamous Doctor Momo on his secret island. My memories of this time are hazy. Once my brain power was increased, and I was given thumbs attached to my flippers, I became ravenous to learn, and read all the books that Captain Bemo had in the library aboard the *Naughty Lass,* and most of those on the island owned by Doctor Momo.

I did skip a number of his more graphic erotica books, as these tended to arouse me, and there were no female seals in my vicinity. You see, with the increase in my brain power, my sexual desires had increased as well. This waiting around for a female to be in heat, that was a bore. Sex for recreation. I want to state here and now that I'm for it. Long as the partners are willing, then why not.

But I have veered.

The books I loved the most were the ones the sailors owned and shared, the dime novels of Buffalo Bill and Wild Bill Hickok and Annie Oakley. Books about people I eventually met. I might also add that I read a book called *Frankenstein,* and I met the monster of that book, as well. He was really nice. The book only gave one side of the story, and it is certainly not well known that Doctor Frankenstein died in a skating accident. This is how the monster told it, and I believe it. He seemed like a genuine sort of chap, and personally, I have no reason to doubt him.

The book, the biography of Frankenstein and his creation, takes quite a different slant, and gives the good doctor a different sort of demise, but as I said, I'm sticking with the monster's version. I got it straight from his dead lips, and he seemed as sincere as a hard-on.

Pardon my language, but I have been amongst a rough crowd.

FLAMING ZEPPELINS

Before the operation to make me smart, mostly what I remember is eating fish, mating with female seals (of course), and avoiding sharks.

I do not like sharks. Not in the least bit. I have my reasons. One of which is that they ate a friend of mine. Or what was left of him. A talking head in a jar. He was the aforementioned famous Buffalo Bill and my hero, and they ate him. They tried to eat me too.[1]

They did bite me a lot, but I survived and I washed up on the shore that is called Spain and was rescued by none other than the famous writer, Mark Twain.

He is known primarily as a humorist, but since I have known him, he has not been that funny. He seems profoundly sad. I am sad too. I miss Buffalo Bill and Wild Bill Hickok and Annie Oakley and Sitting Bull, and there was also Cat. She was beautiful, like Annie, only she had once been a cat of some kind before Doctor Momo operated on her. He operated on himself as well. He gave himself a horse-size penis. Actually, he literally gave himself a horse penis. I assisted in the operation. He conducted it while awake, under a mild anesthesia. I think he liked a bit of pain. That was Doctor Momo's way.

Then again, that is all part of another story, contained in my diaries, and perhaps someday I will write of them, perhaps as fiction, perhaps as autobiography, perhaps as both.

But this time I'm telling you about, I was way up high in a balloon, and the day grew hot. Along we sailed, like a great orange moth, gliding with the wind, willy-nilly, with no particular place to go. We had escaped being killed by what Mr. Verne believed to be Martian invaders, and what were certainly large octopus-looking things with two assholes. I saw the assholes when we came upon a dead one lying on the beach.

Anyway, we escaped from those eight-armed sonsabitches by boat, then by balloon.

At first I found the whole thing quite the adventure. But after going through a horrible storm that made me think we would crash into the sea, and then to hope we would, I began to feel otherwise. Even when the storm passed, I grew anxious and felt restricted by the constructs of the balloon. Its interior was covered quite briskly and there was little to see on a second tour. You also had to shit over the side, and this is a

---

1   See *Zeppelins West* by Joe R. Lansdale (taken and adapted from diaries and journals by Ned the Seal, plus speculation).

precarious feat at best. And for me, a very heavy seal (which is not to say I am not trim, but I am a seal after all) with my ass dangling over the edge of a balloon while my companions moved to the far side to balance my weight, held my flippers so that my ass would not overload my body and send me dropping, it was, to say the least, an embarrassing situation.

I held it a lot. Which, I don't have to tell you, is not healthy.

With me in the balloon was Mr. Twain, the great writer, and Mr. Verne, also a great writer and an inventor. With him was his servant, friend, and fellow inventor, Passepartout. They were all real nice guys. It saddens me... Well, I will not go there. Not yet.

There was also limited food and water, and though, since the alteration of my brain, I can eat things like bread and honey with a certain delight, it is still not the same as fish, and beyond thinking about fish, which I must confess I am frequent to do, I was concerned about the state of our water. Already we had consumed half of the bottle Passepartout had produced from under a cushion, which was the lid to our food container.

And though he assured us that there was yet another container of the same, as well as slightly different foods in tins, stuffed beneath another couch cushion, I was still nervous about our odds. I confess it also passed through my mind, without any true warranty, I should hasten to add, that for three hungry men, a plump seal might began to look quite tasty after a few days with one's belly gnawing at itself.

This, of course, was most likely a silly consideration, though I did think that once I caught Passepartout giving me the once over, the way a butcher might eye a prize hog at a stock show (or so I've read in dime novels). But the heat, the boredom, the fear of death makes one think and consider all sorts of strange things, and even if I were to know for sure this passed through his mind, I forgive him. I forgive him, too, because I sometimes saw the three of them as long white fish. And I thought about how those fish might taste. All I had to do was get them out of those clothes... Well, you see how it was.

Anyway, I thought about food a lot. I wondered if one of the tins inside the food container under the cushion had fish in it. If it did, I wondered if I could work the can opener, or cut into it with a pocket knife. I have thumbs, and I can do some things you wouldn't imagine a seal might do, but the use of really fine motor skills in the area of grabbing and such is not a specialty. I can pull my dick. I do that well. But I've discovered that this isn't an area of conversation that my companions wish to visit. They have, in fact, asked me not to do it while around them. Somewhere, in all my studies, perhaps due to my being around the foul and perverted Doctor Momo, I never learned that this whole yanking the tow line was a private matter.

Frankly, I still don't see the big deal.

I'm a seal. I don't wear britches. So, well, it's out there when I get ready for it to be. I get the urge, it pokes out.

I suppose, if I wore britches, I might not think about it as much.

But the bottom line is, up there in the air, hot, bored, frightened, I would have given my left nut for a big wet mackerel to slake my urges.

Or a sardine.

Or a tuna.

Or a salmon.

Most any kind of fish.

I looked over the edge of the balloon, down at all that water, begin to think about how much I would like to be there, all wet and sleek and diving down deep, hunting fish.

It even occurred to me to leap from the balloon, but I knew better. My brain had not been enhanced by Doctor Momo for no reason. It worked well, and I had studied much. I knew that from that height, were I to dive and hit the water, it would be the same as diving into a brick wall. I would be one splattered seal.

The wind died down, and the balloon slowed, and the day grew hotter and more miserable. For a seal without water it was murder.

Mr. Twain awoke, and seeing my distress, poured some of the remaining water on his hand and gave me a rubdown with it. It felt good, but its pleasurable sensations were brief. The sun dried me out quicker than a female seal's ass on a hot rock.

We drank a bit more of the water, ate some crackers from the second storage bin — just the wrong thing for such a hot, dry trip — but it's what we had, and tried to make the best of it.

Mr. Twain looked over the side of the craft, said, "Look, Ned, could that be land?"

A gray mist floated above the water and the mist was wide and thick, like a wool patch on the ocean, but at the edges of the mist we could see patches of what looked like shoreline.

"There must be land beneath that," Mr. Twain said. "I would stake my royalties from *Tom Sawyer* on it. If I had royalties."

Mr. Twain stirred Mr. Verne and Passepartout from their slumber, took a look. It was generally agreed that it might be land.

As we floated nearer, it became more evident that it was indeed land. Misty and wet-looking, but inviting, considering how hot we were up there. Outside of the mist, we could see for certain a sandy shoreline, a glimpse of trees. Still, it was quite contained in the mist, like a rock hidden in cotton candy, Mr. Twain said.

"Jules," Mr. Twain said. "How do we go down? We must go down."

Mr. Verne took in the situation immediately, looked up at the balloon and made a face.

"We seem to have made an error," he said. "There is in fact a release valve, but we unfortunately forgot to prepare a way to make it work from within the basket here, monsieur."

"What?" Mr. Twain said.

I wrote on my pad. WHAT? WHAT THE FUCK? THAT'S DUMB.

"I'm with Ned on this one," Mr. Twain said. "That was just plain old shit stupid."

"Actually," Mr. Verne said, "so am I. Not the shit stupid. But in agreement with Ned. I would like to remind everyone, though I provided the money for this device, I was not the one who designed the blueprints."

Passepartout cleared his throat. "You examined them."

"I am not an expert of the blueprints. I am not the builder."

"It is a prototype, my good monsieur."

"So it is," Mr. Verne said. "But now, what do we do, my good sir?"

Passepartout looked up, said, "Well, I fear there is but one thing to do."

"And that is?" Mr. Twain asked.

With a sigh, Passepartout said, "I'll need to climb up there and work the release valve. The problem is, when I climb up, it will distribute the weight in a not so good manner. Like when Ned takes the shit. You must arrange yourselves evenly about the basket."

I wrote:

ONE GOOD THING. I DON'T NEED TO GO RIGHT NOW.

"That is good, Ned," Mr. Twain said.

Everyone else agreed that was good.

"I can tell you this," Passepartout said, "don't let this device tip, or you will fall very far. I am going up now."

Passepartout took hold of one of the cables and said, "I'm going to put my foot on the edge here, so I can take hold of one of the cables to climb. Perhaps you should all move to the opposite side when I put my weight down and start to climb. But you will have to adjust as my weight is redistributed. You will need to do that instantly. And I advise strongly that you do not make with the fuck up."

Passepartout put his foot on the edge of the couch, or the basket as he referred to it, and indeed, the basket leaned in that direction, even with Twain, Verne, and myself on the opposite side. For a moment, I thought we were making with the fuck up.

Passepartout scooted up a cable, pulling with his hands, locking his feet around it for support. As the cable tapered to the center, and his position changed, the basket wobbled. We did our best to maintain proper distribution. Moving this way and that.

After what seemed like enough time for me to have eaten quite a lot of fish, he made it to the release valve, or just below it, where there dangled a hose and a clamp and a lever. He said, "I'm going to let out a bit of the helium. Be prepared for a sudden drop."

He pulled the lever and the hose opened. The hose whipped, and the helium gushed. The hose struck Passepartout so hard in the face, he let go of the cable.

And fell.

He fell to the center of the basket, and the basket slung back and forth, but remained centered. The balloon began to descend.

A little too quickly.

"Too much," Passepartout said. "I must fix it."

Passepartout, pushed upright, put a foot on the side of the basket, grabbed a cable, went up swift and nimble as a monkey this time. The basket shook like dice in an eager gambler's hand. (Note these similes. I read a lot and am quite proud of it. I am, after all, a seal.)

Passepartout fought to get hold of the flapping hose, and finally, after being struck on hands and face by the thing, which was popping about like an electrified eel, he nabbed it. (I like eel by the way. I have had it smoked and it is very good. I like it raw. They can shock you, some of them. You have to be careful. A little fishing tip.)

Passepartout closed off the lever with some difficulty, but maintained his position. He found that by locking his feet against the slanted cable, leaning into it, hanging onto the hose and using the other hand to release the lever, he could maintain a position on the cable and control the release of helium. Still, we were dropping a bit fast, and finally he closed it off.

Scootching down the cable to the basket, he said, "I think that we are low enough for the moment. It might be best that we acquire the lay of the land, and then plan our descent a bit more precisely. Otherwise, to put it bluntly, we might end up with the pointy top of a tree up our asses."

"That wouldn't be good," Twain said. "I like your suggestion."

I wrote:

IT WOULD HAVE TO BE SEVERAL POINTY TOPS TO STICK IN ALL OUR ASSES.

"You are right, of course," Passepartout said.

The descent had created a new problem. Down there was a humid mist, and it rose up and surrounded us. We couldn't really see what was below us, only above us, and up there was the bright orange balloon and the hot blue sky, and as we dropped down into the mist, like drugged bug specimens in cotton, the sky and the sun began to disappear.

It was while I was looking up that I saw something moving through the mist. A big, dark dot. And the dot was growing, descending from on high. And then I saw what it was. I grabbed my pad and wrote.

LOOK UP! A BIG FUCKING BAT, I THINK.

Twain looked up. "Oh, shit."

Mr. Verne said, "My God, a pterodactyl."

I JUST SEE THE BAT.

The beast attacked the balloon.

The creature, bat, pterodactyl, winged snake, whatever, was diving at a rapid rate. Its mouth was open and it had as many teeth as a barracuda.

Perhaps the oddness of the balloon, its bright color (can birds see color? I can since the operation , but before, I saw in black and white) had annoyed the bird. I know bright orange annoys me. I am not overly fond of lavender, either. And there are some shades of green I find irritating.

"Shoooo, shoooo!" Verne screamed at the beast, but we were, as they say, shit out of luck.

The beast hit the balloon with its mouth open; its fangs tore at the balloon. There was a sound like a whale spouting water through his blowhole. The blast of helium hit the creature full in the face and knocked it back.

It screeched, whirled and wheeled in midair, went up into the higher reaches of the mist, out of sight, and at the same time we lurched and wheeled and the basket slung us all over the place.

We were nearly thrown out. Our water and much of our supplies were tossed, and the water canister grazed my head and bounced into Mr. Twain, which made him cuss, and then I was hardly aware of anything.

We clutched whatever we could grab as if it were life itself, and in a sense, it was. The basket dropped out from under us at times, then snapped back under our feet (in my case, I use that euphemistically), as we were jerked about by the wheezing, cable-tugging balloon.

After what seemed like enough time to have had a great meal of fish and a squid, the balloon became less radical in its movements, but more determined in its descent. We would not be choosing our landing area now, and I thought about what Passepartout had said about a pine tree up the ass, found myself tightening my sphincter muscles.

I chanced a look over the side of the basket, saw mist, and then poking up from the mist, what Passepartout had suggested might be there, and what I feared.

The tip of a tree.

Though, at that moment in time, I couldn't tell if it was in fact a pine.

Twelve: Ned's Journal Continues with a Lost Land, Seal Nookie, Fresh Fish and Strange Circumstances

And so we fell, and the tip of the pine (for so it proved to be) jammed through the bottom of the basket, poked right through the wooden floor of our craft until it seemed to rise in front of us like a decorative parlor plant. Then suddenly the pine expanded as the branches, momentarily trapped by the floor of our craft, sprang back into position. Our vessel burst apart, except for the leaking balloon, which still hovered above us, whistling helium out of itself like a slow fart from a fish-filled seal, unlike myself who was fishless and fartless.

(We seals make a lot of fart references. It is not considered rude to fart when you are a seal. Though, I will say that what a walrus passes for gas can be considered very rude in most kinds of company, mixed or otherwise.)

We found ourselves clinging to the limbs of the pine, the shattered pieces of our former airborne ride raining all around us, and slowly above us the bright balloon lost its special kind of air, withered like a geriatric woman's breasts, fell down over us and the top of the great tall tree, concealing us in a rubbery darkness.

Carefully, we climbed from beneath the balloon, clutching at limbs.

It was decided that the others would go to the ground, and that I, being a poor climber, would wait amongst the pine limbs, draped over them like a lumpy rug.

They went down to search for the scattered supplies, and in time, a metal box that had been in a compartment under one of the cushions was recovered. There were all manner of things inside. A pistol. Ammunition. Flares. A first-aid kit. A large hacking instrument. A kerosine lantern wrapped tight with cotton and cloth. A corked bottle of kerosine, also wrapped in cotton and cloth. And, for me, most importantly, a rope.

Mr. Twain climbed up to help me, which for a man his age was remarkable. He removed his coat and shirt and managed a rig for me out of them, so the rope wouldn't cut into me too badly. I was also protected by my vest. The rope was attached to me and dropped over a strong limb. Below, Verne and Passepartout helped lower me down.

While Mr. Twain restored himself to his shirt, and I rubbed my chest with my flippers, trying to dispel some of the rope pain, for in spite of shirt and vest, I had been temporarily indented, Passepartout clambered monkey-like back up the tree, slipped under the balloon. Using his pocket knife to cut the rubber around the cables loose, he managed, with much effort, to push the balloon free of the pine. It dropped to hang in the boughs of another tree.

On the way down, Passepartout, in continued monkey-like fashion, swung over to that tree, and with a bit of effort kicked the balloon loose of that tree. It fell in a flutter and a crash to the forest floor, not far from where we stood.

When Passepartout was on the ground, Mr. Verne said, "And why, may I ask, did you bother with that business?"

"Because we may need shelter," Passepartout said. "I thought the balloon might make quite a good one. At least for keeping the rain off. From the lushness of this island, it is my guess it rains frequently."

Mr. Verne thought about that for a moment. "Of course. Sam, what do you think?"

"What's to think," Mr. Twain answered. "He is as right as rain, so to speak. Thing I'm worried about at the moment is food. What little we had, those crackers, got knocked all over this island or jostled out at sea."

"Tubers," Passepartout said. "There are quite a few of those about. We can dig those up. And we do have matches."

"And, with the sea nearby," Mr. Verne said, "we should be able to wash them and clean them. We might even catch some fish."

"We have quite a fisherman right here," Mr. Twain said, nodding at me.

I pushed my chest out with pride.

A fish would have been good right then.

Several would have been better.

189

Fish are good to eat and they give me solace.

Like masturbation, they relax me.

Did I mention that I think it is okay to masturbate?

"It is my guess that Ned would very much like to dip himself in the sea," Mr. Verne said.

I wrote on my pad:

THAT'S RIGHT. I WOULD. I LIKE THE OCEAN AND SLOW SWIMS AND EATING FISH.

"What a strange place," Mr. Twain said. "Visibility on the ground is good, but the mist, it hangs high up, and from what we could see, almost to the edge of the beach. Can you explain it, Jules?"

"Perhaps the foliage, a number of large beasts. They breathe air in, but they breathe out something quite different, like humans. It maybe makes the mist."

"That doesn't work for me," Mr. Twain said, "but it's better than anything I can come up with it.

I wrote:

IT COULD BE MAGIC.

"I do not believe in magic," said Mr. Verne.

"What we don't understand, even if there is an explanation, might as well be magic. So, I'm with Ned. Magic it is."

We decided to break into two parties. Mr. Twain and I were given the task of taking me to the sea for a dip, as well as a search for food or water. Since we could hear the crashing of the ocean from where we were, there was little chance we might get lost. There was, however, no true trail that we could see, so we assumed our journey might be a tedious one.

It was made a lot more pleasant than it might have been for my belly, but for the discovery of the cruiser. It was popped out to full size, and Mr. Twain and I climbed on board. I worked the switch, and with a hiss it rose off the ground.

"Seems no worse for wear," Mr. Twain said.

"We'll start building a shelter," Mr. Verne said. "Maybe recover some of the food that was dropped out of the balloon basket. You might want to be back here before dark, however, considering what attacked us up there, no telling what there is in the depths of these woods, or even along the beach."

"Daylight won't protect us," Mr. Twain said.

"No, but at least you can see it coming," Mr. Verne said.

"Good point," Mr. Twain said.

"There is the large knife...the machete from the survival box," Passepartout said. "You may have to make way for the cruiser. Take it."

Mr. Verne opened the box, took out the machete and gave it to Mr. Twain.

I felt Mr. Twain and I had gotten, as Buffalo Bill might say, the better end of the stick. Our task, daunting as the undergrowth might be, was child's play compared to finding a few dirty crackers strewn about the forest floor, and possibly a water bottle.

We started out, and it was a rough go. Limbs smacked us, and several times Mr. Twain had to get out of the cruiser and hack us a path. Tired and wheezing, he would gratefully mount the cruiser again, and off we would go. This was our method for some time, inching our way through the jungle, me following the smell of the sea. And let me tell you, dear readers, that smell, to me, was as fine as any whiff of French perfume.

After some time, we burst out of the thick growth and moved beyond the edge of the mist, sweaty and dirty, onto the white sand shore and the sight of waves crashing fast and furious in rolls of foam.

"I wonder where we are," Mr. Twain said. "We must be off the coast of Spain or Italy... But which island is this? It seems unlike any I'm aware of in the Mediterranean."

I took my pad and marker and wrote:

THE WIND WAS HIGH. WE SAILED FAST. WE COULD BE ANYWHERE.

Mr. Twain nodded. "You're right. We could be anywhere."

I stared at the sea and licked my lips.

"Go," Mr. Twain said. "I intend to dampen up, myself."

I pushed my pad against my vest, removed my fez, waddled to the water and went in. It was beauty itself. For now I was sleek and fast and part of the great sea, and in that moment, I was no longer Ned, but just a seal, a creature of instinct and muscle. I dove deep, and swam far, seeing silver flashes of fish. A free lunch, if I could catch it.

And I could.

I ate my fill. It was delightful to have a belly full of fish. I decided to catch more, take them to shore so that they might be carried back. But then, as I rose out of the water, looked back, saw Mr. Twain stripped of his clothes, frolicking in the sea, I smelled something that made my whiskers twitch and my flippers flip.

Seal nookie.

I might have been civilized by a better brain, by experience and books, but when that smell hit my nose, I was nothing more than a horny seal with a little pickle dick hard as a coral reef.

I found her sunning on a rock. Her and about fifty other seals. She flirted with me a bit, finally gave me her rear. I mounted her. And then it was over and she was gone, back into the sea with the others.

I had no real urge to follow them. There was no real regret when they swam out of sight. I was no longer of their world, but I felt empty. I had mated, but it had been nothing more than that. A cheap, sordid moment on a warm rock. I was embarrassed. I hoped, that from where Mr. Twain was, he could not have identified that it was me. Though with the metal cap on my head, shining in the sunlight, it was quite possible that during my moment of digression I was visible, hunkering up there on the rock, wetting my wick like a common beast.

Embarrassed, I entered the water again, found a large fish, nabbed it by the head in my teeth, and swam back to shore with it.

Unfortunately, I ate it before landfall. So, I had to go back and catch another. Luckily, it was an even larger specimen.

I dropped it on the sand just as Mr. Twain was coming out of the sea, nude, dripping, and tired. I made a noise, and he saw me and my fish, and smiled. It was good to see him smile. In that moment, I think he must have felt pretty good. The sea is such a revitalizer of spirit.

I went back into the sea. Went three times. Each time I came back with another fish. Now there were four fish. All were rather large. I had lived up to the praise Mr. Twain had given me.

Mr. Twain dressed while I replaced my pad and pencil, pushed my hat on my head.

We started back, and as we went, the sun dipped down and turned a fiery red. It fell toward the sea, and made a flaming fruit on the far side of the ocean, then melted slowly into the sea. It would have been a strange and beautiful sight, had we been returning to Mr. Verne's beach house, but out here, not knowing where we were, it was hard to feel jovial, and that mist above and beyond, hanging there hour after hour, gave me a sensation of creepiness that made my slick seal hair stand up like porcupine quills, made the long whiskers on my face twitch involuntarily.

"I believe we have let this beautiful sunset keep us from doing what Jules suggested. Be back before dark."

There was, however, still a slash of red in the sky, and we used it to guide us as we climbed onto the cruiser and started back.

Things were good in that moment, but my experiences had taught me one sure thing.

Never feel too secure. Life always has a loose sphincter somewhere, and it will let go when you least expect it, drench you from head to toe. Or, in my case, nose to tail.

Thirteen: Ned's Journal Continues: Back at Camp, Shelter and a Fish Dinner, a Cry in the Night

We were all heroes that day. We had all done well.

Mr. Twain and I returned with fish. Mr. Verne and Passepartout had built a shelter out of the balloon. And it was a nice one. They had cut strips of rubber from it, stretched it over limbs and drooped in on two sides and at the back. Only the front of our shelter was open.

They had found a fistful of crackers, a water bottle, and not twenty feet from where we had crashed, a small spring feeding a narrow, slow-flowing creek.

They had also gathered wood, and using matches from the supply box, we had a fire, and soon, cooking fish. I confess that I did not mention that I had already eaten many fish. I like fish, you see. I like them raw just fine. But cooked is all right. If you have the patience. Having already eaten several gave me the patience.

For the moment we had shelter, water, food, and companionship, and by eating my piece of fish cooked, I could perhaps appear a bit more sophisticated.

It was bad enough I had been driven by my baser instincts to mount a seal I didn't even know, but I had also stuffed my belly like a glutton, thinking not once of my hungry partners. I was grateful that in the end I had had enough ambition to go back into the deeps and bring out dinner for everyone else.

After dinner, Mr. Twain, full of fish, having had a drink at the stream, began to talk, and he was very funny. He gave two of his after-dinner speeches, then recited a very funny story about how it was to go the barber, and finally he quoted aloud from an article he had written called "The Literary Offenses of James Fenimore Cooper."

Mr. Verne was howling, and I was rolling about on the ground, the both of us having read, or attempted to read, the long-winded, aimless tales by Mr. Cooper. Passepartout just grinned. He had not read the stories.

Except for the fact that by having read the Cooper tales we were familiar enough with them to enjoy Mr. Twain's oral article with an expulsion of great soul satisfying mirth, I am of the opinion that Passepartout was, in fact, the luckiest of we four. For unlike us, he had not had the original pain of trying to digest and make sense of the stories.

After a time the cooking fire, which was too warm for comfort anyway, burned low, and the conversation turned to females. Mr. Twain told us of the great love of his life, his wife Olivia, and Mr. Verne told us of his life and loves, but Passepartout was a veritable rabbit packed with sexual adventures. Many of them harrowing and funny, and, I must confess, stimulating.

I, having only a small erasable pad to write with, and being bashful, did not feel driven to try and sort out dim memories of my matings with the female clan before my brain enhancement. Nor did I wish to recall the earlier events of the day, desperately hunching a warm seal on a warm rock in the ocean.

Finally, after being coated in water from the creek by Mr. Twain, (he carried it to me in the water bottle that had been found) I turned in, as did the others. Our beds were soft piles of leaves, the air was warm, our bellies full. Soon, we were fast asleep.

This was our life for several days. Eating fish that I caught, and the roots that the others dug, drinking from the spring and telling tales into the night.

At that moment in time, I felt that our lives were good ones. In Europe, probably all over the world, Martian invaders were wreaking havoc, and here we were, relatively cozy, no immediate worries other than me easily catching a few fish, the others digging up tubers like lazy bears, sitting around the campfire at night telling tales, and me in the dark, when they weren't looking, pulling the old tuber. I suspected they might be pulling tubers as well, but I felt it impolite to ask or lie awake listening.

It was quite the wonderful life.

And it made us all feel guilty.

The lot of us wanted to return to Europe, and see what we, as earthlings, could do to combat this ugly Martian menace. It was my opinion, that if they could be stopped, they might be edible. There could turn out to be a really positive side to the whole thing. A lot of people, and at least one seal, could be well fed on the bodies of those Martians.

After all, it wasn't like eating human or seal flesh.

They were just big octopi, or octopussies. Whatever the term might be.

Kill them. Stop them. Eat them. Sounded like a plan to me.

I don't know exactly how long we lived like this, because I lost track of time after seeing the sun go down seven times, and it is my guess it may have gone down another seven times before fate, as I originally suggested it would, let its sphincter go.

We were asleep, having had a particularly entertaining night of talk and excessive food (I caught a lot of fish that day, not counting the ones I ate while at sea, and we all ate an excessive amount of cooked tubers), and I was dreaming of a fish the size of Jonah's whale when we were startled awake by a cry in the night.

It came from some distance, but it was loud.

"It sounds like someone in pain," Mr. Twain said, rising up on one elbow.

"Or someone who is very angry," Mr. Verne said.

"Or both," Passepartout said.

"Could it be one of those sky monsters?" Mr. Twain said.

"It could be anything, Samuel," Mr. Verne said. "But what did it sound like to you?"

"What I said originally. Someone in pain."

"Precisely."

"Since it isn't any of our business," Mr. Twain said, "I suppose we will check into it."

Mr. Verne was already up, slipping on his shoes. "I think that we must."

Mr. Verne took the pistol from the box, made sure it was loaded, then dropped the box of ammunition in his loose coat pocket.

Mr. Twain picked up the machete, and Passepartout found a heavy but not too long limb to carry as a club. I carried with me only my wits.

FLAMING ZEPPELINS

I doused myself in spring water as a refresher, and soon as Mr. Verne brought the collapsible cruiser into full service, I, along with the others, mounted it. Lighting the lantern from the box, fastening it to the front of the cruiser, we started out, Mr. Verne at the controls.

The sound, which was now more of a groan than a cry, continued, and we pushed on through the dense foliage in pursuit of it.

A part of me thought this a foolish idea, but another part of me, and I almost said the human part of me, for I had been changed considerably by the introduction of a larger brain and by the friendship of others and the addition of thumbs, which was the device that allowed me to pull, rather than lick (on occasion, I still do that) the old tuber, knew we had to give it examination. It might be someone in pain, in need of our assistance. And a gentleman did not sit on his hands, or flippers, when there was a cry of distress.

Or it might be a scary monster that wanted to eat us. And in that case, sitting on your hands, or flippers, is appropriate.

The night was not very bright because of the mist that surrounded the island, but the full moon, like a greasy doubloon seen through cheesecloth, provided far more light than one would have thought possible in a land of mist, and, of course, we had our lantern.

Still, it was not high noon, and we went along, bumping up against trees, having to get out and clear brush (actually, I didn't get out; I would have slowed us down considerably), looking this way and that for a trail.

Finally, we decided it was best to just head to the beach, listen from there, and then find our way back in. Trying to thread our way to the cries in the dark was impossible. But, out on the beach, once we located the cries, perhaps we could ride directly to them. It was my surmise that the sounds were not too deeply in the woods, but along the edge.

We found the trail that Mr. Twain and I had cleared, and once on that, our time picked up. As we neared the beach, we realized that the sound had been coming from there all along, not the woods at all. Something about the island, the trees, the crashing sea, had made the source and distance of sound hard to determine.

Now, we realized they were originating somewhere down on the beach, and that they were moving away from us. Eventually, we came out of the forest and hovered over the sand.

There in the fuzzy moonlight, we could see a horde of footprints. Some of them shoed, some bare. Among them were a few huge prints that did not appear human. There was also the sign of something large being dragged, like a sled. A very big sled. This dragged thing had mashed down many of the odd, nonhuman-appearing prints, but the few of those prints that were visible were well indented, which, from having read Buffalo Bill's adventures, I knew meant that whatever was on the other end of those feet was large and heavy.

"What do you make of it, friends?" Mr. Verne asked.

Mr. Twain climbed out of the cruiser, bent down and touched the big track.

"Well, if this was a Fenimore Cooper novel," Mr. Twain said, "we could not only determine what made this print at a glance, we could probably tell its age, hat size, and the length of its dong. Then we could dig it out, harden it in about five minutes by blowing on it, then ride about in it on the ocean like a boat, having swollen it to thirty times its size by a piece of bullshit esoteric Indian lore."

"You do not like this Fenimore Cooper's work, do you, my friend?" Passepartout said.

"Nope," Twain said.

"I am no tracker, no Hawkeye," Mr. Verne said, "but what we can do, since there are tracks most everywhere, is follow them."

"What if we do catch up with them?" Mr. Twain said.

Mr. Verne paused. "Might I suggest extreme caution."

"That's how I'd play it," Mr. Twain said.

"It would be smarter to ignore the whole thing," Passepartout said.

About that time there came a long loud cry that trailed off into a horrid groan.

Mr. Twain had risen from examining the track. He said, "Perhaps. But can any of us ignore that?"

"I can not, sir," Mr. Verne said. "Though, perhaps, before this night is over, I will wish that I had ignored it."

"Let's get to sneaking," Mr. Twain said.

Fourteen: Ned Passes Gas,
an Incredible Discovery

We had not gone far before the fish I had eaten earlier went to work on me. I love fish, but like most seals, it gives me gas. And it's a foul gas, I might add. But I'll not discuss it in detail, because it has been mentioned before and humans seem somewhat reticent to talk about the natural processes of their bodies.

"Ned," Mr. Twain said, "you keep that up, and you can get out of the cruiser and waddle along."

I wrote on my pad and pushed it around where he could see it. SORRY, MR. TWAIN. I CAN'T HELP IT. SOMETIMES, IF YOU EAT MORE FISH IT WILL SETTLE THE STOMACH. WE COULD PAUSE HERE WHILE I GRAB A SNACK IN THE SEA.

"No time for that, Ned."

SORRY. OF COURSE, YOU ARE RIGHT. BUT IT WOULD TAKE ONLY A MOMENT.

Mr. Twain ignored me, which I suppose was best. We cruised along the beach, and sometimes we rode over the waves as they crashed against the sand. I loved the sound of the waves, the smell of the sea, its white foaming thunder broken only by the occasional moans or cries of that which had awakened, and now, guided us.

As we traversed the beach, the shoreline narrowed, and the jungle trees pushed out closer to the ocean. They were scrawny there, and pale from the leaching of the salt spray.

We could see where whatever it was that had been dragged, had in fact, been pulled into the water, and then around the outcrop of jungle, back onto where the beach became wide again.

Beyond that, we saw the blaze of a large fire. It gave off a great orange glow. And now we could identify what had been dragged. It was high and dry and parked between a couple rows of widely spaced palm trees. It was a ship. A large wooden ship. And, not far off shore, in a kind of cove was another ship. Its black sails were trimmed. On a high mast a Jolly Roger floated in the sea breeze and flapped like a wag's tongue.

What swarmed over the beached ship and the shore around it made our jaws drop. They could only be described as pirates. Of the yo-ho-ho variety. Appearing to be of an age long lost. They looked as if they could have stepped out of some of the old pirate books I had read.

I was so shocked, and secretly delighted, I thought I might shit myself.

And they were jubilant pirates at that. Leaping and cavorting, drunk as flies in a barrel of cider, cutlasses waving about or strapped to their sides, belts stuffed with old-fashion cap and ball pistols, or brandishing old-style rifles about, they danced around the fire to the crude stylings of an old squeeze box, pushed and pulled by a large man in a wide-brimmed hat. His leg looked to be nothing more than a peg of wood.

There was something else. Something large amongst the palm trees. Something I could not identify, but something that moved.

The noise we had been following, the cries, they came from this large thing's quarter. And there was another thing, a screeching sound, and the slash and pop of what sounded like a dozen whips. And when they popped, the thing in the dark cried.

"I suggest," Mr. Twain said, "we ride up in those woods there, and sneak around. I got a feeling being seen head on might not work out too well for us."

"Oui," Mr. Verne said.

So we used the cruiser to glide into an opening in the jungle, began making slow progress through gaps in the trees toward the camp. The jungle rose up dramatically from where the beach had widened and this positioned us high up and amongst the greenery, looking down.

We climbed down from the cruiser, collapsed it and leaned it against a tree. Then we got low and crawled along on the ground until we were at the edge of the trees, up above them on an overlook built over the centuries by sand being pushed in from the shore and the sea bottom. It smelled very fishy. Very nice.

I did not like crawling on my stomach however. There were rocks in the sand and they cut me a bit.

Down below we could hear their laughter and yelling, the cries and groaning of that which was in the shadows, and of course, that miserable music from the spinet box. Some were even singing pirate songs. Yo-ho-ho and a bottle of rum stuff. It was all quite off-key, I might add.

Now we were close enough that we could identify (I don't know if that is the proper word) the great shape from which the cries emitted, the great shape that was the target for the whips.

It was an ape.

Sort of.

The beast was forty feet tall if it was a foot, and very broad. There were chains around its neck, wrists and ankles. A sort of grinding machine had been put on the beach, something from the pirate ship no doubt, and it had a wheel on it, and it was turned by the ape, grinding... whatever...in the moonlight.

I could see the name of the beached vessel written on its side — *Der Fliegende Hollander*. Sitting with their backs against the ship were a number of bedraggled people. A rope ran along the side of the ship, from bow to stern, and other ropes had been attached to that rope, and in turn the people had been fastened to those. They looked as dejected as pet pigs that had been decided on for dinner.

Then, I almost cried out. For I recognized two of the captives.

The Sioux warrior and visionary, Sitting Bull, and the black-haired beauty, Cat — her name being the source of her origin — were among the prisoners.

I wrote:

I KNOW TWO OF THE CAPTIVES. THEY ARE MY FRIENDS. SITTING BULL AND CAT. I THOUGHT THEY WERE DEAD. WE WERE IN THE *NAUGHTY LASS* AND IT SUNK. I THOUGHT THEY, LIKE BUFFALO BILL'S HEAD, WERE EATEN BY SHARKS. BUT, LIKE ME, I SEE THEY SURVIVED.

"I'll be damned," Mr. Twain said.

ME, TOO. WHAT CAN WE DO?

Mr. Twain patted me on the head, said, "Hold your water. Yes, I recognize Sitting Bull now. From photographs. But there is another Indian down there. See the braid? Do you recognize him or any of the others?"

NO.

I turned my attention once again to the great ape, who was working at turning that odd wheeled device, going round and round to the snap and pop of pirate whips.

The beast pushed at the wheel by grabbing onto the bar to which it was chained, putting his back into it.

Around and around went the wheel, and I could discern now that the wheel was some kind of crushing device, and that pirates were feeding something into a space beneath it, and that when the wheel turned, the stuff was crushed, the residue forced through a pipe, into a barrel, beneath which was a hot fire.

Twain sniffed. "Mash," he said. "They're making some kind of liquor with a crude crushing device they've rigged. It looks to be a type of cane they're crushing. Like sugar cane."

"Now it is my turn to be damned," Mr. Verne said.

"Probably discovered the cane on the island, and are as happy as clams about it," Mr. Twain said. "My guess is they were spending time here, resting up, drinking, and they spotted this ship and went out to take it. And did. Had this ape pull it to shore. My guess is, like the cane, they discovered him on the island. Makes sense considering what we've seen here. That great beast that brought us down, for example."

"It's easier to scuttle a ship that way," said Passepartout. "Having it on shore."

"But pirates?" Mr. Verne said. "These people look out of their time. That ship. Both ships. Their clothes. The cutlasses, the cap and ball pistols. Most odd."

"That ship, the beached one, or the one docked off the island, could be our way out," Mr. Twain said. "Provided we could rescue a crew from the pirates. I, for one, couldn't sail a rowboat. Now, if it were a steam craft, and had a paddle wheel, we would be in luck."

"Since there is no paddle wheel," Mr. Verne said, "might I suggest another plan."

"Okay?" Mr. Twain said.

"I didn't say I had one," Mr. Verne said. "I said I suggest we have another. Anyone?"

Mr. Twain said, "I suppose there is only one thing to do, and that's wait. Perhaps, if those reprobates drink enough grog, tire of making more, they will go to sleep. Then and only then can we slip down and free the prisoners."

"Making instant grog," Passepartout said. "Without aging, that is bound to be nasty."

"The cane is probably old, maybe even decayed," Twain said. "That way, it ripens almost instantly. It may not be fine liquor, Passepartout, but enough of it will get you drunk. And there is little doubt in my mind that is their ultimate goal."

"Most uncivilized," Passepartout said.

Fifteen: Ned's Journal Continued:
A Daring Plan, A Surprise Ally,
Bull Goes Crazy

As we watched, the stocky peg-legged pirate we had spotted before came well into view. His wide-brimmed hat hung over his head like a black cloud and a nasty looking pigtail wormed from the back of his head and was draped over the shoulder of his filthy blue coat like some sort of horrid little beast that had died in its sleep. A cutlass dangled at his side. He had a crooked dagger in his broad belt, as well as two old single-shot cap and ball pistols. In the firelight his face looked rough, as if it had been used to sand flooring, then hosed down and left out in the sun to dry.

He said something to the crowd that we couldn't hear, and a cheer went up. As we watched, a barrel was rolled out, tapped, and the pirates began to fill whatever they could find with the liquid, drink it faster than I gobble fish, and believe me, I gobble pretty quick.

"All we can do," Mr. Twain said, "is wait until they're so drunk they pass out, then maybe we can slip in, free the prisoners, and run away, back to our camp and hide."

"What about the boat plan?"

"That's plan B, if plan A goes real well. Plan A never goes real well."

"I hate to suggest it," Passepartout said, "but perhaps the better part of valor is to watch out for ourselves. We can not do for us, let alone many others."

I wrote: BULL AND CAT ARE MY FRIENDS. I MUST SAVE THEM. WITH OR WITHOUT THE REST OF YOU.

"I am sorry to have said such a thing," Passepartout said. "I was wrong to think it. It just came out."

"You were merely saying what all of us, with perhaps the exception of Ned, are thinking," Mr. Twain said, patting Passepartout's arm. "Of course, we will all do what we can, Ned. We know what we must do. But we must be cautious. There's no use going off half-cocked. That will not help us one little bit. We rest here, wait until they are blind drunk."

I lay on my back beside Mr. Twain on the ground, brooding. It is uncomfortable for me to lie on my back like that, but I brood better that way.

"Uh, what are they doing now?" Mr. Verne said.

I rolled over on my belly for a look.

A couple of the pirates went over to the trotline that held the row of prisoners, picked one, a smallish brute of a man, cut him free of the line, brought him over to the pirate who appeared to be their captain, the one with the greasy pigtail and the wide-brimmed hat.

The Captain, as I will call him, looked at the man and laughed. He said something, and the man said something back, dropped to his knees and begged. I couldn't hear him beg, for which I am grateful, but begging was what he was doing. That was obvious.

He was pummeled by a couple of the pirates, stripped of his boots and clothes. When it was over, he lay naked and bloody on the sand.

While this had been going on, ropes were attached to two young palm trees, and with all the pirates pulling, the trees were bent over to where the tops almost touched the ground and they crossed against one another. They were held that way by the horde of straining pirates.

"What are they doing?" Mr. Verne said.

"I don't know," Mr. Twain said. "But I don't like it."

The brutish looking man was swiftly bound to the trees in such a way that one arm and one leg were tied firmly to each tree with thick rope. A small barrel of pitch was produced from somewhere, and with a stick a tad of it was scooped, touched to the tip of the man's penis. This was set on fire. The man screamed so loud I thought I was going to suck my asshole up through the top of my head. Then the pirates let go of the trees.

It happened with a snap and a whoosh. The man's body was torn in half, launched high in two directions. The flaming dick went to the right, a little red blur that sailed way out into the ocean, dropped down like a miniature falling star into the water.

A cheer went up from the pirates.

I looked down at Cat and Bull. In the light from the moon, which was clear of mist out there on the beach, and the flickering of the firelight,

Cat looked nervous as a cat might look. She certainly knew that a very special fate was probably in store for her. A plaything to the pirates, and then the trees.

The others on the trotline looked nervous as well. A couple were actually trembling. Bull was the only one who didn't look in the least bit bothered. He looked as if he might be thinking of supper, hoping for boiled dog.

Watching, knowing what fate might be in store for my two friends, knowing others might die, made me sick to my stomach, and for the first time that I can ever recall, at least for a few minutes, I did not think of fish.

There was a pause, more grog was drunk, then another victim was picked from the trotline. The same ritual occurred, with the same horrible results.

WE MUST DO SOMETHING, I wrote.

Mr. Twain said, "We are four against many. There must be forty pirates. We have one gun. We must wait."

GIVE ME THE GUN. I WILL GO DOWN THERE.

"You are brave, little seal," Mr. Verne said. "No doubt. But if you wish to help your friends, you must wait until the pirates sleep."

WHAT IF MY FRIENDS ARE TIED TO THE TREES AND SET ON FIRE AND SHOT IN TWO DIRECTIONS. THEN HOW DO I HELP THEM? WHAT OF THE OTHERS? I DON'T KNOW THEM, BUT ARE THEY NOT HUMAN? ARE WE NOT HUMAN? EXCEPT, OF COURSE, I'M A SEAL.

"And as humans," Mr. Twain said, "we must know our limitations. If we all die, we will have accomplished nothing."

I started to write again, but felt suddenly fatigued. I did not like it, but they were right. I lay down on my belly and waited.

Two more victims were sent sailing from the trees, but fortunately, neither was Cat nor Bull.

After a time, the pirates bored with the whole matter, drank more, and got into fights with one another. There was even a stabbing, which resulted in a death right there on the shore. Or a near death. The poor man was gutted, and with his intestines hanging out, his partners turned on him, pulled down the two trees, fastened him to them, covered his dangling intestines first in pitch, then in fire, and sent him sailing. He was well lit, and I must confess I found it an amazing sight as his guts strung out long and red and flaming across the dark skyline. A string of the guts caught up in the top of a palm tree at the edge of the shore, lit it on fire, brightening the whole gruesome scene below in an orange-red cast.

Finally, after an hour of drinking and cursing and fighting, the Captain became angry with one of the pirates and slashed the top of the man's head with his cutlass. The blow drove the pirate to the ground, the cutlass hung up in his skull. Balancing on his peg, using his one good foot, the Captain, with a grunt and a shove, pulled his sword free.

Amazingly, the man got up, staggered and fell down. Chunks of his hair, which had been cut by the cutlass blow, fell from his head. The pirates let out a roar of laughter. None louder than the Captain himself. "Good form," he said loud enough for us to hear, and the pirates burst into an even louder peal of laugher.

The pirate who had been struck sat up, put a hand on top of his damaged skull and laughed. Soon, with a wad of bloody cloth stuck to the top of his head, he was laughing and drinking, seemingly no worse for wear.

It was then that I noticed that the great ape had finally stopped turning the wheel, and was leaning against it, looking out at the drunken pirates. The look on his simian face was inscrutable.

I looked at Cat and Bull. Cat was snuggled up close to Bull. And Bull, with one arm around her, looked out at the pirates. His face revealed nothing.

As Mr. Twain had suspected, it wasn't long before the pirates lay all over the beach, passed out. The only people awake were those tied alongside the ship. And, of course, the great red ape.

Mr. Verne pulled the cruiser into shape, and we mounted up, glided down from our hiding place, me at the controls, Mr. Verne holding the pistol. Mr. Twain had the machete, and Passepartout held his club. It suddenly occurred to me that as much as I had wanted to fight, we were not the most apt group. Neither Verne nor Twain were young men, and Passepartout, though younger than they, did not appear to me to be the fighting type. And I, alas, was a seal.

The firelight from the blazing palm gave the shore an unearthly look, as if we were floating along a corridor of hell. The cruiser was quiet, and not one pirate stirred. The prisoners saw us coming but remained quiet. It occurred to me we might slip in, free them, and escape without ever being heard.

We arrived in front of the prisoners, and with me staying at the controls, the others dismounted. Mr. Twain used the machete to cut the rope, and then to free individual bonds.

When I was on the beach, Bull and Cat saw me. Cat almost cried out, but stifled it by placing a hand to her mouth. I could see her smile at the edge of her hand, the firelight in her eyes. Bull looked up and made with a soft grunt. For Bull, that was pretty excited.

After Mr. Twain cut the prisoners free, I counted them. Including Bull and Cat, there were ten.

One of the men, an official-looking fellow in what might have been a blue military jacket and very worn blue pants, came over to us. The other Indian came with him.

The man spoke softly, said, "My name is Bill Beadle, and this is my friend, John Feather. We are glad to see you, as you can imagine."

Twain said, "Thing for us to do is to get out of here quick."

"That's why I'm talking to you," Beadle said. "The ape. He can assist us."

"He can?" Twain said.

"He is not like other apes. But there is no time to explain that. If we free him, he can drag the ship into the water, out deep, and we can sail away on the night tide. The wind is up, and we should be able to make good time. This man," Beadle pointed at a tall, lean fellow wearing a dirty cap and soiled whites, "is the captain. He's called the Dutchman."

The Dutchman nodded.

"But the ape," Mr. Twain said. "Why would he help us, without whips I mean?"

"Trust me for now," Beadle said.

Bull said, "Borrow knife."

Without getting an answer, Bull took Twain's machete, and stalked toward the sleeping pirates.

Twain called to him as softly as possible, but Bull wasn't listening.

Faster than you could say let's scalp somebody, Bull began to systematically cut the throats of sleeping pirates.

All I can say is we were stunned. We stood there amazed as he went quickly and quietly from one to the other, and soon the ground was littered with gurgling, thrashing pirates, clutching at their oozing throats.

He must have cut the throats of seven or eight before any sort of alarm was aroused, and by this time, he had picked up one of the old-style rifles from the ground, and had stuffed two cap and ball pistols and the machete into his belt.

He immediately went to work with the firearms.

Bull lifted the rifle and shot one of the pirates full in the face, from less than twenty feet away. There is no need for me to describe the gruesome results, other than to say the fellow, not a pretty sight to begin with, went from grimacing and growling and drawing a sabre to suddenly looking as if a cherry pie had exploded in his face.

Bull tossed the one-shot weapon aside, drew the pistols, and as bullets rained around him, shot first one man in the temple, by walking right up to him (and keep in mind, this man was firing away and seemed to be in a position impossible to miss Bull, but did) and when this man fell from Bull's shot, another who was armed with a sword decided to make a run for it. Bull gave him a warning shot. Right in the back of the head.

Now we were all scrambling for a hiding place. The bullets were storming about us like windblown hail. Twain darted for the opposite side of the ship, and I followed with the cruiser, but what we found there were more pirates, staggering up from their inebriated slumber.

Mr. Verne, who had come around on that side with us, went to work with the pistol, fired five shots in rapid succession, popping off three pirates, sending the other two shots somewhere out into the ocean, or perhaps smacking into a palm tree. He jerked the box of shells out of his pocket and began reloading. While he was about this task, a pirate with a sword charged down on him. Mr. Twain leaped forward, and luckily slid up under the attacker's arm before the sabre could come down on Mr. Verne, caught the pirate's wrist, and began to wrestle with him. I scooted around behind the pirate on the cruiser, and knocked him down.

Mr. Twain stepped on his hand, liberated him of his sword, and stuck him with it through the throat.

"The ape. Come now."

It was Beadle. He had picked up a piece of driftwood, and I could see that it was covered in blood and brains. Mr. Twain leaped onto the cruiser, as did Beadle, who said, "Fine device," and we flitted over to where the ape was chained to the wheel.

All around us pirates were yelling and attacking, but those Bull had killed provided weapons for our group, and considering what they had seen the pirates do, the folks from the trotline attacked with a fury generally reserved for sharks, who I hate, but I believe I have mentioned that.

I saw Cat leap on a pirate, take him down, and with her teeth she tore at his throat. A spray of blood leaped high and wide and splattered her, coating her black hair with gore. But she was already up, springing onto the back of another pirate.

Down the beach a bit, I saw Beadle's Indian friend on top of a pirate, pounding him in the head with what may have been a coconut.

The air stank of blood and shit, and just the faintest hint of salt spray and fish from the ocean. Believe it or not, the smell of fish made me hungry.

A bullet tore past Mr. Twain's shoulder and grazed my nose. It made me mad. I wished I could have a pistol, because with my flipper backing it, using my thumb, I knew I could fire it. But I had what I had. My head and my ass, and so far, pretty good luck.

When we reached the ape and the wheel, Passepartout was already there. He had secured a sabre from one of the pirates, and was chopping away at the wheel where it connected to the chains on the ape's wrists.

"Good man," Beadle said.

"I can't stand to see such as this," Passepartout said. "Even if he chooses to kill me, I must set him free."

The ape was very close to Passepartout, and watched the Frenchman at work in a way that could only be described as grateful; unlike most apes, his face was full of human expression. In fact, on close examination, he seemed less apelike than he had appeared from a distance.

There was something different about the shape of his head, the very human eyes (which, later, in better light I saw to be green), the thin lips and the full ears with lobes. He stood more upright, and unlike apes, who have small penises, this guy had a goober that looked like a four-foot switch handle hammer, testicles like grapefruits.

210

I want to add here that I couldn't help but notice. I mean, it was hanging out there for all to see. It's not that I go around checking out other people's or creatures' equipment, but this couldn't help but be noticed. Really. It was big. No shit.

By the time we arrived, Passepartout had chopped away enough of the wheel that the great ape could tug with the chains and cause the wheel to creak and snap, allowing him to pull his hands (paws?) free of it. The chains still dangled from his wrists, and chunks of the wheel dangled from the chains.

While we floated about, keeping a kind of guard, Passepartout went to work on the lower part of the wheel where chains were fastened to the ape's ankles. In short time, he had made swift work of the wood, allowing the ape to jerk those chains free as well.

The ape turned toward the remaining pirates. The chains that were on his ankles were also hooked together, so he could not move swiftly, but he could move quickly enough, in a hopping fashion.

As he hopped, he swung the great chains fastened to his wrists, the chunks of wood fastened to them. He swung them and struck pirates and knocked them about. Shots were fired at the ape, and no doubt at least a couple of them hit him, but it didn't slow him down. He hopped and swung and shattered flesh and bone like a mad wife smashing dinner plates.

I looked up and saw that the pirate captain was hustling up the hill and making good time in spite of his peg leg. I made a barking noise, pointed with my flipper. Mr. Twain saw the Captain's back just before he was enveloped by the lush greenery at the top of the hill.

"It can't be helped," Mr. Twain said, stepping down from the cruiser. "It doesn't matter now. Our business here, bloody as it is, is through. It's not what I had in mind, but after Sitting Bull got the ball rolling, there wasn't much choice."

About that time the gentleman of mention appeared, blood-splattered, a fistful of scalps dangling from his left fist, the machete in his right hand. Cat trotted alongside him, her beautiful, gore-stained black hair wadded up around her head.

Bull gave the blood-covered machete to Mr. Twain, said, "Thank you."

"You're welcome," Mr. Twain said, tossing aside the pirate sabre to take the machete. "I suppose."

"Little dull. But cut fuckers good."

"I'll have it sharpened."

"Bull do it. Get done right."

"Thanks. I'll let you."

Mr. Verne arrived. "It looks as if we have won," he said. "We have killed most of them, and the others have darted into the woods. Who would have thought it?"

"I think Mr. Bull killed about a third of them himself," Mr. Twain said.

"Kill more," Bull said, "but tired. Hungry. Got anything to eat?"

"I'm afraid not," Mr. Verne said. "But perhaps now we can find something."

The ape appeared. The chains made his movements jerky, but he looked happy. The ape said, "Now, that is exactly what I've been waiting for. The precise moment to take my vengeance on these low-grade sea urchins, these coconut heads of the ocean. And I must tell you, I enjoyed every bloodthirsty moment of it. I am invigorated. After being so tired at the wheel, I thought I might drop down and die. Now, I feel as if I could beat the living shit out of twenty more, fuck a hole in a watermelon, and give head to a pack of monkeys."

Our group sat in silence. Me, because I had to, Bull because he preferred to, and Cat because she thought the incident funny. I could tell the remainder of the crowd was shocked that an ape might speak, and that in so doing would have such strange and vulgar language at his command.

I, being a seal who could write and think like a human, and who had experienced many an adventure with beasts who had been transformed into men or women (Cat was an example) and who could talk, was less impressed.

"You would do that?" Mr. Verne asked the ape.

"Do what?"

"You know? With monkeys."

"It's an expression," the ape said. "I really don't have a thing for monkeys. Or watermelons."

"Damn," Mr. Twain said. "A talking monkey."

"I am neither monkey nor ape," corrected the red-furred creature.

212

FLAMING ZEPPELINS

"And the name is Rikwalk."

"That's quite a name," Beadle said.

"Well, it's really very common where I come from."

"And, if I might inquire," Mr. Verne said, "Where is that?"

"Mars," said the ape.

We all stood on the beach considering that. I thought I was beyond surprise, but this did surprise me. We remained hushed and still, listening as it were to the crash of the sea on the shore, the cry of the birds and the loud thudding silence of death.

Sixteen: Ned's Journal:
The Ship Sails Again, the Thing
in the Hold, Rikwalk Gets Pants

"Did you come with the invaders?" Mr. Verne asked.

"Not exactly," Rikwalk said, "but it is a long story."

"I suggest we wait on it," said John, "push the ship to sea. Lest our escaped pirates return, possibly with reinforcements."

"I doubt he had any," Beadle said.

"Still, I have had all of this island I prefer," said John Feather.

"Speak good white man talk," Bull said. "Like me."

"Thank you," John Feather said. "College."

"And like our friend Rikwalk here, I presume you have quite a story yourself," Mr. Verne said, smiling at John Feather.

"Oh," said John Feather, laughing. "You can not imagine. But like Rikwalk's story, Beadle and I will save it for later."

Rikwalk said, "I will pull the ship to sea, and then it is up to the Dutchman here to sail it."

"I can do that," said the Dutchman. "The remainder of my crew will help me, and they will train the rest of you where your assistance is needed. But that will be minimal. It takes few to sail my ship."

"Work for me," Bull said.

Using tools from the ship, Rikwalk was released from the chains, and we all loaded onto the ship, taking what weapons we could scrounge from the remains of the pirates.

The great ape, using the chain attached to the front of the ship, pulled us out to sea.

He had a bit of tough sledding at first, but when he reached the water, and the ship glided in behind him, it went well. He waded until the water was beneath his armpits and we were enough at sea to let the waves carry us out, then he swam back to the ship, scuttled up over the side like, well, like an ape. His weight was such that this maneuver caused the ship to list to that side.

Once on board, once on the ship balanced out nicely. Once it came up, the sails were hoisted. The wind caught in the canvas and took us out quickly.

When I looked back, I saw, sailing above the jungle, a strange colorful creature that looked more reptile than bird, and yet, somewhat birdlike as well. It was our old friend the pterodactyl, or one just like him.

The cruiser had been put up, and I was raised up on my ass, leaning against the rail. I reached over and tugged on Mr. Twain's coat.

He turned for a look, said, "I'll be goddamned."

Mr. Verne and the others looked now.

Bull said. "Firebird. Me hear of it."

The pterodactyl descended into the mist that covered the island, and was gone.

"I would like to know what other beasts dwell there," Mr. Verne said.

"I'm glad we left," said John Feather. "The pirates were beast enough for me."

"I wonder where they came from," Mr. Verne said. "They looked, well, out of time. In fact, this ship, this crew, looks out of time as well."

"They are," Beadle said. "But again, I'll explain what I know later. Each for different reasons. For now, I suggest we get well out to sea, rest a bit, see if the Dutchman has some food, and afterward we can talk."

"Yee haw," Bull said out of nowhere.

Most of the sailing was left to those who knew how to sail. In the battle with the pirates, not a man from the ship had been lost, and each of them knew his business. They scuttled from rope to canvas, and the Dutchman, tall and noble-looking, stood at the wheel. If he didn't know what he was doing, he sure looked as if he knew.

We helped where we could, but after a point, we were more trouble than we were worth. That being the case, a number of us naturally drifted together. Mr. Twain, Mr. Verne, myself, Mr. Beadle, John Feather, Bull and Cat, and the great ape Rikwalk.

Mr. Beadle determined that we all (I dismiss myself from this group) might be a smidgen more comfortable, as he put it, if we could talk Rikwalk into wearing something over his sizeable member.

It is my belief that this had less to do with modesty than with embarrassment. Comparatively, human penises are worms while Rikwalk's member was an anaconda. I read about them in books. They are big snakes, by the way. Real big snakes.

I, who am not particularly endowed, do not go about with my tool poking out except when I mean business, as you might surmise. And I do not wear clothes, unless, for some reason, I feel sporty. I do like my fez, though. I thought it made me look like a seal with an attitude.

However, I must admit, in all honesty, when I was not mentioned as someone who should wear something over myself, I had a flash of insecurity. A sort of, hey, if you want him clothed, what about me? I'm naked as the proverbial jaybird here and no one's concerned.

But I let that go. I reached down inside myself and found that reservoir of strength I knew I had, and pulled it up tight, secure in my manhood and in the necessary size of my equipment.

After all, I am but a little seal, so what should one expect?

Right?

Rikwalk is a giant. Proportionately, there is no real difference.

Well, maybe a little.

Perhaps more than a little.

Still, it's the not the meat, it's the motion.

Right?

That's right, isn't it?

I believe that's right.

I really do.

Anyway, the matter was broached, and Rikwalk took it well. In fact, he seemed to like the idea. Some sailcloth was found, and some rope, and Rikwalk was appropriately tricked out in a large diaper-style adornment. Cat said she didn't see it as an improvement. Bull thought this was very funny.

When Rikwalk was attired, Mr. Beadle said that he had something interesting he wanted to show us in the hold, and that there was a story to go with it, but he thought it might be interesting to have Rikwalk tell us his story first, and upon its completion, he would take us into the interior of the ship, show us what he wished to have us view, then tell us a tale about himself and John Feather.

This all seemed rather exciting (less exciting than our previous experiences, but a sort of excitement you would look forward to), and so we gathered ourselves on the deck near the mainsail, the moon low down and bright, the sail above us beating in the wind like a hummingbird's wings, a cool salt spray blowing across the deck, and we sat, and Rikwalk talked.

Ned's Journal Ends

Part Three:
Heroes Unite

Seventeen: Rikwalk's Story, Beadle's Tale, the Thing in the Hold

Once upon a time, on Rikwalk's world, in Rikwalk's universe, at a specific angle of dimensional division, this happened:

On one of many planets called Mars, where the universe splits sideways and turns cattycorner and anglewise, there was a rip in the sky and things fell out of it.

There were other rips, and into these rips, things fell up, and out of some of the rips, more things fell down.

Ups and downs. Rips this way and that.

Besides the rips, the ups and downs, what was happening was that, like a hand slowly balling up a sheet of paper, the fabrics of times and spaces were being wadded one into the other, and all of existence was soon to be no more than a tight wad of all things known and things unknown. The Wild West, Flying Saucers, Rock and Roll, Super Heroes, all manner of times, yesterdays and tomorrows, real lives and imagined lives, and as the wad grew tighter, these worlds, these things, would cease to exist.

It wasn't a pretty picture, and this is how Rikwalk discovered there was a picture, and that things were coming together and coming apart.

So Rikwalk is living on Mars, you see, and not the Mars that Twain and Verne look up and see. Not the Mars from which the invaders came to ravage the world of Twain and Verne, but another Mars. Not the Mars that is worn out and sandy, near airless and waterless, but a lush Mars, ripe as a nubile virgin in stretch pants. A Mars crisscrossed by canals and greenery and strange animals and shining cities in which lived what to our eyes would appear to be sophisticated giant apes with big dongs.

But there are other Marses. Some with apes. Some without. Some with the invaders. And some without anything but hot, red soil.

These Marses, these universes, these dimensions, it's like there's a train on a track, and under the track is another train, and they're alike and run the same way but inside the train people do different things. Some times the same people, or apes, or insects, or creatures, but these beings are multiplied, taking different paths, unaware of their counterparts, or their differparts. And say alongside the train, if you could slice into its metal skin, slice it real thin, you would find there's another train in there, running parallel with the first train. Each train (each universe) and its contents (think humanity, apeanity, insectimanity, etc.) believes it is the Union Pacific and no other Union Pacifics exist. But if you could hold a special mirror to the top of the train, you would see that, in fact, there's a train on its back, its smokestack meeting the stack of the other, and its wheels turning on a track that is touching ground that should be sky in the other universe.

And don't forget that train on the bottom of the track. Don't forget that. And on the sides, under the skins. Don't forget them. And, understand, that from all these trains are other trains, atop, abottom, and asides.

It's all in the angles, baby. And, from one train's angle, the other angle does not exist, and yet, all angles exist.

Omniscient narrator is getting a headache, baby, so he's gonna back off and say this:

Say on one train operations are as smooth as married sex, but on the other, well, it's more like adolescent boys trying to determine which hole what goes in. And on some trains, they can't even get their pants down, or haven't figured out they ought to wear pants.

Say there's a warp in the track. A bad warp. Call it trouble with the universe. Maybe a black hole caused it. Something we don't understand yet. Time(s) and Space(s), for whatever reason, begin(s) to collapse on itself.

So this train, running on this track, hits the warped stretch and bumps up into the train below. Or maybe the warp throws the train off the tracks, and the train on the bottom, and the one on the top, and the ones on the sides, all come together. Now, finally, they are aware of the other. And it's not a happy awareness.

Rikwalk's Martians called themselves the Mellie and they called their planet Mars.

And so Rikwalk, he's living on his Mars, and things are good. He's got a job operating one of the locks on one of the canals, and it's a good job. He's making good pay, doesn't work hard, gets a little overtime, has a wife he loves, one of the good ones that hasn't stopped giving head after ten years of marriage, and he's got a daughter and a son, two groodies and a zup[1]. And one day he's out at the lock, ready to check the water depth with a dropping gauge, and he hears something that sounds like a runner's tendon ripping from too much tension, looks up, sees a fiery orange-red rip in the sky. At first, he thinks he sees the sun, but it isn't. Not even close. It's a glowing rip to nowhere.

A boat in the lock is suddenly sucked up and through the rip, falls out of sight into orange-redness. The rip widens, and Rikwalk is sucked up, like a dust mote in a vacuum cleaner. Sucked right up toward the glowing rip in the sky.

Rikwalk goes through it, comes down in a place he doesn't know. The boat isn't there, and he doesn't know where in hell it went. Another exit?

Actually, he comes out, not down. Because in spite of going up, coming through the rift, the exit is to the side, sort of, and it has this ripple effect going. Like a heat wave.

Rikwalk falls out, hits the ground, the orange-red rip closes up like a tear in a persimmon pushed together by a cheating fruit salesman.

Now there is just this thin as razor-edge, orange-red line in the air, and when Rikwalk reaches out to touch it, hoping to go back through, to take his chances, try and fall down into the waters of his lock, the line vibrates and tightens like an old maid who's considered the deed then changed her mind.

No more split.

No more glow.

Not even a line, man.

"So you see," said Rikwalk, "the rips came and went at first, and then some of them started staying. You could see holes in the sky, and sudden

---

1   Martian farm animals on Rikwalk's Mars. One gives milk, the other gives eggs. That's all you need to know.

rips in the air right before you. All sorts of people and things came out of them. Some of the stuff I saw made the hair on my ass stand up.

"I decided to look about at first, and for a moment, I thought I was still on my world. But it was a horrible world of the living dead. They walked about. They attacked people."

"Living dead?" Verne said. "What do you mean?"

"Mellie. Apes to you. The dead were rising from their graves and they were trying to kill the living, eat their flesh."

Ned wrote: WOW. FLESH-EATING APES WITH BIG DICKS THAT SPEAK ENGLISH.

"The dead," Rikwalk said, "they are not sweet to smell. And there's no reason I can offer to explain their rising. You died there, you came back. A virus maybe. Caused by the splits in space and time, perhaps. I don't know. But let me address this matter of speaking English. On my world, this language you call English is Mellie. I have no explanation for it being the same language. A few words, expressions are different. But it's mostly the same. Why? Shit, I don't know. It just is. But from a few books I've seen here on board ship — and I'll explain my being on the ship earlier as I come to it — we have a better approach to spelling."

"I think we all get the idea," Beadle said. "Sort of. Just go on with your story."

Rikwalk nodded. Said: "So there I am. Pursued by the living dead, shuffling along, their hands held out, the hair on their faces falling off, their tongues thick and black. And I'm running like a bastard. They're after my ass. Want to eat me. Or kill me and turn me like them. If they don't eat all of you, you get up and you're hungry. And we're not talking wanting a slice of doonbar loaf and two pieces of bread."

"What's a doonbar?" Mr. Twain said. "Is that English?"

"Sorry," Rikwalk said. "That's one of the different words. It's kind of like a turkey. Only not."

"Close enough," Mr. Twain said. "Go on."

"They want Mellie flesh. No cooking. No seasoning. On the hoof, fresh and hot. And when you turn, when you're like them, even if your legs are cut off, you'll crawl after your prey."

"Was everyone on that world dead?" Twain asked.

"No. There were plenty dealing with the problem, same as me. Let me tell you something interesting. After a short time, people went back to work. Like always. They just carried weapons. You see, you could kill them if you burned them or cut off their heads. So people carried big knives. Thing about the dead, they're not very strong and they're not very fast, and smart isn't even a minor factor in the equation. On a smart scale of one to ten, they're not on it... Yes, Ned?"

Ned held up his pad.

THAT'S SCARY.

"Yes, it is, Ned," Rikwalk said. "It's even scarier when they're chasing you."

"But that doesn't explain how you're here," Twain said.

"No. It doesn't. So I'm on this world that isn't my world, but it's similar, and I'm doing the best I can to survive, and the sky, it starts to be marked all over with rips, like lesions. And finally, one day, sick of it all, sick of dodging and fighting, I stepped into one of the rips."

"That shows you have some real plums," Twain said.

"Or that I'm stupid. I could have fallen anywhere. Up, down, sideways. Actually, I did end up anywhere. I stepped through a slit in time, and fortunately, did not fall, just stepped sideways, ended up in Beadle's world."

"Couldn't the dead follow?" Verne asked.

"They did. They followed me in. A few of them. I dispatched them. The wound in the sky closed. True, another wound would open somewhere else, but there was no telling where it would lead. Back to the dead world. My world. Your world. Any world. Shortly thereafter, I met Beadle, John Feather, and Steam."

"Steam?" Passepartout said.

"Perhaps it's best if I let Mr. Beadle take over the story," Rikwalk said. "Then I'll finish, and then we'll all finish with a look in the hold."

"The Dark Rider," Beadle said. "He was the problem."

"With what?" Twain asked. "What kind of problem?"

WHO THE FUCK IS THE DARK RIDER?

"Bad language, little seal," Mr. Verne said.

I'M SORRY. BUT WHO THE FUCK IS THE DARK RIDER?

"The rips in the sky, tears in the universe," John Feather. "You name it, Dark Rider was behind it all. If he wasn't sticking his dick in someone's asshole, he was poking it through time, waving it in space."

"Interesting expressions," Verne said. "Very American sounding. You are American?"

"Where I come from, we are Americans. But I have no idea if the America here is the same."

"Well, you speak American," Twain said. "I should know. I'm American. You cuss like an American. Only Americans truly know how to cuss. Cussing is an art, and not to be used without intent and discrimination. My wife cussed, but bless her soul, so poorly it was hardly worth hearing. It requires true training and timing to cuss properly."

"You and Verne exist in our world," Beadle said. "I thought I should mention that."

"Really?" Twain said.

"Yes. You write books."

"Same alike here," Twain said. "But I must apologize. You were talking about this Dark Rider fella."

"We don't know much about him. But not long ago, we went back to where we battled him. Went back after we recovered and repaired Steam, and we found his diary. You see, we defeated him. It's a long story and I don't want go into it, but we did. We left the scene of the battle, recovered, went back and found the diary."

"Again," Twain said, "sorry to interrupt, but who is Steam?"

"I'm coming to that," Beadle said. "As I said, I won't tell you the whole of mine and John's story.[2] But I'll tell you some. I'll give you some background. I'll link to Rikwalk's tale. The world Rikwalk came into was as chaotic as the world of the dead. Maybe more so. On our world, time and space were ripping and collapsing at an alarming rate. Maybe it's like that on a lot of other worlds, but this one, strange as it is to me, is nothing like what our world became. There are fewer rips. Less collapsing.

"Me and John Feather were part of an organization. I formed it. There was me and John, two others. You need not know them, know all the past. But we were trying to set wrongs right. When our world started coming apart, all manner of things came through the rips, and

---

2   Beadle's world and his and John Feather's adventures and greater background for his story are provided in the dime novel, *The Steam Man of the Prairie and the Dark Rider Get Down* by Joe R. Lansdale. Another version of this story, based on Ned the Seal's translation of a more detailed story told to him later by Beadle, is available in some rare book collections as *The Steam Man of the Prairie and the Incredible Vampire Traveler from Beyond*. The Lansdale version is more readily available.

we decided to use our man of steam to correct them."

"A steam man," Twain said. "We have dime novels about such things. Steam horses. Steam this and steam that. Jules here, who is far better than a dime novelist, has written about such. I have been in such a machine. A boat designed by Jules, built by Passepartout. It ran at extraordinary speeds. It also came apart."

Ned wrote furiously. THERE IS NOTHING WRONG WITH DIME NOVELS. I LIKE DIME NOVELS. I SELDOM THINK OF FISH WHEN I'M READING A DIME NOVEL. WHEN I READ FLAUBERT, I THINK OF FISH A LOT. I LIKE MR. TWAIN'S AND MR. VERNE'S NOVELS. I DON'T THINK ABOUT FISH WHEN I READ THEM.

"Point taken," Twain said. "And thanks for the compliment."

"Yes, Ned," Verne said. "Thank you."

"Sorry, Beadle," Twain said. "Done it again. Please go ahead. You were saying about correcting the bad things on your world with the use of the steam man."

Beadle nodded.

"Steam was a big metal man. He didn't have brains. Didn't have a heart. Didn't have courage. He was a machine. Built forty feet tall, not counting his conical hat. He was twenty feet wide and tin-colored. Powered by steam. Puffed steam when he walked. He was strong. He could tear trees up by the roots, toss big boulders, wade furious streams. You see, we were his heart, brains and courage, me and John Feather, our two friends. It saddens me so much to think of them I can hardly speak of it. It was the Dark Rider who killed them."

"The Dark Rider was our nemesis," John Feather said.

Beadle nodded. "I believe he is responsible for the rifts in our world, and for that matter, all the worlds. Time travel was not meant to be. It makes holes in the fabric of time, makes it look like Swiss cheese."

Ned wrote: THAT'S CHEESE WITH HOLES IN IT. I LIKE CHEESE. NOT AS MUCH AS FISH, BUT IT GOES WELL WITH FISH. DO YOU HAVE ANY CHEESE OR FISH? I ENJOY A STORY BEST ON A FULL STOMACH. I HAVE EVEN BEEN KNOWN TO EAT OLIVES.

Everyone present admitted they had neither fish nor cheese nor olives.

VERY WELL. BUT, IF YOU THINK OF ANYTHING YOU MIGHT HAVE THAT A SEAL WOULD EAT, AND IN MY CASE THAT'S QUITE

VARIED, PLEASE SPEAK UP. REALLY.

Beadle went on with his story.

"We fought this horrible man who traveled through time, and we defeated him, forcing him through a rip in time, where we hope he will forever be trapped. When it was over, we got out of there. Meaning the place where we had been tortured and the both of us nearly died, this place where the Time Traveler had been holed up with a group of monster men called Morlocks. We went away from there and licked our wounds and repaired Steam, and when me and John were strong again, we went back.

"The Time Traveler was dead, or lost, out of the way, and we had suffered great indignities at his hands, and at the hands of his Morlocks, but still, we went back."

"Couldn't help ourselves," John Feather said.

"Couldn't," Beadle said. "We went back to maybe see if he had somehow survived. But the rip, it was closed up, and there was no sign of him. But in the rubble of what had been his hideout —"

"— it was rubble because Steam destroyed it," John Feather said. "With me at the controls."

"Yee haw," Bull said.

"That's right," Beadle said. "Yee haw. We found what was left of the time machine in the rubble, and we dug it out and pulverized it. We found the diary.

"From the way it read, he had once been whole. His mind good, but the time travel, the things that happened to him, they changed him."

"He turned evil as an old boll weevil," John Feather said.

"That's right," Beadle said. "And all that time traveling, bringing the Morlocks through time, it punched holes in the fabric of things. Anyway, there we were, with the diary, looking through the rubble, and we decided to leave, and the world tore open."

"The bottom fell out," John Feather said.

"And we dropped through," Beadle said. "Splashed in the ocean. But we were lucky. We were near the shore and Steam landed on his feet. The water was up to his neck, but his feet were on the bottom. The water didn't get in. He was built airtight and we had done a lot of repairs. The fire didn't go out. We were able to walk him toward shore."

"This is where I must butt in," Rikwalk said. "Somehow, I came through the same rip with them. Or right behind them. I was on their world already, and I remember seeing the man of steam from a distance. I didn't want to get close, not knowing them. And I saw them go through the rift, and I thought, shit, bad luck for them. And then the rip widened. And I started to run, but it widened faster than I could run, so I was sucked in too. I fell in the ocean, swam toward shore. I saw the steam man ahead of me. Beadle and John Feather were inside Steam, though, of course I did not know that, nor did I know them at the time. Steam was walking onto the shore, moving toward the curtain of mist. That catches my story up for now. Please, Mr. Beadle, Mr. Feather. Continue."

"But then luck turned on us," John Feather said.

"Seems to be the story of our lives," Beadle said. "Turning luck, mostly turning for the bad. There were pirates on the shore. You know the boys. You've met them. They quickly surrounded Steam, and using ropes, they were able to take him down. You see, we had used what steam he had left to fight the current and make shore. He just didn't have the strength. And they got Rikwalk."

"They saw me swimming," Rikwalk said, "and it was a battle, that current, and when I came onto the shore I was so weak I couldn't stand. I crawled, gasping for air. They pounced on me like fleas. If I had had my full strength, I would have killed them all. But like Steam, I had used all my reserves. They chained me. They fastened me to the wheel. And then they whipped me. I really didn't have a choice but to help them."

"We were all in a weak condition," Beadle said. "And for the most part, John and I were already weakened. Our battle with the Dark Rider. The torture. Our world coming apart. We were quite the mess. Then Steam playing out. We were at the pirates' mercy."

"I suppose the pirates arrived out of time and space from some other place, through a rip in time," Mr. Verne said.

Beadle nodded. "So I believe. They made slaves of us for a week. They had us bury gold, they made us help them make their grog. My guess is after they had enough barrels of grog for their ship, we would have been disposed of. Lucky for us, they drank what we made as fast as we made it."

"That was lucky," John Feather said.

"What about the Dutchman?" Passepartout said.

"He came the next day. The pirates spotted the ship, and took it over.

Some of the Dutchman's men were killed. The ship was grounded on the reef. It wasn't until today that the pirates worked it off, beached it, and then had Rikwalk drag it ashore."

HOW DID BULL AND CAT GET ON THE SHIP? I THOUGHT YOU WERE EATEN BY SHARKS WHEN THE *NAUGHTY LASS* BLEW UP.³ I DO NOT LIKE SHARKS.

Ned turned his sign toward Bull. Bull, though he seldom gave sign of it, could read basic English well. He said:

"Not eaten. *Naughty Lass* sink. Real shit time. Go down faster than white whore in buffalo camp. We get away. Boat pick up. Kill two pirates before get hit in head. Get even with their asses."

"I'll say," Twain said.

The Dutchman suddenly appeared. A sailor had taken his place at the wheel. "I couldn't help but overhear," the Dutchman said. "I believe that I fit into the story about here. When we saw the pirates, knew we could not outrun them, and that we would be engaged, we pushed Cat's hair under a big hat. I gave her a large shirt to pull over the one she wore, to hide her attributes. When we were ashore, we stayed as close to her as we could manage, trying not to allow too much scrutiny of her body. But you can only hide a figure like that for so long. I think the pirates were starting to think she might be a boy they could learn to love, and then, as fate would have it, the wind blew her hat off. They pulled up the long shirt, looked at her rear, looked down her pants. I'm surprised she was not raped."

"Actually," Beadle said, "the pirate captain saved her. He didn't give a reason, but he had the men leave her alone. I believe he thought to have her for himself later on."

"Now he has an island full of monsters to call his very own," Verne said.

"What happened to Steam?" Twain said.

"They robbed what they could find inside Steam," Beadle said. "They stuck him in the hold of the Dutchman's ship. I don't know why. Maybe they thought to dismantle him. Sell off the metal. Melt it down. I don't know. It took all of the pirates and us as well to drag him over the side, and push him down into the hold. They weren't easy with him, and he may be damaged down there."

"So that's what you wanted us to see in the hold?" Twain said.

"Yes," Beadle said.

Twain and Verne, taking turns, with the occasional comment from Passepartout and sign writing from Ned, told their story, about the Martian invaders, how they had come to the island.

Rikwalk said, "I would like to, on behalf of the Mars from whence I come, apologize for these other Martians. They give us a bad name."

"Apology accepted," Twain said. "But I'm still curious about why you speak English."

"I'm afraid I can't shed light on that," Rikwalk said. "I have ideas, but nothing concrete."

"Shall we take that look in the hold now?" Beadle said. "I'm curious to see how Steam weathered his drop down the chute."

"I'll conduct that tour," the Dutchman said. "After all, it is my ship."

They followed the Dutchman to a pair of closed doors positioned and bolted shut in the floor of the deck. Beadle unbolted and opened them. There were stairs. They went down with the Dutchman in the lead.

The Dutchman lit a lantern hanging on a peg, and in the middle of the hold's floor they saw an amazing sight.

A giant metal man with a conical hat, like a funnel turned upside down.

"Steam," Beadle said. "If not in the flesh. In the metal."

And so it was.

Big.

Tall.

Silver.

Stained-glass windows for eyes.

Steam.

Eighteen: At Sea, the White Cliffs of Dover, the Invaders Seen from Afar

The morning arrived clear and crisp. The sea was calm and the wind was smooth. The sailing ship moved swiftly. Flying fish glided, porpoises leaped. A cool wind was not only in the sails, it was in the faces of its crew and passengers.

Ned, his nose hanging over the rail, wet with spray, full of the smell of salt, was in heaven.

Twain, Verne, Ned, Passepartout, John Feather and Beadle had joined the Dutchman, the ship's captain, on the foredeck. They stood there while the Dutchman maintained the wheel, observed sky, sea and sails.

Rikwalk was seated down below, but his head almost reached the wheel deck. His red fur was crusted in places with salt. And in the bright morning light, wounds could be seen. Someone, the Dutchman perhaps, had treated them with black grease to keep out infection and dirt.

While they talked, Twain and the Dutchman smoked long black cigars.

Twain said, "Does anyone know where we are? I suppose we are not sailing at random."

"The Island of Mist, as the pirates called it," the Dutchman said, "was off the southwest coast of Africa. So, we are moving north along the coast of Africa."

"My God," Twain said. "The balloon sailed that far?"

"It must have," the Dutchman said, "because that's where you were. And along the coast of Africa is where you are now."

"How amazing," Verne said. "And even more amazing, I saw an actual flying dinosaur."

"So it seems," the Dutchman said. "It is said, that in the depths of the

Congo there are dinosaurs, and even an ape near the size of our hairy red friend. I do not know that it is true, but it is said. And if there are such things on the Island of Mist, I suppose it's possible."

"And where do you sail?" Rikwalk asked.

"I am at your disposal. As for me, it matters not where I sail. I am to suffer ill fate. Storms and pirates. But I never die and the ship never sinks. And I always end up back at sea. No matter how often I dock, fate always leads me back to the ship and to the open sea. I am cursed."

"My God," Twain said. "You're not that Dutchman, are you?"

"I am."

"The Flying Dutchman?" Verne said.

"The one and only. That's what the ship is called. It is written in German, my ancestry, on the side of the ship. I am not Dutch at all. But like many Germans, I am lumped under the label."

The term Flying Dutchman didn't register with Rikwalk, so they filled him in. They often had to stop and fill him in. He was, after all, a Martian. An English-speaking Martian, but a Martian.

"But I thought you couldn't stop sailing at all," Passepartout said. "Isn't that the legend?"

"There are many legends," the Dutchman said, "but I am not a legend. I am sadly real. I can stop, and because I can, I thought at first there was no curse, that the witch had failed. I was wrong. First time I stopped and went ashore, I was shanghaied, hit in the head and tossed on my own ship, which was stolen. I eventually wrested it from the thieves, but I was wounded horribly. I survived, and I was still at sea. One day the sky opened up in front of me, and my crew and I sailed through a rift. It was not a dramatic event. We merely seemed to glide through a red rip in the sky, onto other waters that looked to be the same as the ocean we had been on moments before. I thought it was an optical illusion. Like a mirage. It was just another in a long line of events and disasters. I was in another time and place. This place. Then there were the pirates. I no longer fight my fate. There is no use."

Ned wrote:

THAT'S TOUGH. THAT EATS THE BIG OLD FAT DONKEY DICK BUNCHES.

"You can say that again, Ned," the Dutchman said. "I was cursed by a witch because I seduced her daughter. You want to know something?

It wasn't worth it. She wasn't that good, and she wasn't that clean. Even pussy isn't worth this."

Twain, Verne, Passepartout, Beadle, and Ned paused to consider this. No one agreed nor disagreed. It was like a Catholic cursing the Madonna. That kind of criticism was not taken lightly. Even in the face of indisputable evidence, men find it hard to turn against pussy, so silence ruled. Ned did not write.

Verne cleared his throat. "So can you sail us to Europe?"

"If that's what you want," the Dutchman said. "But why would you want to if it's covered with those Martian machines?"

"Because we should do something," Verne said. "And because they are bound to be all over the world. My guess is you will face them yourself eventually, and I am warning you, they are formidable."

"Most likely I will face them," The Dutchman said. "And I will struggle against them. And I must ask myself again and again why I even struggle. No matter how it ends, I will be at sail again. I can not die. The ship can be damaged, but never destroyed. I have even tried to kill myself. Tried to cut my own throat. I suffered a horrible wound. It healed. I have been wounded many other times in many different ways. But no matter how violent the wounds, in time they heal, and I live. And I continue."

WHY DON'T YOU JUST SET FIRE TO THE SHIP AND BURN IT UP AND YOU WON'T HAVE TO SAIL IN IT ANYMORE?

The Dutchman was quiet for a time. "I hadn't thought of that, Ned... But then again, a wind would probably just blow the fire out... But I could try it."

WHEN WE ARE OFF THE SHIP. RIGHT?

The Dutchman did not answer. He seemed lost in thought.

"You can really just drop us off most anywhere," Twain said.

They sailed on, though they slept nervously for a few nights and sniffed for smoke. Ned did a lot of apologizing, but after a couple days they decided that the Dutchman was not going to set fire to his ship, least not while they were aboard.

They hoped.

Several days more and they could see the English shoreline. The land stood out high and white in the sunlight.

"The White Cliffs of Dover," Verne said.

"Correct," the Dutchman said.

They were at the wheel with the Dutchman again, Verne, Twain, Ned and Passepartout. Rikwalk lay on the deck, his head cradled on his arm, sleeping. Beadle and John Feather were in the hold, finishing up repairs on Steam. Bull and Cat were below as well. They were below a lot. They were not making repairs on anything. Bull explained it once this way: "Hair pie."

"I decided to bring you here, to these shores," the Dutchman said, "because I thought if the Martian machines land here, or in America, they have a better chance of being defeated by the English or the Americans than anyone else."

"You are saying the French can not defeat these machines?" Verne said. His and Passepartout's faces scrunched with irritation.

"I am saying, if the machines want a croissant or a bottle of perfume, France is the place to be. If they want a fight, England or America or Japan is the place to be."

"I take offense to those remarks," Verne said.

"I really don't worry about who I offend or don't," the Dutchman said. "I live forever, unfortunately. I go on and on, and no matter what is done to me, I live. Stab me. Shoot me. I will endure."

"I have no interest in any such solution to an insult," Verne said. "Though I doubt you would endure a shot to the head."

"It was not meant to insult you, Mr. Verne, or you, Passepartout. But I no longer worry about insults. It was a statement of what I believe to be fact. And though I believe in the individual Frenchman's bravery, and you have demonstrated your own, as a country, when it comes to war, you lack a certain something. Perhaps you are too individual."

"That is one way of saying it," Verne said. "But I am not sure I like that better."

SEALS ARE SURPRISINGLY TOUGH, Ned wrote: WE ARE NOT FRENCH.

"I have no comment on the general toughness of seals," the Dutchman said, "but on an individual level, you, my friend, are a tough little seal. And smart as well. I am giving your idea serious consideration. About the fire, I mean."

Ned made a facial expression that might have been a grin.

"I don't even like croissants," Verne said.

"Don't lie," Twain said. "I've seen you eat them."

"I've eaten them, but that doesn't mean I like them. I tasted them. I didn't swallow."

"I like them," Passepartout said. "And I refuse to feel shame for myself. Or the great country of France."

Ned wrote: I AGREE. FRENCHMEN, ENGLISHMEN, AMERICANS. WE ARE ALL THE SAME. EXCEPT ME. I'M DIFFERENT. DO THE FRENCH LIKE FISH?

"Well, yes," Passepartout said.

THE FRENCH ARE A-OKAY BY ME... WHAT KIND OF FISH?

"Most any kind," Passepartout said.

ARE YOU SURE YOU ARE NOT A SEAL?

Passepartout laughed, then the others joined in.

Ned, proud of himself, made with the strange seal grin again.

They sailed along the English Channel, and from the sea they could see black smoke, and even once, in the distance, what they thought might be one of the great Martian stalking machines.

"I suggest we sail up the channel a bit, find an appropriate place to go ashore," the Dutchman said. "But, if I were you, I would stay with me, take to the sea. Forget the idea of fighting these machines."

"Unlike you," Verne said, "we are willing to take our chances trying to do some good here. And sir, if I may bring it up again, for someone who maligns the French, and for someone who can not die, you seem determined to stay away from the fight."

"I find little purpose in much of anything," the Dutchman said.

"That is sad," Verne said. "Very sad."

"Have it as you wish," the Dutchman said. "You, Mr. Twain, I could let them off here, sail you to America."

"I would like that," Twain said. "But I assume America is dealing with these same machines. If I'm going to try and do something, it might as well be here."

"But what can you do?" the Dutchman said.

"You have been a pessimist too long," Twain said. "I am not alone. I have my friends. Ned, Passepartout and Verne. And new friends as well, Beadle and John Feather, Bull and Cat.

"Bull and Cat not leave ship."

It was Bull. He was coming up the steps that led to the wheel deck. Cat was with him.

"You're staying?" the Dutchman said.

"Me stay. Cat stay. We like ship. Stop get supplies. Go back to sea. Help sail boat."

"The Martians, they will come to sea eventually," Verne said.

"Bad things always come. Always find. Men from rock in sky come, me and Cat fight. But now, we sail. Like life. On land, always cocksucker want trouble. Bull tired of trouble. Like big boat. Help out. Learn chess from Dutchman. Hump Cat. Good life."

"Me-ow," Cat said.

"Well then," Twain said, "we wish you luck, friends."

Bull stuck out his hand and took Twain's. "Bull and Cat wish friends luck. Bull miss Ned much. Ned is brave."

"And sweet," Cat said, giving Ned a kiss on the nose.

The little seal stuck out his chest.

"Much luck," Bull said. "You need it."

There was a hiss from below, and out of the open hold came a puff of steam followed by a shiny point of silver metal. Then Steam's head, his multi-colored, stained-glass eyes appeared.

Steam climbed out of the hold and in a moment was on deck, walking slowly toward them. It was disconcerting. Steam was a great tall man of metal, but there was something about him that made him seem like a living thing. When he walked, his body moved the way a human's does. It turned its head in an inquisitive manner, like a man looking for a certain street. It was hard to believe there were men at the controls.

Steam stopped, stood still. A trap in his bottom opened up, a ladder poked out, and down it came Beadle and John Feather.

"He works fine," Beadle said as he climbed up on the wheel deck.

"We used some of the wood down there," John Feather said. "I am sorry we did not ask. We actually broke off a few cabinet doors and put them in the furnace. We can only offer our apologies. We should have asked. But then again, we are desperate, sir."

"Apology accepted," the Dutchman said. "But had you asked, and had I said no, would you have done it anyway?"

"I suppose we would have," Beadle said. "We feel that we must. We want to go ashore, help our friends here deal with the Martian machines. And we want to find our way home. Such as it is."

John Feather said, "We're not so sure we have a home anymore. Our world was in bad shape. But if we could study the diary of the Time Traveler in greater detail, perhaps with the help of scientists, or science-minded people, we could figure out what is happening to the universe. If our theory that Time Travel is causing rips in time and space is true, perhaps we could find a cure, so to speak."

"I know people who might help us," Verne said. "A number of them. I am no slouch in scientific matters myself, and Passepartout, my butler, is more than a butler. He is a genius."

"Why, thank you, monsieur," Passepartout said.

"It is only the truth," Verne said. "Passepartout here is the author of many an invention."

"The boat fell apart," Twain said. "The balloon was designed poorly."

"There were flaws," Passepartout said. "But they did work. Had I had more time, more experimentation, those problems would not have occurred."

Ned began writing.

THERE ARE SCIENTISTS IN AMERICA WHO FIXED IT SO BUFFALO BILL COULD LIVE ONLY AS A HEAD IN A JAR. THEY ARE SMART. I REMEMBER SOME NAMES. MORSE. PROFESSOR MAXXON.

Beadle nodded. "We may need them as well. But for now, we have Steam, and we have a new mission. John Feather and I, we are soldiers of a sort, and we are at our best when battling for the common good. So we look forward to being put ashore."

"These Martians," Twain said. "They have the machines, but they also have a kind of...what would you call it, Verne?"

"Ray," Verne said. "A beam of light that destroys."

"The machines are fast, and they are strong," Passepartout said. "So my friends, you will be in for a fight."

"We're ready," John Feather said. "We've no place to go back to, really. No way to get back if we could. Our friends are dead. We have new friends here. We are ready to do what we can. Besides, you saved our lives. We owe you."

"I intend to prove that Frenchmen are as brave as anyone on the face of the earth," Verne said.

"Oui, Oui," Passepartout said.

Ned wrote:

I HAVE SEEN THE MARTIANS. I SAW THEM THROUGH THE GLASS IN FRONT OF THEIR MACHINES. THEY LOOK LIKE AN OCTOPUS. I SAW A DEAD ONE. HE HAD TWO ASSHOLES.

"That's true," Twain said. "Very much so."

Ned wrote some more.

WE WOULD BE JUST LIKE IN THE DIME NOVELS. PALS, WORKING TOGETHER TO DESTROY THE BAD GUYS. THE BAD OCTOPUSSES. OCTOPUSSY. OCTOPIE. YOU KNOW WHAT I MEAN.

"We do," John Feather said.

Ned wrote again.

YOU KNOW, I MIGHT COULD EAT A MARTIAN. I LIKE OCTOPUS.

"I think I'd let that one go," Verne said. "You don't know where they've been."

"Mars," Twain said.

"Yes," Verne said, "but where on Mars? They could have some very vulgar habits, you know. They could live up an animal's ass or roll in shit or eat it by the pound. We don't know a thing about them."

"You don't know anything about Martians," Twain said. "They could be very clean."

Rikwalk appeared, rubbing his eyes.

"Sorry," he said, "all that work at the booze wheel has exhausted me."

"That's all right," Twain said. "I've been thinking about you speaking English, trying to come up with a reason. But all it does is make my head hurt."

"I believe that at one point in time, explorers from Earth were on Mars," Verne said. "Perhaps when Mars was in its infancy. I have even thought that apes from Earth may have come with the earthlings. For experimentation, I'm afraid. The apes were perhaps advanced, maybe even modified to speak. They learned English. Perhaps they mated with an indigenous Martian species, and you, my friend, are the results."

238

Rikwalk nodded. "I suppose that is possible. The Earth we know is an empty world. Dried up and burned up by the heat of the sun. Our scientists have suggested a collapsed ozone layer, but no one knows. There is a theory that apes came from manlike beings, or that their genetics were somehow entwined with ours, but again, no one knows this for a fact. Man, on our world, does not exist. Just their bones. We, of course, have people who have studied this extensively, as well as our language, and at some point in time, it just occurs as if we came into existence. And, though there is evidence of man, it has long been assumed that he was our inferior ancestor. From the reconstructions I've seen in museums, you beings look much like those reconstructions. Though there are some differences."

"Like what?" Twain asked.

"We had no idea that you were...mostly hairless. We assumed that you had a mild coat of hair."

"What I would like to know is why our Martians have invaded our Earth?" Passepartout said.

"The reason all invaders invade," Twain said. "Greed."

"Perhaps their world is dying," Verne said.

"White Man kill Indian 'cause him want land," Bull said. "Him fuck up land. Shit-eating white bastards."

"I do not think he means you," Cat said.

"After what I saw him do with that knife to those pirates," Twain said, "I certainly hope not."

Bull made a grunting noise. It could have meant anything.

"I believe," the Dutchman said, "we are coming to a good place to set ashore. I'm going to need all hands, including passengers, to help. So, all hands alive."

Nineteen: On Shore, a Hunt for Fuel, Separated, Horrible Events

There were great white birds everywhere, and they screamed at the sky and soared above the sails. A black bird, perhaps a crow, appeared, fluttered and landed atop the center mast.

"Not a good sign," Twain said.

He and Verne were working at pulling ropes, lowering a sail to the command of one of the Dutchman's mates.

"On this ship," Verne said, "I would assume that bad signs are consistent, considering the captain and his crew are doomed."

"Question is," Twain said, "does his curse extend to us? Are we now part of his crew?"

"I hadn't thought of that," Verne said. "I hope that if there was a curse, it applies only to those who were with the Dutchman's ship at the time he seduced this witch's daughter. And could be the Dutchman is no more doomed or cursed than you or I, except in his mind."

"Could be," Twain said. "But I'll be glad to leave this ship, nonetheless."

The ship edged toward shore, and when they were some distance out, a great rope was attached to the bow of the ship, and Rikwalk dropped over the side, grabbing the rope, first swimming, finally wading toward shore, pulling the great ship forward. His strength was remarkable, like that of an elephant.

Twain and Verne watched this event. Twain said, "I'm glad he's on our side."

Rikwalk pulled the ship to shore. Those who wished to disembark did so. In the cruiser came Verne, Twain, Ned, Passepartout. The cruiser floated over the side of the ship, dropping down, blowing over the water near the shore, and finally onto land itself.

Beadle and John Feather disembarked inside of Steam.

Steam, puffing and wheezing, strode down the gangplank. He walked through the shallows and onto the shore, stood there in the sunlight, shiny as a fresh minted coin, a coil of steam slowly vaporizing around his head.

Bull and Cat waved to those on the shore from the ship.

"Keep powder dry," Bull called, placing his arm around Cat.

"You too, my friend," Passepartout called.

Inside Steam, Beadle and John Feather caused the metal man's arm to lift, and with a creaking noise, wave good-bye.

The Dutchman called out, "Good luck, friends. And now, if you would be so kind, Rikwalk."

Rikwalk took hold of the rope and pulled, tugging the bow of the ship around. He pulled the ship out to sea. When it was as deep as he could go, when the water was up to his armpits, he let go of the rope, swam behind the ship and pushed. When the ship was moving comfortably on its own, Rikwalk swam back to shore, shook himself and joined the others, stood beside Steam. He was almost as tall as Steam, but the metal man's conical hat stood ten feet higher than Rikwalk's head.

Rikwalk leaned forward and pressed his face against the stained-glass eyes. That way he could look inside, see Beadle and John Feather at the controls. They waved at him, said, "Pee-Pie," as he moved his face away.

John Feather turned to Beadle, said, "Man, that was some creepy shit. A big ape eye looking in on us."

"I'm glad he's on our side," Beadle said.

As they watched the ship sail away, the sky turned dark and split wide open, making a tall, wide, purple wound. And before you could say, Holy Shit! Look out, goddamnit! the Dutchman's ship sailed through the crack in the sky and out of sight, as if falling off the face of the world.

The split did not widen.

And it did not close.

"It's worsening," Beadle said from inside Steam. "This world will soon be like ours."

"Bless them," John Feather said.

After watching for a long time in astonishment, the split did close. Slowly, as if curtains were being pulled together.

The gang was torn up about it, but knew there was nothing they could do. After a few words of complaint, a cry of lament, they decided to get on with things.

"We don't know that where they went is bad," said Twain.

"That's true," said Verne. "They could be anywhere."

"But it could be bad," Passepartout said.

"Yes," Verne said. "It could."

Ned, though distraught at what might be happening to his friends, Bull and Cat, bucked up and took a dip in the ocean to dampen himself, as well as nab a couple of fat fish. When he was finished with that, they started on their journey.

It was suggested by Beadle, and decided by the group, that everyone, with the obvious exception of Rikwalk, would ride inside of Steam. It was not a gentle ride. Beadle and John Feather sat in spring-loaded seats and worked the controls, and when Steam stepped, the whole machine jostled. There were a couple of hammock-style seats in the machine, and Ned claimed one of them immediately. The other was tossed for. Twain won the toss. Verne and Passepartout made do with sitting on the floor near the controls.

Though being cautious was wise, and back roads were taken, hiding something the size of Rikwalk and Steam didn't seem likely. But neither did it seem smart to abandon such a machine, and, of course, there was no thought of abandoning a friend like Rikwalk.

As Steam strode along, Rikwalk walking beside the great machine, they could see that the road was littered with the bodies of both humans and animals, horsedrawn transportation lay wrecked all about.

Inside Steam, Twain said, "I'm all for a fight. I want to fight. We have to fight. But maybe walking right into their midst isn't such a good idea. And now that I think about it, I really don't want to fight that bad."

Ned wrote: WE CAN HIDE OUT LIKE RATS IN THE COUNTRYSIDE. THAT MIGHT BE A GOOD IDEA.

"You're right," Verne said. "We can't act like rats. We're men."

NO. I WASN'T KIDDING. I MEANT IT. LET'S HIDE LIKE RATS. AND I'M A SEAL.

"What I am thinking," Verne said, "is we make it to London, try and find Herbert. He is a smart man, and has access to a lot of scientific equipment. Perhaps together, and with the aid of all who are present, we can come to some conclusion as to how these invaders can be defeated."

"Who's Herbert?" Beadle asked.

"Herbert Wells," Verne said. "H. G. Wells. The writer and scientist. A good friend of mine."

"I'll be damned," Beadle said.

"What?" Verne asked.

"Well," Beadle said. "He's a writer on our world as well. But not a scientist.

"And I don't know if you and Samuel know one another on our world. Or even if you know Mr. Wells. In fact, I think the timing is a little off. I'm not sure. I'm no expert on such things. But there is much overlap between your world and ours. We too have invaders. Saucer machines. They came through the rips. They're just one of many problems. I'm afraid it may be too late for our world; too many rips, too many invaders. But if we can't get back to our home, can't save it, perhaps we can save this world."

Ned wrote: YOU TALK A LOT LIKE A DIME NOVEL.

Beadle grinned. "If you say so."

"We are going to have to find fuel soon," John Feather said. "And I suggest after we make a bit of mileage, we stop for the day, hide out, and travel by night. We're less likely to be discovered that way."

"I agree," Verne said.

The others chimed in in agreement.

Ned made a noise that sounded somewhere between a burp and bark. Later, lying there in the hammock, he tried to squeeze out a silent fart, but didn't make it. It burst out like a foghorn blast.

Ned wrote: EXCUSE ME.

They went on for many miles, fanning Ned's fart, trekking down a back road, and finally they came to a forested area. Light was seeping out of the day like water running through fingers. They walked Steam off the road, inside a grove of trees, geared him down. They got out and went looking for wood to stoke the furnace.

"We'll need a good supply," Beadle said. "It's a long trek, it takes a lot to maintain steam power. Night is falling, so we must hurry. And for a time it is nice to be free of the gas in the machine."

Ned wrote:

I'M SORRY. I SAID I WAS SORRY. WHAT MORE CAN I DO?

They split into wood search groups.

It was decided that Rikwalk, the strongest, was to stay and protect Steam, and to serve as a lookout.

Rikwalk pulled up a small tree, beat the dirt out of the roots, peeled off limbs with his bare hands, made a club of it. Then, with the club across his knees, he sat with his back to a great oak and waited, lost in his thoughts, spinning out happy scenarios of home, his job, his wife.

"Are you all right, Rikwalk?" Beadle asked.

"I am as good as I can be. At least I am among friends. But I think of home. My family. My job. My life. I miss it. I wonder if I will ever return to it. I'm not even on a version of my own world, but another world. You are at least on your own world."

"Not exactly," Beadle said. "In many ways, it's just as alien here for me and John Feather as it is for you. Buck up as best you can, my friend."

Beadle left Rikwalk, and joined John Feather. Verne and Passepartout formed a team as well. The gathering commenced.

Twain decided that he would start a pile, gather good dead wood and then have Steam and Rikwalk come into the forest to get it. The way the trees grew, there was path enough for the big machine and the great ape, and it beat hauling the wood back in shifts.

Ned, dismounted from the cruiser, could only carry a few sticks in his mouth at a time, so it was a tedious process, him wriggling about. But Twain couldn't help but admire the dauntless seal's efforts. He knew the debris of the forest floor had to hurt Ned's belly, but the seal did not complain.

As they searched for dead wood, without realizing it, Twain and Ned ventured some distance from the others and from the pile Twain had made. Just as Twain was about to turn back with his armload of wood, he noted that the woods had thinned, and a farmhouse and barn could be seen, surrounded by a rock fence. Twain said, "I don't know about you, Ned, but I'm so hungry I could eat shit and call it gravy."

Ned wrote: I DON'T WANT SHIT TO CALL GRAVY, BUT I COULD EAT SOME FISH. I COULD EAT MOST ANYTHING. EXCEPT SHIT.

"I believe you're taking me a bit too literally."

I WOULD REALLY HAVE TO BE HUNGRY TO EAT SHIT. GODDAMN HUNGRY. I'M PRETTY HUNGRY NOW, BUT NOT GODDAMN HUNGRY. I DO NOT WANT SHIT.

"Got you. No shit."

Twain dropped the wood. "If we can find someone here, someone who will help us, supply food for our journey, it could be just as valuable, maybe more valuable than the wood. Let's have a look around, Ned."

Ned clapped his flippers together and barked.

They trekked back to where they had left the cruiser, and mounted up. From the woods to the farmhouse was a short trip by cruiser. Upon nearing it, they were shocked to discover that a portion of the house and the stone wall had been blown away.

"The machines, they've been here," Twain said. "We should look for survivors."

They left the cruiser outside, went inside the house and looked.

Nothing.

They used the cruiser to check the grounds and the barn. No one.

"Perhaps they got away."

Ned wrote: OR GOT ALL MELTED. DON'T SEE ANY CHICKENS EITHER. HOGS. WHAT HAVE YOU.

"Ah," Twain said. "A dead horse."

Sure enough, behind a hedge row lay a horse, bloated, dead and stinky.

"I suppose we could have some horse meat, but I don't know, it looks a little —"

Ned was writing:

RANK AS THE ASS END OF A WALRUS. I'M NOT EATING THAT.

"Have no fear, Ned. We will only eat fresh horse."

I COULD EAT A DOG.

"Hopefully it won't come to that."

OR A CAT. IF IT IS COOKED RIGHT.

Back in the house they found a bag of flour and a bag of sugar. There were some dried meats and some canned goods, but little else. When

245

Twain opened a cabinet, he leaped back. A body tumbled out.

It was a little girl, about six. She was starting to rot away. She was still in the position in which she had died, clutching her knees, her head bent.

"My God," Twain said. "She must have crawled in there to hide, was too frightened to come out. She sat in there until she starved. My God, what she must have seen. How horrible it must have been. Can you imagine being so frightened you would rather starve?"

PERHAPS SHE DIED OF FRIGHT.

"I suppose that's possible. Poor thing. We must bury her, Ned. I'll go out to the barn, see if I can find a shovel."

YOU'RE NOT LEAVING MY ASS HERE. I'M GOING WITH YOU.

They went out to the barn on the cruiser. They found a shovel. Twain eyed a wheelbarrow, and some dried vegetables hanging from the rafters.

"If we use the wheelbarrow, we can haul some of these vegetables, the flour and sugar, back to Steam."

WHY NOT JUST PUT IT IN THE CRUISER?

"We will pack the cruiser as well, but I suggest we take all we can. There's room in Steam for a lot of stuff, and who knows when we'll need it."

"First, we'll take care of that poor child. My God, it makes me think of my own tragic family."

I AM SO SORRY.

"Me too, Ned. Life just keeps throwing darts."

BUT WE KEEP DODGING.

"You are one remarkable seal, my friend."

THANKS. YOU ARE NOT SO BAD YOURSELF. ARE YOU GOING TO WRITE ANYMORE ABOUT HUCKLEBERRY FINN? OTHER THAN THE ONE WHERE THEY GO TO AFRICA BY BALLOON. I DON'T COUNT THAT ONE.

"Not your meat, I take it."

I REALLY THOUGHT IT BIT THE HIND END OF A MOOSE. BUT I SURE LIKED *HUCKLEBERRY FINN* AND *TOM SAWYER*. I LIKED *THE PRINCE AND THE PAUPER*. I LIKED *A CONNECTICUT YANKEE IN KING ARTHUR'S COURT*. HAVE YOU EVER THOUGHT ABOUT WRITING A BOOK ABOUT A SEAL?

Ned paused to erase and write again.

I WOULD READ A BOOK ABOUT A SEAL. I THINK A LOT OF PEOPLE WOULD. I THINK IT WOULD SELL A LOT. SEALS ARE INTERESTING. I CAN BE FUNNY TOO. I KNOW SOME JOKES.

"It's something I will consider seriously, Ned. And, yes, seals are interesting. Later, I can hear your jokes. But for now, let us go back to the house and attend to this rather dreary duty."

Back in the farmhouse, Ned pulled a blanket off of a bed with his teeth and dragged it into the kitchen area where the little girl lay. Twain, using the shovel because the body was too decayed to touch, rolled the little corpse onto the blanket. He wrapped the blanket around the body, and Ned jerked down some curtain cord with his strong teeth, and Twain tied up the ends of the blanket.

Gently, Ned holding the blanket in his teeth at one end, Twain lifting it at the other, they carried the corpse outside. Twain started to dig.

It was hard there, and there were plenty of small stones. It took considerable time to dig a grave deep enough to contain the body, and by the time Twain finished, he was covered in sweat, his great mane of hair plastered to his head like a tight bathing cap.

They lowered the unfortunate victim into the confines of the earth, then, with Twain using the shovel and Ned pushing dirt in with his flippers, they covered her up.

Ned used his flippers to push some of the rocks into a pile, to form a sort of makeshift marker at one end of the grave.

"Sleep well, darling. May angels attend thee. Even though I doubt there are any, and if there are, they're nasty little shits and God is a malign thug."

THAT WAS A VERY NICE CEREMONY. YOU ARE NOT A RELIGIOUS MAN, ARE YOU?

"Not when God allows children to die. Mine or any other. God can kiss my ass."

THAT'S NOT VERY NICE.

"I suppose not."

IT IS A VERY DIRTY ASS RIGHT NOW.

Twain turned, brushed dirt from the seat of his pants. It had collected there during the two breaks he had taken while digging the grave, sitting with his back to the fence.

"Well, Ned. We should gather our goods and try and find our friends and Steam. It is growing dark."

Ned made a noise, a barking sound.

"What, Ned?"

Ned clapped his flippers.

"What?"

Ned wrote:

BIG GODDAMN MARTIAN MACHINE.

Twain looked over his shoulder. And sure enough, stalking between the house and the woods was a machine, striding about like a three-legged spider. From that distance, they could not see the Martians behind the view glass clearly, but they could see bloblike shapes working the controls.

"In the house, quick, Ned."

They leaped onto the cruiser and geared it toward the house. The house wall was torn open on one side from previous Martian attacks, so it was easy for them to glide inside.

They collapsed the machine and rolled it against the wall near a bedroom window at the back. Then, sitting to the side of the bed, their backs to the wall, they listened.

It was then that they heard the sound of guns in the distance. "My God, the British are fighting back," Twain said.

This thundering went on for a time, shaking the cottage, causing the window to jar so fiercely, for a moment it seemed as if it would break free of its moorings.

Eventually, Twain rose, and leaving Ned to wait in the bedroom, slipped into the kitchen, where the wall was broken down.

Out in the dark, Twain could see the machine stalking about, a light glowing from its head and flashing over the landscape. The head wheeled on its gears and sockets, and the light shot out in Twain's direction.

Jumping back, Twain hoped he had not been spotted. He crouched low against what remained of the kitchen wall, half expecting a ray to strike and cause the whole thing to crumble down in a heap on top of him.

The light rotated away, and Twain eased his head around the broken wall for a peek. The machine was stomping off into the darkness. He was glad to see that it was not moving toward the woods where the others and Steam waited.

Back in the bedroom, Twain briefly and quietly reported to Ned what he had seen. There was the continuous sound of gunfire now, and it seemed to be moving closer, as if being pushed along by a current. Then, abruptly, the thundering of guns stopped.

Looking out the window, Twain saw a strange sight. A white mist appeared to be rising out of the distance. He could see it clearly in the moonlight, and soon it was like a gossamer gown thrown over the face of the moon.

"Smoke," Twain said. "Explosions. And now silence. I fear the Martians have knocked out the gun batteries. The goddamn shit-eating dick-sucking bastards."

WAS THAT ONE WORD?

"No."

WHAT NOW?

"Our only recourse is to return to Steam. Taking our goods with us. I'm going to look about in the house a bit more. Living out here in the country, perhaps there is a bird gun."

Twain looked about, but found nothing of the sort.

Outside, Twain took hold of the wheelbarrow handles and started to push. Ned mounted the cruiser, which was also packed with goods, and floated alongside of him.

To the north, they could see not only smoke now, but great fires, and there were distant cries as well.

"The machines are winning," Twain said.

At the edge of the woods, Twain found pushing the wheelbarrow a hard go. The ground was too mushy. He managed it to the spot where they had left the pile of wood and stopped. "I'm leaving it here," Twain said. "We can get Steam to come for the wood and the barrow. There's a path here. It might be tight, but he can make it. I'm all tuckered out."

Twain climbed on the cruiser, and Ned geared it along the trail, toward where they had left their friends, and Steam.

But when they arrived on the far edge of the woods, near the road, neither Steam nor their friends were about.

Lying in the road with its legs bent and twisted and broken was one of the Martian machines. The club Rikwalk had made for himself was stuffed through what had been the face glass of the machine.

Twain climbed down from the cruiser, went over for a look. It was dark, but near the machine lay a Martian. It looked as if something had taken hold of it and squeezed until what was inside of it had come out the top of its head.

Steam.

Ned slid the cruiser over close to Twain. He wrote: WHY DID THEY LEAVE?

"I don't know," Twain said. "But they wouldn't have left us had they not had to. My guess is, from all the marks in the road here, the place was swarming with machines. Steam got this Martian and Rikwalk got the machine. And then they fled. It was the smart thing to do. I would have done the same. They were most likely outnumbered."

Ned slapped a flipper to his side, pointed with the other.

Lying in the woods was another machine. Twain climbed onto the cruiser, and they glided over for a look.

This machine had been bent up too, and this Martian pilot had suffered the same fate as his partner. He lay near the machine, part of his body draped over a log.

"Steam just reached inside the glass, took him out like a baby grabbing a chocolate," Twain said. "Then, he squeezed him."

IS THAT MARTIAN SHIT HANGING OUT OF HIS TWO ASSHOLES?

"I doubt it's flour gravy, Ned."

THEIR SHIT IS THE WRONG COLOR.

"I suppose they might say the same about ours. And my guess is that shit is mixed with a lot of other things. Blood. His guts. And we're seeing it in moonlight... I can't believe I'm standing out here discussing Martian shit with a seal."

WHAT DO WE DO?

"We go on."

INTO THAT MESS.

Ned pointed a flipper down the road. At the far end of it and beyond there were great red and yellow flames lapping at the darkness with the enthusiasm of a hound licking an ice cream cone.

"I suppose we must find our friends. They will be worried about us. They might even circle about to find us."

"They think you're dead."

Ned and Twain whirled at the sound of the voice.

The speaker came staggering out of the woods holding his head with one hand, a rifle with the other. It was Jules.

Twain leaped from the cruiser, grabbed his old friend, who suddenly collapsed to the ground.

"Jules. My God, man, what happened?"

"As you might suspect, the machines, my friend."

"Where are the others?"

"Gone on. We were looking for wood, then we were looking for you."

"We were detained by a machine. Ned and I were trapped in a farmhouse. We had supplies. But then we found this business."

"They came on us suddenly. Steam was stoked up, though. Wood had been brought back and there was a fire in his belly. Or wherever the damn fire is. The machines saw us. Rikwalk took to them. He scampered up the side of one, tugged it down by hanging off it, letting his weight take it to the ground. He shoved a tree into it.

"Steam stomped the machine, grabbed the Martian out. Steam and Rikwalk got another one before the others came. Ten machines. Rikwalk and I decided we would detain them. There was a rifle in Steam. I took that and dropped out. The others were reluctant that we should do what we intended, but Rikwalk and I wanted them to go on. Passepartout knows how to reach Herbert. Herbert is the only reason to go to London. He is the only one who might save us. Our very planet. Either him, or Professor Challenger, if he can be found. But we sent them on. Rikwalk and I scampered into the woods, and the machines tried to follow. A ray was shot at me. It missed, but it hit a tree near me and the tree fell and I was hit.

"I don't know why I wasn't finished off. Maybe they thought I was dead. All I remember was hearing Rikwalk yelling at them. Trying to get them after him. I passed out. Then I awoke to the sound of your voice, Samuel. I have no idea what happened to Rikwalk. But I fear the worst."

"If Wells is our best bet," Twain said, "I suppose we too should head that way, into London. If Steam doesn't make it, then we must. And frankly, being a smaller target may work to our advantage."

"Agreed."

There was a little first-aid kit inside the cruiser, and Twain, using the meager resources of that kit, bandaged Verne's head.

Then, with Ned at the controls, they were off.

Twenty: Ned's Journal:
Flaming London, Reunion, We Take a Captive of Sorts

The great fire before us made London seem near. But it was not. In fact, it was not only London that burned, but much that surrounded it. We cruised silently through many a charred village. Humans and animals lay littered about like tossed garbage. Carts and other vehicles were crushed and burning, and homes were often little more than rubble. There was a stink that rose up from the dead that was almost unbearable. Fish, when rotting, do not smell that bad, and in fact, rotting fish, if dipped briefly in seawater, and then eaten, really aren't that bad.

We had food in the cruiser that we had taken from the farmhouse. It was simple but acceptable under the circumstances. There had been a couple tins of dried fish in the wheelbarrow we had left in the woods, but neither Mr. Twain nor Mr. Verne wanted to go back after it.

I wanted to go back after it, but they overruled me. Sometimes democracy is not all it is cracked up to be.

But there were some potted meats and some dried cheeses that stank, and we ate that with some bread near hard as hammers, and drank water from a bottle Mr. Twain had taken from the farmhouse. It was better than sticking a sharp stick up your ass and cranking it, but only a little better. In fact, if you could grease that stick with butter, it might even have been the better deal.

We spent several days traveling, and along the way we encountered a couple of destroyed Martian machines.

"Steam," Mr. Verne said. "He got some more."

"He's been lucky to miss the rays," Mr. Twain said.

"He didn't always miss them," Mr. Verne said. "I saw him lose one of his metal fingers to one, right before I bolted into the woods. He's as fast as the Martian machines. It's really quite remarkable."

"When they get to London, what are they going to do? Put him in their pockets? They can hardly sneak about with that big tin man."

"I have no idea," Mr. Verne said. "But Beadle and John Feather, and my good friend Passepartout, they are resourceful."

"No doubt."

We traveled by night and slept by day. Sometimes we slept in the woods, or down in gullies, and on occasion in abandoned or near-destroyed farmhouses.

Finally one morning, just as light was slipping through the shadows, we came to signs that told us we were on the outskirts of London. I would normally have been excited. I have always heard of, and have of course read much of London. But now I knew there would be nothing fine to see. From where we stood, was a view of black churning smoke and spits of flames, and even from that distance, the smell of death.

"We should find a place to hole up for the day, and even the night," Mr. Twain said. "We need to be rested. Tomorrow we make London. Such as it is."

We did find a place. A small grove of trees. It was comfortable enough, and we slept away the day, awakening at nightfall.

It was decided we wouldn't travel this night, or the next day. Instead, we would rest, eat plenty of food before proceeding on our journey.

We had a cold supper of canned meat, hard bread and water. There was little water left in the container, and it was decided, though it was dark, that we should venture out of the grove and cross over into the village to look for water.

On this last night before entering London, we had chosen to sleep outside the village for the simple reason that at night the Martian machines roamed such places looking for survivors. But with our water running low, and me needing a rubdown and feeling dehydrated, we took the cruiser back into town, came to a house where we found a water pump and were able to fill our bottle and douse me good.

We had no sooner accomplished that than we heard movement amongst a pile of ruins not far from us. Mr. Verne had the rifle Beadle had given him, a kind of scoop-cocking affair that Mr. Twain said resembled an American Winchester. He lifted it and listened.

No doubt about it. Something was moving amongst the debris near us, behind what remained of the ray-blasted walls. And it sounded huge.

We scampered back onto the cruiser and glided behind the remains of a cottage. Mr. Twain leaned out from the edge of the wall for a peek.

"My God," he said.

"What is it?" Mr. Verne said.

"Ned, bring the cruiser out into the open."

I hesitated for only a moment, then did as Mr. Twain instructed. Coasting out from behind the cottage I saw a wonderful sight, and even though my vision was clouded by night, there was enough light from the stars and the scattered fires from the burning village for me to know exactly what I was seeing.

Rikwalk, squatting, staring at us. When he saw us, he let out a whelp and came running, thundering along on back legs and front knuckles. In that moment he looked like nothing more than a huge gorilla.

As he came to the cruiser, he snatched Mr. Twain out of it, hugged him, set him on the ground, then did the same with Mr. Verne. I was third. Grabbed from the floating cruiser and hugged furiously, he placed me back gently behind the controls.

Mr. Twain and Mr. Verne remained on the ground. Mr. Twain said, "My god, you are all right. We feared the worst."

"And so you should have. But here I am."

"Come, let us go back to our place in the grove," Mr. Verne said. "We can talk there. We have food."

"So when they came, and I saw they were after you, I yelled to them, and they came after me —"

"And I thank you for that, my brother," Mr. Verne said. "It was a brave and noble thing to do."

"No. Not at all. You would have done the same. I ran, and they pursued. I went deep into the woods. On our world, my Mars, there is much foliage, and we use it to travel from place to place. There are even nets amongst the great trees for lounging, and many of our people go there for leisure, and there are homes built there as well. I live in such a place, not far from the locks where I work...worked. So I felt right at home. Except the trees are smaller... And it wasn't home."

Mr. Twain reached out and touched Rikwalk's huge hand. "Easy, friend. If there is a way for you to return to your Mars, we will help you do it. I promise that."

"I know," Rikwalk said.

"Please," Mr. Twain said. "Continue with your story."

"There isn't much to tell. They pursued me through the woods, firing their rays, knocking down trees, causing a fire. I found a creek bed, and though I'm large, it was deep enough that I was able to make some passage down it, and then scamper up and into the trees. High up, amongst a thick growth of leaves, I hid. Wondering if the tree I was in would be hit by one of their rays.

"It wasn't, but as the machines came through, one of them smashed against the tree where I hid, and the might of the machine caused it to shake, and then the machine, somehow standing on two of its metal tentacles, used the other tentacle to grab the tree, and the machine pulled it up by its roots and threw it."

"My God," Mr. Verne said.

"The tree went for some distance and came down hard. Fortunately, I was on the clear side of its fall, and I was spared. I thought it had been grabbed because they knew I was in it, but it seemed that they were merely clearing a path, and the tree I was in happened to be blocking it. I stayed there amongst its limbs until the machine and its companions departed. When I was sure they were gone, I slipped away and have been moving slowly toward the town you call London ever since. I followed the road from a distance, not traveling on it itself, going mostly by night, sleeping in the day, but keeping it in sight as a kind of guide."

Mr. Twain told him of our adventures, and when he was finished, he said, "We have decided to rest through this night, and all of tomorrow. Then when tomorrow night falls, we go into London. We felt, tired as we were, we should try and rest as much as possible. We have food. Can you use some?"

"I am famished, my friend. I found a number of canned goods, but I had to beat them open on a rock. A lot of the contents got splattered. I've mostly lived off bugs and worms, which, frankly, to me are a kind of delicacy, though I prefer them slow-grilled in garrodo[1] fat."

"I will not even ask," Mr. Verne said.

---

1   A farm animal raised for meat and milk on Rikwalk's Mars.

Rikwalk grinned. We gave him the food we had left, and he polished it off greedily. With his belly as full as he could manage, and with half the water from our bottle in his stomach, he lay back and was immediately asleep.

It would have seemed that traveling by day, being up by night, we would not have been able to sleep as well. But it was quite the contrary. I lay next to the collapsed cruiser, and there, with a pile of leaves for a pillow, fell into a deep sleep. When I awoke, it was in the exact same position I had lain down, and my awakening was to the singing of birds and bright rays of sunlight lacing between the boughs of the trees.

The day was hot. I felt as if I were a dying bug specimen in a bottle, killing fumes rising up from the bottom of the bottle, the lid corked, and me with no place to go. Only the stink we encountered was not that of the killing jar, but that of the dead who lay bloated in the village and along the roadside.

It occurred to me, though I tried not to dwell on it, that odds were good that we might soon join them.

We stayed in our grove most of the day, talking, trying to plan strategy, but there was little to plan. The obvious and smart thing to have done would have been not to go into London, but to hide out and stay hidden.

But we were determined to reach Wells, and possibly find a way to get rid of these horrid invaders. We also spoke of Bull and Cat, the Dutchman, his ship and crew. Where were they? Had they lived through their traveling to another world? Was it another Earth? Mars? Hell? Would we ever know?

And what of Beadle and John Feather and Passepartout, the big machine they called Steam?

Had they traveled by night?

Could they have sneaked into London?

Finally, that sort of talk and consideration died out and we began to talk about things that had nothing to do with our current situation. Twain talked of his losses, and how his humor had almost dried up. Verne talked of frustration with his publisher, how they did not want him to publish a very dark novel he was writing about Paris. Rikwalk talked of his family, his world, and how he missed it. He spoke so eloquently, when he finished, I missed his Mars as well.

And I spoke of fish.

I know. It's a simple thing. But I like fish. I think about them all the time. I was also hot, and at some point we made our way back to the village and watered me down with the pump, filled our water bottle, and managed to find a few tins of food. We carried these back to the grove, and waited there until nightfall. Talking. Eating. Dozing. Dreaming. Fearing.

And so the night came and we started out. Rikwalk knuckled alongside the cruiser, and we hovered over the countryside, not far from the road, ever on the lookout for the machines.

About the same time that night fell, a fog rose. It misted whitely across the land as if it were some kind of mystical dragon. It seemed to coil and writhe over the landscape. Soon, we found ourselves inside it, wrapped up by it, and once again, I thought of those insect specimens balled up in cotton, waiting for death.

I thought, Would it be so bad to return to the sea?

Out there I could live free.

I couldn't keep my hat, since it wouldn't last in the sea, or stay on my head for two shakes. But I would be amongst my own kind. Except for the fact that they would not be as smart and wouldn't have books, and the metalwork on my head, though resistant to rust in general, might be ruined by too much water and too much salt.

It was a hard thing to consider.

No fez.

No books.

But there would be fish.

My thoughts were exploded when Rikwalk whispered.

"There. See the light?"

And we did. It was high up and fanning about. The light from the head of one of the Martian killing machines.

There was a hill in front of us, and we went tight against it. I settled the cruiser down on the ground, and we stood inside it.

Rikwalk lay down on the ground and rolled on his side, let his back rest against the base of the hill. It was the only way he could not be conspicuous.

There were dead sheep lying about the hill, under the fog, as if it were their blanket. They had been hit by rays and were missing heads and limbs and had head-sized holes punched through them. The holes were clean and cauterized. The Martians, not distinguishing the sheep from humans, had destroyed them along with everything else in their path. The sheep were bloated and bug-infested, and they stunk to high heaven, and the fog held the stink down close to the earth.

The machine was on the other side of the hill and above us, slicing into the fog. We could see its light. Then we could see more lights. I kept my flipper close to the cruiser's controls, lest we should need to spurt away.

Of course, the cruiser, though reasonably fast, was nowhere near as swift as the stalking machines, but it was more maneuverable. I tried to keep that in mind as we waited and trembled. At least I was trembling. I don't know about the others.

One of the tentacled metal legs stepped over our hill, made us gasp for breath. The leg almost came down on top of us. And then the machine stepped again, bringing forward its other legs. It scuttled like an amputee spider. We stayed pressed against the hill. Soon, above it, there appeared three flying wedge-like crafts with big bright red lights in the front of them.

"My God," Verne said. "They have new machines. They've got flying machines. They look to be two- or three-seater crafts for those big octopusses. Ocotopussies. Octopi. Whatever."

I wrote and held it close to my companions so they could see it. Well, I don't know if they actually could see it there in that foggy darkness, but it made me feel good to write it.

LOOKS LIKE WE'RE FUCKED. WHO'S FOR GOING BACK TO THE SEA? SHOW OF HANDS. WHAT SAY WE FIND A TROPICAL ISLAND WITH SEXUALLY WILLING SEALS? NATIVE GIRLS FOR YOU GUYS. RIKWALK, I GUESS YOU GET TO FUCK A MONKEY.

"We're not dead yet," Twain said, either in response to my note, or just because he thought it was appropriate.

I'm sure that could change at a moment's notice.

"Come on, they've passed us," Twain said. "We should move forward."

I don't know how we made it, since we saw numerous stalking machines that night. The flying wedges as well. But I suppose the fog, which was at first a nuisance, turned out to be our ally.

Well before daylight we arrived on the outskirts of London, no worse for wear, except in the department of exhaustion, due primarily to fear. Rikwalk showed no signs of exhaustion, and unlike us, who had been riding, he had been under his own power.

But he did show sadness. The look on his face, illuminated by burning London buildings, was enough to make me cry. Which, strangely enough, is an ability I've acquired. Maybe it has something to do with the way Doctor Momo wired my brain. But there have been many changes in me since the old days, which, frankly, are harder and harder for me to remember. I do remember quite well my preoccupation with fish. That hasn't changed much.

I still think about seal nookie as well.

I think that's healthy. Don't you?

We glided into London, staying close to the ruins of the city — for much of it now appeared to be ruins. Now and then we would see a human dart out from behind a wrecked building, cross our path with a wild glance, then disappear like a roach into a building across the way.

"Mankind is on the run," Mr. Twain said.

The sun rose and bathed us in morning light. Under other circumstances I would have found it beautiful, but for now I wanted back the night. I even welcomed the fog we had lost just outside of London. Now all our natural cover was gone.

Just as we turned a corner, trying to make our way down an alley, we saw one of the machines scampering along after us, flaming sunlight at its back.

Rikwalk said, "Go. I'll handle this. Give me the weapon, Mr. Verne."

Mr. Verne, without really thinking, handed him the rifle he had taken out of Steam. It was practically swallowed by Rikwalk's hand.

Rikwalk, sticking the rifle crosswise in his teeth, grabbed the wall of one of the buildings with his strong hands, climbed up hand over hand and foot over foot like...Well, he climbed like an ape. Rays blasted around him and bricks shattered and rained down on us.

We glided behind the building, down the alley. I didn't want to leave Rikwalk, but he had been so demanding, without thinking, I had done as he asked.

Above us, we heard the snap of the rifle, and then another snap. I looked back, and the machine had turned the corner and started toward us. But now, the glass that made up the windshield of the machine was shattered. I could see one of the creatures slumped over the gears, the other laboring to maintain his seat, green ichor spraying out of his head as if it were powered by a pump and firehose.

The machine dodged left, caught itself on one of its spidery legs, wobbled, wheeled, fell on its back with a smash.

I looked up. On the roof of the building was Rikwalk. He had the rifle in one of his hands, probably having fired it with his little finger; in his hands the rifle looked like a large toothpick.

"Hey," Rikwalk said, "I hit him. I don't know how, but I hit him."

"Come on down," Mr. Twain called.

I geared the cruiser over there, and Mr. Twain and Mr. Verne leaped out and climbed on top of the machine. Behind the cracked glass lay the dead Martians. Again I was reminded of squid or octopusses…octopi… octopussies. Whatever. Nobody in our group could figure that multiple octopus thing out.

Anyway, the asswipes were dead.

Rikwalk climbed down, gave the rifle back to Mr. Verne.

"You are some shot," Verne said.

"I hate to admit this," Rikwalk said, "but the first time the weapon went off, total accident. Second time I just pointed. I can't believe I hit them. Both shots. Beginner's luck. Twice. It's the first piece of luck I've had since I scored with my wife before she was my wife. That's not for common knowledge by the way. We wouldn't want the kids to know that."

"We'll never speak a word, monsieur," Mr. Verne said.

"Here's the door," Mr. Twain said.

I eased the cruiser up and on top of the machine and glided over to where Mr. Twain was pointing. The machine lay on its side, and beneath it, where the legs were connected, was a sealed round doorway.

Mr. Verne climbed up there as well. He said, "Yes. It appears to be screwed on."

"There must be some way to unscrew it. If we could get inside, figure out the gears."

"Damn, Samuel, that could be a very good plan."

Rikwalk said, "Let's see."

With the tips of his fingers and his thumb, Rikwalk was able to turn the screw. The door came out like a plug.

Mr. Twain and Mr. Verne climbed inside. I could see them through the glass. The machine was wide enough they could stand up inside. They dragged the Martians out, tossed them on the ground.

Mr. Verne said, "I'm going to try and gear it up. See what happens."

"They had two at the controls," Mr. Twain said. "Maybe it takes two."

"Maybe so. We can try it. Ned. Will you come inside?"

I climbed off of the cruiser and collapsed it. With Rikwalk's help (he shoved my ass with the palm of his hand), I wormed my way inside. He screwed the lid back onto the machine behind me.

Mr. Twain and Mr. Verne climbed into the strange chairs, which were designed for larger bodies, and lying sideways, they began to work the controls.

The spider legs thrashed, sending Rikwalk scuttling for cover. After a few trials, Mr. Verne was able to get one of the machine's legs bent and underneath itself, and with another push of a gear, the leg lifted the machine.

It immediately crashed on its side.

This event continued in repetition for a few moments, crashing hard enough that the already shattered glass shattered even more. Finally, a large chunk of it fell out.

I was being thrown around like some kind of ball, from side to side. My fez got knocked off, but I scrambled around until I recovered it.

I finally got hold of a grip bar on the side of the craft with my teeth, and held to it like I had hold of a whale.

Right then, I could have eaten a whale.

When I'm scared, I get hungry.

Frankly, I pretty much stay hungry.

After what seemed a little past forever, the machine stood. It wobbled at first, but in short time Mr. Twain and Mr. Verne had it. They stalked about the alley for a time, making the machine do different things. They slammed against the alley walls a bit, but before long they were operating it in a pretty smooth manner.

"It's actually simple," Mr. Twain said. "You just move these pegs the way you want it to go, and once you get it up, well, you point it in the direction you like with this gear, and it walks. You don't really need to work the legs individually then, unless you want them to do something specific. Like lift them tentacles higher, reach out and grab. That kind of business."

"That bit is worked with this," Mr. Verne said, touching another lever that moved side to side.

"It's kind of fun," Mr. Twain said.

Through the glass we could see Rikwalk. He grinned. "I think I should not stay too close to you. At a glance, you can pass as a Martian machine. I can not. Though, I might add, neither of you look like Martians."

We could hear Rikwalk well through the gaps in the glass. Mr. Twain called out, "Not looking like a Martian is a good thing in my book."

"Right now, it is better if you do look like one," Rikwalk said.

"Now," Mr. Verne said, "we find Herbert."

I wrote:

AND AFTER THAT, COULD WE FIND SOME FISH?

"Quite possible," Mr. Verne said. "And if not fish, food of some kind."

YIPPIE!!!!

Ned's journal ends.

Twenty-one: Big Ben, a Battle, Friends, the Sky Gets Ripped

"We'll hide in plain sight," Twain said.

"How's that?" Verne said.

"Like in Poe's story, 'The Purloined Letter.' They couldn't find the letter because it was not actually hidden. It was in plain sight. We can not only walk amongst the invaders, we will not be recognized."

"I think one good look at us and they'll know we're not Martians."

"Okay. It's not perfect, but it is a plan. I suggest that our next plan is to find out how the ray device on this works, how to aim it."

"And since you'll be doing that," Rikwalk said, "I'll climb on top of a building here."

Ned wrote:

AM I SAFE IN HERE FROM THE RAY?

"I should hope so," Twain said.

"Proceed toward the tower clock," Verne said to Rikwalk through the hole in the glass. "Herbert has a home and laboratory near there."

"I'm a little more conspicuous than you two," Rikwalk said.

"Oh, right you are," Verne said.

"I suggest you go directly to the tower if you can," Rikwalk said, "and I'll work my way there by whatever path I can find. It's a bit hard for an ape my size to stay out of sight."

After Rikwalk went up a wall, disappeared atop a building, Twain and Verne went about trying to find the device to work the ray. It didn't take long. They managed to blast down the side of the building Rikwalk had just vacated.

"I really didn't mean to do that," Verne said.

"I gathered," Twain said.

They worked with it a bit more, and soon they could aim it well enough, if not expertly. But they discovered they had the walking part down pretty well. They maneuvered the machine out of the alley and around the corner and out into the city proper.

In the distance, they could see the great tower clock, Big Ben. Ned glanced out and up, saw Rikwalk moving along a building top. Large as he was, he was moving quickly, shadowlike. Soon, he was out of sight.

"What say we point 'er at the big clock," Twain said, "and go."

Many great Martian war machines hustled about the city, and our heroes went forward rapidly, trying not to get too close, trying to move in the direction of the tower as swiftly as possible, thinking Martian and hopefully looking Martian, but making sure they didn't get too close to their metal comrades so that they might be seen clearly through what remained of the view glass.

They saw a huge machine pause, turn its "head," and look at them. It turned its glass-fronted noggin from side to side like a curious animal. The creatures behind the glass were practically pressed up against their windshield, trying to figure out what it was they were seeing.

nickbic. that is not some of us, it is not. i can see that, i can. earth goobers. that is what we see, it is.

you are right, sumbuma. it is not what it should be, but is what it is. booger things. creepy things that walk this ground. they are in one of our machines.

greenless things. let's make them pretty like us. give them two assholes.

yuk, yuk, yuk.

going to melt them good, is what we are going to do. can I do it?

you did the last.

did not.

did too.

did not.

They never finished their argument. Twain fired the ray from their machine, struck the Martian device solid. The windshield was knocked off whole. The machine twirled around on its legs so hard it practically braided them.

The machine went down.

"It was like before," Twain said. "They appeared to be quarreling."

Ned wrote:

QUARRELING CAN BE BENEFICIAL AND EVEN HEALTHY. BUT QUARRELING TOO MUCH, AND DURING TIMES OF STRESS AND IN TIMES OF NEED, IT CAN REALLY FUCK YOU UP. WITNESS THE MACHINE IN QUESTION. IT'S JUST SO MUCH JUNK NOW. IT IS BETTER NOT TO QUARREL. IT IS BETTER TO SIT DOWN OVER A DINNER OF FISH AND DISCUSS YOUR PROBLEMS. FEMALE SEALS ARE CONSIDERABLY MORE WILLING WHEN THEY HAVE FILLED THEIR BELLIES WITH FISH.

"I'll believe that," Twain said, working controls, helping the machine race down the street.

Other machines and their occupants had witnessed the destruction of one of their own machines by another, and now they were rushing toward our heroes.

Our heroes had the lead and —

FIRST PHASE OF THE RACE

— they're off, and down the street they go, leaping, darting, weaving, and, oh shit, had to leap over some downed carts, and one tentacle went into a dead man's body, and that sucker is hung on the end of it now like a wad of chewy tobaccy on the bottom of a boot. It's throwing off our heroes a bit, and —

SECOND PHASE OF THE RACE

— here they come, the Martians, and there are seven machines, and those green, multi-tentacled, two-assholed sonsabitches, they can really work those things. Running their machines like goddamn deer, they are, closing, closing, closing —

THIRD PHASE OF THE RACE

— four to the right, three to the left, and, with a shake of the tentacle, our heroes' machine is free of the dead body, and now Twain and Verne, they've got their gears pushed all the way forward, and they're working the balance controls, and whoopie, sudden stop, and —

FOURTH PHASE OF THE RACE

— Martian machines go, oh shit, because the humans (one assholed mother-father-uncle-aunt-hive-fuckers) have stopped short, and they have tried to stop short with them, and the results are the big-double assed Martians are being smacked against their windshields.

squirty ass juice and sweaty nut balls, cries one.

One machine loses control, topples into another, their legs get entwined, down they go, thrashing about on the street and up against buildings like a stuck pig kicking out its last.

No time to help their comrades. they're down. way down. and frankly, they don't give a damn. they aren't big on sentiment.

Martians turn about angry, tentacles on those ray levers, baby, but the humans, they are gone. done took off like the proverbial and legendary spotted ass ape —

THE WINNERS!

— bounding along toward Big Ben they go, and inside the machine, Twain, he actually says, Wheeee!

Of course, it doesn't matter. The winner gets dick.

And the losers, they are not in a mood, so to speak.

And furthermore, or meanwhile, as is said in the story trade, our erstwhile heroes approach the tower clock, and right off they see there's good news, and there's bad news.

Good news:

Rikwalk, going his own way, over buildings, down side streets, sneaky as a Paiute Indian in a war party, has made the tower clock. He's there.

That's the good part.

Now for the bad news:

Rikwalk has been seen. He's scuttling up the side of the tower, gripping a Martian by one of its legs. He has somehow broken into one of the machines (scuttled up it, smashed the glass with his fist, pulled out the Martian), and he's dragging the creature with him up the side of Big Ben.

He's a fast climber, Rikwalk is, and way up there he goes.

But there's more bad news:

Machines are closing in on him.

He works his way to the top of the tower, and there, holding the Martian, he begins to use the creature as a thrash rag, slinging him from side to side, bouncing him off of the clock tower, calling out names in English and in a language our heroes do not recognize.

Rays cut the air around him.

Zip. Zip. Zip.

Rikwalk can feel the hair on his body singeing, the rays are so close. He's so certain he's about to buy it, he can imagine his ancestral apes sitting on the limb of the great tree of life, dicks in one hand, the other over their eyes, their mouths open, but silent.

Rikwalk starts leaping up and down on the side of the clock, hanging on to it with one hand, dangling the Martian with the other, making primitive ape sounds.

"Ooohhh, oooohhhh, fucking shit. Ooohhhhh, oooohhhh. Eat my shit. Ooohhh, ooohhhh. Cocksucking octopussies."

"We've got to help him," Twain says.

Ned, who has his eye pressed against a smaller rear window turns, writes:

WE STILL HAVE MARTIAN MACHINES ON OUR TAIL.

"One thing at a time," Twain said.

Verne says, "Turn it. Quick."

And they do. Now they're facing the machines that are in pursuit. They fire rays. One of the machines takes a hit. It's charred on the side and part of the glass is melted out, but it keeps on coming.

The two that fell, they're still down, struggling to free their entwined tentacles.

A ray hits our heroes' machine.

It shakes. More of the glass falls out. Now there's just a sliver of glass in the right-hand corner.

Ned thinks: Must think of happy moments. Fish. Fish. Fish. Nookie. Nookie. Nookie. Fish. Fish..."

"Turn it back," Twain says. "Run this thing like a bastard."

And they do. Sprinting their way toward the tower.

"We'll have Rikwalk leap on top of us when we get there," Twain said.

"I don't know that's such a good plan."

"You come up with another, let me know."

Their machine sprang across the vast expanse of bricks and cobblestones toward the tower; sprang so hard the tentacles extended out in front of it like arrows being shot. Cement and brick popped up, this way and that, snapping like shrapnel.

It was quite the show, the way that machine leaped.

The Martians had never seen anything like it. They didn't know the machines would do that, and they had built them.

got to give it to the humans, they are working that machine some good, they are, the one-assholed pieces of cosmic shit.

yes. (cough) damn. i'm getting a sore throat.

mind the controls.

i'm minding them.

mind them better.

are you trying to tell me how to (cough)...i'm not feeling so good.

now that you mention it, neither am i.

By this point, there wasn't much left of the Martian corpse in Rikwalk's hand, having slammed and smashed it against the side of the tower clock like he was dusting a rug. He threw the creature's remains down at one of the machines attacking him. But it missed and fell splattering into the street.

Primitive ape behavior had taken over. Rikwalk ripped off his pants. He grabbed his dick and shook it at them. He dropped his dick and shit in his hand and threw the shit. He hit the windshield of one of the stalking towers, blurring the sight of the Martians inside.

The others closed in around the tower. They couldn't miss with their death rays now. They lifted their heads, pointed their rays up.

Rikwalk waited for the big pop.

One moment, he thought, I am standing here, and the next moment I'll be nothing more than a blazing hairball with a hand full of shit (for he had filled up again).

He opened his eyes, determined to take it head on.

Then he saw bounding toward him another Martian machine.

Behind it came five others. In the distance, lying in the street, he could see two others struggling to extricate themselves from one another.

The machine running toward him was the one containing his friends.

He raised the shit-filled hand, said, "Howdy, and so long."

The Martian machines had the clock surrounded now.

They aimed their rays.

And Big Ben struck the time.

That close, the whole earth shook.

Rikwalk certainly shook.

And he fell.

The rays blasted the air where he had been.

Rikwalk let go of the handful of shit. He wasn't that fond of it anyway.

He grabbed at the side of the clock tower, slipped (shit is greasy), grabbed again, and this time he caught a ridge, and hung there. Rikwalk dangled like a comma in a sentence.

"*Help!*" he said.

The Martians were surprised by the ape's sudden drop and his loud yell. They tried to refocus their attack. And would have too, but now, things had really changed.

Not only were our heroes coming —

But so was Steam.

Only he didn't know it yet.

You see, Steam was pressed up against the other side of the clock tower all the while.

Way it worked was like this:

The Martians thought he was part of the tower. A kind of statue standing next to the entryway. Standing tall. A symbol that let loose a bit of smoke from its top from time to time.

They didn't know he had fire in his belly. They didn't know he could move.

Steam stood there, hands on his hips, in plain sight all through the night and through the morning, like a statue, being passed by the Martian machines. The Martians had looked at him as if he were part of the clock tower.

Inside, where Beadle, John Feather and Passepartout waited, Beadle said, "Sometimes, I'm so smart I amaze my own goddamn self."

"You the man," John Feather said.

But that was then and this was now, and Steam, he moved.

Because, you see, inside of the metal man, Passepartout said, "That yell. No one sounds like that but Rikwalk. That's his strange voice. I'd know it anywhere."

"Then we have to help him," Beadle said. "No matter what the cost."

Beadle and John Feather put their hands on the controls, moved them. Steam stepped away from the clock, turned and walked around the edge of the tower, in the direction of the cry.

Simultaneously, all about and above them, the sky began ripping open in rips of red and blue, purple and yellow, and one rip of a very nice color that was somewhere between green and blue.

Twenty-two:
A Ferocious Battle, Strange Happenings,
Herbert Wells

"It's happening," Beadle said, seeing the rips through the stained-glass eyes of Steam. "Worlds are coming asunder."

"We must concentrate on the matter at hand," Passepartout said. "All else can wait, or happen without us."

"Oh, it will do that all right," Beadle said. "See there."

Passepartout looked.

A large boat came sailing out of one of the rips, hit the street, slid, crashed into a building across the way.

"That's just the beginning," Beadle said. "Just the way it started on our world. And look there."

One of the Martian machines, near the blue rip, was straining against something unseen. Then it seemed to stretch. And then —

— it was sucked up through a crack in the sky like liquid through a syphon hose.

Old cracks were closing, and new ones were opening.

"The rips still have a hard time staying open," Beadle said.

"If our experience is a common one," John Feather said, "that will change."

But there was no more time for discussion. They had rounded the clock tower. Now they were looking directly at Martian machines. The machines had congregated at the front of Big Ben. Their round heads and their thick windshields were lifted skyward, toward what dangled from above.

Rikwalk.

Steam looked past them at the machines racing toward them. One of them was manned by none other than their friends Twain, Verne and Ned the Seal. They were clearly visible through the hole where the glass had been.

FLAMING ZEPPELINS

The Martian machines near the clock tower were so intent on their hanging prey they had not even noticed Steam's arrival. Steam grabbed the nearest machine by one of its vining legs, jerked it off the ground, and gripping it with both metal hands, began to swing it.

Steam whirled it over his head, came around and struck another of the devices full smack-a-doodle. The Martian machines slammed together hard, exploded glass, green ichor, assholes and tentacles.

The remaining machines turned on Steam, who stood holding one metal tentacle. Rays were fired. One ray struck the metal behemoth in the neck, sliced through it like a hot knife through butter, came in like a burst of light through a bullet hole, hit Passepartout in the head.

His head went —

— POOF.

Nothing more.

A little explosion. A poof. Then there were black ashes settling to the floor. The remainder of his body collapsed, kicked and quit.

"Goddamn," John Feather said.

Another ray struck one of the stained-glass eyes. Glass shards sprayed. Glass hit both Beadle and John Feather. A large piece went through John Feather's cheek and lodged there, the tip of it poking through his gums, against his teeth.

Beadle snatched at the controls. Steam rushed forward, hunkered down. His fists flew.

And they made contact. The sound of metal on metal was deafening. Sparks flew from the blows. Martian machines went to pieces, were knocked about.

A ray was fired. Steam lost the metal tip of another one of his fingers.

Verne's, Twain's and Ned's machine was right on top of the melee now. But instead of joining in they wheeled their machine and sent rays flying back at their pursuers.

Rays jumped out of the Martians they were attacking. The sky was dotted with light. There were so many rays, and they came so fast, it was as if someone were tossing stiff confetti.

And then a strange thing happened.

The foremost pursuer fell.

Just fell over.

Toppled and hit the ground with a thud, went skidding along on the pavement, sparks leaping up like startled red and yellow frogs.

"What the hell?" Twain said.

But there was no time to wonder. In the background, the two machines that had entangled their legs were now disengaged. They were up and coming.

Everyone and everything weighed in.

It looked like a bar fight.

Steam was throwing machines this way and that. Verne, Twain and Ned were too close to use their ray, feared they might hit Steam. But they swung one tentacle like a whip while they supported themselves on the other two.

They snapped it here. They snapped it there. Shattering windshields, popping exposed Martians. They scooped with it, jerking Martians out of broken windshields, slapping them on the ground, grabbing machine legs, tugging them out from under the machines, smashing them to the turf.

"They're not that quick-witted," Twain said. "They can build a machine, but they don't have imagination. They fight like sissies."

The other machines arrived.

The brawl went on.

The Martians didn't mind using their rays close in.

But this didn't work well for them. They quickly wiped out three of their own allies.

A few Martians escaped from broken windshields, or screwed open the plug trap doors, hustled down ladders (Ned thought: Hey, where's our ladder? How come we don't have a ladder?), scuttled onto the ground, looking for hiding places.

They didn't find many.

Twain and Verne were pretty good shots with their ray. They cooked the Martians on the street bricks quicker than Ned could write:

FASTER, FASTER, KILL, KILL.

There was a pause now.

The calm after the storm.

Steam extended a hand.

The machine extended a tentacle.

They shook.

Then, without really talking about it, the Martian machine Twain and Verne operated clambered up on top of Steam, stretched two tentacles high, clung to Steam with the other, coiling it around his head like a constrictor crushing its prey.

The tentacles grabbed hold of Rikwalk, who had climbed down even closer, and lifted him on top of Steam. Rikwalk climbed down the metal man quickly, stood happily on the ground.

No sooner was this done than Steam made a noise and froze up like a rust-encrusted bolt.

A ladder was dropped out of Steam's ass. Beadle and John Feather climbed down, John pulling the glass from his cheek as soon as he descended.

Twain and Verne caused the Martian machine to coil its legs beneath its body, bringing it down to the ground. They unscrewed the plug and came out, Ned dragging the cruiser after him.

"Out of fuel," Beadle said. "We'll have to leave Steam. We were operating damn near off residue. We're lucky we lasted as long as we did."

"I think it's time we leave our machine as well," Twain said. "We're a little conspicuous. And it's taken a lot of damage."

"We are close to Herbert's home," Verne said. "We must try to find him. Where is Passepartout?"

"He is gone," Beadle said. "A ray struck him. He never knew what hit him."

"My God," Verne said. "Passepartout. My butler. My friend."

"I feel for you, sir," Beadle said, "but now is not the time to grieve. We must move on."

The cruiser carried them all except Rikwalk. It was a tight fit in the device and it moved more slowly than usual, bearing the excess weight. It barely skimmed above the ground. But it carried them.

Rikwalk ran beside them, using his foreknuckles to propel him.

As they went, they were surprised to see Martian machines lying about. Both the stalking machines and the triangular flying craft; several of them had crashed, tearing apart, spraying the premises with residue of Martians.

"What happened to them?" Twain said.

"Perhaps there are freedom fighters," Beadle said. "People working from the shadows, like us."

"It's not that shadowy right now," Twain said.

They wound down amongst broken, smoking stones, along damaged walls and trampled gardens, and finally came to a row of houses. The homes had all suffered damage, but appeared to be in reasonable condition.

Verne pointed at the largest of the row. "That is Herbert's home. We'll check."

"Careful he doesn't shoot you for a looter," Twain said.

Rikwalk crouched in the courtyard, a sharp eye out for machines, as the others tried the door.

It came open.

They went inside.

Verne slumped. Though the house looked fine from the outside, inside the back wall had been knocked down, and the interior had been gutted by fire. The floor was littered with charred remains.

"Damn," Verne said. "Our last hope. Another friend gone. God. Is life worth living anymore?"

"It hasn't been for me for a long time," Twain said. "Until now. Until we banded together. With a cause. We have a reason, Jules. I almost forgot it's better to go down fighting than to not fight at all."

"Right now, I am all out of fight," Verne said.

Rikwalk yelled out from the courtyard.

Twenty-three/Epilogue:
From the Journal of Ned the Seal:
The End of It All, Almost

When we went outside, me on the cruiser, the others on foot, to respond to Rikwalk's cries, we were surprised to see that above the courtyard a triangular machine was wobbling in the air.

"We have to flee," Verne said.

"No," Rikwalk said. "Watch. It's lost control."

The machine vibrated violently, sailed past us, dipped into a house across the way, exploded in a ball of fire. The heat from the explosion made my whiskers curl.

"Something is happening to them," Verne said.

"No shit," Twain said.

"Microbes."

We wheeled at the sound of the voice.

Standing at the back of the courtyard was a stocky, mustached man.

"Herbert," Mr. Verne said.

"I am surprised, but glad to see you, my friend," the man said. "Your head is bandaged."

Mr. Verne said, "It's nothing, Herbert." Then to us: "This is H. G. Wells, gentlemen."

I wrote:

I READ *THE TIME MACHINE*.

"Holy shit," Mr. Wells said. "A seal that can write."

"A long story," Mr. Verne said.

IT WAS A GOOD BOOK.

"Alas, a bit of reporting on my part, Mr. Seal, and part of a greater concern, that story is. But that is not a story for this moment."

We paused at this mysterious reply, but Mr. Wells offered no more explanation.

"We saw the house," Mr. Verne said. "We thought you were dead."

"Come. We are still not safe. This ape, is he trained?"

"Oh my, yes," Rikwalk said. "But I don't do tricks."

"My God," Mr. Wells said. "He talks. A seal that writes, and an ape that talks. And a big ape he is."

"It's a convoluted story," Mr. Verne said. "These are my friends: Mr. Beadle, and John Feather, Ned the Seal, and Rikwalk, from an alternate Mars; this is Samuel Clemens, better know as Mark Twain."

"Amazing," Mr. Wells said. "We will share our stories. But not here. Come, the back way."

We went through the courtyard gate, around to the back of the house where it had been knocked down.

Mr. Wells said, "I see that the fuel cell worked in Passepartout's design for the cruiser... Where is Passepartout?"

Mr. Verne hung his head. Mr. Twain said, "Rubbed out."

"I am sorry. Your family, Jules?"

I thought: The family jewels? Now is that a proper question?

"My wife and child left me long ago."

Oh. Never mind, I understood now.

"They felt I was too preoccupied with stories and reporting the events around me. They ran off with Phileas Fogg."

"I never liked him," Mr. Wells said. "Too, I don't know... Too too. Come. Look at this."

Mr. Wells bent down and pulled back a large piece of wood, and underneath it were stairs.

"They didn't destroy the basement. I've been hiding down there. I was down here when the house was attacked. Come. I have lights controlled by the same type of fuel cell that runs the cruiser. It's quite comfortable, actually."

"You clever rascal," Mr. Verne said.

"Of course."

We went downstairs, me by cruiser, Rikwalk narrowing his shoulders. Fortunately, it was a wide opening, and he was able to make it, though the stairs creaked in a frightening manner under his weight.

Mr. Wells pushed the board back over the hole, and we remained in the dark until Mr. Wells managed his way downstairs and hit a switch.

The room lit up.

Above us and along the walls were long bars that generated light.

The room was huge. Packed with rows and rows of books. They rose all the way to the ceiling and there was a rolling ladder that went around the room to give access to them. There was also a lot of fine, comfortable looking furniture. Through a doorway I could see a lab, and beyond that, another open doorway and another room.

"Please, sit," Mr. Wells said. "Rest."

There was plenty of space. I climbed down from the cruiser and stretched out on a lounge. I lay there as if I had been harpooned. The events of the last few days were catching up with me. Mr. Twain and Mr. Verne sat and sighed, feeling the years creep up on them. Until that moment, they really hadn't had time to be old, and I hadn't actually noticed how elderly they seemed. Mr. Verne's beard, which I presume had been dyed black, now showed silver at the roots near his face, and it was the same for his hair. Mr. Twain had grown a bit of a beard, and it matched the white hair on his head. The lines on his face were as deep as ditches.

Beadle and John Feather found soft chairs. They sat back and stretched out their feet. Rikwalk curled on the floor, rested his head on his arm.

"I feel like an old dog crawled up my ass and died," Mr. Twain said.

"That is unique," Mr. Wells said.

"If I was any more tuckered out, I'd have to be buried," Mr. Twain said.

"We will try to hold off on that," Mr. Wells said.

"This is incredible," Mr. Beadle said. "All that destruction above, and here you are, safe and sound, thank goodness."

"It is quite the haven," Mr. Wells said. "But I have had my adventures on the outside as well. I was out scrounging for more food today. I have a large supply set in. I even have a refrigeration machine that is run by the fuel cell I discovered that operates the cruiser. It is amazing stuff. It is not an invention, I might add, but a discovery. Anyway, I was out scrounging, and I saw more and more of the machines crashing. Martians dying. I took one of the machines apart one night, and I found many things of interest inside. I have them in the laboratory. They are very advanced technologically. But that aside, they are not as smart as one might suspect."

"You said something about microbes," Mr. Verne said.

"Exactly," Mr. Wells said. "Fate has stepped in to weigh on our side. The Martians do not have our immunity to such simple things as a summer cold. All manner of diseases that we deal with every day are little devils to them. They are over-laden with our microbes, and now they are dying. It is just a matter of time, and it is all over."

"My God," Verne said. "That is why they are starting to collapse, why there were so many dead Martians lying about."

"Correct," Mr. Wells said. "It started a day or so ago, and I've been waiting them out. Though, foolishly, I went about trying to secure even more food today. It was an unnecessary chance, and, alas, I had no real luck. Within a week, I predict, the invaders will be no more."

"Then all we do is wait," Mr. Twain said.

"Of course," Mr. Beadle said, "happy as that all is, we have the problem of the rips."

Mr. Wells nodded. "Yes. The rips. The tears in time."

"You know about all this?" Mr. Verne said. "How did you know what they were? Beadle and John Feather told us. They are from another time. As is Rikwalk. But how did you know?"

"Because of the Time Traveler. The star of my book *The Time Machine*. I reported his adventures as he told them to me. He was my friend once upon a time. I fear he is the cause."

"He is," Beadle said, and told Mr. Wells the story he had told us.

"It appears it is too late to do anything," John Feather said, "if there is anything that can be done."

"Possibly," Mr. Wells said. "But it would involve traveling in time. I feel almost responsible. I made a hero out of him, and a hero he was not."

"You could not have known," Mr. Verne said.

"We have the Time Traveler's diary in the machine we abandoned," John Feather said. "It might help."

"Yes," Mr. Wells said, "it might. The last time I saw the Time Traveler he had grown quite mad. He left, and I never saw him again. But now, Mr. Beadle, I understand what has happened to him."

"Yeah," John Feather said, "we fucked him over good. But he had it coming."

"No doubt," Mr. Wells said. "But once he was my friend. And whole. A good man. I must give him that."

"You don't get as bad as he was without some character flaw somewhere," Beadle said. "And I doubt it was just bad bathroom habits. Early on, he was askew. It just took stress to show his true character."

"Perhaps, but what matters is this," Mr. Wells said. "If we can travel the paths he made in time, reversing the energy on the machine, we can pull the corridors back together as we travel through. Tighten up the universe. Stop this collapse. I think."

"If that is true," Mr. Beadle said, "If it can be done, we would need a time machine to make it work. And we would have to know all the paths the Time Traveler took."

"Right you are," Mr. Wells said. "Remember, he was my friend. I know a lot about him. A lot I did not report in the book. As for where he went, and how to follow, a companion machine would naturally be pulled into those corridors. The idea is to follow the paths, then reverse them. Close the time tunnels off."

"He traveled so much," Mr. Beadle said.

"Then," Mr. Wells said, "so will we. But not until this Martian menace is certainly defeated by our heroic microbes."

"And how will we travel through time?" John Feather said.

"In this room, I have the plans my friend used for his machine, and I have applied them to the very structure of this room. There are still a few things to be done. Areas to be sealed. But in the very comfort of this room, these rooms, in fact, we, sirs, can travel through time."

I wrote:

THAT IS SOME REALLY NEAT SHIT.

"Yes, Ned," Mr. Wells said. "It is."

A week later, living off the supplies Mr. Wells had put aside, we ventured out one day near evening. London was in flames, but there were people trying to put out some of the fires. A fire engine drawn by four huge, tired horses clunked by, wearing men hanging on the sides of it. It was somehow reassuring to see vestiges of civilization returning. Soon, I presumed fish markets would be back in business, and fish could be purchased at most any time of day. The idea of that intrigued me. Any time of day without swimming about for them. A very merry idea, indeed.

The wrecked Martian machines were everywhere.

So were a lot of people.

They had come out to finish off the few Martian survivors, beating them with bats and clubs. And they looted anything of interest they could find in the machines.

In a huge pile near Big Ben, near where Steam still stood, they had piled Martian bodies and were burning them.

We joined in, dragging the invaders to the pile.

Well, I actually watched. I wasn't suited for moving too swiftly over the streets on my belly. I rode about in my cruiser.

I wrote a lot of notes about what people should be doing.

No one gave me any mind.

Maybe it was becoming too dark to read my signs.

No one asked about me or about Rikwalk, who was carrying the stinking Martians by the armload to the pyre. They had other concerns and had become accustomed to strange things coming through the time and space rips. And it was obvious to them that Rikwalk and myself were helping dispose of the Martians.

I did see one dead dinosaur lying nearby. A long very big thing with tree trunk legs that looked something like the Brontosaurus I had seen in books, but his head was different. And he was brightly colored, like a bird. He had started to decay. It was my guess the creature had come through a rip and gotten into a battle with a Martian machine, and had lost to a death ray. Part of his chest was gone. The tip of his nose, about the size of Rikwalk's head, was rolled up against a wall and was covered in happy flies.

The body of Passepartout, or what remained of it, was pulled out of Steam, stinking and dissolving, and put on the pyre along with the invaders. It was all that could be done under the circumstances. The diary of the Time Traveler was rescued and kept by Mr. Beadle.

According to Mr. Beadle, it was lucky it had not been destroyed, as much of the machine's interior had been sabotaged and stripped of anything worthy by looters. Even Passepartout had been stripped of his shoes, jacket, and pants.

Mr. Verne said a prayer for Passepartout, and we watched his remains climb to the sky in smoke.

And that was that.

When the day was done, we made our way back to Mr. Wells' home, avoiding others lest they might want to follow us and take our food. People had worked together on this day, but there was an air of anarchy, and we did not want to be recipients of it.

It wasn't really much trouble, our going our own way without interference. We had Rikwalk with us. No one wanted to mess with him. And Mr. Verne had returned Mr. Beadle's rifle, which Mr. Beadle carried with an air of authority.

Still, we came to the street where Mr. Wells lived, and snuck into his basement cautiously. Just as I was about to drop downstairs on my cruiser, I looked up and saw a dragon fly across the face of the partial moon.

Not a good sign.

A Week Later — Ned's Journal Continued

And now I sit me down to write on the night we leave. Mr. Wells says we can move through time, and we can move through space, so we will actually change locations, not just travel through time.

That being, coming back could, I presume, result in complications.

Shit. I don't know. I am a Fez-wearing seal. Not some goddamn mathematician or scientist. I can barely boil water.

The room has been sealed and a special door has been fastened above the stairway where before there was only a large gap and a board to cover it.

The door is huge so that Rikwalk can come and go.

Out there, the world is coming apart.

We have water and food in here. Enough to last for some time. Even some canned fish, which is a good thing.

When the last bit of work is done on the machine — and this is being supervised by Mr. Verne and Mr. Wells, and the actual work is being accomplished by Mr. Beadle and John Feather — we will set asail on the seas of time.

If fate is with us, we will fix that which needs fixing.

If fate is not with us.

Then we will die trying.

Not on purpose, mind you. I mean, I'm going to try and live. Even if the world is full of harpooners and dinosaurs and pigs that fly and venomous snakes the size of Big Ben and a dragon that can fly across the face of the moon.

But you get the idea. This is heroic dime novel stuff.

And maybe you don't get the idea.

Maybe no one will read this.

That bothers me. I have used my best penmanship.

Of course, if the journal is in the machine with me, how will anyone read it?

Maybe later it will be read.

If we survive.

Even if we don't survive.

Maybe a flying pig will read it over our dead bodies. It could happen. Provided the pig can read, of course.

I really must rest.

I have been awake for way too many hours.

Ah, Mr. Verne is calling to me. They need me for some last-minute repairs. (I don't know what I can do, but I'm glad to do it.)

And then, after we eat, canned fish, I hope, we're off.

I'M BACK

Damn thing wouldn't start up.

Isn't that typical. Someone crossed a wire or something.

But, hey, we haven't given up. A short break. A nap. And we'll try again.

And if there was someone out there who could wish us luck, someone who could read what I write as I write, I would want them to do that right now.

Wish us luck, I mean.

Luck is always good.

It would be nice if the machine worked, of course. That would be pretty handy, actually.

I have faith it will. And when it does, it will plunge us backward and forward through time, plugging holes like the little Dutch boy putting his finger in the dike. (I read that story in Doctor Momo's library long ago, and I am very proud of my reference to it. I think it is very appropriate, don't you?)

Ah, they call again. The nap is out. They are certain they have it, now.

Someone dropped a fish down there in the wall wiring, they say. They're not naming names, but they have an idea. The fish shorted out the wires. But now all is good. I hope they didn't toss the fish away.

We are going to gather in the main room, sit on the couch, the control box in Mr. Wells' lap. He will flip a switch, twist a dial, and off we will go, a chuggy-whuggy through time.

By God, it will be a great adventure.